# AYA AND THE ALPHAS

## A NOVEL

BERNETA L. HAYNES
LORNETT B. VESTAL

Snake Doctor Press

## ALSO BY
## BERNETA L. HAYNES

*Landrien Moriset*

## ALSO BY
## BERNETA L. HAYNES & LORNETT B. VESTAL

*Eve and the Faders*

Aya and the Alphas

Copyright © 2022 by Berneta L. Haynes & Lornett B. Vestal

Originally published in the United States in 2022 by Snake Doctor Press.

First Edition: June 2022

ISBN 978-1-7359850-5-3 (paperback)
ISBN 978-1-7359850-7-7 (ebook)

Printed in the United States of America

snakedoctorpress.com

*To every black woman and little black girl who dreamed of more...*

# PROLOGUE

Eve stared at the dark face of the woman lying next to her under the moonlight. Blades of grass poked through the sheet they lay on, while the music of crickets and owls surrounded them and a light breeze rustled through the tree canopy. A typical late spring night in Valparaiso, Indiana.

She glanced at the house in the distance and groaned. "I forgot to turn the light off in the kitchen." She couldn't afford to waste any electricity, precious as it was to come by nowadays. "Let me hop over there and turn the lights out real quick," she said, getting up and dusting off her pants.

Carmen rose and grasped Eve's arm. "Let Jesús get it. Maybe he and that boyfriend of his are in there cooking themselves a late snack." As Carmen stepped to the side, her long braids and dress flowed in the breeze.

Eve closed some space between them and cradled Carmen's face between her palms. Gazing into the woman's eyes didn't bring her the joy she expected.

"What's wrong?" Carmen whispered.

"Nothing. I was just—"

"Thinking about her. As usual."

Eve offered an apologetic smile. "I'm sorry. Was it that obvious?"

"Yeah. I don't need to hear your thoughts to know what you're thinking half the time. It's written all over your face. Do you even want me here?"

"Zoey and Gabe are my past. You're my now," Eve replied, bumping her nose against Carmen's as they held each other's gaze.

Carmen smiled. "Good. Now let's get back to what we were doing." She slid her hand down Eve's jeans, while her other hand grabbed a fist full of Eve's locs. Gently, she brushed her lips against Eve's neck.

Eve encircled Carmen in her arms and lowered her to the sheet on the ground. As she lifted Carmen's dress and kissed her stomach, she pushed aside thoughts of Zoey and Gabe. She moved to Carmen's breasts and shoulders. "We could go in the house where it's more comfortable."

Carmen grinned. "What's not comfortable? It's cool out here, all the nice noises, it smells wonderful. I don't get this much nature in Oakland."

"At least you have an actual government out there."

"That's the beauty of being part of the Coalition."

"Except you have to deal with Orson," said Eve. "The man gives me the creeps, thinking he's some sort of god who saved the world and all. If I had a dollar for every white man like him I've met…"

"Okay, this political talk is killing the mood."

Eve chuckled. "Fair point. Where were we?" She resumed kissing Carmen's stomach, moving to her thighs. As she parted Carmen's legs, a loud buzzing interrupted the silence and startled them. They looked around for the source of the noise.

Carmen retrieved the phone from the far end of the sheet and handed it to Eve. "It's your phone. Why didn't you leave it inside?"

With a shrug, Eve looked at the caller id on the old

cell phone. Her eyes widened in surprise. "Kendrick?" she answered.

A deep voice, loud and full of panic, came from the other end: "Eve, I'm coming to you tonight. It's not safe for me and the kids here anymore."

Standing up, Eve pressed the phone against her face. "Slow down. What's going on?"

"Aya's a fader. Probably more than that, actually. I'm on my way to get her back from them—"

"Them?"

"I don't have time to explain right now. But I'm getting her and we're coming to you in a few hours. Be on the lookout."

Before Eve could ask any more questions, the call ended. *A fader but probably more...?*

"What's the matter? Who was that?" asked Carmen, on her feet now and fixing her dress.

"An old friend. He's bringing his family here tonight—something's happened."

Carmen sighed. "I guess that's it for our plans."

Eve gathered the sheet and half-empty wine bottle from which they'd taken turns sipping. "I'm sorry."

Carmen rolled her eyes and scratched her head. She slipped her feet inside some sandals and inhaled. "Well, I'm going to head home. You can update me tomorrow."

Eve rose. "No. You can stay the night."

She kissed Eve's forehead and met her gaze. "It sounds like this is some serious shit. I'd rather be out of the way. I'll check in with you tomorrow." Air whipped around her as she vanished.

"She's gotten much better at that disappearing act," Eve muttered, noting how well Jesús had trained Carmen to teleport.

With the sheet bundled under her arms and the wine

bottle in her hand, she looked at the stars and marveled at the serenity of the night sky. She shook her head. "Everything is so still and quiet out here in the country, while all hell is breaking loose just an hour away in Chicago."

# OF FADERS AND ALPHAS

# *1*

*THREE DAYS EARLIER…*

A bearded man bent over and gawked at fourteen-year-old Aya Wright as she lay in the middle of the street. With a panicked glance at the gathering crowd, he stepped back and shouted something to a woman who covered her mouth and shook her head in wide-eyed dismay.

Head throbbing and back aching against the concrete, Aya blinked and looked from the man to the crowd circling like a curious flock of geese. Her gaze swept over the stone houses lining the street. It had started to drizzle, and she squinted as the drops of rain hit her face. She couldn't be sure, but she would've sworn that before she blacked out that only a few clouds had been taking up space in the vast blue expanse. It hadn't been raining before the taxi hit her. How long had she been lying here?

She winced, recalling the pain of the car crashing into her and the cracking sound her legs had made before she collapsed.

"The son of a bitch made an illegal left at that red light," said a dumpy man, gesturing toward the traffic light.

"The girl was in the crosswalk."

Aya observed a woman crying and shaking her head, while a bald man pointed his index finger into the chest of the bearded taxi driver. Another woman, forehead creased in concentration, knelt and turned her ear to Aya's face.

"Hey, y'all?" The woman turned to the crowd, and all eyes settled on her. "She's still breathing. Look, she's awake now."

The taxi driver hurried to Aya. "Girl," called the taxi driver in a thick Nigerian accent. He squatted next to Aya. "Can you hear me?"

She nodded but groaned from the sharp pain this tiniest motion sent from her neck to her back.

"Can you speak?" he asked.

With a cough, she nodded.

The crowd gasped, and the woman who was crying wiped her face. The taxi driver leaned over Aya and put his hand under her to lift her up. But he froze when the teary-eyed woman hollered out. "No, don't move her. Wait for the ambulance."

As the taxi driver pulled his hand away, Aya tried to lift herself. The impact of the car had caused her left arm to contort to an unnatural angle, and blood had spattered near her head. Yet she sat up after some effort and extended the hand on her unbroken arm to the woman leaning over her.

The woman gawked at her in stunned silence, while the crowd reacted with shocked exclamations and drew back in unison.

"Fine," mumbled Aya, struggling to rise. "I'll help myself up then." She wiped dirt off her sweater and frowned at the fresh rip at the knee of her favorite jeans. When she felt the sharp pain in her left arm, she stared at it in horror. She couldn't move her arm.

"We need to get you to a medic," the woman

exclaimed.

"You shouldn't be awake, not even standing," said the taxi driver. He looked at her as though he was looking at an apparition.

"He must've been going at least forty or fifty when he hit her like that," the bald man remarked. "I saw the whole thing. I don't understand."

To her surprise, when she tried to raise her left arm again, it moved with faint pain. She could feel her bones shifting, returning the arm to its normal angle. Gasps spread through the crowd as they watched with alarm.

Meanwhile, a strange stiffness settled into her legs, but she was happy to find they still moved with no pain. *How am I not dead?* She noticed the looks on the faces of the spectators turned from confusion and awe to fear. Remembering what her father always said about scared people in large groups, her heart began to race as she looked from scared face to scared face. *I need to get out of here.*

"Child...what are you? How is it possible—"

Aya took off running before the taxi driver could finish his question. She ran as fast as her skinny legs would carry her, turning down an alley and looking back until she could no longer see the crowd. She turned left at the end of the alley, fled along the empty street of demolished homes, and sped up before turning right at the next block.

When she approached a three-story greystone house—one of only three houses standing among the rubble of demolished homes—she rushed up the stairs to the front door. She dug inside her pants pocket for her keys, but they weren't there. "They must've slipped out. Damn it." As she gave four quick knocks, she glanced over her shoulder. *Hurry up, Malik. Come on!*

A ten-year-old boy opened the door and shot her a skeptical look. "Why are you knocking so damn loud? You

11

know Dad's sleeping. Why didn't you use your key?" said Malik, staring at her through huge brown eyes that resembled her own. "Hey, why are your clothes so dirty?"

"Get out of the way." She pushed him aside and hastened inside the dim house.

"What's wrong with you?"

"I think people might come looking for me."

"Why would people be looking for you?" Malik asked.

Ignoring him and eager to escape his presence, she headed upstairs to her room.

He followed, closing the door behind them when they arrived at her room. "What happened?"

Aya removed her shoes and walked over to her dresser to get some fresh clothes. Stopping at her reflection in the dresser mirror, she examined her face and marveled that there was not one blemish or mark from the accident. Just a bit of dirt and gravel in her hair. How was it possible? *I can't be one of them. Everybody's going to think I'm a freak.* She turned to Malik. "Tomorrow, let's go to the old South Shore Cultural Center. I need to show you something."

"Show me what?"

"You'll see." Aya cast him a dark look. "Now run along and leave me alone."

Shrugging, he walked to the door and mumbled. "If you're in trouble, I'm telling Dad."

Aya threw one of her shoes, and it breezed just inches past his head. "Whatever, loser."

Standing at the door, he gave his sister the finger just before bolting out the room.

She changed into the clean clothes and rubbed her left arm.

A light midday rain commenced as Aya and Malik made their

way to the old South Shore Cultural Center.

Their father had told them the lavish building once functioned as an exclusive country club for white residents of the old South Shore neighborhood. No black and Jewish people were allowed in the club during those days. But after working and middle class black people trickled into the neighborhood and affluent whites poured out, the city purchased the property. The center quickly became a gathering space for black people from all walks of life, rich and poor and everything in between. Future political leaders, including a United States president, got married there. Well-to-do black professionals golfed there, and teenagers hung out on the shore during the hot summer afternoons, while newcomers toured the elegant building and the serene nature trail lining the lake.

That reality might have been lifetimes ago, a time before Aya arrived in the world. She and Malik only knew of this history from the stories their father told of the old days. Long abandoned after the center was now only a shell of its former glory, just like the neighborhood it was housed within. Just like the entire city.

"Are you recording?" Aya yelled, peering from the rooftop of the center. The wind whipped against her face, and she squinted. She thought about when she'd come to the center a week ago and stood on the second floor balcony. She'd been leaning against the railing when it broke and sent her crashing to the first floor. She'd assumed she was lucky to survive with no injuries other than a mild headache. But after the car accident last night...

Malik stood in the tall grass three stories below, holding up his phone's camera to capture her. "I'm recording," he yelled. "But this is crazy. You're going to kill yourself. And when you do, I'll tell Dad it was all your idea."

"Make sure you hold the camera steady and keep it on

me the whole time."

He shook his head in exasperation and mumbled to himself, "She's really lost her mind."

Aya stepped to the edge of the rooftop, inhaled, and counted to three.

"Hey, no wait. I changed my mind. Whatever it is, I believe you. You don't have to show me. Let's just go home and—" His voice caught in his throat as she took a hesitant step off the rooftop. Gasping, he managed to hold the camera steady, following her quick trajectory to the concrete ground. The loud thud and cracking sound from the impact reverberated in his mind. It happened so fast Malik wasn't sure he'd caught it all on film, nor was he sure what he'd witnessed. He stared at his sister, his hand trembling around the phone. "You said keep the camera on you, right?" The words hurt his dry throat as they came out. He noticed with horror that her head and arms were twisted at a strange angle.

The phone slid from Malik's hand and fell onto the wet grass.

He ran to his sister and dropped to his knees. Thrusting his short arms around her, he cradled her broken body, rocking a bit as tears formed in his eyes. But something struck him as he looked at her face.

"Shouldn't there be cuts? I saw cuts on her face at first..." Frantically, he shook her. "Aya? Can you hear me?"

The stillness of her body sent him into convulsions of grief. "Aya?" he pleaded, shaking her.

When she coughed, he fell back.

Aya blinked and opened her eyes. Her head throbbed as it had the night before, so much she was confused and wondered if she was still in the middle of that street with all the people standing over her. Then, she met her brother's disbelieving face and saw the cultural center behind him. *Oh, right.* With more ease than last night, she pulled herself up and snapped her arm and broken leg into place.

Malik's mouth hung open while he watched her stand straight and, using both hands, snap her neck into place. At the sound of the bones cracking, he cringed and dry heaved.

She turned to him. "I'm a fader, Malik."

He nodded, still bent over and dry heaving.

"Pull yourself together. Where's the phone? I told you to keep recording."

"What if you'd died?"

"I must be one of them," she mumbled. "Malik, I must be a fader."

In response, Malik crouched over on his hands and knees and lost what little food he had in his stomach.

She grimaced. "Gross."

He wiped his mouth clean with his jacket sleeve and got up. "Holy fucking shit."

"You can't tell anybody, Malik."

All he could do was nod.

She gave him a stern look. "Good, now where's the phone?"

Standing in his front yard, Kendrick Imara Wright—some people called him by his childhood nickname "Go"—looked at an outdated electronic tablet and brushed his index finger across the screen. He scanned the news headlines and absently stroked his graying beard that presented a stark contrast to his brown skin. He stopped and skimmed a few stories about the Unified International Security Forces clashing with opposition groups in China. "The whole damn world is a mess." Kendrick groaned, shaking his head.

The next headline pertained to a recent Coalition concert held to raise money for displaced refugee faders. A photograph of Orson Remington III and pop singer Faye Lennox, standing together on an arena stage, accompanied the headline. "The Coalition's PR machine never stops," Kendrick muttered, rolling his eyes before scrolling to the next headline.

When a low battery warning flashed in the center of the screen, he pressed the power button to turn off the tablet and slipped it inside the side pocket of his army fatigues.

"Mr. Wright!" someone called out to him.

He turned around and spotted a kid running toward him. "Jamal, if you're looking for Malik—"

"People are coming," Jamal panted, stopping to catch his breath. The boy bent over and rested his hands on his knees while his little body lurched with every pant. "They're heading this way."

"What are you talking about? What people are coming?" asked Kendrick, his eyes narrowed on the boy.

Jamal pointed. "There."

Kendrick's gaze followed the boy's finger directed at the approaching crowd. He counted at least two dozen people and some soldiers scattered among them. "What's happened?" he barked at Jamal but kept his eyes on the crowd.

"I don't know. Something about Aya."

Kendrick rose to his full, towering height as the group reached him.

A short woman in her late fifties was the first person to address him. "Where is she at? Where is Aya?"

Bewildered and defensive, Kendrick folded his arms across his chest. "I don't know. Probably out with Malik. What's all this about, Mae?"

"I saw her get hit by a car last night," said a younger woman standing next to Mae. "And she got up like nothing happened."

"I thought she was dead for sure. She damn well should've been," a man exclaimed.

Kendrick searched the crowd for the source of the voice. "Hit by a car? What are you—"

"There ain't no way she should've gotten right up," the younger woman went on.

"She's one of them," Mae insisted, a wary look in her eyes.

The crowd grew louder, a cacophony of voices shouting demands at Kendrick. He stared at the frightened and worried faces of people he'd pledged to protect. These were people who trusted him...until now. He wasn't sure what he could say to them to undo what they'd seen or heard about his daughter.

When he raised his hand, the crowd fell silent. "Why didn't you all come to me last night?"

"We..." the younger woman began and glanced around for help.

Mae cut in again. "We had a meeting. We didn't want to just go accusing you of anything. We respect you. You're a good man."

"But we know what we saw," the younger woman finished.

Panicked thoughts darted through Kendrick's mind. "I'm sure this is a misunderstanding. There has to be some other explanation for what you all think you saw."

Mae stepped forward, leaving less than a foot of space between them. Her voice was gentler when she spoke this time. "There's no other explanation, Go. You weren't there. You didn't see it. Any of us would've been dead if we'd been hit like that. She's one of them. All of these people know it, and I think you know it. You have to turn her over."

He studied the woman's lined face and looked at the crowd. "This is an outrageous accusation." Kendrick's deep voice ricocheted off the buildings lining the street. "For you all to come here and accuse my daughter—"

Mae placed her hand on his arm. "Let us at least take her to headquarters for examination. If she's not one, then we'll know for sure. But if she's one of them, we'll figure out what to do. This isn't about hurting you or your family. It's about protecting everybody here. You can understand that, can't you? You've sworn to protect this city, Go. Please do this right."

Kendrick sighed, trying to quiet the thoughts running through his mind. He pointed to the soldier who'd spoken earlier. "You. Come with me."

The soldier nodded and stepped forward. Uncertain looks sailed across several faces, while others appeared relieved.

"As for the rest of you, we're looking into these allegations." Kendrick offered the crowd a reassuring nod, and they began to disperse. He grabbed the young soldier by his arm and took him aside. "This is my baby girl we're talking about. If any harm comes to her—"

"I don't want to imagine what you'll do," the soldier interjected.

"Damn right you don't."

"Got it, sir." The soldier looked at Kendrick with something akin to pity.

"I can't believe we've done this four times and you're still alive. This is so cool." Malik grinned and rubbed his tapered hair—the only haircut Kendrick had the patience to give him.

Aya snapped her neck and arm into place. She looked at the marble balcony above. The impact of the fall still stung a little, like a slap to the face, but she knew that sting would diminish in minutes. "Hand me the phone."

He gave it to her without question. "You should watch them. It's even cooler on video. I added some slow motion to one of them."

She watched each video and deleted them before returning the phone to Malik.

"Wait, where'd they go? I thought you wanted the recordings. You deleted them? Those videos would've made us famous if I posted them online. Ugh. You suck." Disheartened, he followed behind her to the front entrance of the center.

"I changed my mind. Look, this isn't something people will take lightly. You should've seen their faces last night. Like I was a monster. That's just not something I want to deal with right now. I only shared this with you because…well, it's not like there's anyone else I can tell."

"Besides Dad. Can I tell him?" His voice dripped with excitement.

"No. I'll tell him myself when we get home."

They walked through the overgrown grass leading to the steel gate. Crouching to reach the crawl space under the gate, they slipped through the narrow gap.

"What happens when Dad finds out?" asked Malik. "You think he'll freak out?"

She shrugged. "I don't know. But if you say something to him, I'll kill you myself and *you* won't be coming back to life."

"Hey, can we go to the library before we head home? I need to look up something."

"It can't wait?"

He shook his head. "You know how I figured out how to connect the phone to the NeoNet? I think I've found a way to connect to our TV so we can get more channels. I found a book on quantum wireless sig—"

"Fine, we can stop at the library," said Aya, looking straight ahead at the lights in the distance. "It's dark, so let's be quick."

They walked along the crumbling sidewalk and

dodged tall weeds sprouting from the cracks in cement here and there. But they stopped at the sound of vehicles, voices, and boots against pavement.

Malik looked at his sister. "We spent the whole day here. What if there's been an attack?"

Aya watched the small lights grow larger with every passing second.

"Stop! You there!" a man yelled. Flashlights illuminated the silhouette of the gate.

Malik turned to his sister and reached for her hand, but all he grabbed was air.

"Aya?" he whispered, looking around. "Where are you?"

"What are you doing over here, Malik?" said a large man dressed in fatigues. "You know this area is restricted. Nobody is supposed to be here."

"Did you see my—"

"You kids are going to kill yourselves fooling around in these old buildings. Come on." The soldier grabbed Malik's arm to escort him to an old Humvee.

Meanwhile, the other soldiers turned on their flashlights and lifted their rifles. They scattered about the grounds like dogs in search of something or someone.

Sitting in the backseat of the vehicle, Malik watched the soldiers hunt and wondered where Aya had gone.

Kendrick sat at the kitchen table and gazed out the window. He looked at the man sitting across from him and tried to remain calm. Terry Jackson, Major and Company Commander of the Chicago battalion of the People's Army. A man of few words, Terry brought a manic sort of passion to maintaining order. For this reason, Kendrick knew what Terry was going to say. He waited in silence.

"First Sergeant Wright, you understand this is a

serious offense?"

Kendrick nodded.

They exchanged glances, each one waiting for the other to say something. Terry adjusted his posture while Kendrick leaned back. "Goddamn it, Go, you'll be charged with conspiracy against the People's Army. We're not like the New American Army on the East Coast Front who fight alongside fader freaks. Any fader activity is to be reported—"

"And that person is subject to immediate arrest." Kendrick adjusted his posture to make sure he was taller than his commander. "I know. But she's not a fader."

"Go, with all due respect, there were eye witnesses."

"It was dark. Things get murky."

"Are you going to sit here and try to convince me that dozens of witnesses were all wrong?"

"Regular faders don't have the ability to heal themselves, Terry. You know there's only one fader who has that ability. The world learned that after they tried to assassinate him."

"Go—"

"Orson's the reason everything changed. He's the reason we're even having this conversation."

"Well, him and Eve Cooper. Let's be honest, if she'd never exposed that agency...you know what? That's not the point. The point is even if Aya isn't a regular fader, she's still one of them and potentially even more dangerous than the regular ones."

Kendrick became even more rigid and glowered at Terry. "My baby girl is not dangerous. You've known her from birth. She's not some monster."

He shook his head. "It doesn't matter. We're taking her to headquarters. From there, the professionals can have a look at her."

"Damn it," shouted Kendrick, slamming his fist

against the table. He rose and towered over the commander. "I won't let my daughter become a science experiment."

Three armed guards rushed into the kitchen and grabbed his arms to restrain him.

"I suggest you stand down, soldier. Let's just sit here calmly and wait for them to find your children." Terry folded his hands together and rested them against the table. "Stand down."

"Fine," muttered Kendrick, jerking himself loose from the clutches of the guards. He resumed his seat and sat as erect as before, laying both palms flat on the table.

Not taking his eyes off Kendrick, Terry gestured to the guards to leave them. "We're the epicenter of the Midwest Front. We can't afford to appear weak on our policy against faders. It'll weaken the unity among the factions in our region, a fragile unity that General Harris worked her ass off to achieve. Does that mean anything to you?"

"Are you questioning my loyalty to our people?"

Terry scoffed. "What I'm saying is we can't afford to squabble among each other. We can't afford to let anything weaken us, Go. You remember what happened in East Pakistan? When word spread that one of the villagers had the power of Orson himself? That the villager was the so-called 'second coming'?"

"I remember it well."

"Good. Because I'll never forget how that village mysteriously burned down. Not only did the attackers show the fader no mercy, they didn't spare a single soul in the village. They turned the whole place into rubble."

Kendrick frowned. "Don't leave out the main part, Terry, the part where it was all a lie. That man didn't have Orson's power. He was just a regular fader, trying to live a normal life, until a nearby village and some of his people turned on him for being a little different. Just like you're all turning on my kid now."

"Go, I assure you Aya will not be harmed. We're going to play this one close to the chest, out of respect for you and to protect everyone. But we have to take this accusation seriously," said Terry, a pleading look in his eyes.

"You think you can protect her from General Harris? You know what'll happen to Aya if that crazy bitch gets hold of her."

Terry closed his eyes and took a deep breath. "I'll do what I can. Right now, I'm doing my best to calm fears. But you know how people get about this sort of thing. Tamping those fears around here is the only way to defuse General Harris. As worked up as people are now, I'm just as worried about word of Aya leaking out to the other areas." He stopped when the phone rang and buzzed in his pocket. "Commander Jackson speaking. Yes. You found the boy, but no sign of the girl?"

Kendrick leaned forward. "They found Malik?"

Terry cleared his throat and rubbed sweat off his forehead. "Okay. Keep all search parties going. It's imperative that we find her. Roger that." He pocketed the phone and stood. "We'll find her, Go. I'll do what I can to protect her. Until then, you're on house arrest." The commander walked around the table and laid his hand on Kendrick's shoulder. Not a moment later, he departed from the kitchen.

Kendrick listened as Commander Jackson's footsteps grew more distant and the front door clicked shut.

When the soldier released Malik's hand, he entered the quiet house and retreated to his room. As Malik plopped on the bed, he pulled out the cell phone and opened the files folder to determine if he could retrieve the deleted videos. But there was nothing there. "The cloud. Maybe they're in the cloud," he said, turning onto his back.

A knock came at the bedroom door. "Son, are you asleep?"

"No," Malik replied, sitting up and closing the cloud app on the phone. "I didn't think you were home."

Kendrick entered and closed the door before hurrying to his son. He knelt to meet Malik at eye level and placed his palm against his damp cheek. "The soldiers didn't hurt you, did they?"

He shook his head, taken aback by this warm gesture from his typically stoic father. "Where's Aya at? Is she okay? They told me they were looking for her. What will they do to her, Dad?"

Kendrick sat on the bed and put his arm around Malik. "Your sister's smart and resourceful. You and I have to be strong for her right now. I'll clear all this mess up, and then things will return to normal in no time."

The door opened and shut with a bang, startling Kendrick and Malik. They leaped up and turned to the source of the interruption. Yet there was no one else in the room. In an instant, Kendrick whipped out his pistol. He took a few steps forward, his pistol pointed at the semi-transparent form appearing before him. His finger rested against the trigger.

"Don't shoot, Dad," whispered Aya, raising her hands as her form became less transparent. Second by second, each of her features grew more solid and defined.

The gun hit the floor with a loud thud, and Kendrick ran to his daughter. He scooped her up in his arms, burying his face in her hair. "Aya, my God."

When Kendrick released her, he stared into her big brown eyes. "Malik, hurry and close the blinds," he said, not tearing his gaze away from his daughter. "So, it's true. My little girl's a fader."

"When they came for us, I disappeared without even trying. I was standing right next to Malik, but nobody could see me." She wiped away tears.

"It wasn't the first time it happened, was it?"

"No. It happened a few times before, but I didn't know what to make of it. And then last night, when the car hit me—"

"Aya, why didn't you tell me?"

She sniffled. "Because then you'd have to lie to everyone. You'd have to lie and pretend I'm normal when I'm not."

He grabbed her hand. "You're just Aya. That's all that matters to me. There's no lie I wouldn't tell to protect you, baby girl."

"What are we going to do?" asked Aya.

"We'll hide you. For now. Obviously, you can't hide forever, but we can find a way to hide you until I can figure something out."

"But how are we going to do that?" Malik asked, and they both turned to him. "Have you seen all the soldiers watching the house?"

Aya lowered her eyes. "I'm going to turn myself in."

The look on Kendrick's face went from fear to surprise. "You're so much like your mom, the same huge eyes and determined look. But there's something else, something I should've told you—"

The sound of boots thundering up the staircase caught their attention. Soon, a deafening banging at the door followed. "Open the door, or we'll kick it down!"

Aya looked at them, from Malik's terrified face to her father's proud face. She held their hands as the soldier kicked open the door.

Kendrick pushed both his children back, placing his body between them and the soldiers. He counted at least a dozen guns pointed at them.

"Come with us, girl," ordered one of the soldiers.

"This is an unnecessary amount of force," Kendrick shouted. "She's a child."

"Dad, don't," said Aya, shaking her head. Without another word, she looked away from him and followed the soldiers. When she reached the door, she turned to her father and brother. They were holding hands while tears rushed down their faces.

"Keep walking," the soldier barked.

Aya ignored him and stared at her father. "Dad, you said there's something you should've told us. What was it?"

Standing behind her, the soldiers watched the exchange with quiet curiosity.

Kendrick took a few cautious steps forward, looking at the soldiers who had their guns pointed at him. He leaned close to Aya and whispered, "I'll tell you another time."

# 2

Orson buttoned his blazer jacket, stiffened his posture, and waited for the long-winded man at the podium to finish.

"It is my esteemed honor and privilege to introduce to you the Chief Minister of the Human and Post-Human Coalition for Peace," said the man, extending his hand to Orson. "Please give a warm welcome for Mr. Orson Remington."

Orson pushed his abundant chestnut hair behind his ears, and a charming smile sailed across his face. Everyone in the room rose and gave a thunderous round of applause as he stepped forward and shook the man's outstretched hand. Orson's brownish-green eyes, accented by dark eyebrows, swept over the crowd. Political leaders, scientists, engineers, international press, CEOs, and other important people from all over the world. All waiting for him to speak.

Accustomed as he was to the spotlight, Orson still despised these types of formal events. The attention was intoxicating but, after a while, it all grew dull. What did people gain from lavishing admiration and praise upon strangers, he wondered? What primitive craving did such performances satisfy? It was all rather tedious, but he reminded himself it was a necessary part of the job.

"What a warm introduction, although I'm not sure I'm deserving of it," Orson began, feigning modesty. "I'm just a privileged twat from Westminster who decided to try my hand at world peace."

The crowd laughed.

"Good to know you're a light-hearted lot," Orson replied, smiling and adjusting the microphone on the podium. "It gives me great pleasure to be here with you at the European Space Agency. It looks like the Director General of CERN is here today also, probably to beg me to return to my old engineering job." He spotted the director near the front row and caught his eye. "However, I'm rather busy these days, so no thanks, Director."

The crowd cheered and applauded.

"Twenty-something years ago, our world looked very different, didn't it? You all have heard the story innumerable times—the Great Turn that began in 2020 and lasted fifteen years, turning our world upside down. We've all heard the story a million times, but it can't be told often enough. After all, we must never forget those traumatic years from which it likely will take another century for us to heal. So let us revisit for a moment what our world looked like just twenty years ago in 2025.

"Important thought leaders like my old friend, the late great Charlie Ford of FordTech, had stalled in their research about the genetic origins of the post-humans, then called faders. With no answers as to the origins, how could governments hope to identify and, I daresay, control this seemingly new type of human? How could they quell the fears of regular humans who feared these superpowered individuals and even worried that post-humans might make them obsolete, extinct? The answer is they couldn't quell the fears and, inevitably, countries descended into chaos as our species experienced one of the most significant identity crises of our entire history.

"None of us were sure whether our species would make it another decade without ripping each other apart over unfounded hatred, paranoia, and scarce resources. Worse yet, the glue that had held us together, the United Nations, dissolved. We were alone and lost." He paused for effect, and the silence that descended over the assembly hall was anything but comforting. "Then from the ashes of the United Nations rose the Human and Post-Human Coalition for Peace, reminding us we're in this together. The Coalition reminded us that we needed to turn our attention from identity wars to resource development, to energy. The longer we ignored our energy crisis, the longer the world's corrupt leaders would be able to exploit divisions and hoard power, leaving us fighting over scraps. We needed to work together to create the world our children and grandchildren deserve."

The audience applauded, and Orson noticed several wet faces. He caught the gaze of the brunette sitting in the second row on the right and gave her a curt nod as she wiped away tears.

"Realizing my calling lay beyond Downing Street, I abandoned my post as Prime Minister in 2031 and later stepped into the role of Chief Minister of the Coalition. Under my leadership, the Human and Post-Human Coalition for Peace partnered with the Remington Center for Science to revolutionize the energy industry. Through a significant amount of hard work and diligence, we made the impossible possible: nuclear fusion energy for all nations and territories willing to join the Coalition. In 2035, with thirty nations and territories already signed on, we officially ratified the Coalition with the London Agreement.

"As I stand here today exactly ten years later, I'm proud to say that through fusion energy and cooperation, we successfully ended our global dependence on fossil fuels.

Against all odds, we prevailed. That we are here today is a testament to the resilience and ingenuity of our species when we work together."

The audience cheered as Orson smiled.

"But our work is not over. In honor of the ten-year anniversary of the ratification of the Coalition, I am pleased to announce the launch of Ares One, a project to establish the first permanent Mars-based station. Over the next five years, the Coalition, in conjunction with various international space agencies—including the European Space Agency, CNSA, RKA, and CERN—will harness fusion energy to explore the farthest reaches of the universe beyond this blue dot. Ares One is a momentous first step toward ensuring the long-term survival of post-humans and humans alike. With deeper exploration of the opportunities on Mars, we can ensure humankind will survive millions of years into the future. This is what we can achieve together."

Cheers and whoops accompanied applause booming around the room.

He raised his hands, and a brief hush fell over the crowd. "As always, humanity forward together," said Orson, reciting the slogan of the Coalition. He stepped away from the podium and beamed at the crowd, watching as they rose to give him a standing ovation.

The applause and cheers transformed into chanting. "Orson," the crowd repeated in unison.

With a final wave, he turned to resume his seat.

"Sir," Thomas Taylor called, approaching him before he could sit. "Can I have a word?"

Following Thomas off the stage, Orson walked down the aisle. He shook hands and engaged in small talk with the throng of people lining the aisle. The job required that he at least pretend to be sociable. He stopped at the second row to greet Faye Lennox. She brushed her dark shoulder-length hair behind her ears and shook his hand.

After a brief exchange with the pop star, he said his goodbyes and hurried through the crowd with his UISF officers flanking him. When the balmy, musky Paris air hit him, he exhaled.

Seated across from Thomas inside the self-driving limousine, Orson gazed at the Pont Marie. A couple, wrapped in one another's arms, stood at the far end of the bridge. Orson observed them for a moment before turning to the head of his private security. "What was so urgent, Thomas? I have lunch reservations with members of the Coalition's General Assembly in fifteen minutes, so make it quick."

"We intercepted agitators in Chicago and discovered a video that appears to have been posted on the old web on June 2$^{nd}$."

"Yesterday? And we're only finding out about it now?" asked Orson.

"Yes, sir. It was uploaded on an old YouTube server, so it takes us a while to comb through those. It's already at a million views. The video's very popular in areas controlled by opposition factions."

"I don't have all day, Thomas. Are you reaching a point?"

"The video shows a teenaged post-human girl with an amazing ability."

Orson scoffed. "I've seen lots of post-human abilities. What makes this girl's ability so amazing?"

"Sir, just please take a look at this video."

A quiet and stoic man, Thomas was one of the most observant people Orson had ever known. Thomas watched people like a cat waiting to pounce. He knew if Thomas was concerned, he should take it seriously. "Okay, show me the video."

Between the limousine's two backseat rows was a small computer. Thomas pressed the power button on the computer's holographic keyboard, and a three-dimensional figure materialized in front of them. A hologram of a small girl with puffy ponytails.

Orson watched in awe as the frail girl jumped off the roof of a crumbling old building. She crashed onto the ground with an awful thud. Moments later, she stood, no blood or wounds visible anywhere on her. Again and again, she jumped and each time miraculously survived the fall.

"Fascinating. She appears to be able to regenerate and heal herself from fatal injury. Besides me, there aren't any post-humans with that ability. Is this in the U.S.?"

Thomas turned off the video. "Yes, sir. In Chicago, the center of the Midwest Front. What do you think?"

"Are we sure it's not a fake?" Orson stroked his chin and looked out the window. "It could be a ruse of the opposition. It wouldn't be the first time they doctored a video in a foolish attempt to bait me. They are so bloody predictable."

"That's possible, sir. But it's probably wise for us to investigate to be sure."

Orson loosened the cuffs of his sleeves and glanced at his reflection in the window. He patted a fussy section of hair at the top of his head. "At least twice a year, these fools propagate tales of a revolutionary figure who will unite opposition groups against us. Each time, we waste resources investigating their claims only to discover the so-called revolutionary is either human or a run-of-the mill post-human propped up by opposition groups or religious zealots. Each time, these so-called revolutionaries fail to unite our enemies against us."

"You're saying you're not sure why we should care about this girl?"

Orson nodded.

"I understand, sir. But this girl could be an alpha. She's exhibiting extremely rare post-human abilities. While I know the video's authenticity is questionable, consider for a moment that none of the other videos we've seen before showed a person exhibiting the ability of regeneration. I'll also remind you that the Midwest Front is very hostile to post-humans. They're not likely to be interested in making this girl a revolutionary of some sort."

"Are you sure about that last bit, Thomas? After all, your countrymen have a propensity for unbridled rebellion and theatrics."

Thomas smirked. "Nobody knows rebellion better than the Texan sitting here talking to you right now. But from what I've learned from my sources, the Midwest Front is openly opposed to all post-humans. They've all but jailed or exterminated them in that region. So I can't see any chance they'd try to make her their leader. If anything, they're probably hunting her right now."

As the limousine arrived at the Château de Versailles, Orson looked at his watch and thought about the lunch for which he was already several minutes late. "We don't want to raise the flag of another alpha. And if we're to believe this video, we obviously can't easily eliminate this one as we did the others." He adjusted his jacket.

"So, what should we do, sir?"

He groaned, annoyed about having to make such a weighty decision on the fly. "Send a special ops team into Chicago, but inform them that they are to be as inconspicuous as possible and speak of this to no one outside their team. No one from the Coalition should be briefed on this mission. Let's keep this quiet for now."

"Got it," said Thomas.

"I want to know if this girl is an alpha. From my

observations so far, there's only one alpha in this world, me."
Orson scrutinized his reflection in the mirror over the seat
and slicked down his eyebrows. "Contact the tech team
immediately. This video must be scrubbed clean from the old
web, as well as any website on the NeoNet. Have our people
contact every major search engine to remove it and have it
erased off all social media. Make sure that this girl is
contained."

Orson stepped out the limousine and left his most
trusted ally to handle the problem. Now it was time to go
make nice with Coalition leaders and assuage their concerns
about the upcoming General Assembly election.

Orson removed his suit jacket, threw it over his shoulder and
casually strolled around the fountain in the garden, thankful
for some alone time after lunch. While the rest of the
Coalition's General Assembly and French parliament
members gathered in the conference room to celebrate the
launch of the Ares One station, he lost himself in the
quietude of the garden. The sound of the water drowned out
all noise from the conference and streets outside. As he
closed his eyes and enjoyed the quiet, his mind wandered to
the news Thomas had delivered. Was the girl an alpha? "Is it
even possible?"

"Is what possible, Orson?" a woman asked, her voice
melodic and smooth as silk.

Smiling, he turned and met the gaze of his vice-
counsel, Diya Narang. Early in his tenure as British Prime
Minister, his Downing Street Chief of Staff, Madhavi Nehru,
introduced him to a slick solicitor who had completed her
doctorate in political science at twenty years old at Oxford
University and interned for high profile firms focused on
post-human rights. It hadn't taken Orson long to become
fond of Diya, whom he came to view as more intelligent than

just about anyone he'd ever met. He swiftly hired her as his political aide. Fifteen years later, he considered it the wisest decision he'd made in his life.

"You're not feeling hesitant, are you?" she asked. One hand brushed her long black hair behind her ears, while she held a half-full glass of red wine in the other hand.

"No, no. Just thinking," he said, nonchalantly waving away the subject. He gave her a long hug and kissed her cheek. Stepping back, he studied her burgundy cocktail dress. "Diya, you look stunning as always."

"I could say the same for you." She looked him over and sipped her wine. As she took his extended arm, they walked around the garden, a comfortable silence elapsing between them. "Look, I know I can't scan you. You're the only person whose mind I've never been able to scan. But I can read your body language very clearly. What's bothering you?"

"The Coalition has achieved so much in these past few years. It's all happening so fast—"

"Orson, I don't think that's what's bothering you. There's something else going on."

"You really do know me better than I know myself sometimes, Diya. What I tell you stays strictly between us. Understand?"

Diya looked around as though to make sure they were still alone in the garden. "Yes. Now, out with it." She took his arm as they resumed walking.

"I've been alone in my abilities for years. No one else has abilities like or to the extent of mine."

She nodded.

"I've been notified of the existence of a young girl who displayed the ability to regenerate and survive certain death. Until today, I believed this to be an ability that only I possess. But this girl…"

"She could be another alpha." Detecting some subdued excitement in his tone, Diya placed her palm against his cheek and stared into his eyes.

He tilted his head away. "There's also a high likelihood this all will turn out to be another false alarm."

"If she is an alpha though..."

"It's imperative we locate and extract her before any of our enemies do. We don't need opposition maniacs acquiring this girl." He ran his hands through his hair and sighed.

"You're not concerned about opposition forces getting hold of her. What's bothering you is the very real possibility that you're not alone, that you're not so special after all."

He smirked. "Oh, I am special. That's unchangeable. Nevertheless, that child will not become a new symbol to unite our enemies. I can't allow that."

Diya shot him a concerned look. "May I remind you that I cautioned peace with our enemies?"

"I know. Don't worry." He turned to face her and smiled. "As always, I will not stray from the path of peace. You have my word."

"Good." She looked into his eyes while he caressed her hair.

"If she's an alpha, then I've found my protégé. I'll teach her, train her to use her skills. She'll see she doesn't have to be alone like I was." He stared at the sky. *If she's not an alpha, then the tree has to be cut at its roots. She'll suffer the same fate as all the others who claimed to be alphas.*

"Orson, I don't want you to get your hopes up like the other times."

He met her eyes, kissed her hand, and flashed a charming smile. "You worry too much, Diya." In the next moment, he shot up with such velocity it created a whirl of dust around him. Traveling so fast that he looked like a jet trail, he soared high above the city until he faded out of sight.

Aya's shackled hands rested on her lap while she looked out the tinted window of the city hall building, one of the few remaining buildings on LaSalle Street. She stared at the bombed out building across the street. Like nearly everything else downtown, the Thompson Center had been reduced to rubble before Aya was born. The once vibrant area her father had shown her in pictures had become nothing more than a ghost town of shuttered buildings, boarded-up shops, and busted skyscrapers. The country's "second city" all but destroyed by years of violent conflicts with the Eastern Front, commanded by the President of the United States.

"After the first clashes, most of the people packed up and went to the west and other more stable areas," her father had said as they were driving through the city one morning. "The rest, like your mom and me, scattered into the many neighborhoods in the city to live in areas run by the People's Army. In those areas, suddenly we had no running water anymore, very little electricity, no real government, everything outside the city in ruins. The clashes kept happening, so much that I soon got used to hearing explosions in the night. Only when the People's Army joined with neighboring factions to form the Midwest Front did things get better. As bad as life is now in the city, it's nothing compared to what life was like during those years before. Trust me. Maybe one day your generation will rebuild this place."

She'd always hated going downtown. Downtown represented all of the ugliness and cruelty of the world into which she had been born. Why couldn't she have been born in a Coalition country, she wondered? Photographs of those places reminded her of her father's old photographs of Chicago before the Great Turn that began in 2020 when the world learned about faders. Sometimes, she dreamed about moving to one of these shiny cities, having access to all the food she couldn't get in Chicago. She could go to some of the museums she'd read about in school. That world also had places called boutiques, full of fabulous clothes like the ones Faye Lennox wore in her music videos. One day, she would move there and leave all this ugliness behind, she told herself. But this was home...no matter how much she wanted to escape, she didn't want to leave the only home she'd ever known.

As this thought faded into a memory that involved her and Malik walking along the lake, Aya exhaled and her eyes grew heavy with sleep. She'd been awake for nearly twenty-four hours, and she was starting to feel it. Just as she dozed off, the door opened, and she sat up straight. Two guards entered, followed by a tall, middle-aged woman adorned with military ribbons and stars on her collar. She'd pulled her long locs into an austere bun.

"Hello, Aya," said the stern-faced woman with cat-like brown eyes set against beige skin. "I assume you know who I am." Her monotone voice lacked anything resembling emotion. She sat and looked across the table at Aya.

"You're General Gwendolyn Harris. My dad told me about you." This was the elusive woman her father sometimes spoke about in hushed tones.

"I'm sure he has. But more to the point, I'm the Central Commander of the Midwest Front. Do you know why you're here?"

She kept her eyes glued to the woman and nodded.

"You've been accused of being a fader. A fader who's the daughter of one of our most squared away senior ranking sergeants, no less. Do you know that in this region we've outlawed faders? Anyone with the abilities you've displayed is subject to summary arrest. Additionally, anyone with knowledge of the existence or whereabouts of a fader has a duty to report this information immediately to People's Army forces."

Aya lowered her gaze.

"Now, honestly, I find it hard to believe we could have a fader right under our noses all this time and not know. So I'm going to ask you one time, are these accusations true?"

She studied the handcuffs surrounding her wrists. "Yes."

"Hmm. From witness accounts, you appear to be capable of more than the average fader. Is that true?"

Aya remained quiet and didn't look at the woman.

"As it is, we'll run the appropriate tests with our medical staff to see what other abilities you have. You should consider yourself lucky. I don't usually pay accused faders personal visits. But I respect your father's service as a respected member of the People's Army." She reached to lift Aya's chin.

"Is he in trouble?" Tears glistened in her eyes.

"We'll take into account the fact that he has cooperated with us. He and your brother are officially under house arrest at this time."

"But they're innocent. They had no idea about my abilities."

She cleared her throat. "Your father's en route to city hall now for further questioning with Major Jackson. He'll be handled accordingly."

Aya glared at the woman, who looked more and more like the witches in the fairy tale books she'd read years ago. "Why am I not in jail?"

"You're high priority. We know that faders have the ability to disappear, but you apparently have the ability to heal yourself. This isn't a common ability, so that makes you special. A target. If word gets out of your existence, it could spell trouble for our base area." General Harris stood and glanced from the guards to Aya. "We're protecting you and ourselves by keeping you here rather than in jail."

As the door closed behind them, Aya trembled with sobs. She cried until her head drooped to the left a bit and she drifted to sleep.

The loud clanging of the door opening and closing interrupted her short slumber. When she opened her eyes, she found herself staring at more armed guards and a man in a white lab coat. An unnerving smile spread across the man's face as he looked at her.

"My name is Doctor Fischer," he said, his voice soft in a way that sent chills through her.

The guards approached, lifted her out of the seat, and led her out the room. They shuffled down a poorly lit hallway toward an elevator, Doctor Fischer ahead of them. After the guards deposited her on the floor in an empty room with glass walls, Doctor Fischer observed her from an adjacent room. He was accompanied by medical staff and lab technicians working busily at outdated computers and equipment. The guard stood watch beyond the door.

Doctor Fischer stared at her like a hawk. "A teenaged girl capable of such things. You know it's fascinating that over all the years of studying and researching and probing, we still don't know why your kind exists. How such abominations developed."

Aya frowned at him.

"But let's forgo the small talk for now and get started," he went on. "Can you show us how you disappear?"

She shook her head.

"Don't be shy. We're not going to hurt you."

Inhaling, she tried to concentrate. *It's not going to work.* She sighed. "I can't do it, sir. I haven't learned how to—"

"Give it another try."

She closed her eyes and tried once more. "I'm telling you it won't work like that."

"I will not ask again," he warned her.

Aya got up with her hands still cuffed in front of her and went to the glass wall. "I said it won't work." She glowered at him and made sure to emphasize each word. An inexplicable sensation flooded her, coursing through her chest and limbs, and she pressed her hands against her throbbing forehead.

There was a voice. It sounded as though it was coming from a speaker in the room. A shrill voice verbalizing all the thoughts swimming around her mind. The voice sounded nothing like her own, yet it was speaking her thoughts. It was telling her to fight, that something was coming...

Wobbling a bit, she looked at the dull ceiling light that seemed to be growing dimmer. She dropped to her knees, holding the sides of her head and pressing her eyes shut, trying to block out the voice, the thoughts.

"What's wrong? Get up. Get up, now," Doctor Fischer ordered. "If I have to come in there you'll be sorry, girl."

Barely had the doctor's threat registered when the lights in the lab began to flicker, followed by a thunderous boom from the floor above them. Aya opened her eyes, surprised to find the voice was gone. She gathered her wits and looked beyond the lab, but it was too dark now to see much outside her room.

"Get on the ground," shouted a guard standing near the door. "Code red, code red, we're under attack. All civilians stay down."

Another guard bolted into the lab, blood spilling from a gash in his neck as he gurgled out, "Cys!" He slumped to the floor near the door.

She ran to see what was happening on the other side where the doctor had been moments earlier. Gunfire rang out, and she ducked to the floor. Four men, some of the largest and most menacing men Aya had ever seen in her life, entered the lab.

Three of the men appeared to have modified robotic limbs where their normal human arms and legs should have been. The bald one with a half-robotic face had a crimson red-eye on the metal side of his face. Another one had a normal face and a head full of dark hair but a fully mechanized body. They wore military-styled combat gear and wielded guns that resembled no weapon Aya had seen before. She noticed the words "kill" and "death" burned into one man's metal forearms.

Shrinking away in a corner, she watched the man with the metal arms smoke a cigarette as he fired his weapon upon the guards.

When the guards returned fire, they either missed or the bullets had no effect on the cys. Meanwhile, the cys fired at the guards and at any medical staff unfortunate enough to be in their kill range. Aya watched in horror as she realized their guns fired something that looked like light. The remaining guards all fell to the ground, one by one.

The shooting ceased, and the cys looked around at the bodies scattered around the room. One of the cys spoke in a deep and resounding voice. "We've located her, sir." He turned toward Aya and studied her.

The throbbing headache returned, and she winced.

"The girl is over there," he said. "Secure the floor and I'll retrieve the bounty."

Pressing her palms against her forehead, Aya collapsed to her knees. She wondered if she might die from the pain. She was sure she'd never felt pain like this.

While the man approached her, the other cys executed any remaining guards and medical staff as they continued their onslaught of the facility.

One refrain sprang to Aya's mind as the man came closer to her. *Get out of my head, get out of my head, get out of my head.* "Get out of my head!" she yelled, desperately pulling her hair.

Chairs, debris, and lab items strewn about the floor vibrated and shook with increasing violence before levitating off the ground. None of it deterred the man.

On her knees, Aya pulled furiously at her hair and ripped out a few plugs of it. *Get out of my head.* She let out a primal scream, stopping the man in his tracks. He and the other cys looked down in terror. They were hovering several feet off the floor, as if suspended by an invisible string. The one who'd approached her grasped at the air and searched around, his expression one of bewilderment and confusion.

The voice in her head grew louder, and she continued pulling her hair and wailing. *Get out.*

When Aya screamed again, a powerful shockwave shattered all the glass walls around the room and slammed the floating men against the concrete walls of the lab. Two of the men's bodies contorted upon collision with the wall, while one man crashed through the wall and fell into a boiler room on the opposite side. The impact knocked the last man unconscious, and he hit the floor in the hallway.

With ragged breathing, Aya stumbled over and passed out.

# 3

Squinting from the dull ache across her forehead, Aya opened her eyes and was shocked to see the sweating face of her father looking at her.

"Are you all right?" he asked, holding her in his arms. "Did they hurt you?"

She rubbed her forehead. "They tried."

He grinned. "That's my girl."

She moaned as searing pain shot through her forehead.

"What's happening? What's wrong, Aya?"

"Right before the men attacked us, my head started hurting."

Standing at the doorway and holding her hand, he looked down the dark hallway. "We need to get you out of these handcuffs and out of here."

Aya stared at her hands, inhaled, and mustered all her strength to free her hands from the restraints.

"Wait here. One of these guards must have the key on him," he said, stepping over the dead cys to get to the nearest guard. A cracking sound stopped him, and he turned to Aya.

"They broke," said a stunned Aya, eyes wide.

"You broke metal?" he asked, returning to her. As

muffled voices sounded in the distance and ringing alarms followed, Kendrick looked around in panic and watched the door. "The men who looked like machines are mercenaries."

"What did they want?"

"I don't know. And I don't know how many more are on the way. Can you make us both disappear?"

"I've never thought about trying to make another person disappear," she replied, unsettled by the fear in his voice. "I don't even know for sure how to make myself disappear. Like when the doctor was asking me to—"

"You have to try. It's our only way out of here. You can do it. Give it a try." He gave her an encouraging nod.

Wrapping one arm around her father's bulky frame, Aya closed her eyes. *We need to hide. We can't let them see us.* In her mind, she repeated this a few times. The voices outside the room grew louder, sending her into a state of terror like what she'd felt when the cys arrived. She waved her hands in front of her face and groaned upon seeing they were still visible. "I don't think it worked on me. Did it work on you?" She received the answer before he said a word—she couldn't see him. Confused, she waved her hands again but couldn't see them this time.

"Good job, Aya," he whispered, holding on to her. "Okay, keep quiet as possible."

Making their way to the door, they stepped over the debris and bodies that lay across the floor. Smoke and other horrid odors filled the air as they entered the hallway and headed toward the sliver of light at the end.

People's Army forces dashed past them, the leader barking orders at the others. None of the soldiers noticed Kendrick and Aya rushing in the opposite direction. They stopped at the sliver of light that turned out to be a door. With a light push, it slid open. Casting another glance over their shoulders, Kendrick and Aya bolted from the city hall and ran along Randolph Street. They became visible again and kept running, stopping when they reached an old Chevy pickup truck four blocks away.

Out of breath, Kendrick bent over and gestured for Aya to hurry inside. As she strapped herself into the passenger seat, a pair of arms wrapped around her from behind.

"Aya!" said Malik, grinning as wide as ever.

Kendrick turned the key in the ignition, and the truck made a knocking sound but started after two attempts.

Malik released Aya and tossed aside the heavy blankets he'd used to conceal himself on the floor. He made himself comfortable in the backseat.

Aya wiped her wet cheeks and sniffled, looking from Malik to Kendrick.

"It's all right, baby girl. Where we're going you'll be safe," said Kendrick. After a look out the rear-view mirror, he peeled onto the street and sped through a red light.

The truck traveled along empty city streets, passing boarded-up and bombed-out buildings.

"Are we stopping by the house?" she asked as he turned left onto South Canal Street. "Won't soldiers be waiting for us there?"

He frowned. "No, we're not going there. They know I'm smarter than that. The People's Army will expect us to flee the city. That means the main expressways are probably crawling with soldiers waiting for us. So we're taking the city streets and then the back roads until we get to the Indiana border. I need to take you somewhere far from here. This attack was to capture you, and I'd bet money Orson was behind it. For the life of me, though, I can't figure out how news of you leaked beyond Chicago so fast."

"Um..." Malik coughed, picking at his nails. "I

might've uploaded a video on YouTube on the NeoNet and old web before we left the cultural center."

Aya glared at him. "I told you not to share those videos with anyone. You little idiot." She reached back and tried to hit him over the head a few times, but he dodged the blows.

"Cut it out now before you make me run off the road," Kendrick barked.

Aya unlocked her seatbelt and leaned over the front seat. As she connected with two blows, Malik brought his arms up to shield his head.

"Aya, stop it. I'm not going to say it again," said Kendrick. "I believe you've hit him enough for the both of us."

Fuming, she settled in her seat and folded her arms across her chest.

"Now what's this video he's talking about?" Kendrick shot her a cross look.

"I wanted to prove to this moron that I have abilities, so I made him record me jumping off the roof of the cultural center."

"Jumping off the—" Kendrick yelled.

"But I deleted all the videos, so I don't know how Malik posted—"

"Cloud storage, sis," Malik teased. "It's already at two million views, since yesterday."

"Two million? Are you serious?" Aya's eyebrows retreated into her hairline, and she turned to face him again.

He grinned. "Yeah. I pulled up the analytics map. People all over the world have watched it."

"Quiet, both of you." Kendrick's voice boomed, and they sunk in their seats. "Malik, I'm not even going to explain how stupid that was. I'm just hoping Aya got a few good slaps in because it's the least you deserve right now. I swear I don't know where I went wrong with you, boy."

"I'm sorry, Dad."

"As for you, Aya. I can't believe you would be so foolish. What were you thinking?"

"Can I just—can I say one more thing?" Malik ducked when Aya turned to slap him. "The funny thing is when I checked for the video today, it wasn't there anymore."

"What do you mean it wasn't there anymore?" asked Kendrick.

"Before the soldiers came to take us downtown, I checked YouTube. I couldn't find the video anymore. It's like I never even posted it." He grunted in frustration. "It's bullshit. I figured it'd hit a billion views in a week."

"Language, boy."

"Wait, why wouldn't the video be there anymore?" asked Aya, sitting upright and looking at her father.

A dark look came over Kendrick's face. He turned right onto West 33rd street and checked his rear-view mirror to make sure he wasn't being followed as they passed through the vacant streets of the southwest side. "Something strange is going on. From the cys to the video being removed. This has to be Orson and the Coalition. None of the U.S. factions use cys. We can't afford them. Not to mention, who else would have the ability to wipe a video from the internet?"

"But I thought Orson supported faders," Aya remarked. "Why would he send his cys to attack me?"

"Unless they weren't there to attack *you*."

"I felt like their leader was in my head, like he was trying to read my thoughts or something. He must have been another fader. Can cys be faders, too?"

"It's possible. He may have been a fader with telepathic abilities. It's one of Orson's key abilities."

She looked out the window as the truck turned south onto Halsted Street. "Why me? I didn't ask for any of this.

The cys killed all those people."

Kendrick put his free arm around her and kept his eyes on the street. "All right, I have something to share with you two. Something I was about to tell you the other night before the soldiers interrupted us. I didn't think it was possible, but it makes so much sense now." He measured his next words. "Right before your mom died, I made a promise to her to keep you safe."

Malik sighed. "You've told us this before. You remind us at least once a month."

"Keeping you safe meant keeping her secret. Your mom was a fader. She could become invisible and had extraordinary telepathic abilities. Twenty-five years ago when we met, revealing herself wouldn't have gotten her killed. But it still would've brought her trouble, some discrimination and such, that sort of thing. So she decided to hide it, even from me.

"When we met, I'd only been in this city for a couple of years. I was a new recruit in the U.S. Army and wanted to make a new life away from where I grew up in Texas. Valerie was tough, funny, and smart. Very Chicago. While we were together, the world changed very fast, from a vast majority of people not knowing about faders to the world we live in today. It wasn't long before being a known fader meant being in constant danger. Your mom worried that if people discovered her we'd be in trouble, especially given my status as a sergeant first class in the army."

"This was during the Great Turn?" asked Aya.

He nodded. "Yes. By 2031, a year after you were born, the military had seized what was left of the government. The soldiers operated with a ruthlessness we'd never seen, and it became increasingly dangerous to be a fader here. When the military fractured for the final time five years ago, a violent anti-fader element led by Gwendolyn Harris took control of the People's Army and consolidated the region into the Midwest Front. This was when we realized Valerie was no longer safe here. To protect her and the family, we hid her fader identity from everyone, even from our own children.

"But Valerie got more and more worried about someone finding out about her. No matter how much I tried to reassure her she was safe, she was scared to death that she'd be detected one day. So she searched for and discovered an underground network for faders who wanted to leave the Midwest and flee to the Northeast—that's where the New American Army fought side by side with faders. The South was too unpredictable, controlled by militias from town to town and only some of them were friendly to faders. Valerie didn't want to move to another war-torn military-controlled area, even if it was fader-friendly. The only other option was to flee to the Coalition West, so that's where she headed."

"Why didn't we go with her?" asked Malik.

"Valerie knew that if I left before my term was up, the People's Army would hunt me down as a deserter. I wanted her to take you two with her, but she thought it was too dangerous a journey. She planned to send for you when she got settled, and then I'd join when my term was up a couple of years later. But she never made it to the Coalition West." He exhaled and silence elapsed between them.

"You knew I would be different? You knew, and you didn't tell me?"

"No, baby girl, I couldn't know if it would pass along to you or your brother. I had no idea it was even possible. It's never been clear whether being a fader is genetic." Kendrick checked his rear-view mirror to ensure no one was following them as they made their way out of the city.

"Will I be one, too?" Malik asked.

"Time will tell, son."

Aya stared out the window and Malik pondered his possible fader abilities.

"I must admit, Aya, as much as you're like your mom, you're also very different. She only had two abilities, fading and telepathy. From what I know, it usually takes people longer to discover a second ability, and some never do. You have several abilities already it seems."

She thought about how she'd shattered the glass and destroyed the lab with her mind, about how she'd hurt the cys without even touching them, how she'd broken the handcuffs. Telekinesis. Invisibility. Apparent inability to die. Strength. What else was she capable of?

"You might be something the world has seen once so far. An alpha." A proud smile settled on Kendrick's dark face as he gave her hand a little squeeze.

But Aya didn't smile. Instead, she looked out the window, lost in her thoughts and trying to understand everything that had happened and what she'd learned about her mother.

Orson and Diya stood on the patio overlooking the sparkling Mediterranean as soft jazz music and a salty breeze filled the air.

"Mr. Remington," said Doctor Yousef Rouhani, head physicist at the Remington Center for Science and former professor at the University of Tehran. Wine glass in hand, he approached them with a smile creasing his tan face. "Now that we have the Mars station, what's next? That brain of yours seems to never stop looking for new adventures."

"Right now the focus is on the Mars station, so let's not get ahead of ourselves," Orson replied, turning to the old man.

Diya sipped her martini and smiled at them. "Orson's

being coy. But what he means to say is the future holds many possibilities. All thanks to Iran's breakthroughs in quantum computing, which paved the way for Quantum Valley's and the Remington Center's development of the quantum internet, or NeoNet. Doctor, your work innovating pathways for using quantum computing to make fusion a reality has opened up a world of possibilities I'm sure none of us dreamed of."

Doctor Rouhani toasted her with his wine glass. "Ms. Narang, I could listen to you speak all day. No wonder Orson has kept you by his side all these years." He toasted them once more and drained the remaining drops of wine from his glass.

Orson beamed at Diya but was interrupted by one of the servers who whispered something in his ear. He sighed. "Even during my impromptu holiday, it's all work and no play. I have to take a call in a moment, but before I step away, I should add that Diya is correct. Were it not for your discoveries, I'm not sure where we'd be right now."

"Indeed." Diya lifted her glass and nodded.

Orson cleared his throat and sat his glass on the railing. "Pardon me for a moment." He hurried to the villa's private office on a separate floor from the gathering. When he sat at the desk, he pushed the button on the computer screen and a hologram of Thomas appeared in front of him. "I hope this is important. I was in the middle of a conversation I was actually enjoying."

"Yes, sir. I wanted to give you an update on our target in Chicago."

Orson waved his hand with an air of impatience. "Go on."

"Our contractors weren't able to capture her. They're now in the custody of the Midwest Front."

"Will the Midwest Front be able to trace anything

back to us?"

"Well, I'm sure the fact that we sent cys will raise suspicions. But our men know the protocol and will keep quiet."

"What of this girl?" asked Orson. "How did she manage to evade capture?"

"She's more powerful than we first thought. She critically injured three of the cys. She's telekinetic, sir. Our men, even the telepathic one, didn't stand a chance against her."

"Bloody hell," Orson mumbled, sitting forward. "She's an alpha."

"Our informants tell us the child is now on the run with her father and her brother. From what I've learned, her mother died years ago."

Orson stroked his dark hair and scoffed. "I want to know everything about this child. I want a complete file on her. We already have several international news sites questioning the removal of her YouTube video. Conspiracy theories will proliferate if we don't handle this matter with urgency. We need to get in front of this now before it blows up in our faces. My brother and his communications team are working on a spin claiming the footage was altered. But while they're working on that, we need to find out as much as possible about this child."

"Yes, sir. We've asked our American allies to keep us abreast of where she pops up next. There's no telling if she is hiding in the city or the back country. If we're lucky, the Midwest Front will lead us right to her. They'll be searching high and low for her. We'll find her. We won't...how do you guys say it...'cock it up' next time."

Orson half-smiled. "I don't know, Thomas. We're dealing with an alpha. Acquiring her won't be easy, and standard capture methods won't work."

"True. We'll get more intel and figure this out. I'll update you later."

Orson rose as the hologram faded away. He'd wondered when he might discover someone with abilities equal to his own. How long he'd waited for that day, and it had arrived at last.

At dawn, Kendrick's pickup truck pulled into a gravel driveway leading to an abandoned farmhouse. The white two-story house sat tucked away about a mile down a dirt road outside Valparaiso, Indiana. As the truck bucked to a stop and Kendrick turned off the engine, Aya yawned and stretched her arms. Malik blinked awake and looked out the window.

Studying the landscape, Aya noted the almost endless expanse of fields and weeds. She couldn't see the burned out trailers in the park they'd passed along the highway a couple of miles away before turning onto the gravel road. Barren flat fields stretched as far as she could see, broken up here and there by narrow roads and quiet highways. "Why did we stop? Did we run out of gas?"

Staring straight ahead, Kendrick rested his hands on the steering wheel.

"This is our stop. Let's go." He yawned as he stepped out the truck. "It's been years since I've driven out the city. Even one hour on the road feels like a journey nowadays."

"This place is empty," said Aya.

"And creepy," Malik muttered.

Kendrick went to the passenger side and opened Aya's door. He offered her his hand. "There's nothing to fear. Come on."

Malik stared at them from inside the car, and Kendrick chuckled. "Dad, this place looks like those houses I've seen on some of your old scary movie DVDs. I know what comes after this scene."

Kendrick stifled a laugh. "Boy, we don't have time for this. Out. Now."

Malik lowered his head and stepped out. He pressed himself against them. "All right. I'm just saying this never goes well in the movies."

Kendrick grabbed Malik's hand and walked both his children to the porch. The porch sat low to the ground, with two steps leading to a screened door and a large sitting area a short walk to the left. An old swing bench and a rocking chair comprised the sitting area to the left of the door. A faded and empty terracotta pot sat on the porch railing.

Aya looked around the porch. It was so different from the smaller porches in the city. Despite the eeriness of the house, she found the porch inviting. She rubbed her hand against the wall, noticing the paint had peeling off parts of the wood. The window was shattered and boarded up.

Instead of knocking, he said, "It's Kendrick Imara Wright. I've arrived with someone you'd like to meet."

Aya and Malik exchanged bewildered looks.

"He's lost his mind. Obviously there's nobody there," Malik mouthed to her but made sure not to make a sound.

"Dad?" asked Aya, tugging his sleeve.

He shushed her and spoke louder to the door. "I don't remember the old password. But, uh, you can ask me a question to verify it's me."

Malik shook his head. With his index finger, he made a circular motion around his ear. "Cuckoo," he whispered to Aya.

The door creaked open and a small woman emerged, causing Aya and Malik to retreat in fright.

"Someone actually lives here?" Malik muttered to Aya, not tearing his eyes away from the mysterious woman.

The woman, mere inches taller than Aya, appeared to

be in her early-to-mid-thirties but for her grayish-white locs that hung to her shoulders. Her hair provided a stark contrast to her brown face. With her arms folded across her chest, she stood aside, and they entered the dark house.

As soon as they were inside, she latched all three locks and turned to them. At once, her face brightened with a smile and she pulled Kendrick into a hug.

"Easy there. Don't squeeze the life out of me," he gasped.

Standing on the tips of her toes, she planted a kiss on his cheek.

"Eve Marie Cooper. My God, woman, you really don't age."

"Don't let the looks fool you. I still have the body of a fifty-year-old woman, aches and all."

He laughed.

"Anyway, I haven't seen you since Valerie—" She glanced at Aya. "She showed me so many pictures of the kids. They were so little then, my goodness." She put her arms around them, and they winced.

Malik grinned, while Aya stiffened and squirmed.

"You did tell the kids about me?" asked Eve, looking at Kendrick with concern.

"I planned to tell them one day," he replied.

She scoffed at him but smiled at Aya and Malik. "I'm Eve, an old friend of the family. I'm sorry for the mess. I usually keep a tidier home, but I didn't have too much time to clean up, given the short notice and all."

Aya surveyed the immaculate dining room to the right and wondered what mess the woman was speaking of, since the place was spotless. As she detached her attention from the dining room, she stared at Eve. Something felt warm and trustworthy about this woman, but there was also a slight edge to her. An edge Aya couldn't quite put her finger on.

"Hey," Malik said, stepping forward. "Why does this place look so busted from the outside?"

Kendrick threw him a disdainful look. "Boy, if you don't remember your manners."

Eve smiled and put her hand on Malik's head. "No worries, Kendrick. I can handle kids."

"I'm just saying what everybody was thinking," Malik mumbled. "Is nobody else wondering what happened to the boarded-up window that was there a minute ago?"

Eve laughed. "Come on, let's have a seat in the living room."

They followed her to a dim room containing an old, cream-colored sofa resting between two worn lounge chairs and facing a fireplace. At the far end of the large room, a door opened into the kitchen.

On the fireplace sat two candles and a framed photograph between them. Drawing closer, Aya looked at the three people in the photograph. The people's style of dress reminded her of some of the photographs she'd seen of her father and mother, taken in the old days before Aya was born. Recognizing the woman in the middle as Eve, Aya looked at the woman in the room and then at the photograph. How was it that little else had changed about Eve other than her hair?

Before Aya had time to ponder that question, two bookcases caught her eyes. Built into the wall next to the fireplace, the bookcases rose from the floor to the ceiling. A small stool sat in front of the bookcase. Aya marveled at the collection of books. She had never seen so many books.

"Go ahead and have a seat." Eve gestured to Aya who had drifted toward the bookcase.

Nodding, Aya joined Malik on the sofa and grimaced when she sat. The sofa proved to be much harder than it looked.

"Yeah, sorry about that. I should've replaced that sofa years ago before all the stores closed," Eve remarked, making herself comfortable in one of the lounge chairs.

"So why does the house look all messed up on the outside?" Malik asked again and sat on the edge of his seat.

A sly smile sailed across Eve's face, piquing Aya's interest.

"Eve is a fader. During the Great Turn, she was probably the most famous fader besides Orson," Kendrick explained, standing near the window.

"Famous? What happened?" asked Aya.

Eve's smile disappeared for a moment. "That's a long story for another day."

"She helps faders in the Midwest looking to escape persecution," Kendrick continued. "She helped your mom years ago, and she's helped countless others."

"Wow. That's bad ass," exclaimed Malik.

"Boy, if I have to tell you one more time to watch your mouth."

"Sorry," Malik said. "But that still doesn't explain why the house looks like—"

"This boy doesn't give up," Eve interrupted, chuckling. "He must've hung around too many of your army buddies. Cuts to the chase and has a foul mouth just like them."

Kendrick winked at Malik. "He's just hard-headed and spoiled rotten."

"Valerie's doing, I'm sure. Malik, what your father meant to say is because I'm a fader I have certain talents. Among them, I can help people see what I want them to see. It's not a talent I like to use, other than to make this house appear vacant and rundown."

"Why would you want people to see it like that?" asked Malik.

"To not attract any unwanted attention. To encourage any passersby to keep on driving."

Malik nodded. "That's so cool. You know Aya's a fader, too. Also, I like your hair and your sweater."

Eve looked at her over-sized purple sweater. "Why thank you. I see you have your father's charm, too. But I don't know why he's standing by the window instead of joining us over here. Come have a seat, Kendrick."

"Do you live here alone, Ms. Cooper?" Aya asked. "It must be scary being out here by yourself in this big house."

"Call me Eve, dear. And no, I don't live here by myself. There's one other person here for now, but he's asleep. Jesús sleeps like a log. And my friend, Carmen, pops in and out from time to time. You may meet her at some point while you're here." She looked at Kendrick. "Are you going to stand there the whole time? Join us, will you?"

Kendrick didn't move from the window but turned to them. "Eve, this is only a stop for me and Malik. We need to get on the road soon."

"What—we're not staying?" asked Malik.

"No, son, I'm afraid we can't."

"I already got word about what's going down. I had Jesús check with our contacts there a few hours ago, after your call interrupted my evening with Carmen. I'm offering you a place to rest today, and then you can leave first thing tomorrow morning. Besides, I'm basically a stranger to Aya, so you should at least stay long enough to let the girl warm up to me."

Kendrick caressed his beard. "All right."

"Good," said Eve, smiling. "We can talk about everything over breakfast. I know you and Malik have a long journey ahead. But until then, bring your big butt over here and sit down."

In the dining room, a corner nook—consisting of benches built into three walls surrounding a large wooden table—served as the main sitting area. There was a smaller table in the adjoining kitchen. Bright light streamed through the window that overlooked the front yard. Eve had prepared breakfast and disappeared to the barn, leaving Aya, Malik, and Kendrick alone for a while. They ate in a voracious manner, so accustomed to ready-to-eat meals they usually had in Chicago. It was nice to eat regular food like toast and scrambled eggs. Kendrick made omelets on the rare occasion he could get his hands on some eggs, but his culinary skills paled in comparison to those of Eve.

After finishing her food, Aya stared at the last page of the tattered old paperback book lying open on the tabletop. "Let the ears of a guilty people tingle with truth, and seventy millions sigh for the righteousness which exalteth nations," she read aloud from *The Souls of Black Folk* for the second time and closed the book. "What time is it, Dad?"

Kendrick, sitting across from her and enjoying a cup of coffee, glanced at his watch. "It's eleven thirty-eight. Why?"

Aya's eyes widened. "I finished that book."

"What?" he asked. "You opened it not even thirty minutes ago before we started eating."

A huge grin spread across Aya's face. "I know. That's my point."

"You mean you read that whole book in less than thirty minutes?" said Malik, scrambled eggs dangling from his mouth.

She nodded. "Yeah. How awesome is that, huh?"

"Damn, Aya. Why didn't you do any of this before now?" asked Kendrick.

She lowered her eyes and sat. "I didn't know I could do it. My head's kind of spinning—I should sit."

Malik looked confused. "You are sitting."

"Oh," said Aya, dizzily and realizing she should probably hold off reading anymore books for the day. She hadn't felt this dizzy since her telekinesis incident with the cys. "Dad, do you think I could always do these things and just didn't know?"

"Maybe. I'm sure Eve will help you understand more about yourself." Kendrick placed his hand on top of hers. "Why don't you go out there to the barn and help her with the chickens? It'll give you two a chance to talk some."

"I don't know. She seems busy. I don't want to bother—"

Kendrick held her hand and squeezed it gently. "Aya, you're going to have to talk to her, eventually. Trust me, she could probably use some help in the barn."

Smiling, Aya nodded and hopped up. "Wish me luck, Shrimp," she said to Malik.

He frowned. "Don't call me that."

She stuck out her tongue and made a face at him before heading out the kitchen. As she arrived at the front door, a stocky man descended the stairs. She marveled at his midnight black hair—the most hair she'd ever seen on any man—and how it flowed down his back. "You're Jesús?"

Jesús brushed his hands through his hair and yawned, stopping at the bottom stair. "Yeah. I'm Jesús Barrera. I'm assuming you're the girl Eve said was visiting from Chicago. You're Valerie's daughter."

Aya smiled. "Yeah, that's me. I'm Aya. My dad and brother are—"

"Standing right there, I presume." Jesús looked over her head.

Kendrick and Malik stood in the doorway of the dining room.

Jesús came forward, and Kendrick shook his

outstretched hand. "It's nice to meet you, son. Eve has told me a lot about you."

"Only the good parts, I hope," Jesús joked. "It's nice to finally meet you, Mr. Wright."

"Kendrick or Go is fine, son."

Jesús' brow furrowed in confusion. "Come again?"

"Some folks call me Go," Kendrick explained.

Jesús seemed perplexed. "Well, it's good to meet you, Go. Is Eve around? She told me to make a store-run this morning, but I overslept obviously."

"I was just on my way to talk to her in the barn," said Aya.

Jesús smiled. "I'll come with you."

The barn was a short walk across the paved driveway and at the side of the house. The fresh white paint job and new roof indicated the barn was new or had been updated, compared to the house.

"How did your dad get that nickname, by the way?" asked Jesús.

Aya grinned. "My grandmama was known for always telling him," she said, pausing and affecting what she believed to be the accent of an older woman from the south, "'Kendrick, go on over there and get me some water' or 'Kendrick, go on over there and grab me the remote', or 'go get me some ice water', and so on. So one day she told him to do something, and he got mad and said, 'my name might as well be Go'. She agreed with him, and that's how he got the nickname Go. Isn't that funny?"

Jesús laughed and shook his head as they approached the barn.

"What are those things on the roof there?" asked Aya, staring at the flat dark gray squares on the barn's rooftop.

"Solar panels," he replied. "Our main source of electricity out here. I helped Eve install them some years ago when the windmills stopped spinning."

"Windmills?"

He pointed at the large white structures in the distance. "The People's Army started disrupting the electrical grid and cutting gas off in the outskirts. Luckily, my dad did maintenance work and knew a thing or two about solar panel installation. He was big about living off the grid, and he taught me. I put those up there for Eve years ago."

"Why would the People's Army do that? It doesn't make sense."

Jesús smirked at her. "You're young. But one of the things you'll learn soon is that people with power often seek more of it. It's about control."

They stopped, and a black cat emerged from the barn door that was ajar. A rather large dog followed behind the cat.

"That's Baldwin." Jesús pointed at the cat as it rubbed against their legs. The dog, however, kept its distance. "The Plott Hound's name is Miss Sandy."

Eve came out, holding a chicken in her arms, and smiling at them. "And like most who find their way to this old house, Miss Sandy and Baldwin came years ago as strays in need of a home. They've been here since."

Aya knelt to encourage Miss Sandy to approach her. The dog trotted forward, put her ears back and lowered her head for Aya to pet her. She rubbed the brindle-colored dog's head. "I always wanted a dog."

"Well, consider Miss Sandy your new friend," said Eve, hands on her hips after releasing the hen. "Now, I don't suppose you two have come out here to help me with these chickens."

Jesús shook his head. "I definitely didn't. I came to see if you still needed me to go on a store-run."

"Of course I do."

"As you wish." He gave a mock curtsy and vanished.

"What just happened?" asked Aya. "Did he just—"

"Fade and teleport? Yes. Now, why don't you come on in here and give me a hand." Eve turned to the barn, leaving Aya to marvel at what she'd witnessed.

Miss Sandy and Baldwin trailed behind Aya as she followed Eve.

The next morning, Aya woke up in a cold sweat. She leaped from the bed and looked around in terror. Where were the cys? She'd seen them standing over her, one with half a metal face and glowing eye. Beads of sweat rolled down her damp forehead as she realized she was alone in the room. She exhaled and collapsed onto the bed.

For a while, she stared out the window and watched the rising sun's orange glow shine against the field. Her father had described how corn and lush green soybean crops once covered the field. Now, other than Eve's small garden next to the house, the field consisted of weeds, tall grasses, and wildflowers.

Voices sounded from downstairs, catching Aya's attention. As she sat there on the bed and listened to their conversation, it occurred to her that she could hear every single word they were saying, as though they were standing in the same room with her. Puzzled, she tried to recall if her hearing had ever been so sharp. *Weird.*

She quieted her thoughts and listened:

"You've been too kind to me already, letting us stay here."

"Kendrick—"

"But I want to hit the road as soon as possible."

There was silence followed by some sighing.

"Where to?" asked Eve.

"East."

"Okay. But I can't see what a few days of staying here can hurt, Kendrick."

"I can't risk waiting too long, not while I'm still this close to Chicago. I'm AWOL and a deserter from the People's Army. They'll find me if I don't get as far away as possible. I have friends in the New American Army who can protect me and Malik."

"I've hidden your truck. The same way this house is hidden. How could they know where you—"

"I don't want to take any chances. You don't know these people like I do. I only joined the People's Army to keep a close watch on the anti-fader crowd."

"So you'd know when it was time for Valerie to run," said Eve. "I know it's been five years, but I still can't believe she's gone."

There was a pause, followed by a sigh from Kendrick.

"That bitch, Sage. What she did to Valerie still haunts me—"

"Eve—"

"When I teleported to Eden's Paradise—or whatever bullshit name they called that place—and met Sage, I knew what she'd done to Valerie. I remember it like yesterday."

"You never told me what you did to Sage to stop her," said Kendrick.

Eve inhaled. "I didn't have to do anything. Lee Kwon showed up at the same time—you know that's how I met Lee. He'd been hunting the so-called 'parasite fader' who killed other faders to take their abilities."

"He killed her?"

"Lee did what I wasn't sure I could do. There was no other way to stop that mad woman."

Silence passed between them again.

"I think about Valerie every day." He sighed. "But keeping Aya and Malik safe is my main priority now. Malik and I are better off far away from here with the protection of the NAA, and you're the only one who can protect Aya."

"I know. I know. So, where east are you headed?"

"Philly. I have a buddy I served with in the U.S. Army before transitioning to the NAA. He's been holed up there for years now with his wife."

Another pause ensued, followed by some shuffling and patter of feet against the hardwood floor. Aya closed her eyes as she waited for them to continue.

When Eve spoke again, her voice sounded lighter. "I got a new jacket for you, Kendrick. You don't want to be seen with those People's Army patches on your clothes out east."

There was more shuffling and movement.

"Not a bad fit."

"I also have some new ID cards for you and Malik in case you run into any highway patrols. While you're on the road, look for triangle signs if you need to stop for gas or otherwise. Triangles mean 'friendly to faders'. No way People's Army will be in those areas. There's a triangle patch on your jacket, too."

"How do you get this stuff?"

"The network of those of us who smuggle faders has gotten more organized. I made sure of that."

"But do you ever even leave this house, Eve? How have you even managed to keep yourself off the radar for all these years?"

"Jesús is my vessel to the outside. He puts his talents to use in exchange for my kind accommodation."

"You're full of surprises," Kendrick replied.

"So I've heard."

"How are things with you and Carmen?" he asked.

"She's still Carmen. She keeps trying to convince me to settle down with her."

He laughed. "You might not look it, but you're not getting any younger. Maybe you should take her up on the offer."

"Spoken like a man," Eve said, chuckling. "Carmen and I have a good time. I prefer to keep it simple like that. I'm still not sure I'm into monogamy."

"And you women call men players."

Aya opened her eyes and looked out the window, thinking about the conversation and her mother. Just like her mother had gone away, her father was going away tomorrow. Would she see him again? Would it turn out as it had with her mother?

She'd hoped Eve might change her father's mind about leaving. But from the conversation it was clear he was determined to get on the road without delay. Tears flooded Aya's eyes as she realized her father and her brother would be leaving soon.

Aya stood on the front porch and watched her father and brother pack gear inside the cab of the truck. She sensed it was the last she'd see of them for a long time. Eve wrapped her arm around Aya, while Jesús passed them to deposit two gas cans onto the truck bed.

Kendrick approached Eve and Aya, and Malik followed him. A look of great disappointment clouded Malik's face, and he kept his gaze lowered. During breakfast, Aya thought he'd seemed angry. Now he appeared dejected. To cheer him up, she stuck her tongue out and frowned at him before winking. He cracked a mischievous smile.

When Kendrick pulled her into a tight hug, his massive arms enclosed her. "I'm going to miss you so much, baby girl."

She squeezed his waist, suppressing the tears that had welled up. "When will you be back?"

"I already told you I'm not sure. But we'll be back. Don't worry." He kissed the side of Aya's head, flattening her puffy ponytail. "I want you to listen to Auntie Eve, all right? Do as she says. You're in good hands now."

Eve grinned. "Your dad's right. But don't ever call me 'auntie' anything."

Looking at her father, Aya tried to hold in tears, but she had no strength left to fight them. The tears gushed down her cheeks, and she leaned her head against his waist again.

"I love you, Aya. It'll be okay. Everything'll be okay. I promise. This is just temporary, okay? Until I figure out a permanent move for us."

"Maybe far away, to one of the Coalition countries where the People's Army can't find you?" she suggested, thinking about the things she'd read about life in the Coalition countries. "We can have a nice house, and I can go to a real high school where they have dances and sports teams, and I can see Faye Lennox in concert. And nobody would care that I'm a fader. We can live normal lives, like the stories you told us about the time before the Great Turn."

He cast her a sad smile. "Maybe. We'll see."

Sniffling, Malik joined them in a group hug.

Aya pulled him close to her and leaned her head against his. "Don't get into any trouble, Shrimp."

"Stop calling me that," he shouted but smiled at his sister, his cheeks as wet as hers.

After standing there for a few minutes, enveloped in one another's arms, the three of them let go and wiped away tears.

"Thank you for dinner last night, Eve," said Malik. "You're a way better cook than Dad and Aya." He made a face at his sister, and she shoved him.

Meanwhile, Kendrick shook hands with Jesús. "Pleasure meeting you, son. Keep these two out of trouble, eh?"

Jesús nodded. "No worries. I will, sir."

Next, Kendrick turned to Eve, who had moved to the doorway on the porch. In silence, Eve and Kendrick regarded one another with concern. Observing the worry on their faces didn't fill Aya with confidence, but she also knew that her father was a man of his word. If he said everything was going to be okay, then she believed he would do everything possible to keep her safe. Leaving her here with this strange woman would keep her safe, he'd said. So she wouldn't protest. She wouldn't insist upon going with him and Malik. She'd obey his orders because his orders had kept her safe so far.

"Thank you for everything, Eve. When things get quiet I'll come for her."

Eve squeezed his hand and looked into his warm eyes. "Just try to make it to Philly in one piece. Hopefully, the extra gas can keep you on the road without many stops. It's dangerous out there. Like I said, look for triangle signs and stickers, and then you'll know you're in slightly friendlier areas than Chicago."

"And just in case, I have my trusty rifle with me and enough ammo to take out a hundred men," Kendrick replied.

"Whatever you say, Rambo." Eve planted a kiss on his cheek. "Now get on out of here."

He held her gaze for a moment. With another reassuring smile at Aya, he ushered Malik to the truck. Aya, Eve, and Jesús descended from the porch and lingered in the driveway, watching and waving as Kendrick reversed the truck.

Aya thought about the old days of exploring the streets of their South Shore neighborhood. Memories of the beach and swimming in Lake Michigan, playing hide and seek with Malik in the ruins of the old South Shore Cultural Center...all of it rushed to the front of her mind as she watched the truck fade into the distance along the country road. All her fondest memories hitched a ride with her father and her brother, leaving her in the middle of nowhere with two strangers.

# 4

From the skybox in Cape Town Stadium, Orson watched a rugby match between the Central Lynx and the Free State Badgers. Blade Sonani, a stout and boisterous man whom Orson had groomed to lead the Coalition's General Assembly, sat opposite him as they chatted about the upcoming election.

Beneath Blade's boisterous exterior lay one of the most self-contained and regimented men in South Africa. He woke up every morning at four o'clock, went for a run, enjoyed a morning cigar, and by six o'clock headed to his office for meetings. With minor variations, Blade repeated this same routine every day. Though not a fader, his potent mix of magnetism and efficiency propelled him from a short-lived trial attorney career to President of South Africa and eventually General Assembly president in the Coalition.

Now that Blade was approaching the end of his first term in the General Assembly, he'd become more anxious and sought constant reassurance that Orson could gather enough votes to secure him a second term.

"I will be honest, Blade. There are a few holdouts. Those who think you're perhaps too close to me to be impartial. Not to worry, I have some meetings lined up later this week. I'm sure I can bring them to my line of thinking. You have nothing to worry about, mate."

Blade cast him an uncertain look and blew out smoke. "I'll take your word for it."

"On to less troubling topics. I've told you my parents never took me to sporting events when I was a kid. It was all beneath them. My brother and I were adults before we ever went to a football match. We took Mother to one last year for her birthday. Cornelius thought it would be a good laugh. The woman hasn't stopped complaining about it since."

Putting out his cigar, Blade smiled and shook his head. "Mothers are a handful, eh?"

"My mother more than most, I assure you."

He lit the cigar again. "You should go out there one day and try your hand at a good game, Orson."

"I prefer darts, less violent. Also, I'm not that much of a team player."

"A man like yourself, not a team player? Rubbish," Blade retorted, blowing out thick smoke.

"That's a common misconception people have about me. The reality is I prefer to do whatever it takes to get things done, without consulting a cadre of people."

"Yet you're a politician, which requires teamwork and consulting people. Some would say you are one of the most brilliant politicians the world has ever seen."

"You're too kind, Blade." Orson refilled his glass, while Blade inundated the room with more cigar smoke.

"You're still an anomaly to me after all these years. But look, while we're back on the subject of politics, I've almost forgotten. Some members of parliament are having a fancy cocktail party later today. Perhaps you'll go with me later?"

"A date? I'm honored but you're just not my type."

He frowned, not amused by Orson's quip.

"Yes," said Orson, smirking. "Of course I'll go."

"Great. I promise not to keep you there too long." He took a puff of the cigar and turned his attention to the game. Not a minute later, he jumped out his seat when the Badger's fullback tackled the Lynx's second receiver.

Orson applauded the team's skillful tackle. "I must say, Blade, football is much more entertaining. These rugby boys are a bunch of meatheads."

Blade's eyes were glued to the field, but he threw a sideways look at Orson. "My good man, you're much mistaken. There's no greater sport. I believe you're angry a rugby player stole your girlfriend in prep school, no?"

Orson laughed. "That's still a rather tender spot, I admit."

"She wasn't worth it, my friend," said Blade, giving Orson a sarcastic pat on the shoulder.

They had a good laugh, and Orson took another sip of his Scotch. He looked at the field and wondered how many of the players were post-human. The country, with its horrid racial past and class divisions, had seen their fortunes turn as of late. Just as it had for the rest of the continent, nuclear fusion had brought South Africa peace and prosperity. Orson viewed the successful introduction of fusion to this once political hotbed as one of his major accomplishments and as a way of making amends for his country's past harms against South Africa. Indeed he counted Blade as a close ally for leading the country's transition to fusion.

"Orson, I know we're not going to discuss work. But I'm still worried about the election. I've heard President Chen wants to run against me. Is there any truth to these rumors?"

"You shouldn't worry about that."

Blade sucked his teeth and scoffed. "Doesn't China have enough to keep them busy, with the Children of Mao separatists in Shanghai and Hong Kong causing upheaval? I do not understand how you trust them, Orson. They *did* try to assassinate you during your Prime Minister days."

"My brain and skull regenerated, which is why I'm still here despite that assassin's bullet. And that bullet came from the separatists not from the Chinese government. That's common knowledge now. China is an asset to the Coalition, and they share our vision of a future of peace through collaboration."

"That's not the point. To replace me with Chen, to trust people who tried to kill you. What a foolish thing—"

"You're not being replaced, Blade. It's only speculation, and it's total rubbish. You'll have the votes. I assure you."

He regarded Orson with concern. "A man is only as good as his word. I trust your word, so do not let me down. I made you the man who supposedly brought fusion and a future to the continent. Because of my endorsement, all of Africa honors you now for this gift. I am a man of my word."

"For that I'm grateful, Blade. As I said, don't worry. Your position is safe. Anyway, you have a country to run, mate."

"Yes, and I'm doing a damn good job at it," he replied, his smile not reaching his eyes. "But you're aware that losing the GA President title will call into question my credibility with parliament, where my brand is international diplomacy. Losing this election would weaken that brand I have spent so long cultivating. I cannot afford that. You understand that, yes?"

"You have my word. You'll remain GA President. I'll see to it."

Blade offered a curt nod and a smile before turning to the field. "On a less serious matter, how is that lovely aide of yours, Diya? A pretty face and a nice ass, that one."

Orson smiled. "She's doing fine. And, yes, she does have a wonderful bum. I should know."

Chuckling, Blade took a puff of his cigar and stared at the field. "A beautiful lover and immortality. My man, you truly are a god amongst men."

Orson grinned and sipped his Scotch.

As the game wore on, they chatted about women, the merits of football versus rugby, whether Scotch was a "rich white man's" beverage, and what sort of flowers Orson should buy his mother for her birthday next week. When the Badgers scored, tying them with the Lynx, Blade hopped up and pumped his fist in the air with glee.

"Sir, Thomas is here," said one of Orson's guards. "He'd like a minute of your time."

Orson waved the man away, drained the rest of his Scotch, and excused himself. As he hurried from the skybox, he wondered if Thomas had more news about the girl. In the week since the video, the trail had gone cold.

He passed a couple of fans who gaped when they recognized him as he reached the entrance to the café. The guard stepped aside, and Orson scanned the room until he spotted Thomas sitting at the bar.

A young blonde approached Thomas and tried to spark up a conversation. Orson almost pitied the woman as he watched her smile fade into a look of disappointment. When Thomas was working—and he was always working— nothing could distract him. Not even a beautiful and flirtatious woman. She quickly rejoined her friend at the other end of the bar, and the two women cast uncertain looks at Thomas.

The formidable directness and seriousness of Thomas made him more tolerable to Orson than most people. He understood Thomas' taciturn nature. As Thomas had explained once, it stemmed not from a lack of things to say but rather from years of encountering "insufferably stupid people who talk ad nauseum about nonsense." Orson hadn't argued with that assessment of people. Indeed, he figured it was the insufferable stupidity of people that had enabled him to control them all so easily.

Nevertheless, Thomas' ability to refuse perfectly fit women still mystified Orson.

As he watched the bartender refill Thomas' glass, Orson cleared his throat and approached the bar. "It's good to see you, mate."

Thomas stood and greeted him with a cordial smile that vanished as soon as it appeared. "Orson."

"Would you like to join me and President Sonani for a few drinks in the skybox?"

"I'll stick with my water, sir." He tapped his glass.

Orson smiled. *Of course it's water.* He knew Thomas preferred to always keep his wits about him. To this day, he hadn't seen Thomas take even a sip of alcohol.

"But, sure, I'd be happy to join you both as long as you promise to keep Blade from talking me into a coma."

"I can't make any promises there." Orson laughed. "So what brought you here? I thought you and Cornelius were meeting today about the girl."

"Yes. I wanted to fill you in about that." Thomas resumed his seat, and Orson sat next to him.

"What's the news?" asked Orson, although his attention drifted toward the two women at the other end of the bar. They smiled and averted their eyes.

"We still haven't seen or heard from the girl." Thomas finished his glass of water and shook his head when the bartender asked him if he wanted a refill.

"Miss?" Orson beckoned to the bartender before she turned to another customer. "Two drinks for those ladies there. Whatever they like. And I'll take a Scotch."

"We're looking as hard as we can, sir, but nothing so far," Thomas went on, ignoring the interruption.

Orson sighed. "What are you doing to find her?"

"Our failure to retrieve her just before she disappeared has put the Midwest Front and other terrorist factions on high alert. Who knows who might be hiding the girl or trying to smuggle her out of there. Meanwhile, the People's Army has beefed up patrols and imposed an area-wide lockdown with checkpoints. Nobody can come in or go out. So I can't imagine whoever's hiding her will be able to keep her hidden for too long. We're monitoring the area twenty-four-seven, sir."

"Good. Good." Orson looked at the women again and raised his glass to toast them. In return, they raised their cocktail glasses and smiled at him.

"But we have another problem. The New American Army, assuming we were behind the failed mission in Chicago, has accused the Coalition of betraying the ceasefire deal."

Orson's eyes flashed on Thomas. "Bloody American terrorists. I'm not bending the knee again. That ceasefire is all I'm giving them, and they can thank Diya for it. If they threaten action against us, they will pay the price." His cheeks reddened, and his nostrils flared enough to make Thomas wince.

"For now, it's just the New American Army, not the whole Eastern Front, pointing the finger at us. So far, the People's Army and the rest of the Midwest Front haven't turned their attention to us." Thomas paused. "It's nothing we can't manage as long as we get in front of it press-wise. I'm mentioning it now because we know how potent this accusation can be if they go to press with it. We need to preempt them."

"Put Cornelius on it right away."

Thomas nodded. "Already done, sir. He's on it."

"Good. In terms of finding the child, let's give it some time. Let her feel comfortable just enough for her to slip up and lead us to her. Meanwhile, we should keep tabs on her father and brother. Didn't you say he's AWOL now?"

"Yes, sir. We could take them, her father and brother. It would pressure her to come forward."

Orson shook his head. "No, too hasty. That may come later, but let's be patient for now."

"Yes, sir."

"Now," said Orson, patting Thomas on the shoulder. "Care to grab a pint and watch some rugby? Oh, and tomorrow morning remind me to order my mother some flowers. It's her seventy-second birthday next week."

"Will do, sir."

"What's the verdict on that pint?"

Smiling, Thomas shook his head. "Thank you. But I'm going to stick with water."

"So serious, mate. Always so serious." He draped his arm around Thomas' shoulders, and they returned to the box where Blade was watching the game intently.

Loud cheers went up around the stadium and Blade hopped up and pumped his fist into the air, while Orson applauded and sipped his drink.

As Aya experimented with her newfound abilities, her spirits brightened in the days that followed Malik's and Kendrick's departure. She kept herself occupied practicing her fading skills, trying to move things with her mind, and speed reading and memorizing Eve's books. She read every book in Eve's extensive library and committed each one to memory. Two hundred and twenty books. Excited to show off one of her new gifts after finishing the last book one sunny afternoon, she ran downstairs to grab Eve from the living room.

"What's going on?" Eve placed a half-empty wine glass on the side table and followed Aya. "What in the world is all this about?"

"Choose a book, any book," said Aya, standing in the middle of the library with a big grin.

Eve put her hands on her hips. "Why? What are you up to?"

"Go ahead." Aya bounced off the balls of her feet. "Pick one and open it to any page."

Looking sideways at her, Eve went to the bookcase and picked up a book lying flat on a middle shelf. "Okay, this one, *Parable of the Sower* by Octavia Butler. What am I supposed to be doing?"

"Open it and tell me what page you're on."

"All right. I'm looking at page two fifty-eight, the opening of chapter twenty-one. So what?"

Aya frowned as she concentrated. "Give me a second." She recalled the faded words on the page of the book. Then she closed her eyes and recited the passage verbatim. "The self must create its own reason for being. To shape God, shape self…"

Eve's eyes widened. She read the passage and stared at Aya. "Incredible."

Aya smiled. "I read it yesterday. Why do you have so many books by that Octavia woman?"

"Well, she's a legend, and she's my favorite writer. Hold on, you're saying you read this entire book yesterday?"

Aya bobbed her head. "And some others. I can recite passages from every book in here."

"This is just…wow. Let's try another book." Eve wandered to the bookcase nearest the window. Her hands drifted over the spines of several books and stopped on one. "Ah, here we go." She pulled the book from the shelf and opened it to a random page. "Isaac Asimov. I'm looking at the next-to-last paragraph on page two-forty-two of *I, Robot*."

"Every period of human development, Susan, said the Co-ordinator, has its own particular type of human conflict," Aya began, closing her eyes. She stopped for a moment, trying to recall the next sentence. As she went on, she opened her eyes. "...as the economic and social environment changed."

Eve regarded her with deep admiration.

"What does economic mean?"

"Good lord. Did they teach you kids anything? It's a complicated term based on a lot of bullshit ideas. It's best discussed after I've had a couple more glasses of wine." Eve put the book on the table and smiled at Aya. "This is a rare talent. I never knew anyone else who could do this."

"Anyone else? You mean, you can do it, too?"

Eve nodded. "At your age, I was mainly just a faster reader than the average kid and could memorize things with greater ease. I was in my late twenties when I developed it to the level you're showing. I bet you'll make a damn good English teacher someday."

"You think?"

Eve sat at the table. "Absolutely."

"Cool. I loved tutoring the kids back home. But I never thought about being an English teacher," said Aya, sitting across from Eve.

"Well, now that we know you basically have a top-notch eidetic memory—"

"Eidetic?"

"A type of visual memory, honey. Now that we know your visual memory is probably better than that of every other person on this planet, I think you're ready to try something even more exciting." Eve stood. "Come with me."

Excited, Aya took Eve's extended hand, and they exited the library.

When they descended the stairs into the dark and muggy basement, they found Jesús painting an old coffee table. He'd pulled his long hair into a ponytail, and beads of sweat lined his forehead. White paint was spattered on his jeans and the sleeve of his shirt. Not bothering to remove his headphones, he glanced at them and continued painting with gentle strokes along a corner of the table. Soft rock music hummed from his headphones.

Eve pulled off his headphones and leaned toward him. "I think Aya's ready to try teleportation, Jesús."

"What?" Aya gawked at Eve. "I'm ready to try what?"

"She looks kind of skittish to me, Eve. I don't know."

"From what I know so far, she can fade and she's telekinetic. Not to mention she has the same memory ability I have, and I didn't even train her to do it. I think it's time to push the envelope, see what all she can really do."

Jesús nodded, laying the paintbrush in the pan. "Okay. But what makes you think she's ready for the next level?"

"I have a hunch she's something different than other faders," Eve said to Jesús while casting Aya a warm smile.

Jesús and Eve exchanged a knowing look and seemed to communicate silently with one another. Aya watched them, pondering the meaning of the last statement. "I've been meaning to ask you something, Eve. Why am I able to do all these things?"

She put her hand on Aya's shoulder. "That's the smartest question you've asked so far. Most faders have two or three abilities at the most."

"But I have more than that—"

"Yes, it's not very common, but some faders can learn other skills. It takes lots of training," said Eve.

"I didn't train, though. I just keep finding out I can do things. It's a little overwhelming."

Eve smiled. "I know the feeling. But we can talk more about that later. For now, I want you to work with Jesús. He's the best teleporter I've ever known. That's what makes him my window to the outside world."

Jesús removed the rubber gloves and dusted himself off as he approached Aya. He lowered his head to meet her perplexed eyes. "Let's just try it one time, Aya. You'll be fine."

Aya looked from him to Eve.

"Jesús has teleported millions more times than I can count. He's an expert. I've only known one person who was as good or better." Eve paused with a look of despair for a moment. "Trust me, you're in good hands."

He turned beet red. "Well, I don't know about all that. But I know what I'm doing, Aya. So don't worry," he said, extending his hand to her. "Besides, Eve will kill me if I let anything happen to you."

Aya grasped his hand.

"Now, tell me where you want to go."

"Where I want to—you mean I can go anywhere?" She thought for a second about all the places she'd dreamed about visiting. The cities with towering and shiny buildings. The museums and libraries. The forests in Asia and the deserts in Northern Africa. She blurted out, "Egypt. I always wanted to see the Sphinx. I read about the ancient Egyptians when I was younger. The pictures looked so cool."

"Well, that's a new one for me," he replied, smiling. "But sure, we can go there. Close your eyes and hold tight."

Behind her belly button, she felt an unpleasant tug, like she'd eaten some bad food and her body wanted to expel it. The queasy feeling rose to her chest as the room began to shake and an eerie silence enclosed her. Panicking, she tried to clutch the table but couldn't find it. Everything was dark and still.

A vaguely familiar language filled Aya's ears. Arabic. A family in their neighborhood in Chicago spoke Arabic, and she'd learned a few words and basic phrases. *Wait…I feel normal now.* She took deep breaths, noting the queasy feeling had disappeared.

"You can open your eyes now, Aya."

When she opened her eyes, she looked straight ahead at the Great Pyramids of Giza. Her mouth hung open. "How did we—"

"Go from standing in the middle of Eve's basement to a bedrock of ancient civilization?"

Aya looked around, absorbing the new sights, smells, and sounds. Dozens of people passed them on the narrow sidewalk and stopped to point and stare. "The pyramids seemed a little bigger in all the books. Hey," she said, turning to Jesús, "where's the Sphinx?"

"We're standing on top of it." He looked at his feet and then groaned. "The fade must've worn off as soon as we teleported. Damn it. Let's fade again so no one can see us."

Aya, not paying him any attention, peered around with her mouth open. "I can't believe I'm actually in Egypt!"

"Yeah, you did it," he said, watching the growing crowd below. "Um, Aya…"

She turned to him. "Hey, you said I did. What do you mean by that?"

"*You* teleported us."

"But—"

"As it turns out, Eve was right. You have some natural gifts, it seems."

The toothy smile returned to Aya's face, and she spun around with her arms extended and reaching out to the blue sky. The warm Egyptian sun hit her face, and a feeling of pure freedom washed over her. "Where else can we go?"

"We can go anywhere, on Earth that is. I already tried to teleport to the moon once, but I couldn't do it. Plus, there's no atmosphere on the moon, so we'd die."

She smacked her lips. "Why would you try to go to the moon? That's stupid."

"You clearly lack imagination. Why wouldn't I try to go to the moon? It's awesome."

"Yeah, but there's nothing up there. There are much more interesting places. Like the Serengeti. Let's go there."

"Girl, you want us to get eaten by lions? You're nuts."

"Not any more nuts than you wanting to go to the moon. Besides, I read about it when I was younger, and I always wanted to go. Please. Can we go?"

"I'm going to end up dead messing with you. But I suppose we need to get out of here before we get arrested."

The police gathered below and began shouting at them.

Jesús grabbed Aya's hand. "Well. What are you waiting for?"

They disappeared once more, and Aya felt the familiar tug before they reappeared in the Serengeti National Park in Tanzania. The wispy tall grass rose around them, and the hot sun beamed down on their exposed arms. She surveyed the lush, endless landscape.

"This is the coolest thing I've ever seen. Look, Jesús, a baby wildebeest." She pointed toward the animal that was standing about ten feet away. Taking Jesús' hand, Aya ran to get a closer look at the creature before it hurried away.

Jesús looked around, searching for the rest of the herd. "If that thing's alone, some big ass cats or hyenas can't be far away. Or a mama wildebeest."

"It's afraid of us."

"It probably should be," replied Jesús, still searching the area. "I don't know why I never thought about coming here. I guess I'm usually busy handling things for Eve and all the faders who come to the house for refuge. This is the first time I've teleported just for fun in years."

Aya tugged at his shirt sleeve. "Let's sit up there and watch."

Without further thought, she climbed the tree while Jesús watched from below and kept an eye out for any predators. At the top of the tree, Aya gazed at the vast open land that went as far as the eye could see. "Jesús, there's a pack of hyenas over there." She pointed eastward. "I can see it off in the distance. Look, there are buzzards flying overhead—something must have died."

He shook his head. "I might be next to die from this heat. It must be two hundred degrees out here. I wish you'd said the Himalayas or something." He rolled his eyes in frustration and pushed up his sleeves. Not without struggle, Jesús climbed up the tree and rested on a thick limb next to Aya.

They rested in the tree for hours and watched herds of animals come and go and even spotted a pride of lions lying about in the shade of one of the few trees.

"I didn't think lions were that lazy. They're just lying around. Actually, this is kind of boring now." She yawned. "Hey, you think we should try a big city like London or Shanghai? That could be cool."

Jesús sat up. "Maybe another day. Let's stay put here for a bit." After a pause, he started a discussion about lions and how they compared to the other big cats of Africa.

As the conversation continued, they transitioned to talking about growing up poor and life after the Great Turn.

"I was born in 2019, near the start of the Great Turn in the Western Wastelands in Arizona. Back when the existence of faders first became common knowledge to the rest of humanity. It was a few more years before everything went to hell after that. I was very young when things collapsed completely around the country. I don't really remember how any of it happened. But my family became homeless and that's how we lived for years in the Wastelands. Just moving from place to place. I learned all the ins and outs of the underground world, of faders and fader allies, people in criminal trades. My family had to learn that world to survive."

"My dad told me stories about the Wastelands," said Aya.

"It was a tough place. We survived by trading and smuggling illegal stuff from the Coalition West to militias of the east. Medications that had become difficult to get, weapons, unauthorized cy spare-parts, non-perishable food, all kinds of contraband."

"My dad said people in the Wastelands sold our people drugs and lots of bad stuff."

"We sold people what they needed. There was no other way to make it in the harshest place in the country. After armed militiamen killed my parents—when a deal went wrong—I was alone. For the first time ever, at thirteen, I had nobody. Somehow I made my way to the Midwest because other faders said there was a woman in Indiana who could help me. I ended up at Eve's safe house. She saved me."

"She does that a lot, huh?" asked Aya, thinking about how her father had said Eve helped her mother. "Does Eve have any friends? She seems kind of alone. And that picture on the fireplace looks like it was from the old days."

He looked sideways at Aya. "Eve's been through a lot of things, lost a lot of people. She doesn't like to talk about it."

She wished he'd say more but then remembered her father's advice. He'd told her it's best to stay out of grown people's business, and that seemed wise for the moment.

Jesús put his hand on top of hers and remained quiet as the bright orange glow of the setting sun highlighted his face. They enjoyed the quiet for a while until he yawned and said, "It's time to head home."

Sitting on the old porch swing, Eve sipped wine while Jesús smoked a joint in silence. After regaling Eve with vivid descriptions of their adventures, Aya had fallen asleep on the living room sofa.

With Baldwin and Miss Sandy sitting at their feet, Eve and Jesús stared at the night sky that looked like a black blanket of crystals with a giant pearl lingering in the west. Crickets chirped and wind rustled through the tall grass.

"Do me a favor, will you, Jesús? Go check the generator in the morning. The power went out for a few minutes when you two were gone, so I was expecting the generator to kick in. But it didn't. It wasn't a big deal, since the power came on within minutes. But I noticed the generator's been doing that a lot, not switching on when we need it. We might want to get another one at some point."

Smoke rose from his nostrils. "The battery probably just needs recalibrating. I'll look into it tomorrow."

"Oh and, before I forget, Aya is using a lot of water. She knows we rely on rainwater, right? I can't remember if I mentioned it to her. Anyway, give her another tutorial on how to conserve our water."

"Got it, boss. Hey, have you heard from Go?"

"He's settled in. Apparently, his friend is getting him a post in the NAA."

"Maybe Aya and I can teleport to Philly and visit them?"

"I suggested that to Kendrick. He thinks it's best for her to lay low here for now. I don't plan to tell him she just traveled to Africa with you." Eve chuckled.

Nodding, he took another drag of the joint and remained quiet.

"You got something on your mind, Jesús. Spit it out."

He exhaled. "The girl's been cooped up in this place for days since her family left. She needed that trip, but it's not enough. She's going to get restless."

"Are you approaching a point, Jesús?"

"I think she's ready."

Eve sipped wine and stared into the darkness ahead. "Hmph."

"She's mastered teleporting quicker than I expected. Plus, she told me what happened in Chicago. Did you know she can't even be killed, Eve?"

She continued staring ahead at nothing in particular.

"And she learned how to speak my first language fluently in a matter of a few minutes. Took me eight fucking years to get to that level of complexity...in my own language."

Eve laughed and wine spittle landed on her robe. "I promised her father I'd keep her safe. Now you want her to join you on your nightly missions?"

"Why not?"

"I trust you, Jesús. You grew up with little to no protection in this harsh world. You know how to handle yourself. But Aya was protected from the harshest realities of it. She's not ready for what's out there. Here, she's safe. Here, I can protect her."

"Eve, things have changed out there since the night of the attack. Aya and her family are definitely lucky to have gotten out of there that night. It's getting worse, and I don't think we can just sit on the sidelines. The Midwest Front has been on high alert since the attack. They've amped up their efforts to find nearby faders. Usually, we get a fader passing through every couple of days."

"It's why we haven't seen a drifter since Kendrick and Malik left us," she muttered to herself, understanding his implication.

"Word is they're rounding up faders at rates we haven't seen in years."

She nodded. "Which is exactly why she's safer here."

"Eve, are you listening? These missions are more dangerous now. What you asked me to do is something I can't do alone. She's special. Her abilities are extraordinary. I know she can handle herself."

"I agree that she's special. But she's also a kid. Even if she's invincible or whatever, she's not mature enough to manage this situation." The near empty wine glass dangled in her hand that hung over the side of the swing.

Jesús put out the joint in the ashtray on his lap, sat up straight, and faced Eve with an impatient look. "I know you let Aya's mom head west several years ago, and you still regret it to this day. But you can't blame yourself for her death. Everyone knew how dangerous the Western Wastelands were at that time. Her mom made a choice."

She sat the wine glass on the floor of the porch, and Baldwin sniffed it. Eve's scathing look made Jesús wince.

"All I'm saying is I need help to pull off this caper, Eve. And we got a girl in there who's damn near invulnerable, who's like y—"

"Jesús…"

"I promise you the army won't capture her. Look what happened in Chicago, the stuff she saw. The stuff she did. She beat cys. Cys. Hell, I run when I come across those freaks. She fought them and lived. Look, what I'm saying is her innocence—if that's what you're trying to protect—is already gone."

Eve walked off the porch. Her head turned upward to the sky.

Jesús remained seated on the swing. "I'll guard her with my life. I promise you. Eve, she can help us."

"Okay, she can go with you tomorrow night, if she wants to. I'll brief her on everything, so she can make the decision on her own. And if she does decide to go, you just make sure the army doesn't kill you and snatch her away. You hear me?"

He lit the joint again, took a puff, and rose to join Eve. "I hear you. Now take a hit of this," he said, passing her the joint. "You need to relax."

Eve took a couple of drags and smiled at him before passing it back. "Changing the subject...how's it going with that boyfriend of yours?"

"Rashaad?"

"What? You have more than one boyfriend?" Eve grinned.

Jesús laughed.

"I like him. You two are cute together, always cuddled up in front of the fire in the living room last winter. I haven't seen him here since the night before Kendrick and the kids arrived."

"Rashaad wants something serious. I don't right now. You know how that goes," Jesús replied, before taking a last drag of what remained of the joint. He coughed and blew out smoke. "Let's light another and stargaze for a while."

Thinking about Carmen, Eve laughed and discarded the finished joint in the ashtray he'd brought with him from the porch. "You ain't said nothing but a word, boy."

He pulled another joint from his pocket, lit it, and passed it to her. "You know, Eve, I sometimes wonder if there are other planets like ours, planets with creatures that can do what we faders do. It's what I think about every time I see a clear night sky. Are we alone? Is the answer to why we exist up there?" He took a puff and passed to Eve.

"Who knows, darling? Who knows?" She glanced sideways at him. "You think Aya will say yes to the mission?"

He coughed. "Yeah. I think she'll jump at the opportunity to do some good. That child has heart."

"Let's just make sure Kendrick doesn't find out. He'll shit a brick," she said, laughing.

After an hour, they retreated to the living room. Jesús carried a sleeping Aya to her room and tucked her in, while Eve poured herself another glass of wine and stretched out on the sofa. They had a grand plan to save some faders, and Aya was their secret weapon...they hoped.

# 5

Aya dragged the yarn through loop after loop with a methodical rhythm. After Eve taught her how to crochet, she'd decided to make matching scarves for Malik and her father.

Eve leaned against the pantry door and watched the girl, as though waiting for her to speak. "Aya, you still haven't responded to Jesús' suggestion. I know this is a lot to ask of you, but it's also a great way to test your abilities. What's your answer?"

"I don't understand why you need me to go, that's all. I would just get in the way," said Aya, not looking up as she continued crocheting. *I don't want people's lives in my hands. What if I mess up and people get hurt?*

Jesús sat across from Aya at the kitchen table and gestured for Eve to take a seat. "I already told you why, Aya. The People's Army has about a hundred faders and their families all locked up at the old Racine Correctional Institution right outside of Milwaukee. They're cracking down all over the region, part of the Midwest Front's efforts to prevent anyone from hiding faders."

Eve came forward and sat on the other side of Aya. "And we want you to help us break these faders free tonight."

"It's a bigger job than I've ever done on my own. After seeing your teleportation skills yesterday, I think I could use your help. That's why I want you to be there," Jesús said.

Aya put aside the yarn and crochet needle. Her eyes darted from Eve to Jesús. "As your sidekick?"

"It's okay if you don't want to do it," said Eve. "It's dangerous, and there'll be a lot of People's Army forces in that area since they're on high alert. This won't be an easy task. But considering the number of lives we can save, it's worth trying."

"I keep wondering what Dad would want me to do. I think he'd tell me to do what it takes to save innocent people." She smiled, thinking about her father's booming voice. "I can hear him telling me I'm just like my mom, telling me to follow my gut. And Malik would tell me not to be a wimp."

"So that's a yes?" asked Jesús. When she nodded, he fist pumped the air.

Aya inhaled. "So where are the people going to go— the ones we free? And how are we going to get them there?"

"A girl who gets straight to the point. I like it. Eve has a contact in Atlanta. He heads a fader militia group there that helps the New American Army sometimes. They're willing to help the folks locked up in Milwaukee. So I was planning to teleport some people to Atlanta. I can take at least two people per trip. But since you can teleport, too, I figured we can get everyone to Atlanta in half the time it would take me doing it alone."

"What if we could take everybody at the same time?"

Eve's eyes widened. "I like the way this girl thinks, Jesús."

"Bold, but if you think it's possible, let's do it. I say we just aim for taking a few people at a time," he replied, standing up. "I'm going to go pick up some items to make sure we're prepared. Be ready at nine tonight."

Aya resumed crocheting and tried not to worry about the upcoming mission.

As the afternoon wore on, they decided to take a walk through the fields. Humid June air brushed through the overgrown grass, birds sang, and crickets chirped along with them. It should have been growing season, but all the large agriculture corporations had abandoned the fields twenty years ago after a series of power grid failures. While authorities never confirmed it at the time, general rumor spread that cybercriminals were behind the grid failures. Local governments blamed faders. Yet Congress and national authorities questioned whether it was the work of the nation's long-time enemy and constant bogeyman, Russia. Others believed it indicated the biblical end times were approaching.

Within a few years, small farmers emptied out of the state and emigrated to surrounding states that had managed to stabilize their grids—largely by turning over ownership of state power grids to a few major energy corporations. Yet any stability in the region proved to be fleeting.

Before long, the entire region collapsed as power grid after power grid inexplicably went down, exposing local bureaucracies and the federal government as incapable of handling a major energy crisis. A crisis exacerbated by rising tensions between regular people and faders. By the mid-2020s, the Great Turn was in full swing. The years leading into the terrible thirties saw the ascendance of the Midwest Front, a military faction comprised of many former local officials, law enforcement, and military servicemembers—that is, all those who hadn't fled the unprecedented social upheaval and violence of the region.

Like many small towns in the country, Valparaiso

became a ghost town after the Great Turn—more recently, the People's Army of the Midwest Front had turned off the windmills, flushing out the few people left in the countryside. Soon nature reclaimed the fields and open land. Tall weeds standing as high as Eve now covered all the old farmland.

In the years since she moved back to her family home after her father's death, Eve had learned to live with minimal interaction. Her carefully cultivated hermit lifestyle had kept her off the radar of Orson and the Midwest Front.

After everyone she'd lost, she assumed she was meant to be alone until Jesús arrived. In exchange for shelter, he helped her tend to the several acres surrounding the house and they began supplying help to faders looking for a safe haven. Sometimes they enlisted the help of their fader visitors to maintain the home, assist with repairs, care for the garden, and look after the chickens.

Besides Eve, Jesús, and Aya there were no other people around for almost fifty miles northwest to Chicago. Eve's safe house, situated outside Valparaiso and some twenty miles from the nearest interstate, remained hidden away from anyone who wasn't looking for it.

As Eve strolled through the towering weeds, bright green against the clear blue sky, she stared at the brave girl that had arrived so unexpectedly. "Aya, are you sure you want to go through with this? The mission tonight."

Aya nodded.

"You know you don't have to say yes just to impress me. It's okay if you're not sure, if you want to back out of it."

She met Eve's gaze and stopped walking. "I remember when they captured me. I remember how horrible it was when I was with them, how they treated me like I was a freak."

Eve remembered that feeling too well. "To regular people who hate faders, you are a freak. A threat, something to be controlled or eradicated. That's the reality, especially in this region. It's what led to the final split of what was left of the U.S. military. Some military people didn't like the faders. Others were fine with us, even wanted to help us.

"Unfortunately, the ones full of hate won in this region. It's why I set up my home as a safe house, as a way to help my fellow faders and provide them safe passage to somewhere they can be free," said Eve, staring in the distance at nothing in particular.

"You help them get to the Coalition areas?"

"Not always. Not everyone trusts Orson and the power he wields in the Coalition countries. I'm not saying the so-called 'Free World' doesn't have its rewards. But there's something about Orson's power there that just doesn't sit right with me."

"It still seems better than here," Aya said and then lowered her eyes in embarrassment. "I don't mean here at your house. I mean in our country. I like it here at your house, and I'm glad you let me stay. The People's Army probably would've tracked me down if Dad hadn't brought me here."

"I know what you meant. Most of the faders who stop through here are on the run from the People's Army. They usually only stay for a couple of days before heading to the Coalition West. Most of them go to Washington. But some linger for weeks, long enough to work up the nerve to hit the road again. Sometimes Jesús offers to teleport them. But sometimes folks prefer to take their cars with them, so they drive."

"I bet you're a hero to a lot of them. You're probably like a legend to other faders."

"I'm not a hero. Just another fader trying to help," said Eve, smiling. "Besides, most people don't even know I exist. I may as well be a ghost."

"You're a hero to me, and my dad trusts you. He wouldn't have left me here if he didn't trust you."

Eve blushed. "Such a charmer, you are."

"How do you keep the house hidden though? You never explained how you can—"

"Control perceptions? It's something I learned to do by accident in my mid-twenties." They continued walking as Eve described the time she woke up in the hospital and nobody recognized her. "It took me a while to understand how it worked. How could I change the way I looked to people? But, eventually, I realized I could control perceptions. To be honest, it scared me to learn I had that kind of power."

"Can I be honest too?" asked Aya, interrupting Eve. "I'm scared. Not of my power. But this mission. If that place, the prison, is as bad as you and Jesús say it is…"

"I'm glad you're scared. That's good. You'd be foolish to not be scared."

"What if we mess up, and some of the faders get hurt?"

"I think you're tough enough to handle this, and Jesús has been doing this type of thing since he was a kid. He's crafty and knows how to deal with soldiers and armed guards." Eve gave her a reassuring pat. "Also, he knows there'll be hell to pay from me and Kendrick if he lets you get hurt."

Silence elapsed between them, and they looked at the red glow of the setting sun.

"Why do they hate us, Eve? Do regular people feel like we'll rule over them, like Orson does? That's what Dad says the soldiers think."

"That's part of it, I suppose. Orson believes that, through the Coalition, he's given peace and stability to the world. Maybe he has in *his* world. But this country hasn't known peace or stability since the Great Turn. All we've known is chaos."

"We need our own Orson here," she said and sighed.

"I just want to be normal again. It's not fair."

Eve lifted the girl's chin and looked into her big brown eyes. "Listen, girl, you can't change who you are. You were never normal. You didn't know you were different until now. Yes, there are assholes who hate us because of the abilities we have. That's on them, not us. You hear me? Even if you were normal, people would still find some reason to hate you. Being a fader is part of who you are, and it makes you more powerful than most of your enemies."

Sniffling, Aya hugged Eve.

"Oh...oh, well. Right. Okay," Eve stammered, unaccustomed to sudden displays of affection.

After Aya released her, they resumed walking for another half hour and talked about Kendrick and what the countryside used to be like before the Great Turn.

In the living room, Jesús rummaged through the old backpack he always carried on his outings. He was in full mission mode, reminded of his younger days when he and his parents used to smuggle illegal items for the military. The adrenaline rush of it, the sense of purpose, all surged through him so much that he could've sworn he was ten feet tall. His hand slid along the length of a wooden baseball bat, the Louisville Slugger his father had given him when he was seven years old. The only physical remnant from his childhood, the bat now served as his weapon of choice during missions. With a firm grip on the bat, he closed his eyes and took a deep breath. "Tonight is just another mission. You'll be fine," he muttered.

He gave a start when he opened his eyes and saw Aya standing at the doorway. She wore an amused smirk and folded her arms across her chest. "At least I know I'm not the only one who's freaked out."

"You ready?" he said, sitting up straight.

After a nod, she approached him and looked at the large backpack. "You look like you're preparing for battle."

"I am." Jesús held up an old tablet, swiped it, and tapped the GPS icon.

"How are you using the internet with the grid down and everything?"

He tapped on the small black object connected to the side of the tablet. "Through this cell phone. I have a friend in Atlanta who gave me this phone for emergency use. I keep it turned off most of the time because I don't want the People's Army or anyone else to track us out here." He swiped across the screen again. "The GPS doesn't show the prison's specific location—it hasn't been accurate since the old days, according to Eve. But it does give us a general sense of where we need to go. Thanks to my sources, I don't think my coordinates are too far off the mark. As soon as we reach the prison, we're going to have to fade. The place will be crawling with guards. We can't be seen."

"I know. We've gone over this like five times already."

He turned off the tablet and slipped it into his bag before shutting off the phone and standing up. "Just reminding you. If they see us, we're dead. Well, I'm definitely dead. Maybe not you since you're—"

"I got it."

He smiled. "All right. A good soldier is always prepared."

"My dad's a soldier. You just steal things."

"Hey, I 'acquire' things, and always for a good cause."

She smacked her lips.

Jesús' smile faded. "I'm serious, Aya. You need to get

these silly ideas out of your head. We have food, don't we? We have clothing? Sometimes you have to steal to survive. That doesn't make you a bad person."

"I get it." She picked at her nails.

"Good. The sooner you understand that this is a tough world, the better," he said, giving her a pat on the shoulder that almost made her lose balance and smiling. "We're not in Kansas anymore, Dorothy."

Aya's eyebrows went up in confusion. "Who's Dorothy? And we're in Indiana not Kansas."

"Damn, kid. You've really missed out on all the fun parts of childhood, huh?"

She punched him in the shoulder. "I'm not a kid. I'm almost fifteen."

"Cut out the fooling around, you two," said Eve, standing at the doorway and wearing her favorite over-sized red sweater. She informed them that she had communicated with their contact in Atlanta. "Lee Kwon confirmed that everyone is on standby and ready for us in Atlanta. They'll be waiting when you start teleporting people back and forth. Be safe and come home in one piece, both of you."

Aya's eyes widened. "You're not coming with us?"

Eve shook her head. "No. I leave these missions to Jesús."

"Do you ever leave the house? I've never even seen you leave or go out for an errand."

"That's a discussion for another time," Jesús whispered to Aya. He grabbed her hand and gave a nod to Eve. "We'll see you later."

An odor of mold filled her nostrils as she struggled to see through the impenetrable darkness.

"Stay by my side," said Jesús, squeezing her hand.

They proceeded with caution toward a sliver of light

Aya and the Alphas

ahead and remained quiet.

When Aya tripped over something, her hand slipped from Jesús' grip and she went tumbling. Her hands swept over the damp, carpet-like surface. Wet grass. "We're outside," she murmured, lifting herself up.

"The prison yard. Shit. I was trying to teleport us inside. That's the door, I believe."

In the thick blackness of the yard, she couldn't see but assumed he was pointing at the light ahead. At once, she hurried toward the light and groaned. She glanced at the small light attached to the corner of the ceiling. Her hands brushed over the concrete wall, searching for a doorknob or latch. "This isn't the way out."

She looked over her shoulder at Jesús, who lingered behind her and retrieved a small flashlight from his bag. Turning to the wall again, Aya extended her arm and gasped as it went through the solid concrete. She took a step forward and walked through the wall.

"You can walk through walls?" Jesús said from the other side. "The only person I know who can do that is Eve."

"Stand against the wall and don't move. I'm going to bring you through," she said, keeping her voice just above a whisper. She reached through, felt around until she grabbed his arm, and pulled him to the other side. Dim floodlights above illuminated the space, and she stared at her arms and hands. She beamed at Jesús. "Holy shit. That was awesome."

"I'll say. I'm already patting myself on the back for insisting that you join me on this mission." He slung the pack over his shoulder. "Now, let's find the holding cells. We need to be quick."

"And quiet. *No queremos provocar la atención a nosotros mismos.*"

"*Sí, claro.* Although we might need to work on your word choice...*provocar?* Hmm...maybe *llamar* or *atraer?*"

"Hey, let's not die first. Then, you can give me another grammar lesson," she said, tugging him toward the stairway.

Wasting no more time, they rushed to the metal stairway leading to the lower levels of the prison. She held his arm, and they faded, allowing them to evade unsuspecting guards as they descended to the lowest level. By her count, they'd passed at least ten guards before reaching the lowest level. It was dark and appeared vacant. Not sure where they were going, they kept walking. The darkness and heavy silence sent chills through Aya, and she clung to Jesús.

They stopped after a while, and Aya wondered how long they'd been trekking through what felt more and more like some awful dungeon from a horror movie. It reeked of mold, accompanied by the sound of dripping water—from where, she wasn't sure—and the faint chirping of rats.

As they kept walking, they entered what seemed to be an abandoned area. Jesús peered around. "I have no idea where we are. I don't see any cameras or any more guards nearby. Seems weird they'd have an entirely unguarded area of the prison. This is going to be trickier than I thought. We can't just waltz around this prison all night."

Not listening to him, Aya closed her eyes and stood still. Her eyelids fluttered and her head moved as though she was listening to slow, rhythmic music. Voices flooded her mind, voices she didn't recognize, chaotic and incoherent voices that made little sense. So much fear and pain and hopelessness in the voices, the weight of them brought tears to her eyes. Who did these voices belong to and how could she help them, she wondered?

Then there came a response, as though one of the voices heard her question. As the realization hit her, she inhaled and tilted her head. *You can hear me? But I'm not talking. How can you hear my—oh, right.* The voices ratcheted up more,

102

and she opened her eyes.

"I hear them, the prisoners. They're in my head. They're saying they're on the third level, in sector C. We have to go left and up."

"Wait. You're a talker, too?" asked Jesús, staring in disbelief.

She shrugged. "Talker?"

"That's what it's called when you can hear people's thoughts and communicate with them without speaking. Eve can do it, too. One thing I never understand is how can you keep yourself from hearing people's thoughts all the time? I've heard stories about some talkers going crazy because they couldn't control the ability."

"Eve taught me how to listen yesterday, but I still don't know how to turn it on and off. I don't know how I turned it on this time." She shook her head and rubbed her temples. "It's so loud right now. My head hurts."

"All right, well keep listening until we reach them. I can teleport us this time."

She grabbed his hand and tried to ignore the throbbing pain in her head. In an instant, they were standing inside the holding cell on the third floor and surrounded by about a dozen people—some asleep, some wide awake. There were no beds in the cell, just a few thin blankets for cushion against the concrete floor.

"Jesús. We did it."

Startled by the sound of Aya's voice, people jumped to their feet and stepped back, looking around for the source of the disruption. The voices grew quiet in her head as she looked at the people, mostly adults and a few children. Some of them appeared frail and terrified, while others seemed ready to fight. Putting her index finger over her mouth, she signaled them to keep quiet. "We're getting you out of here tonight."

Their expressions changed from surprise and fear to hope.

"Aya, I think they have us on camera." He pointed to a camera in the upper left corner.

A flash of red lights and alarms ringing out followed the ominous thud of dozens of guards' boots against the floor. She covered her ears to shut out the piercing noise. *Don't panic. Don't panic.*

"Aya, start teleporting people out of here now. Take two at a time. Do it now!" He snatched her hands from her ears and cupped her face with his large hands. "If you panic, there's no telling what will happen to them. Now do what you need to do. I'll hold off the guards."

The terrified prisoners shouted at Aya, pleading for her to help them.

"Follow the plan," Jesús repeated. "Save these people." He gave her an encouraging nod and disappeared.

When Jesús reappeared in the hallway, he found himself facing four guards. "Hi, boys. I was just checking out the place," he quipped, winking at a tall, attractive guard standing near the rear of the group. "Interesting improvements you've made. Although, I would've added more vibrant colors. White and gray is so basic."

"Shoot him," yelled one of the guards, a bulky man not much older than Jesús. They raised their machine guns and let off a couple of rounds at Jesús as he teleported. Keeping their guns aimed at the spot where he'd been standing, their eyes searched left and right.

Reappearing behind the group, Jesús watched them look around frantically.

"Did you get him?" asked a guard with greasy brown hair. "Looks like you missed."

The bulky one shrugged. "I think—"

Jesús teleported and reappeared in front of the man. Before he could say a word, Jesús pushed him over the balcony railing. A loud clack confirmed he'd hit the concrete floor two stories below. At once, Jesús faded and pushed the greasy-haired guard over the railing. After the second thud, he sighed. "You know you all could just run away now. I wouldn't judge you."

Of the two guards left standing, one fled down the narrow hallway. The other, eyes wide in terror, opened fire on Jesús only to realize a second later that he was shooting at nothing but a wall.

Jesús reappeared behind him and watched the guard take panicked breaths and look left and right. "You might want to look behind you at some point."

When the guard turned around, Jesús swung the baseball bat. With a shocked look and blood spilling from his lips, the guard fell to one knee. This allowed Jesús to deliver a quick head kick, the final knockout blow. The man fell face forward to the floor and moved no more.

Jesús readjusted his backpack and turned around when he heard footsteps. He counted at least ten guards advancing toward him. "Boys, why can't we just sit and talk about this over drinks? There's no need for all this violence."

They raised their guns in unison, and the one woman in the group yelled, "Don't move. Stay where you are."

Not giving them time to open fire, Jesús teleported and materialized in the middle of the group. With a firm grip on his Louisville Slugger, he whacked one guard in the shins and another in the kneecaps.

Once the fight ended, four guards lay on the ground while the woman guard reloaded another magazine in her rifle. Three other guards pointed their guns at Jesús. "Stay where you are, damn it," one of them hollered.

He smiled as the guards cautiously approached him

with their weapons drawn. All the while, the moans of the injured guards grew louder.

"Who are you here with?" asked the guard who had reloaded her clip. "Are you with the Coalition? Are you with the NAA?"

Jesús smirked. "I'm here with Louie."

Looks of confusion spread across the guards' faces. "Who the hell is Louie?"

"Allow me to introduce you."

The guards exchanged uncertain glances.

Jesús used this opportunity to teleport, and the guards fired. Again, their bullets hit the wall. He caught one of the guards with a right hook, knocking the rifle out of the man's hand and causing him to stumble. Jesús spun around with the bat and whacked another guard over the head.

The two remaining guards, as panic-stricken as ever, fired more shots and their bullets missed Jesús as he teleported behind them. "Look, I don't want to hit a woman."

When she pointed the gun at his face, he kicked her in the stomach and swung his bat at the other guard. The force of the swing knocked the guard over the railing, and he fell to the floor below. The last guard, still catching her breath from the kick in the stomach, reached for her handgun.

As Jesús was about to deliver a clubbing blow to the guard, he noticed at least twenty more guards running toward him from both directions. They started firing their weapons, and Jesús teleported in a flash.

Back in the cell, Aya's mind raced with ideas about how to get everyone out before the People's Army called up reinforcements. Taking two or three at a time wouldn't be fast enough. Could she teleport them all at the same time? *I have to at least try.*

Stepping forward, she cleared her throat—trying not to let her nerves get the best of her—and ordered them to hold hands. Once they were all linked, she joined hands with them.

Aya closed her eyes and, through the dark tunnels of her mind, searched. She searched for something to grab onto, something tangible. She didn't know what she was doing or how she was doing it, but she felt herself connecting to the minds of the prisoners. *Connecting? Is that what Eve called it?* She concentrated on the thoughts of those around her. Jumbled words and voices. Incoherent fragments.

*Wait...are there others here? Others outside this cell?* In her mind, she could see a cell different from the one she was standing in now. The cell had beds, and she didn't recognize the faces. As she accessed more minds and more pleas joined the chorus in her head, the words became more discordant. She couldn't distinguish any individual words anymore, but she knew the voices belonged to all the other fader captives in the facility. She was certain of it. *But what do I do now?*

A sudden realization crashed over Aya as she remembered what Jesús had called her. A talker. *I must talk to them.* But Eve hadn't taught her how to send thoughts, to talk to others telepathically. Balling her fists and opening her eyes, she concentrated as hard as she could. Her head throbbed as it had when the cys attacked in Chicago. But she gritted her teeth and focused.

*Hello, everyone.* As though she'd pressed a mute button, they fell silent. For the first time in minutes, her mind was quiet and clear. *You don't know who I am. But that doesn't matter right now. I can get all of you out of here to a safe place. Okay? But you must trust me. Grab the person next to you right now until you're all linked. When I count to three, you're going to feel a little funny. One...*

Jesús reappeared in the cell with Aya and looked around in confusion. He checked his legs and groin area and exhaled. "I'm not shot. My balls are still in place. Oh God, thank the universe." He grasped Aya's shoulder as he caught his breath. "We have more guards coming our way, Aya. We need to—"

*Two...Three.*

His words choked in his throat when he saw electric bolts conjured up in the cell and sparks flying everywhere. The camera overhead exploded, and sparks filled the room. As the ground shook, Jesús blinked and looked at the ground beneath his feet, watching it transform from wet concrete to grass. He stared at the other faders, all of them shaking and scared. His gaze swept over the park.

At least a dozen armed people in fatigues advanced toward them with weapons drawn.

"Piedmont Park, the rendezvous point. My God. Aya, you did it."

She pulled herself to her knees, having collapsed upon their arrival in the park.

"You teleported everyone at one time. I've never seen anything like this before." He pulled her up and threw his arms around her, lifting her off the ground for a moment. "You fucking did it."

The militia approached them and lowered their weapons. "Christ," said a man leading the militia. "I thought we'd agreed to have y'all bring a few at a time throughout the night. We're going to need a bus and all hands on deck for this. How the hell did y'all manage this?"

Jesús wiped sweat from his forehead and gestured toward a very shaken Aya standing next to him. "Aya did it. I'm just as mystified as you are, Lee."

"You're telling me that little ninety-pound girl did this?" Lee Kwon's light brown eyes flashed on her with admiration. "Well, I'll say."

She stared at him. Something about the man—

perhaps his stern face and deep voice—reminded her of her father. She watched him whip out a cell phone, send a message, slide the phone inside his pocket, and hurry to the crowd of new arrivals.

Jesús patted her shoulder. "Let's go help Lee get these folks get settled in. After that, we'll teleport to Eve's."

Too exhausted to ask questions, she nodded. All she cared about now was sleep.

# 6

Turnip greens from the garden simmered in broth on the burner while Eve stirred together some buttermilk, cornmeal, and honey in a bowl. As she poured the mixture into a cast-iron skillet, a loud thud sounded from the hallway, followed by a soft patter of feet against hardwood floors. "I don't know how many times I've told that girl not to play with that dog inside the house. She's been here for a month and can't grasp this one rule," Eve mumbled. "One minute she's saving a bunch of people, and the next minute she's running through here like a five-year-old."

"Would you rather she be broody like most teenagers?" said Carmen, chuckling. She put her arms around Eve's waist and kissed her neck. "You know, I don't understand why you never wanted kids. You're good with them."

Eve smiled. "You just want to lock me down."

"I learned years ago there's no locking you down. But you know I do think about it sometimes. Adopting. I wouldn't want to do it alone though."

"Carmen, you're not going to talk me into having children. I'm not into that traditional family shit. Never was my thing."

She brushed her nose against Eve's neck and giggled. "I know. You're a lifelong rebel."

Eve slid the pan inside the oven and placed the used dishes in the sink before taking a quick look at the greens.

More noise sounded from the hallway until Aya emerged with a big smile. "I was playing fetch with Miss Sandy. She doesn't like to give the ball back."

"You're supposed to do that outside." Eve cast her an annoyed look.

Aya dropped on her chair at the table, and her eyes widened as she took in the presence of the strange woman whose arms were wrapped around Eve.

Carmen removed her apron and pulled Eve close to kiss her lips. "I'll pop in later this evening, okay?"

Eve smiled and, a moment later, Carmen vanished.

"Who was that?" asked Aya.

Eve threw her a fleeting glance. "That's Carmen. I mentioned she might be popping in and out from time to time."

"She's pretty. I heard you and Dad talking about her one night. Is she coming for dinner?"

"Maybe. Anyway, what have you been up to besides messing with the dog?"

"Earlier, I was in the barn. You didn't tell me catching chickens is hard work. They're fast."

"That's why you don't chase them, honey," said Eve, washing a bowl and placing it in the rack.

"But if they run—"

"You wait until they're relaxing. Then just scoop them up, hold their wings down, and be gentle so they know you don't mean any harm. They'll let you pet them or gather eggs with little fight." She approached Aya and scrunched up her nose as a musty odor filled her nostrils. "I guess you must've really been having fun because you smell like them.

Why were you out there anyway?"

Aya lifted her arms, sniffed herself, and shrugged. "I was working on my scarves for Dad and Malik. But I got bored and thought I'd sit in the barn and play with the chickens for a while until Miss Sandy came in there."

"Where are the scarves?" asked Eve, looking at the table and the bench. Baldwin was sitting next to her and busy grooming himself.

"In the living room. I'm halfway finished. Oh, I've been meaning to ask you who are those people in the photo on the fireplace mantel?"

Eve removed plates and glasses from the cabinet. "Which photo?"

"The one with you and the two other people. A really pretty woman with short, dark hair and a man with a bald head and thick beard."

"My two old friends, Zoey and Gabriel Ellis."

"Where are they now?" asked Aya, petting Baldwin.

The loud noise of broth boiling over and spilling onto the burner startled Eve. She hurried to the stove and turned the temperature to low. With her back to Aya, she stood there for a moment lost in her thoughts. Not a day went by that she didn't think about Zoey and Gabriel. Not a day went by that she didn't regret every action she'd taken from the moment she took the job with the Special Procurements Initiative twenty-five years ago. How that one decision had altered the course of her life and robbed her of anything resembling happiness…she never would be able to describe to this child.

"Eve?"

She turned to Aya and smiled. "You go take a shower, and dinner will be ready when you come down. All right?"

Aya nodded. "Is Jesús going to be here for dinner? I need to talk with him about tonight's mission."

"Yes, he's just on a simple errand. You know he's not one to miss dinner."

"What's his errand?"

Thinking about Zoey and Gabriel, a sad smile sailed across Eve's face. "He's picking me up some wine and weed. Stuff you're too young to have any use for. Now go on and get cleaned up."

A tense atmosphere pervaded the Human and Post-Human Coalition for Peace headquarters in London. The tension emanated from Orson, who had been on edge since the surprise press conference from the President of the United States. The last thing he needed on the day of his meeting with President Zǐháo Chen of China was more chaotic news from the United States.

Yet two hours before his late afternoon meeting with President Chen, Orson sat at his desk and watched with increasing anxiety as President Sonia Espinoza Lopez explained that someone had been carrying out nightly missions to rescue captured post-humans from the People's Army. Within weeks, the post-human refugee population on the East Coast and Southeast of the country had doubled as the Midwest struggled to keep control of their fader holding facilities. President Lopez, who controlled the East Coast, called the individuals responsible for the rescues "heroes". Meanwhile, General Harris of the People's Army of the Midwest Front had announced a large reward for anyone who could provide information leading to the capture of the "vigilantes". General Harris and other People's Army top brass blamed the New American Army of the Eastern Front and the Southeastern post-human militias for the prison breaks. For the already divided and struggling country, military tensions were reaching a peak and edging towards an all-out war.

Orson welcomed the final collapse of the former empire. But something else bothered him about the situation. Was the girl behind the rescues? If so, he needed to extract her. Fast.

Sitting opposite President Chen later, he tried not to daydream. For half an hour, he listened as the man talked about brokering a new ceasefire deal with the Coalition and neutralizing the Children of Mao separatists—groups of humans and post-humans who disapproved of the China's relationship with the Coalition, which they accused of engaging in illegal surveillance and questionable peacekeeping operations in non-Coalition countries.

"I assure you I can put a stop to the separatists in Shanghai and Hong Kong. But the newest fusion reactor is of utmost importance, Orson. As long as I have your word that the Coalition will approve the contract for the reactor, you don't have to worry about the separatists."

"Am I to understand that were it not for the promise of another reactor you would not intervene against these terrorists?" asked Orson.

President Chen regarded him with an impassive face.

"But you made your country a member of the Coalition. Do you not approve of the Coalition, President Chen?"

"It's not the Coalition that the resistance has concerns about, Chief Minister."

*It's me.* Orson considered what Diya had told him about the need to employ a peaceful strategy against the opposition. But it all irked him. If he was playing nice with the opposition, how would he ever be able to align all countries under the Coalition? Wouldn't it take violence to achieve that outcome? Yet, as Diya had told him, a violent conflict with opposition forces would make him look like a tyrant. *And that's what my detractors want the people to believe about me. That I'm nothing more than a common villain.*

He sighed and looked at President Chen's lined face. *Diya's right. I have to tread carefully. I must give in to some of their demands.* He reminded himself that though he easily could make these people do what he wanted—that they'd be powerless to stop him if he dared go against Diya's advice—he had to stay true to his overall mission. Peace and a better world for everyone. *Humanity forward together.*

For this reason, Orson nodded. "You will get your reactor. You have my word."

When they rose and shook hands minutes later, cameras flashed and eager reporters buzzed around like a beehive, launching questions like torpedoes at Orson and President Chen. Orson fastened a button on his blazer jacket, while President Chen turned to the audience of reporters.

"It gives me great pleasure to finalize this deal with President Chen, the leader of the world's largest economy. I am very happy to open the next generation fusion reactor in Beijing. This will be the fourth fusion reactor in China. As I have repeated before, it's vital that we deal with the resistance in a peaceful and careful manner to prevent any further loss of post-human and human life. I'm hopeful that this prolonged guerrilla campaign will end, and time will show the Coalition is on the right side of history."

The audience erupted with chatter as reporters threw more questions at him. Orson raised his hand, and the room fell silent.

Displaying his omnilingualism, he spoke highly of President Chen in fluent Mandarin. The crowd cheered.

Taking Orson's hand, President Chen leaned over to whisper into Orson's ear, "I hope I can count on your vote of confidence when the General Assembly election comes at the end of this year."

Thinking about his conversation with Blade last

month, Orson smiled and held President Chen's hand in the air. He caught a glimpse of Diya, her eyes fixed on him with glowing approval. Her admiration and approval were all he needed to feel comfortable with the deal he'd struck with President Chen.

Although, as relieved as he should feel about the deal, he couldn't stop his mind from drifting to the press conference and his growing problem across the Atlantic.

The small crowd dispersed, and the room emptied, leaving Orson standing on the stage near Diya. He busied himself checking his phone as Diya finished her conversation with the few remaining reporters.

Once the reporters left, she approached him with a smile. "Well done. I think we're on the right track with China."

He groaned. "Bloody politics."

"Says the politician," Diya replied, laughing as they headed toward the exit. "I think approving the contract for another fusion reactor to China will ease their pain, especially when you announce at the end of the year that Blade Sonani will remain President of the General Assembly. The reactor should make Chen a bit more willing to forgive your slight, I'd say."

"Diplomacy is so tedious."

"Yes, but diplomacy is why people admire you, Orson."

He entered the elevator after her. "Reactor or not, I all but promised Chen that position. He'll see red when it doesn't happen. It could lead to China opting out of the Coalition."

"And where will that get them? You can take back your four fusion reactors, and they'll return to where they were twenty-five years ago. And they certainly don't want to lose their access to the Q System and NeoNet."

*She's right, I suppose. The Q System alone is enough to keep them in line.*

The Q System, a database developed through the Remington Science Center, compiled, tracked, and monitored the online and public activity of every post-human throughout the Coalition's member nations. At the beginning of the Great Turn, governments realized that faders could be used as potential spies and expose national security secrets. As paranoia set in, governments looked for means to watch or else suppress this new class of people. Border laws became more restrictive and anti-post-human laws proliferated, tearing at the social fabric around the world. For many worried world leaders, the creation of the Q System felt like a miracle that couldn't have arrived too soon. Countries readily joined the Coalition in exchange for the protection the expansive tracking system offered.

"If they lost the ability to track all their post-humans, they'd go stark mad like the Americans. You and I both know, the normies are still terrified of us, but at least for now they know who we are because of the database."

"Which gives them some sense of control and, in general, keeps the peace between us and them. I know, Diya. Don't worry, I'm following your advice on this matter. You've never led me astray before."

She brushed her hair back, and a pleased look spread across her face. Stroking Orson's hair, she smiled at him. "Just doing my job."

The elevator opened, and they dropped their hands to their sides before exiting. They slowed as they approached Orson's office. Thomas was leaning against the wall next to the door and tapping his feet. He appeared positively bored. When he saw them, he straightened his posture and fixed his blazer jacket.

Diya stopped, grabbed the lapels of Orson's suit jacket, and gave him a passionate kiss while rubbing her fingers through his thick hair and leaving it quite messy. "We'll talk later," she whispered to Orson. Without so much as another look at Thomas, she turned around and headed to the elevator.

Thomas said nothing, but Orson noticed a slight frown curled his lips as he watched Diya leave.

Inside the office, Orson removed his suit jacket, hung it on the coat stand next to the door, and seated himself behind a large desk. Directly behind him was a window overlooking central London. As though swiping the air, he turned on his computer and a holographic screen appeared. He sideswiped the images and addressed Thomas in a distracted tone. "Have a seat, Thomas. What can I help you with?"

Thomas unbuttoned his jacket and sat. "Sir, I wanted to give you an update on what's been happening in the U.S."

"Yes?"

"As you know, President Lopez has been singing the praises of the person—"

"The 'hero' who's been freeing post-humans for the last few weeks. Yes, Thomas I'm aware."

"Our inside sources confirmed that several facilities—"

"Prisons. They're prisons, Thomas."

"Yes. Several prisons had their detainees all teleported out at the same time. In some cases, over a hundred individuals were teleported all together."

"So my suspicions are right. It is the girl," Orson muttered, looking at Thomas but still sideswiping news articles.

"There's no typical post-human capable of simultaneously teleporting that many individuals all at once.

All our data on post-humans over the years confirms this point. This is not regular post-human behavior."

Orson stopped sideswiping and rested his hand on the desk. He leaned back in his chair. "Only an alpha would be capable of such feats. And I'm not even sure I'm capable of that."

"Sir, I'm sure the girl is aligned with some underground pro post-human agents. She's challenging the People's Army in the Midwest. From what we've gathered, she seems to be operating near Chicago and the upper Midwest region. I propose we revisit Chicago. Once again, a black-ops mission that can't be traced to you or the Coalition."

"And what do you suggest should be the purpose of this mission, Thomas?"

A smile settled on Thomas' pale face. "I can assume we have some cys that are looking for a little payback for what happened last time they were there. This time we hit her where it hurts: South Shore. Leave no one breathing. We can send in three covert cys teams to draw out the army, one team to take out the unprotected militants, and send in old-world predator drones to bomb everything after our cys have done their work. She'll have no choice but to come out of the shadows. Not to mention we add fuel to the tensions between the fractured armed forces. For all intents and purposes, this will look like an attack carried out by the Eastern Front, since the Eastern Front used old-world predator drones in their last campaign against the Midwest Front—"

"Five years ago before the last ceasefire agreement. Yes, yes. I see your angle." Orson leaned forward. "It was clear from the press conference that these prison breaks have exacerbated tensions between the Eastern Front and the Midwest Front."

"Yes, sir. As you know, the two fronts have had an uneasy truce for years. Using this approach, we kill two birds with one stone: smoke out the girl and destroy any semblance of peace between the two fronts."

Orson cast Thomas an approving smile. "Remind me not to get on your bad side. Between you and Diya, I'm not sure who's cleverer."

Thomas frowned.

"Ah, lighten up. A comparison to Diya is always a compliment. Now then, back to this plan."

"Yes, sir?"

"Set it up."

"On it." Thomas headed to the door but paused and cleared his throat before turning to face Orson. "If I could speak freely, sir...?"

"Of course."

"Please be careful of the company you keep. Even of those you believe to be the most loyal to you."

Orson smiled and propped his elbows on the desk.

"Should I be worried about you or someone else?"

"I'm only saying you'd do well to not be blinded by beauty. Sir."

At this, Orson laughed. "You look after Chicago, Tommy, and don't worry about me. I'm practically immortal, so I doubt I'll find myself on the senate floor like Julius Caesar."

Thomas gave him a curt nod and left the office. Alone and in silence, Orson stared out the window and considered Thomas' warning.

Aya sat below Eve on the second porch step. Eve fussed with her Afro puffs, pulling Aya's head this way and that with the wide-toothed comb. Aya winced and smacked her lips in frustration.

Kendrick had tried to do Aya's hair but to no avail. By the time she was eleven years old, he'd given up any hope that he would be able to fix his daughter's hair in the cute styles her mother had done so many times. "If we were back in the days before the Great Turn, I'd take you to a beauty shop," he'd once told her.

Although plenty of women had offered to do Aya's curly, bushy hair, she'd rebuffed all their offers. They all had ulterior motives—namely, to snag her father—and she wanted no part in their schemes. When she got old enough, she learned to style it herself. Her favorite style? One giant puff on each side and, sometimes, just one big puff at the top of her head.

"You sure you want it back in the same style? Do you always wear your hair like this?" asked Eve, sliding the comb through Aya's hair.

"It was the last hairstyle my mom did for me before she went away." Aya paused. "Eve, what was it like?"

"What was what like?" She made a part in the middle of Aya's hair and tightened the left side into a big puff.

"What was everything like before the Great Turn? I know back then most people didn't know faders existed. I know the stories Dad told me, and I remember things I've read. But what was it like for you, being a fader and all?"

"It was different. I think some people knew about us well before the Great Turn. An old company named FordTech eventually traced the existence of faders a few decades before the Great Turn, so I imagine some people had to have known about us. Anyway, things were tolerable then…relatively. We had cell phones that worked, lots of food, busy cities, a dysfunctional education system, major environmental destruction, and wars that never ended. We had crooked politicians, all-powerful corporations, annoying celebrities like Faye Lennox."

"I love Faye Lennox!"

Eve laughed. "To each their own. Anyway, it wasn't really all that different, now that I think about it. We just stumbled our way through history."

"Are we still stumbling?"

"I'd say so. We just have less order to our chaos now. Nowadays, there are more military factions than anybody can keep count of, and you never know which faction's turf you're on. We're on the brink of another war, this time between the East, led by President Lopez, and the Midwest, led by General Harris."

"What about the South? It seems okay and friendly to us."

Eve shook her head. "The South is pretty much divided, with some states under the control of President Lopez, and a few other rogue states divided among the militia groups whose services can be bought for a fee. Why else do you think Lee has helped house the faders you've saved?"

"You paid him? I thought since he's a fader, he was doing it because—"

"Everybody has a price, child. Nothing is free. Lee needs weapons, and Jesús is good at acquiring them." Eve patted Aya's head and resumed combing.

"Is my dad paying you to let me stay here?"

Eve smiled. "Okay, so maybe some things are free here and there. No, your dad isn't paying me."

"What about out west? California, Oregon, Washington, and Alaska. Dad told me things are nice out there, and Carmen lives there..."

"I don't know if I'd say nice but definitely better."

"They're part of the Coalition, right?"

"Yeah. Personally, I didn't like that region before the Great Turn, and I still wouldn't want to live there. It's beautiful out there, but they have their problems."

"Like what?"

Eve explained how the four Coalition states were dealing with an influx of people fleeing from the Western Wastelands, how the states had erected mostly ineffectual border walls to separate themselves from the rest of the country. She combed out the puff on the right side of Aya's head and moisturized her hair with water and coconut oil. "The world you were born into is tough, but it's always been tough. Unfortunately, people always let hatred and fear control them. That's exactly what helped Orson climb to power and enabled him to create the Coalition after the United Nations collapsed. A lot of faders in the western states that belong to the Coalition see him as the fader who bridged the gap, bringing regular people and faders together in peace to achieve a common goal. All a smokescreen to get nations to buy into his Q System."

"Q System?"

"Child, did they teach you all nothing about the world outside Chicago? Orson created the Q System to track all illegal fader activity, although I'm sure he tracks everyone at this point. Stupid people wanted to feel safe from us and weak faders just wanted to be accepted, so the Q System was basically perfect. I can't even blame him for playing these idiots. Anyway, most of the world fell for his peace and transparency bullshit. But I think his only goal was power, and the Q System and his fusion energy finally gave him that. The man is damn near untouchable at this point. I mean, people have started questioning the Q System more lately, wondering if they handed their governments and Orson too much power in the name of safety. It's a little too late to complain at this point, though."

"Doesn't Orson fight for faders around the world? They didn't teach us much about him in school, but some of the things I've read about him...he seems like he wants to help make the world better for faders. What's not to like about that?"

"Maybe I just generally don't trust a man with that much power. I don't know," said Eve, shrugging. She tied a band around Aya's second Afro puff ponytail and surveyed the two perfect puffs on each side of the girl's head. Reaching forward, she handed Aya a mirror.

Aya smiled as she stared at her reflection.

"Aya, I have something to tell you, dear." Before Eve could get out another word, Jesús burst onto the porch, cursing in Spanish and his face as red as a tomato. Sweat poured down his forehead, his usually neat hair disheveled.

"They're dead," he shouted. "They're all dead!"

"What the hell are you talking about?" said Eve, rising and grabbing his shoulders to calm him. "Pull yourself together and stop pacing. Who's dead?"

"In South Shore, everybody's dead. It's all gone. Burned to the ground."

Aya jumped up and clasped Jesús' arm in a vise grip. "Take me there." Her voice was uncharacteristically low.

"Let's not be hasty," said Eve, giving Aya a gentle pat on the arm to show that she should release Jesús. "Do we know who did this, Jesús?"

"No. It could've been the Eastern Front. Whoever it was, they could still be there, so I don't think we should set foot there yet. We'd be hopelessly outnumbered and outgunned."

Aya frowned. "I can't be hurt. Remember? I'll go by myself."

Eve shot Jesús a threatening look.

"Wait, Aya," said Jesús, meeting her panicked gaze. "We can go together."

"Fine." She held his hand and looked at Eve, before surrendering to that familiar tug in her stomach.

Within moments, they appeared at 78th and South
Shore Drive, mere blocks from the house Aya once
considered home. Smoke filled the air and flames rose high,
brightening the sky. Buildings and vehicles had been reduced
to rubble. Destruction, smoke, and fire stretched from the
lakefront to the old Dan Ryan expressway as far as her eyes
could see.

Aya fell to her knees, tears flowing like a raging river.

Jesús looked around and tried to pull her up, but she
recoiled.

Besides her brother and father, everything and
everyone she knew and loved was—had been—here. The
small children she'd given reading and arithmetic lessons to
on Tuesday and Thursday evenings. The old cultural center
she and Malik snuck into every weekend. The house on South
Shore Drive where she'd grown up and made so many
memories. Her body lurched from sobbing. It was all gone.

"Aya, I'm sorry, but we need to get out of here. It's
not safe."

She stared at the rubble and glowing embers of her
childhood and wiped away tears. In an instant, she felt the tug
in her stomach and found herself standing on the porch at
Eve's house.

Aya drew back as Eve reached for her. "I thought I'd
be able to go home someday."

"I know. I wish I could—" She stopped when Aya
took off, running into the house and slamming the door.

They settled into the living room, where Eve plopped onto
the sofa, lit a joint, and looked at the black television screen.
The old flat screen television hadn't picked up channels in
years, but she'd felt compelled to keep it in the house as a
reminder of the old days. She'd hoped one day she'd turn it
on and it would pick up an antenna signal for some

channels—that is, without requiring her to use her abilities to pick up channels. It would be nice to watch television again without relying on her abilities. Yet on a day like today, it seemed like a silly, mundane hope. She handed the joint to Jesús sitting next to her.

"Do you think she's coming out of that room for the rest of the day? I'm not sure she should be alone right now, Eve."

"She'll be fine. I'll check on her in a bit."

Jesús looked toward the window and a gloomy look came over him. "It was so terrible. The destruction. There was nothing left, just cinders. And the smell…" He trailed off and met Eve's eyes.

"I don't think this was the work of the Eastern Front. I've had a bad feeling since you two started the rescues, but I didn't want to say anything. I didn't want to deter you two from saving those people, obviously."

"A bad feeling?" He handed the joint to her.

"Yes. We knew she was on Orson's radar, since that's why the cys showed up in Chicago. I worried this might make him do something awful."

"You really think Orson—"

"Yes, Jesús. There's always been whispers—all unverified—of Orson retaliating against communities suspected of harboring powerful faders. I bet he doesn't want the competition. Why do you think I've made a point of staying off his radar?" She took a puff, inhaled, and put out the joint in the ashtray on the coffee table. "Honestly, I'm probably not even capable of getting high right now. Might as well save that for a better time."

Jesús relaxed and sighed. "Aya told me about how her father and his army buddies had devastated areas during some of their battles with other factions and the Coalition. I don't think she ever thought she'd see the same devastation firsthand, that it would happen to her people."

Eve looked at the framed photograph on the fireplace mantel. The photograph that had piqued Aya's curiosity. "I'm afraid she's about to learn that the world is crueler than she imagined," Eve muttered, thinking about Zoey and Gabriel Ellis who were standing beside her in the photograph. "We all learn that eventually. Don't we?"

Jesús cast her a dark look. "Are you going to tell her, Eve?"

"I was on the verge of telling her before you showed up."

"Do it soon. She needs to know who you are."

Eve glanced at him and nodded. Sitting there in silence, she mulled her thoughts about the attack. If Orson had done it, how long would it be before he found them? Surely he had his ways of finding even the most well-hidden people.

Shaking off these thoughts, she decided she needed a distraction. She turned on the television, closed her eyes, and searched for a distant signal—usually she could pick up a quantum signal from the Coalition West, but it was never a sure bet she'd find a stable signal and she worried about the risks of detection. Last year, she'd used her limited cyberkinesis abilities to find a strong enough signal to watch the Los Angeles New Year's celebration live. Ever since, she periodically distracted herself with television programs from the Coalition world.

When she found a signal, she focused on it and an image appeared on the screen. "Oh for fuck's sake," she scoffed. "This is why I never bother turning this thing on."

On the screen, Faye Lennox was performing alongside another pop singer with whom Eve was not familiar. Jesús lit the joint again, took a drag, and hummed along.

Aya remained in her room for two days, taking all her meals there, while Jesús busied himself with gardening, errands, and tending to the chickens. Meanwhile, Eve focused on gathering information about the attack in Chicago. It could've been the work of the New American Army of the Eastern Front. That theory seemed plausible, since People's Army forces had shot down several outdated predator drones—a weapon of choice of the Eastern Front—in Chicago during the attack. But Eve wasn't convinced, and she wasn't alone. Lee also didn't believe the Eastern Front was responsible for the attack.

Eve still suspected Orson. She knew it sounded crazy, but she couldn't shake all the rumors of him assassinating faders he perceived to be more powerful than him. The world's leading fader killing other faders...it sounded insane. Yet, besides the Q System, these rumors were part of the reason so many anti-Coalition resistance groups had spawned around the world in the last few years. Was it all mere conjecture and conspiracy, or was there a grain of truth in it?

"What a goddamn mess," Eve muttered, standing next to the fireplace and sipping wine. "Nobody knows what's going on. None of my sources can confirm who did it. The only thing we know now is that tensions between the Eastern and Midwest armies have hit their breaking point. The fallout is going to be big."

Jesús stretched his legs out and rested his feet on the coffee table. "Is your gut still saying it's..." He stopped when Aya appeared at the doorway of the living room.

Eve surveyed her flattened Afro puffs and weary eyes. "Have a seat, Aya. There's something I'd like to share with you."

Aya joined Jesús on the sofa, where he handed her a pillow as a cushion to lean on.

Eve remained near the fireplace, the half-empty wine glass lowered near her waist. "You saved so many people over the last few weeks. I don't know if you realize the magnitude of what you and Jesús accomplished."

"But I couldn't save the people back home, could I? All my friends. Even the people I didn't like, the soldiers who treated me bad. I couldn't save them. They didn't deserve to die like that."

Jesús exhaled. "Nobody deserves that."

"There's something I've been wanting to speak with you about." Eve drained her glass of wine and sat it on the fireplace mantel. Twisting her fingers around one long dreadlock, she fixed her eyes on Aya. At once, Eve's locs started to shrink, the skin on her face began to tighten, and her hair color changed from gray to black. In mere moments, she had a short black Afro and not a hint of a wrinkle in her freckled brown face. She looked like the younger version of herself in the photograph on the fireplace mantel.

Aya shrugged. "You already told me you can manipulate how we see things. Just like you do to make the house look abandoned to outsiders."

"No, this is what I truly look like. If I'm going to be honest with you, I need you to see what I really look like," Eve replied. She grabbed the framed photograph off the fireplace. "This photo was taken in 2020 when I was twenty-five. You need to know about the things that happened to me that year and—"

Aya looked bored. "I already knew that photo was old because the clothes you're wearing in it look old-fashioned."

"Honey, this was one of my most fashionable photos. Faded jeans never go out of style," quipped Eve. She pulled up an ottoman in front of Aya, sat, and placed the glass of wine on the coffee table. "The year this photo was taken is when everything changed for me. That's when the government found out about me. About my abilities. This was before we faders were well known to the public. The government tortured me and later my friends. I got away and ended up a fugitive for a while. During that time, I was violently attacked by a paranoid fader, who slit my throat." Eve traced her finger from ear to ear along her throat.

Aya sat up straight. "I don't understand. What are you telling me?"

"The wound should've been fatal, but it wasn't. I healed almost immediately," she went on, watching a dumbfounded look cloud Aya's face. "I should be dead, but my body healed itself. Just like yours healed itself. Just like Orson's did when he miraculously recovered from the assassination attempt against him in China twenty years ago. They called him the alpha after that. I'm one too. And so are you."

Aya gaped at her.

"After my near-death experience—and even before then—I knew I was different from the other faders. I basically could do anything. Of course, I always figured at least one other fader possessed all the abilities. I figured I couldn't be the only one. And then along came Orson…and now you."

"You're an alpha." Aya rose and glared at Eve. "Why do you just sit in the house all day, every day? You could've been helping us. Jesús could've died on our missions. Other faders could've died while you were sitting here letting us do all the hard work. You had the power to make things better, but you did nothing. Instead, you sent Jesús to do it all for you."

Eve frowned. "Nothing? I let you stay here. I let others stay here out of harm's way. That's not nothing. You need to calm down and have a seat."

Aya remained on her feet and folded her arms across

her chest. "I see now. One alpha tries to save the whole world, and another one tries to forget the world even exists."

Eve breathed in deeply, doing her best to not appear angry with the girl. "You're upset. I understand that. I should have told you sooner. I'm sorry I didn't."

"It's not about me!" Aya yelled and rushed out the room. A moment later, the door slammed upstairs.

"That's the last time she's going to slam doors in this house." Eve picked up the glass of wine and drained it. "This is why I don't have children. That girl is on my nerves."

Jesús shook his head and seemed to suppress laughter. "I never thought I'd see someone tell you off, and I certainly didn't think it'd be a teenager."

Eve cut her eyes at him and got up. "I'll go up and talk to her. But, first, I need another glass of wine."

Eve knocked on the door and, hearing no answer, gently turned the knob. Aya was lying on her stomach on the bed. She didn't move or acknowledge Eve's presence. *Headstrong kid, this one,* Eve concluded, sitting next to Aya on the bed. She held her hand out to pat the girl's back, hoping this would encourage her to sit up so they could finish the conversation.

It worked. She sat up but scooted to the edge of the bed away from Eve and cast her a sideways glare.

"You've been here for over a month," Eve began, her voice as gentle as she could make it. "But I've seen you grow so much over this short time. I knew when we first met that you were like me, that you could do anything you put your mind to. Your dad had already told me about all the things you could do. So I felt it was my job to train you a bit, open the door wider, and give you the freedom to see your potential. And you ran straight through that door. I couldn't be prouder, Aya." She reached out to put her hand on Aya's shoulder, but the girl backed away.

"You're making it about me, but it's not. You have all this power, but you don't use it. My friends in South Shore...you could've saved them."

"We don't know that, Aya. We don't know that I could've saved them. None of us had any warning of the attack."

"Why do you ignore the outside world?"

Eve's shoulders sunk. "I tried to save the world before. It didn't work."

"So you just gave up?"

"You don't understand what it was like before, when they discovered my abilities. I just wanted to be a teacher and not be poor. I just wanted to live in peace. But the world wouldn't let us. So I tried to make it better, to be the hero, and I failed. I eventually lost every friend I ever had, everybody I loved. And I did things I'm not proud of." She turned from Aya, thinking about AJ, Niles, and Samuel. Her thoughts drifted to Zoey and Gabriel, and she closed her eyes for a moment. "You have no idea what I've sacrificed. I think the good I've done over the years has been more than enough."

"It sounds like you gave up."

Anger crashed over Eve, and it became more difficult to suppress the urge to yell at the girl. "Kid, you need to fall back. You're barely out of puberty and have the audacity to judge my life? I've been dealing with this mess since before you were born. And I did what I had to do to survive. I was an advocate for our rights. I opened my home to faders. In my house—*this* house that's been in my family for three generations—faders like you have found refuge, safety, and food.

"Yes, many people are dead, and I probably could've saved some of them. But despite having god-like abilities, I'm not a god, nor do I have a desire to be anybody's god. I don't want the weight of the world on my shoulders, and you shouldn't want that burden either. It'll destroy everything that's good about you."

Aya looked at her hands. "I think you just want to hide from everything. You're afraid of the world outside."

An image of AJ's mangled body, riddled with bullets and lying in the middle of Sheridan Road in Uptown Chicago rushed to the front of Eve's mind. If she hadn't been there to remove the bullets quickly, she was sure AJ would've died, that she wouldn't have been able to heal her and get her to the emergency room in time. Tears clouded her eyes as she recalled how she had cradled AJ's blood-soaked, still body in the middle of the street, how stunned she was when AJ opened her eyes. They'd returned to Chicago after a year in the Caribbean—Eve, AJ, Niles, Samuel, Zoey, and Gabriel—hoping to build a decent life following the closure of the Special Procurements Initiative facility on the west side. But soon hate and prejudice had shattered any possibility of having a decent, peaceful life among regular humans. After the shooting, Eve's friends left her, one by one, as she encouraged them to do what was best to protect themselves while she continued fighting.

"You asked about the people in that photo. They were my closest friends. For a while, we all lived together in a big house in Rogers Park. We'd pooled our money together to buy a big enough place for the three of us. Two other friends of mine, Niles and Samuel, moved into the other side of the house," said Eve. AJ had insisted upon having a lush bachelor pad in Uptown, eager to accommodate her steady stream of girlfriends and her new reality television career. "We were happy. I was doing speaking engagements on news shows and TV shows, informing people about faders and why we deserved equal rights, trying to show them we were just like everyone else. Day in and day out, I was working to convince people to just let us live, while I watched so many of us get shot like dogs, locked up, disappeared, homeless because nobody wanted to hire faders, fader kids kicked out on the streets. But I just knew if they saw enough of us looking like them, living with them, being in relationships with them, being in movies, then they'd come to accept us.

"Then, we all watched our friend get shot in broad daylight and almost die because some asshole considered her and our kind an abomination. An aberration.

"I tried to stay hopeful, but my friends didn't feel the same way. The shooting killed that bit of idealism they were clinging to. Zoey and Gabriel left, emigrated to Greece. Gabe's from a military family, so he had family stationed there. He and Zoey begged me to leave with them. Niles and Samuel left, and I don't know where they ended up. My friend who got shot—AJ—left with one of her girlfriends and went west. We lost touch. I haven't spoken to any of my friends in twenty years, Aya. I have no idea how to reach them, or if they're even still alive. These people were my family, and I lost them all," she said, pausing and rubbing her wet eyes. "So forgive me if I don't think highly of the world outside this house."

"You say you lost touch. Why? Why didn't you just teleport to them? It's not like you had to stay away from them."

Eve lowered her gaze. "I felt like all the bad things that had happened to them was my fault. I was too well-known at that point, and I didn't want to go through the world disguising myself all the time to avoid unwanted attention. I thought maybe if I just stayed away they could have normal, happy lives without worrying about what someone might do to them to get to me. I didn't want to be the reason any of my friends got hurt again."

Aya nodded. "Well, I'm sorry for what happened to you. But I can't sit in this house forever just to sneak out at night to help a few people. I won't let what happened to my city happen again."

Eve closed her eyes in frustration. "You can't save everybody, Aya."

"I can try. I can go to someone who can help us."

"Who?" asked Eve.

"Orson. He has the power to protect faders and put an end to all this fighting between the Midwest Front and the Eastern Front. I heard you and Jesús talking about it—you think the Eastern Front did the attack."

"We don't know that, and your dad's in the Eastern Front now. He'd tell us if the Eastern—"

"Orson can help us stop all this mess. I'm going to him."

When Eve extended her hand, Aya didn't draw back. "Look, there's a lot we still don't know. I want you to stay here and continue to help us get people to safety. Don't you realize how important that work is, helping people to freedom? I want you to stay, Aya. Your dad would want you to stay."

With a frown, Aya turned away and lay on her stomach again. "You can't stop me from leaving."

Deflated, Eve headed out the room. She lingered at the door for a moment. "Dinner will be ready in a couple of hours," she said, and shut the door. *How on earth am I going to explain this to Kendrick?* Eve knew what the girl would do next, and she knew there would be no talking her out of it.

# THE SECOND ALPHA

# 7

Standing in Eve's library, Aya turned over a book and stared at the back cover. Her thoughts drifted from her father and Malik to the dreadful news from Chicago since the attack. Besides the hundreds of confirmed dead, almost one hundred more people remained missing.

As she pushed aside gloomy thoughts, she returned to her father and Malik. Nearly two months had passed since their departure and she'd heard nothing from them, only reassurances from Eve that they were safe and well. *Did they even remember my birthday?* It wasn't every day that someone turned fifteen, so she'd expected at least a call. But July seventeenth had come and gone with no word from them, and she wondered if they'd celebrated it without her. They were probably going on about their lives, not even thinking about her.

She'd asked Eve and Jesús if she could visit Philadelphia, only to be told her father thought it was too dangerous at the moment. "He's trying to build trust with the New American Army in his new post. Although they're fader-friendly, they're still hesitant about newcomers. Give him time to send for you," Eve had said the morning of Aya's birthday, three days after the attack in Chicago. But none of it made sense to Aya, and she grew tired of trying to understand. Instead, she'd busied herself with finishing the scarves for her brother and father and thinking about her next mission. A solo mission.

"Are you sure I can't talk you out of doing this?" asked Jesús, lingering at the doorway of the library room on the day of her departure.

She slid the book onto the shelf. "Yes. I'm sure."

He sighed. "Well, it's going to be lonely here without you, kid. It was nice for Eve to have someone other than me to do all the tedious stuff like turning the compost and feeding the chickens."

Aya grabbed the backpack from the chair and slid it over her shoulders.

Eve approached in the hallway, holding Baldwin in her arms and caressing the yellow-eyed cat. Jesús stepped aside to allow her to enter. A heavy melancholic silence filled the room for a moment. "If anybody tries to do something horrible to you, you tell us. Jesús and I will come and tear some shit up. Believe that."

"I know," said Aya smiling as tears pooled in her eyes. "Eve?"

"Yeah?"

"Tell Carmen I want her to braid my hair like hers when I come back."

Eve nodded, caressing the top of Baldwin's head as he purred.

"It's ten in the morning in London," said Jesús, coming forward. "The Coalition leaders should be meeting right now, according to my contact there. It's the Great or Huge Assembly or some crap like that going on."

Eve shook her head at him. "The General Assembly. By the way, who's your contact there, Jesús? You've never told me."

"A fader I dated a few years ago. He lives outside London now."

Looking at them with unflinching resolve, Aya tightened the backpack straps on her shoulders. "All right. I'm ready."

Jesús turned to her, and he appeared worried. He handed her a cell phone. "Remember to call the number saved in there if you get into any trouble. Go to the hotel address I saved in the phone. The money I gave you is enough for a few nights' stay and food."

"Yeah, yeah, you've told me all this a hundred times." Aya grinned, trying not to look terrified. "Are you still going to visit?"

He cast her a reassuring smile. "I'll send you a message on that phone when I plan to pop into London. So be sure to check the phone each morning for messages from me. At all other times, keep it off so it can't be traced."

"Got it." With a nod to him, Aya slipped the phone inside her jeans pocket.

"Given that he's in a big meeting right now, when you arrive there should be plenty of media and spectators," Jesús continued. "So it's going to be difficult to get to him while he's in the meeting. I'm sorry we didn't have any contacts inside the Coalition to make this easier. You're going to have to figure out how to get his attention."

Aya smiled. *Oh, I know how to get his attention.*

"I'll repeat my advice to you—fade and see if you can follow him until he's alone. No matter what, this is going to be weird for everybody, Aya. Especially for Orson. He won't be the one and only all-powerful anymore, and eventually everyone will know it." Jesús shot Eve a wary look.

She came forward and straightened the collar on Aya's shirt. "Jesús is trying to say you should be careful. Stay alert and watchful."

Aya scoffed. "You talk like Orson's going to try to hurt me or something."

Eve glanced at Jesús and turned to Aya. "Just remember you don't know this guy or his world, Aya. I've told you I have mixed feelings about him, and now I'm telling you to just be smart. Pay attention. Honestly, I'm curious to find out what you learn about him and the Coalition. I'd like to be proved wrong about him."

Silence passed among them as they stared at one another, and Baldwin rubbed against Aya's ankles.

Eve placed her hand on Aya's shoulder. "You and Jesús are the only people who know I'm an alpha, Aya. Not even Carmen knows. Orson probably doesn't even know I'm still alive, and I'm sure it's not for lack of trying to find me. I'd like to keep it that way."

"Okay," said Aya. *She's really too paranoid about everything. Probably from being stuck in this house too long.* She took a few steps back from Eve and Jesús and drew a deep breath.

Aya gazed at them for a while, fearing that this might be the last time she ever saw them. Part of her wanted to call it off, run into their arms, and never leave the farmhouse. But she remembered how easily her father and brother could have perished in Chicago, along with all her old friends. If anybody could prevent it from happening again, it was Orson.

With a wave goodbye to Eve and Jesús, Aya closed her eyes and waited to feel the tug behind her navel.

Sitting at the front of the assembly hall, Orson surveyed the crowd of media personnel, heads of state, economic experts, business leaders, and other dignitaries from all the Coalition nations. Representing over a hundred and sixty countries, the guests had gathered at the Human and Post-Human Coalition for Peace Headquarters for the fourth quarter General

Assembly convening of the Coalition. Orson knew one thing was at the forefront of their minds: the General Assembly president seat.

He caught Diya's eyes and smiled as he recalled their brief conversation in his office before the meeting.

"All the most powerful humans and post-humans jockeying for one seat," he'd said, tucking a stray strand of Diya's hair behind her ears as she leaned against the door.

"It irks you how people feel so compelled to scramble for meager bits of power when all you want to do is bring us peace and harmony."

"It's disappointing and pathetic. But I know that having an election for a new GA President every four years is the best way to maintain my power and ensure the ultimate goal of the Coalition is achieved." He brushed his hand against her cheek, and she looked at him with the most beautiful eyes he'd ever seen.

As Diya explained to him years ago, allowing democratic election rather than appointment of the role of General Assembly president helped reduce the liability of any individual leader becoming too powerful or big-headed. It also helped the leaders to feel more involved in the Coalition's business, and he was more than happy to enable that illusion.

But sometimes he longed to dismantle the Coalition and handle everything himself. It certainly would make things less chaotic and much simpler for him, he surmised. Not to mention it would free up his schedule from needless rituals like today's meeting.

"Humans and post-humans like chaos," Diya said, before leaning forward to plant a kiss on his lips. "They expect chaos, so long as it can be organized and controlled. You know better than anyone how to give them what they want."

He'd pressed his palm against her cheek and stared into her eyes, turned on by how much she understood him. "A world without the chaos of democracy would terrify them." They would not accept that world without a fight, and he had no patience to fight them all.

As he caught Diya's gaze in the crowd now, he winked at her and sipped his cup of steaming hot black tea.

Blade Sonani finished his opening remarks and resumed the seat to the left of the podium. The Russian president, a small man with broad shoulders and a balding crown, headed to the podium. A serious man, he looked as though he was marching rather than walking. Before he reached the podium, he stopped dead in his tracks.

Bolts of electricity sparked around the room, and some people pointed in alarm. Others looked around wide-eyed and confused. Orson held up his cell phone, watching with curiosity as the screen flashed white and black.

As papers blew about the assembly hall and lights flickered, some people rose from their seats and fled to the exit. Orson noticed all the sparks seemed to gather at the center of the room near the stage. A blinding flash caused him to drop his phone, and the entire building went dark.

Terror-stricken people screamed and ran in all directions.

When the lights came on, everyone froze and silence descended upon the crowd. A wiry teenaged girl with dark brown skin and two puffy ponytails was standing below the stage. Besides her t-shirt, jeans, and sneakers, she wore a backpack and a deadly serious look.

Not missing a beat, the video crew turned their cameras on the girl who'd just made a grand entrance.

"My name..." she began, but something caught in her throat. "My name is Aya Wright. I'm here to meet Orson."

All eyes turned to Orson still sitting on the stage and

staring at the girl. He couldn't believe she was here, the second alpha. *Thomas, your plan worked.*

Aya's eyes rested on the man with chestnut hair and green eyes. She recalled his face from news clippings. She studied him for a moment. Compared to everyone else in the room, he appeared composed and unmoved by her sudden appearance. In fact, she detected curiosity rather than fear in him.

When he got up and buttoned his gray blazer jacket, dozens of armed people in fatigues hurried to the center of the room. More of them burst through side doors and the main entrance, making their way to the center of the room. They pointed their handheld railguns at Aya and barked at her to get on her knees. She counted at least a dozen officers surrounding her.

Her heart quickened. "I'm just here to see Orson. I didn't mean to—"

"Get on the ground," one officer repeated. "Now. We're not saying it again."

As Aya lifted her hands into the air, one nervous man fired his weapon.

She couldn't be sure, but time seemed to slow, and the screams of the crowd became muffled. In slow motion, she saw the projectile beam approaching her and put up her hand as though it would block the beam from hitting her face. At once, a cool aura with shades of blue and purple enveloped her entire body. Gasps sounded from the crowd as the projectile beam bounced off Aya.

Onlookers screamed and fled toward the exit. Meanwhile, reporters scattered to a safe distance but continued filming the events live. The officers closed in on Aya, their weapons pointed at her and terror on their faces.

She looked around at them, her mind still racing

about what had happened mere seconds ago. "Always be ready to react," she remembered Eve telling her one day while they practiced telekinesis. "Never let yourself be caught off guard."

With one wave of her hand over her head, the officers' guns flew into the air. Instead of hitting the floor, the weapons levitated above their heads, and the officers looked from their weapons to Aya.

"Enough," came a calm voice. "Stand down."

They halted their approach, and one of them signaled his peers to retreat.

Not moving, Aya kept their guns levitating in the air as they fell back. A couple of officers reached for their levitating guns, but she nodded her head to make the guns leap away from them. She'd gotten a lot of telekinesis practice during the prison missions and, to her delight, it was now paying off. Over her shoulder, she saw Orson coming toward her.

"You can return their weapons to them now," he said, approaching and holding steady eye contact with her.

She regarded him with uncertainty but turned her gaze to the officers. The guns crashed to the floor. After a nod from Orson, the officers scrambled to collect their weapons and rushed from the assembly hall. Her chest heaving in and out, Aya turned to Orson and held her head high. She couldn't believe she was standing face to face with the most powerful fader in the world.

He smiled, an excited gleam in his eyes. "Ms. Wright, I'm sorry about the hasty actions of the Coalition's security officers, but we have to be careful at all times. I'm Orson Remington. It's an honor to meet an alpha."

She shook his hand and, from the corner of her eye, saw the last officer exit the assembly hall. She glanced at the blank faces of the people still in the room, all of them staring at her in silent awe.

A man lingering by the main door of the room lifted his hands and clapped. Other people joined, and soon the entire room erupted in applause.

For the first time in history, two alphas stood side by side, and the whole world had witnessed the event unfold live. In a matter of minutes, Aya became the second most famous fader as headlines dubbed her the "Second Alpha."

At Orson's behest, Thomas escorted Aya from the Coalition headquarters to Orson's home in central London. "Keep her away from the bloodthirsty reporters," he told Thomas before ushering them out the assembly hall. "Diya and I will join you both shortly. I'll keep the reporters distracted here."

Aya followed Thomas, a stocky blond man, as he directed to a black sedan. The noise of the crowd behind them, she glanced at the man and wondered if Eve would tell her to "just play along." As she watched him open the car door, she inhaled and tried to relax. She made herself comfortable in the backseat, and he got in beside her.

When the car started moving, her eyebrows went up in shock as she realized the car had no driver. *This is one of those self-driving cars I've read about.* Fascination and excitement overwhelmed her, and she gazed out the window at the city she'd only read about until now.

Before long, they arrived at Orson's flat, a white stone three-story at the outer circle of Regent's Park.

"Let's go," said Thomas as her door popped open. "Out you go."

They rushed inside the cold house that smelled strongly of vanilla, the fragrance emanating from two candles burning on the living room table. Her eyes drifted from the light brown hardwood floors to the white walls decorated with odd canvases and art pieces. The curious chandelier hanging in the center of the living room caught her attention. Tiny bulbs hung on what looked like slender tree limbs. Two bright blue chairs sat across from a beige sofa and a blue sofa. As beautiful as it all was, it didn't feel as inviting as Eve's home.

Yet she walked from room to room, taking in the home's beauty. Large windows allowing in plenty of natural light in every room, white marble floors in the bathroom, a patio that overlooked the park and street below, a dining room with a stylish and modern long table that sat six people. When she arrived at the kitchen, she went straight for the refrigerator that was full of food—all sorts of vegetables and cheeses. She'd never seen so much food. Eve's refrigerator had been a bit empty, and they'd never had much in Chicago.

Bowls of fruit sat on the kitchen island that doubled as a bar area. *This is how people in the Coalition areas live?* She'd always imagined life in the other world, the world under the Coalition. But this was beyond anything her mind had conjured.

"Can I get an apple?" she asked Thomas.

"Sure you can. Grab two." He lingered near the entry to the kitchen. "Then we can go have a seat in the living room."

She grabbed an apple, bit into it, and stuffed two more inside her backpack.

In the living room, Aya plopped on the plush blue sofa, and Thomas took the chair across from her. A middle-aged woman with bags under her eyes approached and startled Aya. Until that moment, she hadn't realized anyone else was in the apartment.

"Would you like some tea?" the woman asked.

Aya shook her head, amused by the woman's thick accent. It sounded a little different from Orson's accent.

"No, Iris, we're fine," said Thomas.

She offered him a polite nod and retreated to the kitchen.

Silence filled the room, while Aya chomped away at her apple and avoided Thomas' stare. As she peered around the room, she sensed he was watching her like a hawk. "You know staring is rude."

"So is disrupting a Coalition meeting and attacking our security officers."

Aya looked up and fixed a narrow gaze on him. "They attacked me. I defended myself. I came here to see Orson. That's all."

"Yes, I think you made that clear to the entire world." He flashed a smile that looked more like a sneer.

She bit into the apple again. "Good."

As Aya waited in the living room, she chewed her nails from boredom. She didn't realize Orson had arrived until his voice startled her.

"You caused quite the stir, young lady," he said, standing near the hallway behind her.

Aya sat up, blinked, and rubbed her eyes. She turned to Orson, and her eyes settled on the woman next to him. Besides Carmen, this was one of the most beautiful women Aya had ever seen. Long, dark brown hair curtained the woman's face, and her brown eyes met Aya's curious face.

"You definitely made your presence known in a big way, Ms. Wright," Orson went on.

Aya looked at him. "Your men tried to shoot me with…a laser beam."

"Well, yes. They can be a little hasty."

"A little?" Her eyebrows narrowed almost into a straight line, and she stood. "They would've killed me."

"If you could die, that is," said Orson, smirking.

*So he's seen my video. Maybe it was him who sent the cys to save me.*

"I deeply apologize for the ordeal, Ms. Wright. The guard who discharged his weapon has been put on administrative leave until further review. I should add, they're not laser beams. They're called Trenton Mach 9s, or Mach 9, and they're basically handheld railguns developed by the Remington Center for Science years ago. They use small but powerful magnetic charges to fire projectiles, not lasers per se."

Diya stiffened and glanced sideways at Orson. "I'm sure the child doesn't care to know the background of the weapon that almost injured her."

"Yes, well there were many important people who were vulnerable at that meeting, and your entrance was a major security breach, you see. There have been assassination attempts in the past. We can't be too careful." He placed his hand on Diya's lower back. "I'd like you to meet Ms. Diya Narang, my vice-counsel and a prominent post-human figure in her own right. She even interned with Landrien Moriset, the famous American attorney who won the landmark post-human civil rights case in your country decades ago."

"Landrien who? Never heard of them," Aya replied, sitting down.

"They really don't teach American children their history, do they? Remind me to give you a book about Landrien and the great work she did for post-humans at the beginning of the Great Turn."

Aya stared at him, not sure what to say.

Orson looked at Thomas, who appeared to be on the verge of falling asleep. As Orson signaled for him to leave them, Thomas rose and walked past to the patio door. At once, Orson sat in the chair Thomas had vacated and gestured to the housekeeper to bring some tea.

"Are you all right, dear?" asked Diya, joining Aya on

the sofa.

Aya nodded and kept her eyes on Orson. "I'm fine. I just didn't expect for people to shoot at me."

"I'll make sure it doesn't happen again," said Orson, with a sympathetic smile. "But what an extraordinary display of power and skill. You shut down the entire room. Every news outlet is talking about you. I must say you're taller than I imagined you'd be." He paused and looked over his shoulder toward the kitchen. "I see you've helped yourself to my kitchen. Are you hungry?"

Her stomach growled and did a somersault at the very mention of food, but she shook her head. Reminded of the purpose of her mission, she decided to get straight to the point. "Not right now. That's not the reason I'm here."

Orson's eyebrows went up. "Go on, then. Let's hear it. You have a private audience with the Chief Minister himself."

Aya laughed. "Why do you talk like a character out of a comic book? 'The Chief Minister himself'? Who talks like that?"

"The girl has a point there, Orson," said Diya, snickering.

Silent, Orson took a cup of steaming tea the housekeeper offered him and gracefully passed another cup to Aya. As they sat around a mahogany Victorian-aged tea table trimmed in gold, he and Aya quietly sipped tea while Diya looked amused.

Aya tried not to be overcome by the surreal nature of the moment. She hoped her face didn't betray her emotions. After all the events of the past couple of months, it felt strange to be sitting on another side of the world in the home of someone so powerful. Her palms rested flat on her knees as she leaned in closer to Orson. "I came here to ask for peace in my country. I believe you're the only person who can stop the violence. I just want peace and for everybody—faders and regular people—to be safe."

He sat back and a bright smile spread across his face. "You can't imagine how delighted I am to hear you say that. I've spent so long wondering if I'd ever find a way to establish a functional relationship with the factions in your country, to help the post-humans caught in the cross hairs there. You grew up in Chicago?"

She nodded.

Shaking his head, he fixed a sympathetic gaze on her. "I'm sorry you had to grow up around those who hate you, around so much violence. Your voice might be just the thing the Coalition needs, to help us bring peace between not only your country's factions but between the Coalition and anti-Coalition groups around the world."

Excited about his reaction to her request, Aya sat up straight and waited for him to continue speaking.

"Imagine what we, two alphas, can bring to this world if we work together. I have the wisdom and experience. You have youth and vigor. We'd make an exceptional team in this peacemaking work," said Orson. "What are your arrangements while you're here?"

Aya's eyebrows went up. "Arrangements?"

"You're more than welcome to remain at my flat for as long as you want."

She smiled graciously but shook her head, remembering the hotel Jesús had booked. "Thank you, but there's a hotel—"

"This is an expensive city and very different from what you're accustomed to. Save yourself the hotel money and stay here. I have the extra space. I'd be honored to host you."

Surprised by his offer, Aya smiled again. "I'm fine staying at a hotel for now."

"Orson, may I?" said Diya, her voice soft like silk. She went to him, put her hand on his head, and ran her fingers through his hair. He beamed at her as though there was no one else in the room. At last, she turned to Aya. "Dear, you have the Chief Minister of the Human and Post-Human Coalition for Peace begging you to stay with him and join him in the fight for a better world. I think you should at least take the night to think about it. How does that sound?"

Aya regarded the mysterious woman, not sure what to make of her. She looked at the empty teacups on the table and then toward the hallway leading to the kitchen. As she continued peering around, she saw Thomas smoking a cigarette on the patio.

With a long look at Orson, Aya relented, overcome by the surreality of the situation. "Okay. I'll stay the night."

"Fantastic. Iris and my assistants will be more than happy to sort you out," Orson exclaimed, looking as gleeful as ever.

Aya stood at the doorway, and her gaze traveled to the large bed covered in a pastel yellow blanket and two fluffy white pillows. Next to the bed were a large gray-blue comfy chair, a small table, and a floor-to-ceiling bookcase with a step stool in front of it. A sliver of light broke through the bay window where there was sitting space and another slender bookcase.

"This is the guest room," said Orson, standing behind her. "Consider it yours during your stay."

She looked over her shoulder at him and Diya, both smiling at her.

They watched as she ran her hands along the soft blanket and pulled aside the beige drapes. She peeked out at the quiet street, Regent's Park on the other side of it. "This is like a fairy tale," she mumbled, pinching herself to make sure it was real.

"Sorry?" asked Orson. "Did you have a question? Is there anything you need?"

She turned to them and shook her head. "I feel like a girl in a fairy tale."

Orson smiled. "Well, what's mine is yours, Aya. Make yourself at home. We have some new clothes for you in the wardrobe there." He pointed at the freestanding oak cupboard sitting next to the bookcase. "I had an assistant nip some from the nearest shop before you arrived here with Thomas."

She went to the closet and regarded it with fascination. She'd always known closets to be an extra room in a house rather than a piece of furniture. It creaked as she opened it, and she slid her hands over the clothes hanging inside.

"And there's the telly. It's a holographic quantum platform television."

"It's a what?" She cast him a confused look. "I don't even know what you just said."

Orson chuckled. "There are over three thousand channels for you to watch, and your private lavatory is there to your left, attached to the room."

"My private what?" Aya laughed. "Are these words I'm supposed to know?"

"Bathroom, dear," said Diya, smiling. She waved for the head housekeeper, the woman who'd brought them tea earlier. "This is Iris. She'll be the one to sort you out. Let us know if the clothes are your size. Iris, be a darling and run to the market. Let's prepare Aya a nice supper this evening, yeah?"

The woman gave a stern nod and exited the room.

"Hey," said Aya, looking at Orson. "How did you know I was an alpha? When you introduced yourself, you called me an alpha. How did you know?"

He nodded. "In addition to your extravagant entrance, your viral video was fascinating. I've never met another post-human who has the power of regeneration…who can't die. That's an alpha ability."

Aya thought about Eve, and smiled.

"Orson, do you mind giving me a moment alone with Aya?" asked Diya.

He looked from Aya to Diya. "Don't be long, love," he replied with a wink and left.

Diya sat on the bed and pushed her hair behind her ears. "Listen, I know this is a lot. Is there anything I can do for you?"

Aya shook her head. "I'm just…I can't believe how different everything is here."

"For what it's worth, I think you ought to consider the opportunity Orson's proposing here—to join him in the Coalition's peacekeeping efforts. He's practically rolling out the red carpet for you. Just think about it: any other post-human who did what you did today would've been in trouble. But not you."

"Why?"

"Because you're the new alpha. His only equal. It's hard to believe I'm even saying those words." She stopped and looked at her hands, as a somber look sailed across her face. But when she looked up, she smiled at Aya. "You've made quite an impact on Orson."

Something about the woman's smile comforted Aya. "Thank you. I'll think about it tonight."

"Great. I hope you decide to stay with us." Diya headed to the door. "I'll let you get some rest."

Alone at last, Aya pulled a pair of pajamas from the closet and laid them on the queen-sized bed. The pajamas looked like they would fit, although she figured they might be a little big in the middle. She sat on the bed and tried to silence her racing thoughts. Thoughts about all the sights she looked forward to seeing, about visiting the stores and boutiques. Thoughts about collaborating with the leader of the Coalition to make life better for faders and people back home.

She realized she hadn't really thought through the various possibilities of what might happen after she met Orson. She'd assumed she'd have one meeting with him and that's it. It hadn't occurred to her that she might end up sitting in his posh home, contemplating a fancy end of summer vacation offer and the opportunity to work with him. There was so much she could learn from him, she realized. *I'd be crazy not to take his offer to work together. Right?*

Some shuffling outside her door interrupted her thoughts. Orson made his presence known by clearing his throat. "One more thing, Aya," he said, not opening the door. "When you teleported earlier, you know you created a magnetic field disturbance for a few short seconds, right?"

"Right," she answered, puzzled by the inquiry.

"I've teleported myself hundreds of times before. That ability doesn't create a magnetic field."

"I know. I wanted to make a point. You know, get your attention."

Orson fell silent for a moment. "Cheeky."

When she heard his footsteps in the hall, she got up and listened for more talking. But all was silent now. She lay on the soft bed, looked at the ceiling, and mulled over the question of whether to accept or reject his offer. No matter what she decided, she knew her life would be different now, and she didn't know whether to be excited or terrified.

## 8

Orson swiped the holographic screen and scanned headline after headline about Aya as Diya watched him in silence. "The mysterious arrival of an American child at the Coalition," "Unknown girl's sudden arrival disrupts Coalition proceedings," "Orphan, another alpha, or just a lost post-human child? No word yet..." the headlines read.

Diya walked around the desk and stood at his side. "Orson, what do you plan to do with the girl?"

"I only want what's best for her. She's been brainwashed her entire life by Yanks." He continued swiping past headlines and not looking at Diya.

"Come on. Do you think she's a fool?"

He read more news headlines, groaning as he tapped on one article.

"Damn it, Orson." She slapped him across the face.

The slap was hard enough to leave a sting, and he stared at her.

"You sent cys to kidnap that child and then you attacked her city, didn't you? You think she won't put two and two together? This is why I told you peace and nonviolence are the only way."

He rubbed the side of his face. "That's a disgusting

accusation."

She cast him a disappointed look. "You can't really think I'm foolish enough to believe the Eastern Front drone bombed Chicago. You didn't come to me for advice when you discovered her existence, and you made a hasty decision. Twice. I'm assuming it was Thomas' idea." She drifted to his bookcase, turning to him with a hard look. The look on his face was all the answer she needed. "You must follow her lead now. The girl wants peace, so that's what you're going to have to give her. As you know, peace with the anti-Coalition groups is what's best for everyone. I've recommended this for years. If you don't want to be seen as a tyrant, work with this child and carry out your promise to her."

"That child," said Orson, as though he hadn't heard anything else Diya had said, "has teleported hundreds of post-humans to freedom while somehow managing to overcome and evade soldiers and prison guards, again and again. She singlehandedly disarmed all the UISF officers at the Coalition meeting. Video footage from Chicago shows she's invulnerable. She's a lot more than just a child, Diya. She's a bloody alpha, and I doubt she even understands yet the full range of her abilities."

"Orson—"

"I'll broker a deal with the opposition if that's what's best for business. But I will not intervene to prevent war between U.S. opposition factions. If they want to rip each other apart as they've always done, they're welcome to do so. That's their problem not ours."

Diya dropped in her seat. She crossed her legs and tried to keep her expression impassive. "That's where you're wrong. You have an American alpha at your flat now, and she very much cares about whether her country spirals into another war. You heard her, Orson. This is very much our problem now, even if she decides to leave."

"At supper yesterday, she told Iris she's willing to remain with us for a while."

Diya nodded. "Orson, she deserves what's left of her childhood. She deserves a better world. Promise me you'll do right by her."

"I promise," he said, approaching her. He kissed her forehead and smiled. "I've always admired your passion for defending post-humans. I was in my twenties when whistleblowers exposed to the world the fact that governments were hiding the existence of post-humans. But I remember it like yesterday. I remember what it felt like to be feared and hated the world over, never safe anywhere."

"I was a teenager at the time, so I have some memory of it, too," said Diya. "I'm glad the world's different now."

"Being feared and hated, never safe. For this girl, that's been her whole life. It's all she knows." Silent, he tried to fathom the shock of leaving a violent world so abruptly as Aya had yesterday. "I promise you I'll do right by her. You have nothing to worry about. Now, go home and get some rest. I'm sure you barely slept last night after all the chaos."

Squeezing his hand one more time, she planted a kiss on his cheek and left him alone.

As he returned to his desk and asked the computer to connect him to Thomas, he thought about Diya's words. *She deserves a better world.*

"Sir?" said a translucent Thomas. He appeared to be enjoying breakfast in his kitchen.

"The girl has agreed to stay."

Thomas' holograph replica was quiet for a moment. "Have you scanned her, sir?"

"No. Do you think she could be working for the opposition to infiltrate us?"

Thomas shook his head. "Probably not, sir. It seems that due to their own misguided prejudice towards post-humans, the People's Army failed to see her potential usefulness for them."

"A rare diamond they had in their hands, and the fools let her slip away. Fortunate for us."

"Yes. But we need to be careful. We don't know her motivation for showing up here, sir. And we don't know what all she can do. If she's telepathic—"

"I'll block her as I do everyone else. Just continue keeping tabs on her brother and father."

"Sir, the father deserted to the Eastern Front, apparently some time before the girl arrived here."

"Interesting," Orson replied, rubbing his head. "Keep me up-to-date on his activities there."

"Absolutely. Sir, if the girl ever presents a problem to you or the Coalition…what then? Have you given any thought to developing something, a device or facility, to contain someone with your power? I know I've mentioned it before—"

"And my answer then as now is no. Imagine if I created something to take me down and any of my enemies obtained it. With the number of enemies I have, it's not a risk I'm willing to take."

"But, sir, we need to be prepared."

"Sometimes the best tool is psychological." Orson stroked his beard stubble and smiled. "Remember, Tommy boy, even those of us who are invincible still have a weakness. I suspect her weakness is her family."

"Right, sir. Be sure not to let her become your weakness," said Thomas, before disconnecting the call.

For a minute, Orson replayed the conversation in his mind. The People's Army had failed to recognize the potential of Aya, and now they were on the verge of an all-out war with the Eastern Front. Due to his machinations and their own prejudice, one of the strongest wings of the global opposition movement was teetering, and the second most powerful weapon in the world was at his home now. Orson smiled as he rested his head against his palms.

Groaning, Aya pulled the cover over her head when Iris switched on the ceiling light.

"Up you go, Ms. Wright," said Iris, wash cloth in one hand and her other hand on her hip. "I've been instructed to wake you."

"Why?" Aya yawned, keeping the cover over her head to block out the light.

Iris pulled the cover back. "So that you can tidy up for your first day as an esteemed guest of the Chief Minister. Now up you go."

Relenting, Aya rose and stretched her arms above her head, yawning once more. From the floor next to the nightstand, she grabbed her backpack that held her change of clothes and dragged herself to the bathroom. While she showered, Iris laid out a purplish-blue dress and silver shoes on the bed before retreating to the kitchen to prepare breakfast.

Aya's mouth hung open when she came out the bathroom and saw the clothes on the bed. She'd changed into her spare pair of jeans and a t-shirt. Although she preferred her current attire, the prospect of getting all dolled up in such a beautiful dress excited her. She picked up the dress, her hand brushing against the soft and cool satin.

After changing into the dress, she went to the large wall mirror next to the wardrobe. The beaded v-back dress fit a bit too loosely and flared at her nonexistent hips. *I look like I'm wearing a bag.*

There was a knock at the door, and she spun around. "Yeah?"

Iris entered and surveyed her. "Yes, I thought it

would need a bit of tailoring. Come," she said, gesturing for Aya to approach her and turn around. For half an hour, she fussed with needle and thread to tailor the dress for Aya's skinny frame. As she finished, another housekeeper arrived. It was the first time Iris smiled.

"This is my daughter, Lily. She'll sort out your hair."

Aya backed away, looking at the women.

"What is the problem, child?" Iris asked, confused.

Aya shook her head.

Lily looked concerned, while Iris cast Aya a look of increasing incredulity. "Lily's a hairdresser, dear. She's quite capable."

Aya went to the wall mirror, looked at the brushes and sprays in Lily's hands, and turned to Iris. "No offense. But I doubt Lily can do my hair. Thanks, though." Looking in the mirror, Aya combed her fingers through the two Afro puffs. She fluffed them, patted them, then exhaled and removed the bands around them. Holding the bands between her teeth, she combed her fingers through her fine curls once more and gathered her hair together. She replaced the bands around each puff and patted them.

"You're not honestly going to wear it like that?" Lily remarked, staring at Aya with obvious disapproval.

Aya examined her reflection and patted the two puffs. "It's the way I always wear it."

"But if you just let me brush it into a bun..." She stopped, taking in the reproachful look from Aya. "Very well," she said and exited the room.

Iris glared at her. "You should learn better manners, child."

"I'm not a child."

"Whatever you say. Come now and let me fix the zipper on your dress."

Aya stepped forward and turned around. Iris went to

work with the needle and thread, tugging at the dress and almost knocking Aya off her feet.

"There." Iris, standing with hands on hips, appeared pleased with her handiwork. "Now you can say that dress was made for you."

Aya rushed to the mirror and looked at her reflection. "It's...it's so..."

"Beautiful?"

"I've never had anything so fancy." Aya pulled at the dress and scratched her leg. "It feels sort of weird."

"That would be the lace. Very itchy it is. You'll get used to it."

"Come, Aya," said Diya, appearing at the doorway.

Aya slipped her feet inside the silver slippers and followed Iris and Diya to the living room where they were met by a couple of Orson's private security guards.

"Ma'am, should I not finish preparing breakfast for her? I'm sure she'd like a bite to eat before leaving." Iris looked from Aya to Diya.

"No need, Iris," said Diya, smiling at Aya. "There will be plenty of food where she's going."

Aya studied Diya and noticed something else lurked behind the woman's smile. A quiet thoughtfulness that reminded her of Eve. But where Eve seemed to go with the flow, Diya seemed calculating. She was a woman with a plan, Aya surmised.

The security guards escorted them to a self-driving black sedan. Sitting in the backseat across from Diya, Aya looked at the streets teeming with people and the oldest buildings she'd ever seen. As their car swerved through the heavy traffic, Aya grasped the seat in fear and longed for her father's smooth, cautious driving. What would her father and Malik say if they saw her now, being whisked away in a carriage to some special event? *Dad would call me a princess. And*

*Malik would find a way to tease me, like "be careful you don't turn into a frog or something."*

When she giggled at the thought, it drew a confused look from Diya.

"What are you smiling about?" asked Diya.

She choked back a laugh and grinned. "Nothing. Just hoping I don't turn into a frog."

Hordes of reporters, journalists, spectators, and security guards awaited their arrival at the Coalition headquarters in central London. Aya felt dizzy staring at all the people in front of the building. She shrunk in her seat, and her body stiffened.

Diya regarded her with concern. "My apologies for not warning you about the media. I assumed you'd expect it. The media are already calling you 'the Second Alpha'. You're now the world's biggest celebrity besides Orson."

"People are talking about me?" Aya swallowed, thinking about Jesús and Eve reading the headlines at the farmhouse. More than ever, she wondered what they were thinking and feeling right now. After all, she'd left them just twenty-four hours ago and, already, she was front-page news. *Has Dad seen the news? Oh no, he's going to be so mad at Eve for letting me leave.*

"Take my hand, Aya. You'll be fine."

As she took Diya's hand, a guard opened the car door and escorted them through the throng of people and cameras. Aya avoided the stares as they passed through and entered the building. The guard led them to a private room where Orson was talking to a man who looked similar to him. Tall, chestnut hair, well-dressed but heavier in the midsection. The austere man appeared to be a decade or so older than Orson, stood at least an inch taller, and wore horned-rimmed glasses.

When Orson saw Aya and Diya approaching, his face

lit up. "You look lovely. Diya chose that dress for you. I daresay she has a fantastic eye for fashion." He winked at Diya. "Now, let me introduce you to my dear brother, William Cornelius Remington. He's the Coalition's Minister of Information."

"Pleasure to meet you, Ms. Wright," he said, shaking Aya's hand. "Don't mind remembering the title. It's just what a little nepotism can get you around here."

*Well, he's definitely high energy.* She smiled and was thankful when he released her hand from his strong grip. "You can call me Aya."

He nodded. "Duly noted."

"You're perhaps wondering what's all this going on here today and why on earth Iris woke you up at the crack of dawn," Orson said, standing up. "Well, we're going to have a press conference today to spotlight your arrival. Furthermore, we want to highlight the courage and bravery you demonstrated rescuing all those post-humans from the clutches of the opposition in the Midwest. We want to do press around your heroic efforts. Cornelius will tell you all about that process later. But, more importantly, Diya will bring you out to the stage in just a few minutes so that I can announce you. Let her know if you have questions. You're in excellent hands." He whispered something in Diya's ear that made her flush, and he hurried out the room. Cornelius followed him.

Aya tapped her feet against the floor and looked around the room. "I didn't expect all this. What I did wasn't that big of a deal, not compared to the stuff Orson has done."

"Nonsense," Diya scoffed. "You saved lives, Aya. That's worth recognition."

She looked at the woman and thought about the first prison she and Jesús had liberated, how terrified she'd been that she might fail. "I just did what I felt was right."

"More often than not, that takes incredible courage." Diya patted her shoulder. "Don't be nervous. There won't be any questions for you to answer. Just introduce yourself— where you're from—and maybe a few words about why you helped post-humans in your country."

"That's it?"

Diya chuckled. "That's it. Leave all the long-winded epic speeches to Orson. He specifically told me not to prep you because he wants you to be natural." She leaned closer to Aya and whispered in a dramatic tone, "Between me and you, I think Orson doesn't want you to outshine him on the stage."

Aya laughed and shook her head. "Outshine Orson? Like that's even possible."

"You never know what's possible," said Diya, smiling and glancing at her watch. "Do you have any questions before we go out there?"

"Actually, yeah. Why am I wearing this dress? I thought I was going to a—"

"Ball?" said Diya. "That's later. Anyway, don't worry about this press conference. It'll be over in a flash."

"I'm not worried. It's just that these shoes feel like they're cutting off my toes."

"Have you never worn heels?"

"No." Aya kicked off the silver shoes and breathed a sigh of relief as her feet touched the cool concrete floor.

"You can't walk out there without them. I have an idea. How about you put them on and then once we get behind the podium on stage you can take them off again?"

She looked from the shoes to Diya. "Nah. I'm good."

"Very well. I don't suppose it's the end of the world if you walk out shoeless. Let's go." Taking Aya's hand, she led her through the door and into the Chief Minister's Briefing

Room.

Aya's head turned left and right as she took in the room that was little more than a small theater with a stage and podium displaying the Coalition emblem. For a moment, she studied the emblem, the global map with an almost transparent peace symbol overlaying it. A wreath consisting of olive tree branches encircled the emblem.

When she looked up, she saw Orson next to the podium and watching members of the press gather. They fiddled with their tablets, phones, and cameras, while others snapped pictures of Aya and commented about her bare feet.

Diya directed Aya to a chair behind Orson and retreated to the front row in the audience.

"Any reason you're not wearing shoes?" Orson whispered.

"They hurt my toes."

"Ah. Well, I'm fairly certain this is the first time bare feet have graced this hall. You really know how to make waves, don't you?" He smiled at her.

Not sure what to do with that statement, Aya shrugged and replied, "I'll try not to upstage you."

"I see I have some competition today," he teased. "I daresay you already upstaged me yesterday." After a wink to her, he went to the podium and raised his hand to silence the audience. "Good morning, everyone. I called this briefing today to comment on the spectacular events of yesterday. It has been quite a long twenty-four hours since the world met the mysterious young girl sitting behind me. Today, I would like to ask you all to extend a warm welcome to Aya Wright."

Cheers and applause followed as Aya looked at the excited faces in the crowd. *They don't hate me? They're not afraid of me?* Despite what she'd read about life in the Coalition countries, she still couldn't wrap her mind around the idea being a fader made her popular rather than feared.

"Is it true that she's an alpha? Are there two alphas in the world now?" shouted an eager reporter near the back of the room.

Chatter erupted. Still smiling, Orson glanced at Aya whose face betrayed her nervousness. "Yes, it's true. I'm no longer the only alpha in the world. Aya Wright is an alpha."

Gasps sounded around the room. People whispered to one another and gawked at Aya.

"But more than that, Aya is a brave girl who fought for a better world for post-humans in her troubled country. A country where the opposition who call themselves the People's Army have been systematically targeting people for being post-humans. They round up suspected post-humans and place them in prison camps where many perish from barbaric conditions. It's an international post-human rights crisis happening right before our eyes. Yet we closed our eyes to this reality years ago, didn't we? And what's the consequence? We left a young girl like Aya and millions of others unsupported, unprotected.

"Unlike us, Aya never had the privilege of closing her eyes. She decided to take a courageous stance against the grave injustices happening around her. She valiantly rescued hundreds of post-humans from unjust imprisonment. I salute her fearlessness, and I'm honored to be in her presence." Orson turned to her and applauded.

The audience followed his lead, clapping and rising to their feet.

When he turned to the microphone again, the audience members resumed their seats. "Her visionary example is one we should all follow. In fact, it has led me to reexamine the Coalition's posture on international human and post-human rights. We have taken a hands-off approach with those countries outside the Coalition. Brazil, the United States, and Pakistan, just to name a few. But I'm afraid that posture is an error. While I'm proud that the Coalition countries are sanctuaries for post-humans, I believe unfair treatment of post-humans anywhere is a threat to post-humans everywhere, and we must no longer look away."

As he paused and inhaled, choked up by his own words, Aya watched with increased interest. Never had she seen anyone speak with so much passion.

"Allow me to speak directly to the opposition and those who support them." He looked into the camera extending from the ceiling at the center of the room. "Is this the cause you fight for? A cause that treats those with abilities as criminals who deserve to be locked inside cages? Or put down like rabid dogs? Is this who you are? I ask that you look at your actions and recognize the humanity of us all. Moreover, I want you to know that your hatred has no place in a free world. Hate will not win."

Thunderous applause went up around the room as half the audience rose and cheered. The hive-like enthusiasm in the room energized Aya, and she joined in the applause.

"Years ago, I sought to unite humans and post-humans, to help us see our mutual struggle in the face of an alarming rise of violence and an ever-worsening energy crisis. I stand here today as the leader of the Human and Post-Human Coalition for Peace. The key word is peace, something I have envisioned since the Coalition came to fruition.

"Regrettably, that vision has not been fully achieved yet. But Aya's presence has given that lofty vision new hope, new possibility. While it may seem premature, I want to honor Aya Wright with the Human and Post-Human Coalition for Peace Global Citizen Award for her efforts saving post-humans in her country. At just fifteen, she has done more in the service of peace and post-human rights than most of us will do in our lifetimes."

Everyone in the audience stood, and applause rippled throughout the briefing room. Raising his hand, Orson silenced the crowd. Once the room was quiet, he turned to Aya and encouraged her to approach and accept the award.

She remained seated, meeting Orson's eyes, smiling nervously. *Get up, Aya. Get up.* His smile faltered. Taking a deep breath, she got up and approached the podium.

As she took the award made of glass and shaped like the Coalition emblem, camera lights flashed on her.

Aya sat next to Cornelius Remington and across from Orson and Diya in the limousine. She observed the throng of Londoners lined up alongside the street to catch a glimpse of her. They waved and cheered as the limousine passed by.

"You're the highlight of the day, Aya," remarked Cornelius.

Orson wore a look of intense satisfaction, and Aya watched him for a moment. She clutched her Global Citizen Award and looked out the window once more. Holographic billboards flashed in an assortment of hues. The colorful lights reflected off the towering glass skyscrapers juxtaposed to stone buildings that looked older than any buildings she'd seen back home. As she rode and stared out, she noticed the cameras everywhere—above streetlights, on tops of buildings, placed in trees, on the sides of buildings.

"You've been rather distracted since we left headquarters," said Orson. "What's on your mind?"

She looked at him and glanced at the award on her lap. "Being a fader, I didn't know I could feel this accepted. It feels weird."

He smiled. "We don't use the word 'fader' anymore. It's become a favorite slur of those who hate post-humans."

Aya recalled the way General Harris spat the word at her. "Well, if someone wants to use it as a slur, they just better not say it to my face." She met his gaze and smirked. "Besides, 'post-human' sounds kind of stupid, no offense."

With a jerk, the limousine stopped at an official looking building.

"Where are we now?" asked Aya.

Diya smiled. "Buckingham Palace, dear. We're a little late to the reception, so put your shoes on and let's hurry."

As guards escorted them inside to the reception room, Aya's mouth drooped open. She looked from the classical jazz quartet playing sensual music to the endless red carpet and dazzling staircase railings. Applause from at least a hundred people welcomed them into the reception room where the drinks were already flowing.

When Orson asked her to take his hand, he whispered, "Relax. This is my treat to you. Try to enjoy yourself."

Before they could reach a table, a loud voice called Orson's name. Through the stentorian din of chatter and music, Aya heard the voice call his name again. They stopped as a stout, dark-skinned man approached them. A shade or so lighter than Aya, he wore a contagious smile. Aya looked him over, amused by his blinding yellow suit. The man extended both hands in greeting to Orson, and his smile grew bigger if possible.

"Orson, you didn't mention you were adopting our newest little star?"

Diya and Aya frowned at him.

But Orson smiled. "Aya, I'd like you to meet my old mate and the President of South Africa, Blade Sonani."

"Pleasure to meet you, Aya. I saw your entrance the other day, me and around eight billion other people in the world. Quite a splash you've made," said Blade, shaking her hand.

"Blade, shouldn't we have a drink and chat with

President Chen? We don't want him and the Russian president to come to blows tonight, now do we?"

"Can't have that," said Blade, smirking at Orson.

"I'll stay with Aya," said Diya.

Orson nodded. "Perhaps introduce her to some other kids," replied Orson. "I'm sure she wants to mingle with the other kids, right, Aya?"

"I'm not a kid."

Orson fixed an apologetic look on his face. "Ah, yes. Of course, you're not. So do me a favor and look after Diya. She gets a bit nervy around so many high-profile people."

With a wink at Diya, Orson left with Blade to find President Chen and grab a drink.

Diya smiled at Aya and took her hand. "Let's go find a table, since I'm sure those shoes are murdering your feet."

Aya looked around, and her eyes landed on a dark-haired woman in a flashy, sequined dress. Her mouth dropped open, and she stared wide-eyed. "Is that Faye Lennox?"

"Probably. Where?" asked Diya, peering around.

Aya pointed to the woman approaching Blade and Orson across the room.

"That's her. She wouldn't miss an opportunity to elevate herself. You know Orson is thinking about nominating her for the Coalition's Goodwill Ambassador role next year?"

She nodded, barely hearing what Diya said. "I love her music, especially her newest song "This Love Is Loud, But It's Moody". Can you introduce me?"

Diya laughed. "Sure. Looks like she's heading to the drinks now. Come on."

Aya squeaked with excitement, bouncing on the balls of her feet.

Sitting in silence, Aya looked at all the happy people talking and draining glasses of wine. Women decked out in extravagant gowns, others in modest cocktail dresses, while men wore finely-tailored suits. "Everything is so fancy, and these people don't seem to have a care in the world. And there's so much food." She stared at all the serving tables of cheese and fruits.

Diya took another sip of red wine. "I know all of this is very new to you. I felt the same way years ago when I first left home. Less than ten years after leaving home, I was meeting Britain's youngest Prime Minister and being personally mentored by his Chief of Downing Street. Definitely a feat for a poor girl raised on the Indian and Pakistan border."

"You have abilities, right?"

"Like most post-humans, I have a couple. Yes."

"You ever think your abilities just made you luckier than everybody else?" asked Aya.

Diya laughed. "Women and people like us—"

"Like us?"

"Black, brown. Those of us that people like Orson colonized once upon a time well before you and I were born," said Diya, a fleeting frown curling her full lips. "We've spent centuries being unlucky and at an unfair disadvantage, at the mercy of people with bigger weapons. Maybe the universe is finally balancing itself out by giving me and you and millions of other little brown girls and boys these abilities. No longer is power about who has the most advanced society or the biggest weapons. No longer is it about one's social class, religion, or race. None of those things have any bearing on whether one develops abilities. In terms of who develops abilities, it's all just blind luck. It's perfect evidence of evolution leveling the playing field for every human."

"So, you're admitting you just got lucky though."

"Yes, I got lucky. Just like you."

Aya sighed. "What about people living in military-controlled areas? It's not a level playing field for regular people or post-humans living there."

"We still have a lot of work to do, dear. I'm the first to admit that. But be honest: the post-humans there can take over those areas any time they want to and bring peace to their people. Look at what you were able to do. Maybe peace doesn't exist in those areas because the post-humans don't have the courage to stand up to their military oppressors yet."

Aya thought about Eve sitting at the farmhouse and doing so little, hiding from the world.

"Maybe that's what needs to change. The attitude of just sitting back and taking what happens instead of standing up to your enemies," Diya added. "Or maybe I'm thinking too simplistically about it all."

From the corner of her eyes, Aya noticed several teenagers hovering a few feet away from her table. The group, all of whom were around Aya's age, cast furtive glances at her but didn't dare come closer until Diya signaled them over. Before the group reached their table, Diya leaned close to Aya and whispered, "Be nice."

One by one, they all took a seat and pulled some extra chairs from a nearby table.

A boy with curly blond hair said something incomprehensible.

For a moment, the foreign words coming out of his mouth confused Aya. She shrugged, looking to Diya for help. Yet when the boy repeated his question, the garbled words began to make sense. She repeated his words. "Is it true? Are you an alpha?"

He nodded.

*Wait...how can I understand him?* "Yes, I'm an alpha,"

172

she said. "Are you speaking English... or am I speaking another language right now? I'm confused."

"You were speaking German, dear. You and the boy were speaking to each other in German," said Diya, looking impressed.

Aya stared at her in shock. "I've never spoken German before."

"Until just this moment. I've only ever seen Orson learn another language within seconds," said Diya.

"*Orson ist Ubermensch*," the boy interjected, beaming. "*Er ist legendär.*"

A little alarmed at the boy's excitement, Aya replied in German, "He's okay, I guess."

Diya leaned in once more and whispered to her. "In Germany, Orson is considered the embodiment of the ultimate man, a.k.a the Ubermensch. It's weird, I know."

Aya recalled what Jesús had warned her about the cult-like behavior of Orson's followers. She offered the German boy an awkward smile and turned her attention to the others around the table.

"Lukas is a little obsessed with Orson. Anyway, I'm Geni," said a small dark girl speaking in English. "I'm the only post-human in my family. My father represents Somalia in the Coalition." To prove her post-human skills, the girl disappeared and reappeared again to the delight of the audience around the table.

A tan-colored boy with a head of curly dark hair waved his hands around the table, and the dinnerware levitated. "Geni can't do that," he said, grinning.

Aya laughed as they started teasing one another. Her eyes landed on a quiet boy sitting across from her. With a shy gaze and his hair pulled into a long ponytail, he'd caught her attention the moment the group approached. "What about you?" she asked him, and the table fell silent.

"I'm Michio," he answered, also in English.

"So, Michio, is your dad some fancy Coalition member, too?"

"His father is Japan's Prime Minister," said Geni.

Aya nodded. "I see. Do you have abilities, Michio?"

Michio looked at her for a second before transforming into her exact replica. "I can be you, the second alpha," he replied, his voice identical to hers. "Or I can be Mehdi." He transformed again into the boy who'd teased Geni.

"I'm prettier," Aya teased, laughing as Mehdi frowned at her and Geni giggled.

Michio shifted to his normal form again and extended his hand to Aya. "Or I can just be Michio. It's nice to meet you."

She shook his hand and grinned at him. If she were a few shades lighter her cheeks would've been bright red. When she tore her eyes from Michio, most of the smaller kids and teenagers at the party had gathered around her table.

"Show us some of your alpha abilities," one kid called from the crowd.

"Come on, let's see it," another kid said.

Aya got up and walked to the center of the crowd, and they watched her with rapt attention. "What do you want to see?"

"Anything!" Geni shouted.

"Okay." Aya clapped her hands until sparks flew out from her fingertips. "There's that." Feeling encouraged as they cheered, she repeated the demonstration. Yet this time the sparks created an energy ball. The ball glowed with the same faint blue aura that had surrounded her when she first appeared at the assembly hall yesterday. The energy ball floated just above Aya's open hand.

Diya, who'd been sitting and observing Aya's

interaction with the kids, approached Aya with caution. She tapped her shoulder. "I think that's enough, dear. We don't want to blow up Buckingham Palace."

With a sideways look at Diya, Aya dropped her hands. The energy ball ruptured into fine pieces and disappeared to the dismay of the crowd. They groaned with disapproval. Diya led Aya to her chair and invited the group to resume their seats as the rest of the disappointed crowd dispersed. Aya sat and slumped in her chair.

*Is the world big enough for two alphas?*

She turned to Diya and replied, "Why would you ask that?"

Diya's eyebrows went up. "Ask what?"

"You just said—" Aya began but stopped when she realized Diya hadn't spoken. Rather, she'd heard Diya's thoughts. Half-smiling at the woman, she shook her head. "Nothing."

# 9

Orson brushed aside strands of Diya's hair, while her thighs rested against his waist. She straightened the pillow under his head and smiled at him. Morning light pierced through the sheer curtains and cast a cool glow on her brown face, revealing a hint of green in her eyes. "Nobody should be so beautiful."

She smiled. "I'm sure I'm not the only woman you've said that to."

He brushed his hand against her warm cheeks. "Do you wish you could scan me? Hear my thoughts right now? Does it frustrate you that you can't know what I'm thinking?"

She shrugged. "Sometimes. But it's also what I like about you. It's so incredibly exhausting to always know what people are thinking. A bit of mystery is nice now and again." She swept her lips against his nape and closed her eyes as his fingers wandered up her thighs. "Orson?"

"Yes, love?"

"Would you ever give all this up, if I asked you to?"

He looked into her bright eyes. "You mean the Coalition? Leading the world?"

"Yes," she whispered.

Orson's hands rested against her breasts and squeezed

a bit. It pleased him to watch her close her eyes and lick her bottom lip. He slid his hand farther up her thighs, and she moaned with pleasure. "Let's not talk about work now." He'd already slept late but wasn't in the mood to rush out of bed.

Something buzzed on the nightstand, and Diya opened her eyes at once. She looked at the vibrating phone on the nightstand and sighed. "You don't have to answer it."

"It's probably Thomas."

"It's Saturday morning. He can wait," said Diya, pressing her body against him and nibbling at his ear lobe. "Let it go to the mailbox, Orson."

"Actually, it's almost noon." He looked at her, and an amused smile settled on his lips. "You really don't like Thomas at all, do you?"

"No, I don't."

"Why not?"

Diya sat up and rolled her eyes. "Are you trying to ruin the mood?"

He looked from her full breasts to her pouting face and laughed. It always had fascinated him how much his two most trusted confidants hated one another. He couldn't understand why two people who seemed more alike than not despised one another's presence. After a few years of observing them, he assumed it all boiled down to jealousy and competition for his attention.

Grabbing the phone from the nightstand, he read the text message from Thomas: "Aya is in the VR room with Michio. They were playing it after the event yesterday and got up at the crack of dawn to play some more. You mentioned you'd like to meet with her today. Do you want me to tell them to wrap it up?" He sent a quick reply to Thomas before silencing the vibrate feature and depositing the phone into the nightstand drawer.

Diya slid from under the cover and went to the

bathroom.

It amused him that she never bothered closing the door when she peed. He had to admit it endeared her to him. Here was a down to earth woman, not ashamed of anything. Perhaps he should invite Diya to supper with his mother at some point, he wondered. *No, she'll say something to hurt Diya. Then I'll have to spend weeks making it up to Diya.* For his mother, only a woman from good English stock was worthy of her son. Despite this, the words came from his mouth before he could stop himself. "Diya, would you like to join me for supper with my mother?"

In an instant, she emerged from the bathroom and stood at the doorway. "After ten years, you're going to tell your mother about us? Don't you think that ship has sailed? Surely she already knows."

"Of course she knows," he replied, nodding. "Which is why she hasn't stopped hassling me about the 'special person' in my life and asking me when I'll invite you to supper. I'm tired of dodging the question."

She dashed to the bed and leaped onto him, straddling him with the sheet between them. "So tell me, how does she feel about some wild brown girl spoiling her precious son?"

"She's not keen on it. But I think she's trying to be a good sport about it."

Diya laughed.

"I'm serious. My mother's very racist. She doesn't like post-humans either, except for me. Don't take it personally if she's an asshole to you."

"You've told me that before. But in all my encounters with your mother, she's hardly said two words to me."

"She's not a fan of the work events I drag her to, so she usually keeps quiet. You've only met the quiet version of my mother."

"Ah. Well, I'm sure I've encountered worse than her," said Diya, grinning. "But what's the real reason you're asking me this now? Is it because deep down you want her approval of our relationship?"

Silence elapsed between them as he held her face between his palms. He thought long and hard about her question, not sure what to say. "I've had you send flowers to her on her birthday for years. It feels weird to be keeping you away from her. I thought I was doing it to protect you, but maybe I was protecting myself."

"I see then." Smiling, Diya leaned forward. "Next thing I know you'll be asking me to move in here with you." She kissed his lips and slipped under the covers.

*The thought has occurred to me.* He laid his head against her shoulders and closed his eyes. Despite the solace of that moment, he knew he never would leave the Coalition for her. But he figured it was better to keep that to himself.

Aya ran as hard as she could in the virtual reality room at the Coalition headquarters. She darted across the football field as fast as her legs would allow and turned around. As she repositioned herself and caught her breath, she saw the defensive midfielder coming down the field. In one swift move, she flanked him, took the ball, swiveled around, and shot off in the goal's direction. She feinted left away from the midfielder and kept going straight, lining up the ball to where a brawny goalkeeper was moving from side to side. After feinting left again, she shot forward, slowed, and kicked the ball into the air.

As Aya launched her body upwards, she delivered an overhead kick, hitting the game-winning goal. The crowd screamed and her teammates flocked onto the field to celebrate with her.

Michio scoffed. "I don't believe you never played

football until today."

Winded, Aya grinned. "I played a different version with my brother and his friends back home."

"Michio, it's time to go," said a distant voice. The holographic players and the crowd froze, and the virtual reality game came to a standstill. The room cleared itself of the game and returned to its regular state: a giant white and windowless room.

They turned to the door where Thomas stood alongside two members of Michio's security team.

"I guess you have to go now," said Aya, looking downcast.

Michio, standing an inch or so taller, threw his arms around her.

She rested her chin against his shoulder as they remained wrapped in a tight hug. "I'm glad you came to my table yesterday."

"Yeah, that party was lame. But it was fun hanging out with you all weekend. Maybe my father will let me visit again next weekend." He released her and looked at Thomas and the other men. "Too bad they have that very serious guy babysitting you. Does he even talk?"

Aya glanced at Thomas and snickered. "Not much."

Michio laughed before transforming into a replica of Thomas. His smile transformed into a hyper serious expression. "I'm a deeply serious person who does deeply serious work for the leader of the free world," he joked, mimicking Thomas' monotone voice and accent.

Laughing, Aya covered her mouth. "Hey, you're going to hurt his feelings."

"Hurry. You're needed by your father now," said one man, speaking in Japanese.

Michio shifted to his normal form, looking sad as he held Aya's gaze. "I'll ask my father if I can visit again soon."

She leaned forward and kissed his cheek.

He flushed and did his best to keep a straight face.

"Bye for now," said Aya, smiling.

Michio rushed to the men but turned around one more time to wave goodbye.

Once Michio was gone, Thomas cleared his throat. "I hope you enjoyed your game. Orson has blocked some time off in his schedule for the rest of the afternoon. He wants to have some one-on-one time with you today."

Still standing in the middle of the room, she looked at Thomas. "One-on-one time?"

So far, she hadn't spent any time alone with Orson. He was never home, so she'd spent most of her free time getting to know Iris and Lily.

"All right. But I've been sweating and probably stink." She sniffed her underarms and grimaced. "I should probably shower first. Michio and I played a tough game of soccer on legends mode. It was so cool."

"This VR room was personally designed by Orson. It was the first of its kind."

"There's more than just this one?"

"Yes. Many," said Thomas. "He sold the tech. Orson's always creating revenue streams. Some cities use this tech for their city council or other official meetings, and to host events. Museums have used it to increase accessibility. I'm sure Orson will be happy to tell you more."

Aya nodded, surprised that Thomas was in a talkative mood. "I see."

"Anyway, you know where the showers are. Orson will meet you at his office at three o'clock sharp. Don't be late." Without another word, he exited the room.

While picking out her right Afro puff, Aya walked into Orson's office and came to an abrupt stop. "You're wearing normal clothes," she said, staring at Orson who was standing by the window and looking at the London cityscape. His attire included jeans and a solid white t-shirt. "I've never seen you dress like a regular person."

He turned and smiled at her. "It's a special day. Let's take a trip upstairs. There's something I want to show you."

Tucking the Afro pick inside her pocket, she stepped aside and followed him. They went down the hall to the elevator that took them to the top floor. Once there, they walked along a hallway and approached a steel door. The door opened to a staircase that took them to the rooftop of the Coalition headquarters. As they emerged onto the rooftop, she gasped at the view of London. The church steeples and rugged old buildings were breathtaking.

"Beautiful, isn't it?"

"My dad used to tell me how beautiful Chicago was before the Great Turn. This looks like what he described."

"Chicago was certainly a beautiful city years ago. The destruction there was a tragedy all around. I can't imagine what you've experienced, Aya." He looked at the cloudy sky and grasped the railing.

"Did you try to save me in Chicago?"

He stared at her and his eyebrows went up.

"There were some cys who attacked the place where the People's Army was holding me. Your people use cys. My dad said the U.S. Army factions can't afford cys."

"I worried about your safety," he replied, nodding.

"And then there's the fact that my video totally disappeared from the old web and the NeoNet. Did you do that too?"

He smiled, leaning against the railing. "I had it scrubbed from the internet. I feared the trouble it might cause if my world believed an alpha existed among the anti-Coalition forces. Not to mention, I worried for your safety if your anti-post-human compatriots found out about you." He placed his hand on her shoulder and gave her a reassuring pat. "You've experienced so many terrible things over the past two months. It can take a toll. I hope you're able to relax and enjoy yourself here, not having to worry about people hurting you."

"I can't get used to feeling so…"

"Free?"

She nodded. "And playing in the VR room was amazing."

"You're also the only person I've allowed to use the VR room as a personal game room. I thought you could use the distraction. It's sounds like you hit it off with Michio. We'll have to invite him here again," he said, smiling.

Aya ran her fingers through her hair, a rush of embarrassment coming over her.

Orson chuckled. "At any rate, I hope you remain with us for a while longer. Things have been far livelier with you around. I could use a little more vitality and energy around here." With a satisfied smile, he took two steps from the railing. "Now, I know you've teleported many times before, but have you ever flown? Transvection, as some call it."

"Trans-what? No, I never tried to do that."

"Well, you're in for a treat," he said, raising his arms to create a 't' shape with his body. With ease, he lifted himself until he was hovering two feet off the ground.

Aya stared at him, thunderstruck. "We can fly like superheroes from the movies?"

"Yes, but without the silly spandex and blue knickers."

She giggled.

"Do you want to try it?" Lowering himself to the ground, he took her hands and led her away from the railing. "When you arrived at the Coalition meeting, you levitated the guns of all our security officers. If you can levitate an object around you, then you can do the same to yourself. Just focus on levitating yourself rather than an object."

As he spoke, they walked backward. He seemed to have eyes in the back of his head as he pulled her along with him. The wind grew stronger, and she struggled to stand against the force of it.

"I don't think I can," When she looked down, she noticed her feet were not on the ground.

He kept a firm grip around Aya's hands while they floated in the air. "Mind over matter, Aya."

Her heart quickened, and she squeezed her eyes shut. She felt herself moving but couldn't bear to peek.

"Don't fear it. Even if you fell, it wouldn't kill you as you already know. Just let your mind continue to expand as you take command over yet another ability. We alphas are always expanding our minds and capabilities."

Taking a deep breath, she opened her eyes and looked at her feet. The Coalition headquarters, one of the tallest buildings in London—standing several stories higher than the Shard building—was behind her. As they rose higher and higher, she got a better view of the building and its triangular shape amazed her.

"It's a long way down and would probably take a day or two for you to recover if you fell from this height. But I wouldn't let that happen." He squeezed her hands to remind her that he was still hanging on to her. "Trust yourself. This is easy. Remember that you managed to teleport over one hundred people at the same time. That you defended yourself from Coalition officers by using only your mind. You have the power."

Aya inhaled and exhaled, counting to ten as she tried to calm herself.

Orson released her hand and floated to her side.

Giving in to her instincts, she imagined herself as a bird, light and graceful. The air beat against her neck and arms, informing her that she was moving rather than floating in place. She used her arms to pull herself upward while her legs pumped downward. All the while, she soaked in the exhilaration of the air slapping against her and realized it reminded her of swimming in Lake Michigan.

As the gusts of wind lifted her over London, Aya took in the views of the city's steeples and ancient blocks of residential buildings. Higher and higher they rose until they were peering at the entire city from above. Everything below looked like mere toys. This was even more fun than the VR room.

For what seemed like hours, they soared over the countryside and other cities Aya didn't recognize. The air grew chilly, and it frustrated her that she hadn't worn a long-sleeved shirt. Despite this discomfort, she marveled at the serene beauty of the countryside and at the ruggedness of the cities.

As they continued, a grayish-blue expanse appeared. *The North Sea. Wait until Malik knows I've seen the sea.*

Something dropped in her stomach and when she looked down, she realized she was falling. Panicked, she kicked her legs and pumped her arms. In a matter of seconds, she rose and found herself level with Orson again.

"Nice job recovering. The first time I flew I was around your age. I plummeted hundreds of meters over Scafell Pike and recovered just before hitting the ground. It's safe to say falling hundreds of meters onto jagged rocks would've been unpleasant," Orson said with a chuckle. "I would've caught you before you hit the ground. Not to worry."

She looked at him, holding in the urge to vomit.

"We've reached Hoy. Let's stop there." He pointed at

a cliff along the coast.

Lowering his arms, he brought himself to a vertical position.

She imitated him and, with surprising ease, floated downward. Aya watched the landscape become less panoramic every passing second. When her feet touched the ground, her head spun from dizziness. "I don't know how much I enjoy flying."

"You won't say that after you've completed a few more flights."

Once she composed herself, she looked at the water below. Shivering as the chilly wind brushed against her, she wrapped her arms around herself to warm up.

"Aya, look at how much you've gained. An entire world is now open to you. You have more than any girl in this world now."

She half-smiled. "Yeah, but I wish my family could be here to enjoy it with me."

"They can be."

She turned to him with a quizzical look.

"I gave the okay to start the initial talks with the opposition in the U.S." He paused and sat on a grassy patch on the cliff's edge. The wind ruffled his hair, sweeping it over his ears. "We're also starting initial peace talks with the opposition in Brazil, Pakistan, and the separatists in China. These groups have been on a guerrilla campaign against me and the Coalition for years now. It's time to put it all to bed so that we can move onward together, forward. Aya, an end to the chaos, violence, and hate is possible. We can fix things in your home, or you can bring your family here. I admit, I'd rather you stay here."

She pondered the idea. Would her father ever agree to move to London? How would they afford it? Maybe Orson could help her father get a job and a house...

"Let me tell you something that few others know about me, Aya. I searched for years across the entire world for another alpha, for someone else like me. But all I found were average post-humans. You can't imagine the loneliness. I'd searched so fruitlessly for so long that I'd begun to think I might be the only alpha in the world. Until I learned of your existence, another person who'd evolved beyond human and post-human. We are the alphas, the only two of our kind."

A fleeting image of Eve sailed to the front of Aya's mind.

"Unlike every other human and post-human in this world, we can do almost anything we want to do. Think about that."

"You talk as if we're gods."

"In a way, we are. Over the past twenty years, I've been called many things. Savior, peacemaker, unifier, tyrant, dictator, post-human rights hero, tosser, knob, and—a favorite from your country—douchebag. So many different names, I've lost count."

"Why do some people consider you a tyrant?" It dawned on her that nobody had ever explained the so-called bad things Orson had done. *How can helping faders be a bad thing?*

His voice grew quiet, and he looked in the distance. "People spread vicious rumors. People who fear progress and a world where post-humans are equal."

*Rumors like what*, she wondered. But before she could press further, he continued talking.

"But more people than not recognize the good I've done, and that's what matters," he said, with a smug smile.

"Tell me about some of the good things. Why do some people call you a savior?"

"Well," he said, rubbing his hands together and smiling, "with some geo-engineering and my atmokinesis abilities, I developed a way to bring regular rains to countries plagued by droughts. Countries that had seen millions of their people die because of seemingly endless droughts and wars fought over scarce resources like water."

"Atmokinesis? What's that?"

"Weather manipulation. Whatever weather event is occurring, I can channel it and manipulate it."

"You can create weather?"

"No. Only manipulate it. Like…for instance, those rain clouds there." He pointed at the distant gray clouds in the otherwise blue sky. "I can cause rain to fall from those clouds. But I can't make those rain clouds appear if they're not already there."

She gazed at him in awe.

"Since you're an alpha, I bet you could do it too if you tried. Focus on the clouds, clear every thought from your mind, and try to smell the rain. Once you smell it, faintly sweet and refreshing, believe that it's raining. Visualize it."

Following his directions, Aya waited for something to happen, for rain to pour from the thick gray puffs. "I don't think I have that ability."

He smiled and pointed. "Keep focusing and look closer."

Squinting, she noticed a haze just under the cloud and the rain smell intensified. The haze grew denser, and her eyes widened.

"That's just a bit of a mist you created. But with practice, you'll be able to create powerful downpours."

"Malik's going to flip when he finds out I'm like Storm," Aya burst out, grinning before catching herself. She cleared her throat. "I mean, I never knew I could do that."

"You're only learning about the range of your skills. Soon you'll realize you can do more than you've ever thought possible."

"Why do we have these abilities? How long have there been people like us, faders and alphas?"

"I'm afraid that despite all the research and money we've dedicated to answering those questions, nobody knows why some of us are like this. No specific genes appear common in all post-humans, but we have found that mothers can sometimes pass on post-human abilities to offspring. The Remington Center for Science spent billions researching these fundamental questions. We learned some interesting things. For instance, the oldest known post-human, a man named Forrest Sherman, was born in the 1980s. He died just before the Great Turn began. Unfortunately, we don't know if others existed farther back than that and how these abilities originated.

"Some researchers hypothesize that exposure to environmental toxins played a role. Forrest was born and raised in a small community where a toxic nuclear fission plant once operated—incidentally in a small town in the southern state of Georgia. We've found an unsettling number of post-humans grew up near toxic facilities, but nothing is conclusive," said Orson, pausing and sighing. "While some researchers are still investigating, I've decided our energies are best spent on other matters. Namely, the future rather than the past. We post-humans are small in number, less than five hundred million people scattered across six continents. But I believe we can leverage our abilities as post-humans to make the world better tomorrow."

She nodded and remained quiet.

"I have a favor to ask. I would like for you to be by my side for these peace talks with the opposition."

"Orson, I don't think you need my—"

"You're too young to remember when the world learned about the existence of post-humans. The world was on the brink of global war. Economies were in freefall, and humans were in panic mode. Groups and governments systematically targeted post-humans because of our extraordinary abilities, while vigilantes were hunting us in some warped mission to save humanity from us. All of this is why I created the Human and Post-Human Coalition for Peace. The Coalition pulled us back from the brink of annihilation as a species, Aya."

She'd heard this story too many times now, and it was sounding like one of her father's broken records. "You're not the only person who's told me how bad the Great Turn was."

"Well, then I imagine you're smart enough to know how horrible humanity can be to each other. War, racism, slavery, rape, and chemical warfare. Those are just a handful of things our species has done to each other in the name of civilization. That's why we alphas are the key to ensuring things don't go down a dark and destructive path again."

"I just don't know why you think you need my help. I don't know half the things you know. You're this big leader, and I'm just a girl from Chicago."

"No, Aya." He placed his hand on her shoulder. "You're so much more. Never forget that."

After an awkward silence, Orson got up and dusted himself off. "The world is yours. You need only reach out and grab it."

Before standing up, she pocketed a rock she planned to give to Malik. With a glance at Orson, she sighed and wished more than anything her father and brother could be here with her. Maybe it was time for her to pay them a visit in Philadelphia and even teleport them to London. Surely, it was safe to visit them now...

As she stood, she stared at the sky. The rain was gone, and the clouds had passed.

Kendrick's bare arms burned in the scorching late July sun

while he sat on the front porch of an old rowhouse on Osage Avenue in West Philadelphia. The house, situated a block away from Malcolm X Park, belonged to an army friend who had been kind enough to offer him and Malik a spare room. Since their arrival over a month ago, Kendrick had been trying to figure out his next move but sunk deeper into depression as he realized he had no next move.

A half-empty bottle of whiskey made by his new comrades lay next to his foot on the porch step. He picked it up, uncapped it, and swallowed a bit, squinting as the liquid stung his throat and lit a fire in his chest. Capping it up, he coughed and cursed under his breath.

When he looked up, he found Jesús standing on the other side of the porch and leaning against the wood railing. "What the hell...when did you get there?" Kendrick lifted the bottle and looked at the dark brown liquid. "I don't suppose there's anything else in this."

"I teleported," said Jesús, smirking.

"Oh, that's right. Eve said you could do that. Guess I never saw you actually do it. Well, good morning then. Come with some news or just dropping by?"

"A bit of both. But speaking of morning, don't you think it's a little early to be drinking? If I didn't know better, I'd think you were trying to drown yourself in that bottle."

"Look around you, son." Kendrick sat the bottle on the porch step and gestured at the decrepit neighboring rowhouses, all of them in extreme disrepair. "This city's in worse shape than Chicago, St. Louis, and Milwaukee put together. And I hadn't thought it could get worse than that."

"Seems like the New American Army is doing all right holding it together here. At least they haven't been attacked like Chicago."

"Holding it together? There's only one remaining power plant supporting this whole city. We have power outages constantly. Even with the power rations, the outages happen still. And winter will be here before we know it."

"You and Malik can come with me to Indiana."

Kendrick shook his head. "I have responsibilities here as a First Sergeant in the NAA."

"What do you do for them exactly? Eve didn't give me any details."

"The Eastern Front uses the old SEPTA trolley lines to transport personnel, food, firearms, and supplies through the city. I oversee the safe passage of all the cargo. I'm off duty today." He stopped abruptly and changed the subject. "Why the hell did you let her go?"

"Huh? Oh," said Jesús, shifting his weight from one foot to the other. "She insisted. She wanted to ask Orson to help her city."

"Ironic, since in my gut I know it was Orson who did the attack. The Eastern Front had nothing to do with it—I would know."

"Eve thinks it was Orson, too. But I don't know...that sounds like a conspiracy theory to me. It doesn't make sense."

Kendrick groaned. "So Eve suspects Orson, and she let Aya run off to him?"

"If we'd tried to stop her from leaving, she would've left anyway. She was determined, and we thought it best that she leave on good terms knowing that she can come back whenever or contact us for help." Jesús leaned against the railing and ran his hands through the hair he'd left loose for the journey.

"She's so much like her mother. Just as stubborn." Kendrick's voice quavered. "He'll hurt my little girl, and I can't do anything about it. I don't even know how to reach her."

Jesús flinched, taken aback by the deep fear and

helplessness in Kendrick's voice. "She has a burner phone I gave her, and I'm going to meet with her tomorrow in London. That's part of the reason I'm here, to see if you want to come with me."

He groaned and, after a moment, shook his head. "I can't. The Eastern Front might be fader-friendly, but they're still opposed to the Coalition. It would raise suspicions if I went there."

"You know, you and Malik could just leave her altogether and join her in London."

Kendrick was silent. "I don't know what I'd do there. How I'd provide for them."

"I'm sure we could figure something out," said Jesús, scratching his head. "For what it's worth, it appears she's doing well. I'm sure you saw they introduced her and gave her some sort of award at the press conference a few days ago."

"Yeah, I saw. She's never liked being in the spotlight."

"She's a lot like Eve in that way." Jesús smiled. "Look, I'm not worried about her safety. Despite how heavy the surveillance is there, what with that damned Q system, I still have my ways of getting information without being detected. Plus, she knows to contact me if anything goes wrong. Eve and I will step in if we hear anything that suggests she's in immediate danger. Although, after the entrance she made at the General Assembly meeting, I don't think Orson's people are any match for her. I've seen Aya in action. Trust me, she can handle herself these days."

"Eve confirmed you and Aya were behind the prison breaks." Not smiling, Kendrick looked at the vacant street, while running his hands over his head in frustration. "Like I told Eve, I didn't leave her with you all for her to be getting into trouble, breaking people out of prisons and running off to London. You and Eve broke your promise to keep her safe, to keep her hidden."

Jesús inhaled and shuffled his feet. "She would never be content holed up in that house, Go. We didn't want her to leave. But she was devastated by the destruction in Chicago. You had to see what it did to her. She said she needed to do something more, to stop it from happening again."

"I mourned the attack, the death and destruction of it all. Malik's heartbroken that he'll never see his friends again. I know what it did to her." Standing up, Kendrick turned to Jesús. "But now my daughter is with the same monsters who very likely destroyed our home."

"I don't know," Jesús said, hesitating. "Like I said, I'm not as sure as you and Eve are that Orson was behind the attack. It could've just as easily been these Eastern Front folks you call your friends now. I know you think you know these people, but how well do you know them? How are you sure it wasn't them?"

"Sure enough." Kendrick turned away from Jesús. "Everything I've grown to know and love is just about gone. My wife. My home. All I have left are my children."

"You know Eve was worried that when word reached here about Aya, your superiors would put two and two together."

"I've already talked about all this with Eve. She thought they'd figure out Aya's my daughter, see that she's making nice with the Coalition, and it might mean trouble for me here. As I told Eve, I've proved my loyalty to the NAA. Besides, they need as many able-bodied folks as they can get, since the People's Army is preparing for war against us because they think we're responsible for the jailbreaks and the attack. My position here is safe. In fact, as a defector from the People's Army, I'm an asset. The NAA has some talkers here as well, so they did a scan to confirm my loyalty."

Jesús stared at him for a moment. "Go, how are you holding up here?"

Kendrick glanced at the rowhouse and nodded with sad smile. "Ruthie and Dylan are good people. They were happy to put me and Malik up in their extra room. I'm just glad I stayed in touch with them all these years." He stopped and uncapped the bottle. After gulping some more whiskey, he looked at the half-empty bottle and offered some to Jesús.

"No thanks. I'm more of a sacred plant type of guy."

"Son, what the hell is a sacred plant?"

"Weed, bud, ganja, sticky icky, etc…sir."

"Right. But with your abilities, that shit could kill you. You'll end up teleporting to the bottom of the Indian Ocean because you're too high to know where you're going."

Jesús chuckled. "I think I'm good. But that kind of sounds like an awesome adventure. Anyway, Eve's also worried Orson's people might come looking for you."

Kendrick frowned. "The thought has crossed my mind. You think his people know we're here?"

"This is Orson and the Coalition we're talking about. They have informants everywhere—hell, I'd be surprised if they don't know you're here. If you're right that it was Orson behind the attack, this could be the calm before the storm. But let's just hope you and Eve are wrong."

He put his hand on Jesús' shoulder. "Well, when the storm comes, it's going to be a category five hurricane. You can count on that. Orson never does anything small."

Jesús shook Kendrick's sweaty hand. "I'm going to hope that forecast is wrong then. I'll let you know how the meeting goes with Aya tomorrow. Be safe, Go." When he pulled back his hand, he was holding a small wad of cash.

"That's for Aya. Be sure to tell her we miss her, and I love her."

"You could tell her in person, you know."

A sad smile sailed across Kendrick's face. "Maybe next time."

With a final nod, Jesús disappeared.

Kendrick took another sip of the whiskey and looked at the spot where Jesús had been standing mere seconds earlier. *Maybe I should've taken his offer to visit London.* He wondered if he'd made a mistake, just like he'd messed up by not leaving with Valerie years ago. *No, if someone here finds out, they'll never let me back in.* But would that be such a bad thing? Perhaps leaving the country was the best option. As he settled on this thought, it hit him again...*how would I provide for us with no money, in some place where I don't know anyone?*

He walked to the front door, figuring he'd head inside to get a couple more hours of sleep before everyone else woke up.

As he reflected on his situation and how he had no idea what was going to happen next, he tried to suppress a frightening vision of the future. He couldn't lose his children as he'd lost his wife. He'd die before he let that happen, and that's what worried him the most.

During the visit with Jesús, Aya experienced a jolt of excitement about the possibilities ahead for her. Her father might come during the next visit, Jesús told her, and now her mind buzzed with ideas about the life they could build in London.

"Maybe the Coalition will pay me, and I can help Dad get started here," she exclaimed to Jesús, standing in the middle of Hyde Park as the afternoon clouds shifted. "I bet Orson could get Dad a job, too. He could join the Coalition security force, the U....I...um, I can't remember the letters."

Glancing around, he smiled but shook his head. "Don't get ahead of yourself. Your father isn't a big fan of leaving the country. Not yet anyway. Not to mention, he's a little leery of Orson."

"Why?" said Aya, eyes wide. "He's so nice. I mean, a little weird and talks about himself a lot."

"He and Eve believe some of the rumors about Orson. Stuff about him attacking faders who oppose him," Jesús whispered.

"That's crazy. I can't believe he'd do anything like that. The way he talks about bringing us all together and protecting faders—"

"I know. It doesn't make sense to me either. But I'm just saying your father has his reasons for not wanting to move to a Coalition country." Jesús leaned close to her as two women jogged past them, followed by a man walking a Labrador Retriever. "Hey, I'm glad you changed your appearance like I asked you to. I guess Eve did a good job teaching you how to control perceptions."

Aya pushed her hair behind her ears. Long brown hair had replaced her puffy Afro ponytails, and her dark brown skin was now a creamy tan shade. She'd based her look off a combination of girls she'd seen on television.

"Did you keep this meeting a secret like I asked you?" he asked, keeping his voice low. "You didn't tell anyone where you were going or who you were meeting, right?"

She nodded. "I just said I was going to the Tate Modern again. I go there during the afternoon sometimes anyway. But I don't know why you wanted me to be so secretive."

"Well, I might not agree with Eve and Kendrick, but I trust their instincts. It's best to err on the side of caution." He gestured toward a bench and they sat. "So tell me how every thing's going so far, besides becoming an international star."

For the rest of the hour, they talked about everything from Aya's sightseeing to her first time flying to Eve's new project—turning the backyard shed into a guest house.

Pedestrians, joggers, and people shuffling back to offices after the lunch hour passed them, none of them taking any interest in Aya. She realized how refreshing it was to be unknown again and considered she might need to use this ability more often.

Rain clouds drifted in, and Jesús looked at his watch. "I probably should head out of here anyway," he said, standing up and stretching. "How do you feel about popping over to the farm now and again to check in with us? Eve would love to see you."

"She could've come with you!"

He laughed. "You know that's not happening. Carmen still can't get her to visit in Oakland."

"I don't understand her. How can she live like that?"

Jesús shrugged. "Hell if I know. Anyway, I'll let her know you said hi. But if you think about dropping by, just be sure to keep it a secret. Eve wants to stay off the grid." He pulled a small wad of money from his wallet. "Your father, Eve, and I pulled some of that together. I'm sure you're running low."

She pushed his hand away. "No, I'm fine. Orson's covering everything. I still have the money you gave me before I left."

A puzzled look sailed over his face before he smiled. "Well, I suppose it's the least he can do since he's rich."

Aya hugged him and kissed his cheek.

"All right, don't get mushy. You just keep that phone on you and let me know if anything comes up. And keep your eyes open, okay. Eve and your father may be a little paranoid, but they have their reasons."

With a nod, she smiled. "I know."

After a wink and a wave, he vanished and left her standing alone in the park as raindrops hit her forehead. She replayed Jesús' words about Orson and tried to wrap her mind around why her father and Eve distrusted him. *Rumors about him attacking faders? So those were the rumors Orson mentioned during transvection practice?* She wondered if it was possible that she was wrong about Orson.

*Dad trusts almost nobody, and Eve's too scared to leave her house.* They've been through so much that they can't see the good anymore, she concluded. She shook her head and smiled, pushing their suspicions aside. As more raindrops hit her face, she squinted and hurried toward the nearest café. She'd change the world with Orson, she told herself, and she'd prove her father and Eve wrong. A better future was possible…

# 10

As days turned into weeks, Aya watched television, checked out the swans in Regent's Park, and fed the ducks...that is, when she wasn't accompanying Orson to Coalition meetings or touring the city with Diya. Orson took her on more flying adventures and regaled her with tales about all the mistakes he'd made when learning to use and manage his abilities. One incident involved ending up in the hospital with third-degree burns all over his body. Aya shuddered at the thought.

When she woke up one morning in late August with a splitting pain in her abdomen and a pulsing headache, she wondered if it was because of the rocky landing she'd had yesterday upon their return from Dublin. She'd lost her concentration and, from a height of at least twenty feet, crashed onto the concrete driveway in front of Orson's home.

As she sat up, she leaned against the pillow and ground her teeth through the pain. Something felt wet beneath her. She rolled over, looked at the huge red spot on the bed sheet, and cursed under her breath. "Ugh."

Right after her first period years ago, Aya started to notice strange things happening to her body. Every once in a while, a hand or foot would disappear while she showered.

Maybe it happened to all girls her age, she'd told herself, deciding not to dwell on it. She also didn't want to be targeted by the People's Army or anyone who harbored strong anti-fader sentiment, so she'd kept her secret from everyone. Until the night of the taxi accident, she'd never faded more than a couple of times. Until that night, she'd never believed she was anything other than a typical girl.

This morning, she desperately wished she knew a way to use her abilities to alleviate the pain. Eve had suggested shifting into a male for a few days. But Aya had never mastered that level of shifting during her trainings with Eve.

She hurried to the bathroom, slipped out of her soiled pajamas, and rinsed off. Realizing she had no sanitary items, she cursed again and placed a towel in her pants.

Groaning, she plodded from the bedroom to the hallway in search of Iris. *Why is this apartment so damn big?* She stopped outside the guest bathroom, realizing she wouldn't make it to the end of the hallway. Bent over and holding her stomach, she suppressed the urge to cry. Instead of dragging herself farther, she teleported to the kitchen where Iris was preparing breakfast.

Startled by Aya's sudden presence, Iris almost dropped a jug of orange juice. She leaned against the kitchen island and clutched her chest. "Dear, why are you up so early?"

"Do you have any pads and something for period cramps?" Aya winced as a stabbing pain emanated from her abdomen to her thighs.

"How young do you think I am?" The woman smiled and laid the towel on the countertop. "You watch these tomatoes in the frying pan, and I'll make a quick call for you. Spread some marmalade on those toast when they pop up, too."

Aya huffed in frustration and turned over the

tomatoes before replacing the lid. Her head throbbed, and she thought she might buckle to the floor as pain shot down her legs. She poured herself a glass of orange juice, sat on a bar stool at the island and gulped the juice. It brought little relief. *Okay. Tea. Hot things help.* Lucky for her, Iris had already boiled some water.

After submersing a bag of Irish Breakfast Tea in a tall mug of steaming water, she waited several minutes for the tea to steep. When she took some sips, it brought more relief than the juice but not enough.

Although she really wasn't hungry, she forced herself to eat a piece of toast.

Iris returned with a reassuring smile, slipping past Aya to stir the potatoes. "I remember those days. I'm well past my prime now, so those days are ancient bloody history, thank goodness. Just wait till you're my age when you'll have to deal with menopause. You'll wish all you had were a few aches once a month."

Aya flashed her a confused look.

"Anyway, you're in luck, dear. Ms. Narang is on her way and will be here in a few minutes with some painkillers and personal items. I reckon you should pop back in the room to get cleaned up before she arrives. But I recommend you walk rather than teleport. Exercise is good for the cramps. Besides, I've never liked that teleporting thing. Orson did it often to scare me when he was a boy. I find it all a bit excessive when you can just walk a few feet to where you're trying to go."

Aya nodded, grabbed another piece of toast, and hurried to her room.

After taking a painkiller and drinking more tea, Aya got dressed and sat with Diya in the living room, waiting for the pain to subside. As they passed time talking about London,

Aya realized she hadn't spent any one-on-one time with Diya. Indeed, she'd spent most of the past three weeks with Orson's housekeeper, security guards, and Michio whenever he teleported in for more games in the VR room.

Once Aya's pain dulled to a minor ache, Diya suggested a shopping trip. Aya hopped at the idea, longing to see more boutiques in London—she'd popped into a few but never bought anything. In Chicago, shopping mainly consisted of visiting stores that people ran out of their homes or yards, or going to the central market, a cluster of tents with people selling rarer items.

As they stepped inside the store, Aya peered around the huge open room filled with endless racks of clothing. It was bigger than the smaller shops she'd visited.

"Welcome, Ms. Narang," said the shopkeeper. The woman, at least six feet tall, stared at Aya and covered her mouth. "Oh my God, it's you."

Aya smiled but averted her gaze, not yet accustomed to people being starstruck by her.

"Thank you, Nellisa, we'll just browse a bit and let you know if we need anything," said Diya.

Looking at Nellisa, Aya noticed there was something a bit off about her, something she couldn't quite pinpoint. She appeared a little too perfect: shiny dark hair, a smile that conveyed little emotion, ultra-feminine looking, blemish-free skin. She moved gracefully around the store, but her movements seemed a little too graceful and not...human. Struck by the eerie perfection of the woman, Aya watched her with increasing curiosity.

*She's what we call a pretty-borg. She's a human who has paid a lot of money to change most of her human body parts. Her modified body uses biomechatronic prosthetic body parts that look and feel human. To make it simple, she's half machine, half human. She's faster and stronger than a typical person. She's also much prettier than a regular cyborg.*

Aya wondered why Diya's lips didn't move as she spoke. *Are you in my head?*

*I'm not reading your mind. I'm just communicating with you. I'm sorry if it was weird or inappropriate. I didn't want to offend the shopkeeper by talking about her cy status aloud. Some people view cys as a dangerous lot—because of how powerful they are—but cys are like everyone else. Just trying to figure out their place in the world.*

Aya's brow furrowed in confusion. *How can you talk to me in my head?*

"I wish I knew. I tried to scan Orson many times, but it didn't work. You two have the same mental block, an alpha thing. With alphas, I can vaguely sense what you're both thinking. When I try to scan you, I get only a sense of what you're feeling. It's like staring at a picture and seeing the color but none of the detail." She went to a pair of Manolo pumps. "These shoes are to die for. But, alas, I must resist temptation."

"So why could you hear my thoughts when I was responding to you telepathically?"

Diya placed the shoes on the stand. "Because you were responding to me. You were consciously sending that response to me."

"I see. It's like how I was able to communicate to the people telepathically at the prison camps. Orson told me it was impossible to read the minds of alphas, but I couldn't make sense of why those people in the prison could hear me then. You're saying by talking to them telepathically, I sort of gave them access to specific thoughts. Like temporarily?"

Diya smiled and nodded. "I think it's because you intended for them to hear you. I'm still amazed you were able to telepathically communicate to that many people, all at the same time. To think that the post-human community dubbed me the most powerful talker three years in a row at the Post-

Human Image Awards."

"There are awards for being a fader? That's kind of stupid."

Diya laughed. "It's a lot of fun, in fact." She drifted to a rack of cocktail dresses.

As Aya followed Diya, she found herself less interested in the clothes than in all the holographic displays of beautiful models.

"At puberty I noticed I was able to read people's thoughts, hear what they were thinking. Then I was able to communicate with other people telepathically. When it first happened, I thought I was going mad, but I learned how to manage it. I was able to turn it on and off at will. But there soon came a time in my life that I'm not proud of. Even to this day, I regret what I did next." She stopped as her hand brushed against a red dress. "I learned how to use my telepathy to influence others. I could make them do things. Discovering that took me down a bad path during my late teens and early twenties."

"What do you mean?"

Walking toward a yellow dress, Diya stared at the white stitches and blue embroidery. "The more I leaned on my ability, the more I became a monster. You're still young enough to do the right thing with your abilities. Whatever you do, don't get drunk with power. I wish I'd had someone to tell me that when I was your age." She turned to Aya with a sad smile. "I like to think I turned out well enough, but I did hurt a lot of people along the way, including my father."

"You can still apologize to him, can't you?"

"He passed on."

Aya's expression went flat.

"You and I have a lot in common, Aya. We're poor girls who now find ourselves in the halls of power, connecting with the most powerful people on Earth, thanks to our abilities and a little bit of street smarts. But there are some things I hope we never have in common." She cleared her throat and smiled again. "Help yourself to anything you like in the store. I'm paying."

As she watched Diya browse through the dresses, Aya wondered about the details she'd left out of the story.

Orson rested his head against his palms and looked from Thomas seated across from him to the holographic image of Blade Sonani. Blade's transparent figure sat in a chair next to Thomas. The tension in the office was palpable as they listened to Blade air his grievances about the upcoming peace talks.

"While I'm supportive of your decision to convene peace talks with the U.S., it was your responsibility to clear this with the General Assembly—with me—before announcing it to the world. I decided not to publicly express my disappointment about your behavior, which I believe amounts to a complete lack of respect for me and this Coalition. But now you schedule these talks with the U.S. without consulting me or ensuring my calendar is clear. Orson, I will not jump at your every call. Nor will I allow you to treat me like an afterthought. As GA President, I demand respect," he said, glaring at Orson.

"Blade—" Orson began.

"There are members of the Coalition who loathe the idea of allowing the U.S. into the Coalition. President Alabi of Nigeria is furious. As the head of the African Union, she believes inviting the U.S. into the Coalition now threatens the power of the African bloc. She's not the only one who feels that way. I've been on calls for weeks since the press conference trying to ease the concerns of Iran, South Korea, North Korea, Vietnam—"

"You're a man who understands the international

press very well," Orson interrupted. "So you know just as well as I do that starting peace talks with President Lopez and General Harris is the right move to make. Also, let's not jump ahead. These are peace talks, not an invitation to the Coalition yet."

Blade waved his hand and made a phish sound. "What makes you think that the military factions in the U.S. would even agree to a peace deal with the Coalition?"

"Aya came here because she wanted peace after the devastation to her home."

Blade leaned forward. "That girl has clouded your judgment, Orson. I understand giving the Chinese a new fusion reactor and making efforts to establish peace with the separatists there. All that is what China wants, and it benefits the Coalition to keep China satisfied. It's a sensible move. But playing soft with the opposition elsewhere, especially the U.S.? Where's the benefit? My fellow leaders in the African Union aren't happy about the implications of that collapsed empire regaining any semblance of power. You're making me look like an ass in front of my peers, as I have no way of explaining to them this irrational strategy of yours."

"Bollocks. You always look like a wanker to people." Orson laughed, but Blade didn't crack a smile and Thomas shifted in his seat. Clearing his throat, Orson went on. "This is the right move. Poll after poll shows that people feel the opposition movement is a continued threat to global stability. Not to mention, the western part of the U.S. is already under our influence. We now have a shot at ending this quarrel with the opposition globally."

"I understand. But don't you think the opposition will see this as an act of weakness and launch even more terrorist attacks? I don't want that on my head, friend. Plus, the Americans have been tearing each other apart for years now. Their fate was sealed in the London Agreement ten years ago when their president refused to join the Coalition. Let them have their war, and we can pick up the pieces afterward."

Orson shook his head. "Trust me. We're better off acting preemptively. If we can negotiate peace with the U.S., then the Brazilians, the Pakistan groups, the Chinese separatists...think about it. Other opposition sympathizers will all fall in line. If we quell the strongest opposition group—the Americans—we'll be able to make our moves with fewer snags. Once we completely open those borders, we'll have brand new markets.

"Imagine it: Brazil and Pakistan join the Coalition, and China's role in the Coalition is strengthened, quieting President Chen's concerns. The U.S. joins and becomes a global trading partner again, putting you and your fellow Africans in the position to lend to them at very profitable rates. How else will they afford to buy our fusion energy and quantum computers? How else will they afford to access the Q, which they'll desperately want to track and follow all their post-human and human threats? Blade, this is what 'picking up the pieces afterward' looks like."

Silent, Blade rubbed his head and leaned back.

"I know the electric grids across the U.S. are on their last legs, the food supply has all but collapsed, and the opposition there is more divided than ever. This is a perfect time to open up these talks. Where there's chaos, there's opportunity."

"I see," said Blade, folding his arms across his chest. "I see."

Thomas chimed in at last. "If I may add, Aya is our symbol of peace. The Coalition should use her while the public still favors her."

Orson smiled. "Precisely. We have momentum and history on our side."

"Orson, you slick devil. Now that you've explained

your plan, I guess I'm happy that you've managed to get the U.S. opposition to agree to talks. If we're lucky all will go well. Meanwhile, let's hope that the public continues to hold Aya in high esteem." Blade paused as a fleeting look of concern shaded his face. "I have to go now but update me before you act. I'd like not to be caught off guard again."

"Absolutely. Cheers, Blade."

When Blade's transparent figure disappeared, Thomas straightened his posture. He took a sip of water and regarded Orson. "I hope there's an actual endgame."

"Thomas, you know me well enough to know when I feed Blade a bunch of rubbish." He ran his fingers through his thick hair. "But that wasn't all rubbish. Aya is the key, and she's given us a wonderful opportunity. Next week in Iceland, we'll have our first talks in a decade between the U.S. opposition and the Coalition."

"I get it. You're using her to open the doors to peace since President Lopez has heralded her as an American hero. The mysterious teen girl who saved so many people. She's a regular ambassador of goodwill. But I still need to know the endgame beyond what you just laid out, sir."

Orson adjusted his tie and walked around his desk. "This girl's arrival has led a couple of major players in the U.S. to let their guards down. We have a moment now. We can end this guerrilla war campaign with little bloodshed."

"I agree, sir."

Orson walked toward the window. "Ever since the Coalition's rise to power, there have always been whispers of me being an autocratic dictator. Remember when all the journalists referred to the Q and the Coalition as the arrival of the Big Brother state? Outside the Coalition, they continue to call it that to this day, Thomas. Those whispers never stopped, even here. Even after all I've accomplished, after all I've given them, many still view me as no better than bloody

Hitler. I want to quash those whispers and prove naysayers wrong. If we can establish peace with the opposition and with no more bloodshed, do you know what that would mean?"

Thomas offered no response.

"It would mean they were wrong about me. And they would have to finally admit that."

Thomas regarded him with an impenetrable expression.

"I will have their full support then for the Ares One station, for whatever I pursue in the name of peace and stability. This is what I've worked so hard for, Thomas."

"I understand. What do you need me to do?"

Orson approached him. "Keep our informants active in the U.S. and continue to keep the tension high between the Midwest Front and Eastern Front. It will make any peace discussions feel all the more urgent."

"Will do, sir. I just have one last thing to ask. What if the public adoration of Aya fades or something goes wrong, and the opposition amps up their guerrilla campaigns? What then?"

"There's always a Plan B."

With a nod, Thomas rose, buttoned his suit jacket, and headed toward the exit. When he reached the door and grasped the doorknob, he turned to face Orson. "Always a Plan B, sir."

Orson smiled. Left alone with his own thoughts, he peered out the window. With the second alpha under his sphere of influence, and the opposition weakened, how could he lose?

For the first time in many years, he experienced a sense of relief. The end of the loosely connected opposition movement was on the horizon, and it would take little or no violence to reach his goal of unity and peace. He couldn't help but smile. "Onward together, forward," he said, gazing at the cityscape.

Exhausted from shopping, Aya lay in bed as evening rain beat against the window. She examined the rock she'd picked up during her flying trip to Hoy and turned it over in her hand. She closed her eyes, recalling the sound of the wind against her ears as she soared through the air, the smell of the salty sea filling her nostrils. "I think flying is my favorite ability," she'd told Diya earlier while they sat at a restaurant patio after shopping.

"Flying or teleporting are the abilities I wish I had. The freedom of it," Diya had said. "I can fade, and I have telepathy. That's it."

Aya had only practiced flying a few more times since the day they flew to the cliff in Scotland, and she had to admit it was even more exhilarating than teleporting.

As she turned onto her side, she reached for the backpack on the floor and stuffed the rock inside. Her hand brushed against the scarves she'd started crocheting while at Eve's home but never finished. *I wonder what Eve and Jesús are doing.* She assumed Eve was tending to the chickens and Jesús grabbing a midday snack, since it was still mid-afternoon in Indiana. Or maybe Eve was lying on the sofa with a book and Baldwin on her lap, enjoying an afternoon glass of wine— Aya had noticed this was a near daily ritual for Eve. Lost in these thoughts, she remembered she hadn't finished the scarves for her brother and father. She pulled the backpack onto the bed and retrieved the crochet needle and a scarf.

After she got up and slipped into her pajamas, she dropped onto the bed. But before she slid the needle through the first loop, a knock came at the door. She looked up. "Yeah?"

"May I have a moment, Ms. Wright?" asked Iris, opening the door and standing in the frame. "Mr. Remington has asked me to tell you to pack for a trip to China. You'll be leaving with him first thing tomorrow."

Aya's eyes widened. "China? Why are we going there?" *It's probably about the Chinese separatist groups. He said he was setting up a meeting with President Chen this week.*

"From what I understand, there are celebratory events lined up related to some recent deal he struck with the president there," said Iris with apparent disinterest. "If you need me to run pick up some more trousers, knickers, or other items for you, I'm happy to do so, dear."

She shook her head. "I think I have enough. Diya and I bought a lot of things when we went shopping."

"Well, I'm doing the washing now. Do you have anything that needs washing?"

Aya pointed to the pile of dirty clothes next to the wardrobe. "I'm sorry. I was going to bring them to you but forgot."

Iris gathered the clothes and smiled. "I'll have these to you after supper."

Staring at the crochet needle and scarf after Iris left, Aya's lips parted into a smile as she thought about the prospect of traveling to yet another fascinating country. If someone had told her just a few months ago that she'd see anything outside of Chicago, she would've laughed and said they were joking. Not for one moment had she imagined she'd know life outside Chicago, life not sullied by war and conflict.

She pulled the yarn through a loop and started crocheting the scarf, her mind buzzing about the trip to China and getting more involved in the Coalition's peacekeeping work.

## 11

When they boarded Orson's jet, Aya was surprised to be flying with the aid of modern technology. "Sometimes it's important for us to save our energy and live as normies do," Orson told her when she asked why didn't they just teleport.

While Diya, Thomas, and Orson talked business, Aya relaxed and looked at the empty blue sky. So this was what her father meant when he talked about the experience of flying in an airplane? The whole thing felt a bit dull. Yawning after a while, she pulled a scarf and crochet needle from her backpack and occupied herself for the next few hours until she fell asleep.

By the time they arrived in Beijing, night had fallen and the neon lights from the towering skyscrapers flooded the streets teeming with people. Their car wove through the throngs of bright skyscrapers, the tallest buildings Aya had ever seen.

At the hotel, lines of people gathered on both sides of the path to the entrance. Some people shouted Orson's name, while others cheered and yelled Aya's name. Orson smiled and waved at the crowd.

"Come." Diya placed her hand on Aya's shoulder. "We'll be here a week. You'll have plenty of time to see the sights."

"Even in between all the meetings? I heard you and Orson talking about it on the plane." From what she'd heard, the week would be filled with diplomatic meetings, press conferences with Asian leaders and businesspeople, and a chance to view the construction of the Coalition's new fusion reactor. Sightseeing hadn't seemed high on the list of priorities.

"Yes," said Diya. "We're starting off with a meeting tomorrow with President Chen and other members of the National People's Congress. It'll be busy. But I'll make time to show you the city."

Aya thought about the other thing she'd heard Diya whisper to Orson. "You're worried about something bad happening, aren't you? From the separatists here. So you don't want me to go out on my own."

Diya threw her a quizzical look.

"I heard you tell Orson that security forces are on high alert, that the separatists have made threats."

They entered the elevator, and Diya pushed the button for the twenty-fifth floor. "I'm not worried. But it's always important to be cautious."

After exiting and separating from Orson, Diya led Aya to the suite the two of them would be sharing. The suite was almost as lavish as Orson's apartment. Two separate bedrooms, a patio with a stunning view of the city, and a small kitchen that opened into a living room. Whereas Orson's apartment looked classy and a bit old, Aya thought this place looked like something from the future.

She retreated to her bedroom and sprawled out on the soft bed. She thought about what she might see during her time in Beijing. There was so much to see, and she wished she'd had time to create a list. Most of all, though, she hoped to see Michio. She assumed his father would be among the Asian leaders attending the week's events, and Michio might go with him.

But the next day came and went, and she didn't see Michio. Filled with meetings and an elaborate celebration, the first day was busier than Aya had expected. President Chen welcomed the head of the Coalition with a decadent traditional Chinese opening ceremony complete with drumming and holographic displays typically seen during New Year's events.

The celebration didn't stop there. Members of the press invited Orson and Aya to interview after interview, and every press conference saw a gathering of large and jubilant crowds.

Excited as she was, all the activities drained her. She struggled to keep track of the days, which were so packed that she found no time to explore the city with Diya. Instead, she occupied herself with observing Orson and trying to make sense of the man.

He appeared to enjoy the attention. He laughed and bragged about himself during one interview when asked about the Coalition's upcoming meeting in Iceland with the United States' opposition groups. "I'm sure their opinion of me will change," he said. "It may take time, but I'm confident the Americans will embrace me and the Coalition in the same manner as you all have. With Aya there for the talks, I have every hope that we'll come to a resolution that satisfies all sides."

During another interview, he went into a long monologue highlighting his achievements and efforts to bring peace, making sure to praise China. "Since the Great Turn, China has become the most prosperous nation on Earth. The Coalition's grand experiment of social equality has lifted some of the poorest humans on Earth out of dire poverty, and given countless people access to inexpensive, clean, and unlimited energy."

Aya daydreamed as Orson launched into the talking points she'd heard over and over—about the Q system and fusion bringing prosperity in Asia and Africa—since she arrived in the Coalition world.

As one day bled into the next, Aya took every fleeting opportunity to retreat to her room and either sleep, watch television, or think about the meeting with the United States. For weeks, she'd hoped for a meeting with the United States, and now that it was around the corner, nervousness overcame her. If they agreed to join the Coalition, it would change everything. She could go back, help rebuild, and transform her city into one as nice as those she'd seen in the Coalition countries so far.

But what if it didn't go well? *What if I can't help Orson convince them to join the Coalition?* Stretched out on the sofa, she stared at the ceiling as these thoughts ran through her mind and a Faye Lennox music video played on the television.

"There you are," said Diya, walking in and shutting the door. "Why are you hiding in here, Aya?"

Aya sat up and yawned. "I'm just tired."

Diya sat on the sofa and looked sideways at Ayah. "I know it's exhausting. But people want to hear from you, Aya. Having you here is a big deal. I've let Orson know you won't be at the afternoon meeting. He wants to give you a tour of the new fusion plant tomorrow."

Aya nodded.

"How about you and I go out?" asked Diya.

Aya sat up. "Where?"

"We can go to a museum. Or the zoo? It's recently remodeled with an augmented reality room. You'll love it."

"I've never been to a zoo," said Aya.

Diya smiled. "Then zoo it is. Let's go."

Orson stopped in a small courtyard on the grounds of China's newest nuclear fusion plant that would begin operations in three months. Flanked by Coalition officials and two engineers from the Remington Center for Science, he stood before a handful of congressional members, clean energy advocates, and local elected leaders. They listened while he spoke about fusion plants in other Coalition countries and how he hoped this fourth fusion reactor in China would bring even more prosperity and jobs to the country.

As he concluded the tour, the small group dispersed, leaving him with Thomas who'd arrived with Aya during his closing speech. He smiled at them and gave Thomas a pat on the back. "It's a lovely day in Beijing."

Thomas didn't reply but looked at Orson with a typical humorless expression.

Orson shook his head and smiled. "Always so serious," he remarked before turning his attention to Aya. "What a wonderful day this is for that tour I promised you, huh? I have about one hour or less before President Chen sends his subordinates to fetch me. So let's get this show on the road, shall we?"

Aya adjusted her hard hat, her Afro poking out on all sides.

"I'm terribly sorry you didn't get to see your friend, Michio. His father informed me he had school and studies this week."

"He still could've popped over for an hour or two," Aya muttered, disappointed. "Or I could have gone over."

"Maybe we'll take a trip to Japan to see him soon." Orson paused as they entered a hallway. "But I wanted to share with you something you might not have heard about during your time growing up among the opposition. You see, this country is special to me because it shows the promise of the Coalition and my vision. Not long after the anti-post-human element here tried to assassinate me, I gifted them with their first fusion reactor, technology developed by my science center. I've counted China as a close ally ever since."

"Do you think fusion is the reason everyone celebrates you here?" Aya paused and looked up at him. "Or is it because this is the place where everyone saw firsthand that you couldn't be killed?"

Orson's expression flattened, yet his lips curled into a smile. "That's why I like you, so observant and straight to the point for a young person. The point is what I did for the people here in the years following the failed assassination attempt on me, is what I want to do for your country and for the entire world. But there are a lot of young people who were born during a vastly different era here, during the hard times. They're all grown up now, and are still resistant to the Coalition, convinced that we are the problem."

"Are they resistant to the Coalition or to you?" asked Aya, staring at him. "In the meeting yesterday, President Chen said the separatists' anger is more about you than about the Coalition."

His smile faltered once more as he looked at her. "The separatists don't like the change I'm offering. But change will come. It's an unavoidable fact of nature. This reactor is the change that's necessary."

Staring straight ahead, they stopped at a set of steel double doors adorned with a "Restricted Area" sign. He opened the doors and stepped aside to usher them into the Remington room.

Aya looked around the room, and her gaze rested on the tall metal cylinder structure.

"Welcome to the Remington," said Orson, pointing at the two-story cylinder-shaped machine in the center of the room. "Inside the Remington's doughnut-shaped chamber is where fusion takes place. That's where all the magic happens."

She walked closer to the machine and stared at it. Her expression of awe pleased Orson, and he smiled. He needed her to understand the power they possessed as alphas and the responsibility of that power.

"For decades, scientists and engineers alike were stumped about how to make fusion energy cheap, scalable, and affordable. The problem was ignition. What can yield enough power to make the reaction stable and allow sustained fusion to happen? That's what I figured out, using my abilities. Brilliant, isn't it? With the help of quantum computers we were able to plot the magnetic and electric fields emanating from a simple configuration of electrons. To put it plainly, I solved magnetic confinement fusion." Orson's eyes lit up as he approached the machine. "This invention allowed me to make fusion energy available to any countries willing to join the Coalition. So, you see, the opposition is wrong about us. I only want to give the world what my abilities have made possible."

He brushed his hands against the machine and looked upward, marveling at the technology that had changed everything for him. This machine had led him out of the halls of parliament and into the position of Chief Minister of the Coalition, making him the most powerful man in the world.

"I'm showing you this now because I believe we're meant to do this work together. You and I could've taken different paths, yet we ended up at the same place. I don't believe that's coincidence. It's our responsibility to be the stewards of humankind."

Aya glanced from Thomas to Orson. She smiled and shook her head as she replied, "I already told you I'm nobody's savior. Or steward." She paused and took a deep breath. "But I'll stand by you and the Coalition to bring peace to my country and every country like it."

He stepped forward and stood next her, staring at the machine. "Aya, do you know how I realized I was much more than a regular post-human?"

She shook her head.

"Let me tell you a story. One day, I was playing football with my mates at a park. After the game, most of them left because of the extreme heat of the day. But I wasn't bothered by the heat. I realized I could regulate my body's temperature to avoid heat stroke."

While Orson spoke, Thomas perched by the double doors and leaned against the wall.

"I quickly recognized my abilities far exceeded those of the other post-humans my parents secretly introduced me to. The few post-humans I'd met could only make themselves disappear, but I was able to do that and so many other things. It didn't take me long to realize I could do almost anything I wanted to do. Standing in the field on that hot summer day, I simply thought about the sun. I'd always been fascinated with science, you see." He held out his hands, palms up. "I reached out my hands and thought about the sun and its energy. In moments, a small ball of energy formed in my hands. It felt like warm water. I'm lucky I was wearing sunglasses because that little ball of energy created an extraordinarily bright glow. I might've lost my sight had I looked at it without my sunglasses. That's when I realized I was capable of plasmakinesis."

"You made a ball of energy from the sun with your thoughts?"

He nodded. "Something like that, yes. And as I stood in the middle of that football field, I had an epiphany. There I was, a little boy with the power of the sun in the palm of my hands. I didn't know it at the time, but I'd created a sustained fusion reaction. That energy ball would've killed any other post-human. It only knocked me out."

"Knocked you out?"

"My brother found me in the field after reports of an explosion spread through South London. I was unconscious in the hospital for three days. My mother said my body was covered in third-degree burns. But by the time I woke up, I was healed. I can't imagine how much my father had to pay the hospital to keep quiet, or how relieved they were that I didn't hurt any other kids. From that day on, I realized two things, Aya. First, I wanted to become one of the world's greatest scientists. And, second, I was the closest thing in human form to what many people would consider a god. You see that's what you and I both have become through our abilities."

"Sir, the time," said Thomas, standing up straight.

Orson cleared his throat and glanced at his watch. "I'm afraid we're approaching the hour, and I have a supper date with President Chen and state officials. Thomas will escort you to the hotel where you can spend some quality time with Diya. We'll continue this conversation tomorrow, perhaps."

He ushered them out of the Remington room, and they proceeded along the hallway. When they reached the exit, a thunderous explosion came from the direction of the Remington room. Orson grabbed Aya's arm and pulled her toward him.

"Sir, we need to get out of here now," Thomas yelled, his hand on Orson's shoulder.

Not wasting another moment, Orson teleported them seconds before half a dozen smaller explosions engulfed the fusion plant in a sea of flames. They reappeared on a hill and watched in horror, from hundreds of feet away, as smoke and flames rose from the construction site.

Thomas yelled into his phone. "Send security backup

forces out here now!"

Members of the Unified International Security Forces arrived on the hill to secure the area. All the while, at least five minutes passed during which Orson held Aya's hand and watched in silence as the fusion plant burned to the ground. When she squeezed his hand, he turned to her. "Are you okay?"

"Were there workers in the plant? We have to go back."

"No, other than a few UISF officers around the perimeter, we cleared out everyone before our private tour." He wiped her damp cheeks and offered her what he hoped was a reassuring smile.

"Do you think it was the—"

"The separatists? Yes. This was obviously an attack by them." He released her hand and looked over his shoulder. "Thomas, ensure that all active fusion plants across the Coalition countries have increased security immediately."

"But why would they do this now, with the peace talks?"

Orson interrupted her. "Aya, go with Edward. He'll take you to the hotel." He nodded toward the stocky guard standing next to Thomas now.

With a sigh, he watched her leave with the officer.

Aya sat alone in her hotel suite and occupied herself by reading a magazine in Chinese. Trying to forget what had happened earlier, she figured teaching herself to read Chinese would provide a good distraction. But the distraction didn't work because it took her all of ten minutes to become fluent in Mandarin.

After a while, she closed the magazine and peeked outside the room. The hallway was crawling with members of the Coalition's security force, and it felt like she was back in

Chicago again surrounded by military people.

As she returned to the bed and reopened the magazine, a knock came at the door.

"Aya, it's me," said Diya, creaking the door open. She rushed inside and scooped Aya into a tight hug. "Are you feeling okay, dear?"

Taken aback by Diya's uncharacteristic display of emotion, Aya shot her a puzzled look. "Is it true the opposition did it? Did they plant the bomb?"

Diya wore a crestfallen expression. "The authorities think so."

She informed Aya the country had been put on high alert while President Chen met with Orson and the Coalition's General Assembly members to discuss response options. President Chen already had called it "an act of domestic terrorism by the separatists." Diya feared tensions would get worse, with more unpredictable events to follow.

"Orson's asked me to come with him to Iceland for the peace talks. But what's going to happen now? Is he going to call it off?" asked Aya.

She looked over her shoulder. "Can you teleport us out of here to my place in London?" she whispered, rising and glancing over her shoulder again.

"What's going on?"

"I need to speak to you about a couple of things, but we can't do it here." Diya grabbed the television remote control from the nightstand, turned on the television and increased the volume. A holographic image of a woman dancing appeared in front of them. It was a reality show dance competition that had become one of Aya's favorite shows since she arrived in Beijing. "Do you trust me, Aya?"

*Why would she ask that?* She stared at Diya. "Yeah, of course."

"All right." Diya grasped Aya's hand. "Then get us

out of here."

Aya closed her eyes and concentrated until she felt a tug behind her navel. As silence filled the space and the temperature changed, she opened her eyes. She was standing in the middle of a modest living room, bright light shining through the floor-to-ceiling windows. Before she had time to take in the new setting, Diya led her to the kitchen. A small and unkempt old man wearing reading glasses that hung too low on his face was sitting at a table and pouring himself a cup of tea.

"You have to promise me you'll keep this conversation between all of us in this room, Aya. Whatever you do, don't tell Orson about this little trip."

Her curiosity piqued, she looked from Diya to the old man. "I promise."

"This is Doctor Yousef Rouhani, a nuclear physicist who's been working on the technology behind the Coalition's fusion reactors for the past sixteen years at the Remington Center for Science," said Diya.

The man shook Aya's hand, pulled a chair out for her, and resumed his seat. "Please sit, Aya."

Instead of joining them at the table, Diya stood near the window. "Doc and I believe today's attack was an inside job. In the past, the opposition has tried to attack fusion facilities, but the security at these plants is impeccable nowadays. It would be nearly impossible to stage such a surprise coordinated attack like the one that happened today without inside help."

"When you say 'inside job'...do you mean you think Orson or the Coalition blew up the plant?" asked Aya, eyes wide. "Why? That doesn't even make sense."

"See, Doc and I believe the purpose would be to give Orson reason to vote against President Chen's nomination for General Assembly president this year. Orson has

President Blade Sonani deep in his pocket—or he thinks he does," she paused and smiled. "He believes he wields more influence over the South African president than he does over President Chen. China has an independent spirit despite agreeing to join the Coalition."

"Which they joined because they needed the fusion power the Coalition offered," muttered Aya, recalling her conversations with Orson.

"Exactly," said Diya, turning her back to them and staring out the window. "They celebrate Orson for giving them fusion, but it's still China first even if that means sometimes countering the Coalition. Meanwhile, Blade has helped keep other African leaders in line with the Coalition's agenda for now. But even among the African leaders, there are rumblings nowadays. Questions about Orson's leadership, about the mysterious disappearances or deaths of opposition individuals in their countries. Also, I know for a fact that Orson overestimates Blade's allyship and friendship."

Doctor Rouhani nodded. "I've long said Orson's excessive confidence in his ability to charm others is his primary weakness."

"I'm certain that if the opportunity arises Blade will lead the Coalition in ousting Orson and take his spot. He's biding his time. Orson must know this on some level, given his telepathy skills but, for whatever reason, is choosing to play nice enough to discourage Blade from such action. Perhaps he's absorbed some of my advice about diplomacy over the years. Who knows? The fact is he needs President Sonani to quell the growing discontent among African leadership."

"I don't understand," said Aya. "He couldn't just keep Blade Sonani in power without blowing up the Beijing plant? I'm sorry, but none of this makes sense."

Diya leaned against the window, still not facing them.

"With this attack, it makes China look too unstable and reduces the General Assembly's confidence in China's ability to quash the separatists. The General Assembly now will be reluctant to vote Chen as president. It leaves Blade as the only viable option now. Not to mention, the African leaders control the most economically powerful region on the globe besides China. And the combined military influence of the African leaders is currently unrivaled. Orson owes his power to Africa even more so than to the Chinese. He'd be willing to give up a half-built plant in Beijing and the affection of the Chinese people to maintain his goodwill with the African leaders."

As Aya leaned back, her eyes narrowed on Diya. She watched Doctor Rouhani pour himself another cup of tea. "This is crazy. People could've died at that plant today. What kind of a—"

Doctor Rouhani raised his hand to silence her. "The key to Orson's dominance is fusion. During the Great Turn, the European Union was on the verge of economic collapse, and people were in a state of panic because of the realization that people with extraordinary abilities existed."

Aya rolled her eyes. "Ugh. I've heard this story a gazillion times by now. It still doesn't explain why Orson would blow up the fusion plant in Beijing."

"But here's the part I'm betting you haven't heard, and it's why we believe Orson's behind the attack," he said, smirking and stirring honey into his tea. "While Orson was Prime Minister in Britain, there were many attacks against power sources such as old coal plants, wind farms, hydroelectric facilities. All across Europe in particular, some in your country. The attacks devastated the grids and left millions of people without any power. We still don't know how many people died due to lack of power during the two winters that followed the first attacks, but the estimates are in the millions.

"This all stoked the flames of civil unrest, causing even more panic as people blamed post-humans for the attacks. War seemed inevitable as old ideologies rose to prominence again, threatening to take us back to a time many longed to never relive. As you can imagine then, European leaders were quick to welcome the fusion technology the Remington Center for Science had developed and already started deploying in China and throughout Africa. The catch was that each country that received fusion plants had to join the newly formed organization called—"

"The Human and Post-Human Coalition for Peace," Aya said, finishing his sentence.

A dark smile sailed across his face. "Exactly, Aya. Fusion brought stability and electricity back to Europe, reunified the European Union, and everything else eventually fell into place. But, more importantly, fusion gave the Coalition the leverage it needed to establish itself as the world's first global politico-economic international coalition."

"Different from the previous United Nations, which had little real authority over sovereign nations," Diya explained.

"The Coalition created a true world government, an idea that had been mere conspiracy theory before the Great Turn. Most countries joined up, eagerly willing to exchange sovereignty for peace and stability."

Turning to them now, Diya folded her arms across her chest. "We're not saying anything is wrong with a world government. I know from experience the lunacy of borders, having grown up near the India and Pakistan border. But it was the way Orson did it…"

"Through sabotage and coercion. By the time Orson stepped down from his Prime Minister post, he was already the most powerful person in the world. Once he made himself the Chief Minister of the Human and Post Human Coalition for Peace, his power grew." Doctor Rouhani sipped his tea and stirred in some more honey.

Still unable to decipher what any of this was supposed to mean to her, Aya looked from Doctor Rouhani to Diya with increasing confusion and annoyance. "Okay, so what? He still helped make things better for faders. And there's no proof that the fusion plant explosion—"

He chuckled. "I apologize, Aya. I'm a bit long-winded as they say. Here's the 'so what'. Orson owns all the world's sustained fusion technology. New Coalition members received a complimentary fusion plant but generally had to enter purchase agreements for additional plants. He's gotten obscenely rich off his fusion technology and used it to bring all these countries under his control. It's the only technology his center developed that's shrouded in secrecy. How to build and design quantum computers and systems like the Q database are all now in the public domain. But fusion is not."

"We believe Orson wants it to remain that way so that he can remain in power. After all, were he invested in peace, he'd make the information about fusion public," said Diya, drifting to the table where she poured herself a cup of tea. "But there's more to this story. You know already that before the Great Turn, different international security agencies and their internal departments were using post-humans as secret weapons, and there were companies experimenting on them in secret. The Americans led the way with their Special Procurements Initiative, a secret department within their CIA. Britain followed suit.

"Orson was running for Prime Minister and serving in parliament. He had knowledge of the secret task force that tracked down British post-humans and recruited them— often by force—for the MI5. Parliament even authorized contracts with major weapons corporations to perform studies on post-humans in secret and use them for militaristic purposes. Orson personally funded one program called the Harmony Project that advertised itself as aimed at creating harmony between post-humans and regular people. But after some disastrous results, the initial program shuttered." Diya sat and blew on the hot tea. "Few people know that Orson later restarted it in secret and essentially turned it into his own mercenary arm, completely contrary to the aims of the original Harmony Project."

"We haven't been able to prove it definitively," said Doctor Rouhani, "but we're certain Orson used these individuals to stage the attacks on power plants around Europe and elsewhere. He manufactured chaos to enable his rise to power as the bringer of peace, Aya."

"Britain officially ended its special MI5 program a few years after Eve Cooper exposed SPI, leading to the exposure of other such inhumane programs around the world," Diya added.

*Eve Cooper? The same Eve Cooper I stayed with in Indiana?* As Aya recalled Eve's story about her background—"The government tortured me and later my friends," Eve had said—it all started to make more sense. She'd kept quiet about Eve but suddenly wondered if she should mention her. *No. Eve told me to keep my lips sealed about her. She has her reasons.*

"But I know that Orson kept his clandestine team of mercenary post-humans and used them as his own little death squad," Diya continued. "He knew what post-humans were capable of and used it to his political advantage. Members of the Harmony Project 2.0. launched cyber and physical attacks across the globe, not just on power plants. A cyber-attack on New York and the Chicago Stock Exchange crippled your home country's economy. The media quickly blamed post-humans for the attacks. The U.S. economy crashed, and your country faced a depression unlike any it had ever seen before.

That led to the increasingly fractured U.S. Armed Forces taking over your country's government, while the west coast sold their military bases to the Coalition. This all happened just as Orson stepped down from Prime Minister post to become leader of the Coalition."

Doctor Rouhani retrieved a flask from his right pocket and poured some whiskey into his teacup. He turned to Aya after sipping his spiked tea. "I'm sorry about this long history lesson we're giving you. But what we're saying is Orson's responsible for a lot of the instability seen during the Great Turn. Many in the opposition believe this but can't prove it because Orson did such a good job covering his tracks and creating the perfect PR campaign for himself.

"Fusion energy is his biggest and most successful PR campaign, and his most powerful weapon. It brought most world leaders under his control immediately. And for the holdouts, Orson's ace in the hole that got them to eagerly join his Coalition was his Q database. Ingenious really…make the world distrust post-humans and then offer them a system to track post-humans. Imagine how desirable such a product was to a world terrified of what many considered basically a new species of human."

A look of disbelief shaded Aya's face. Everything they were telling her sounded crazy, yet it lined it up with the vague information she'd learned about Orson from Eve.

"Using the Q, the Coalition can track and monitor all the activity of member countries' citizens in public spaces and online."

Aya shook her head. "And people agreed to this? This is all so crazy."

"It is crazy, Aya. But fear makes people do strange things," said Diya, sighing. "They agreed to it partly because Orson didn't tell them the full truth about the Q. That the database is a registry for humans and post-humans alike."

Doctor Rouhani poured more whiskey into his tea. "But he marketed it as a database for tracking post-humans only. Not surprisingly, any human or post-human who has challenged the Coalition has disappeared. How do you think he finds all these individuals? As I'm sure Diya has told you, for years he's been especially keen on finding other alphas. His goal? To neutralize them or eliminate them." Doctor Rouhani took off his eyeglasses and cleaned them.

Diya nodded. "Which, to be honest, is why I'm a little surprised by how much he seems to genuinely adore you."

*My dad, Eve...they were right about him.* Aya's head spun.

Diya sipped her tea and met Aya's eyes. "Orson's accustomed to being different, special. Before the Great Turn, he and his family went through great pains to ensure they kept his abilities a secret. He had no equal. He was one of a kind. Put yourself in his reality for a moment: if you could do anything you want to do and have all this power, wouldn't it be impossible to avoid an inflated sense of importance? A belief that you are superior, a god."

"An *Ubermensch*," said Aya, remembering what the German boy, Lukas, had called Orson during her welcome reception in July. *Because I exist, he's not special anymore.* "He's only nice to me because I'm a threat. If I don't accept his friendship, will he try to hurt me?"

They exchanged uncertain looks.

Diya drained the rest of her tea. "He admires you, Aya. I'll admit he lights up whenever he interacts with you. But Orson can be unpredictable when he feels betrayed."

The fearful look on Diya's face conveyed more to Aya than any words she'd uttered so far. Aya's heart sank. She looked at the tea leaves in her cup, a newfound terror sweeping over her. "Coming to London was all a waste of time."

"No it wasn't. Aya, you're the key," replied Diya,

reaching across the table to grasp Aya's hand. "You're the key to defeating him."

She stared at them, both amused and worried, feeling as though she was stuck in one of Malik's comic books.

After a few minutes of awkward silence, Aya stood and walked to the window. She gazed at the city below. It looked so old compared to the Beijing skyline. She turned to Doctor Rouhani and Diya, both of whom watched her with interest.

Diya shifted in her seat and glanced at Doctor Rouhani before turning to Aya. "We need you to keep Orson in his jovial mood so that he goes through with these peace talks. For years, I asked Orson to seek a peace accord with the opposition. He rejected the idea every time. But since you arrived and expressed how much you wanted an end to the conflict, he's been open to the idea of a peace agreement. You've been able to influence him in a way no one else has been able to."

"How does getting Orson to establish peace with the opposition defeat him, Diya?"

"Well, if the agreement requires him to compromise that will dilute his power. If Orson signals he's willing to compromise, it will show the opposition they might bring him to heel. Also, the more we can dilute his power in the eyes of the public, the more easily we can squeeze him out of the Chief Minister role in the Coalition."

"You think he'll actually compromise with the opposition?"

Diya lowered her eyes and looked at Doctor Rouhani.

"And even if he does," said Aya, "you think he'll give up his power in the Coalition? And what about the fusion tech? If nobody knows how to replicate it—"

"Those plants can work without the aid of Orson or the Coalition's scientists. Once the fusion ignition produces energy, it can last forever in theory. The only thing is we have no idea how to start the ignition, create the sustained fusion. That's what Orson has kept as his most guarded secret. He kept that bit from scientists in his employ. But we're working on that, and we think we're close to the answer. Covertly, my team has been trying for years to figure out the key source to start the ignition. I think someone found out we were up to something because over the last couple of months, most of my team members have all disappeared. I left and went into hiding two weeks ago."

Diya nodded. "Doc and his team are risking everything because they believe people deserve access to fusion energy, whether or not they want to bow down to Orson's vision. His vision that only grows his bank account, company image, and self-absorbed ego."

"What you're asking me to do seems pointless, Diya," Aya said, sighing. "You're never going to take him down."

Diya cast her a pleading look. "You have Orson's ear unlike any person I've seen before. The peace talks can keep people on both sides safe for now and give us a little more time to figure out this fusion thing. Remember when I told you to choose your own path. Tonight, you can choose to leave us and return to your family. Orson will scour the globe to find you again, believe me. You and your family will never be safe. He won't rest knowing there's another alpha somewhere outside his sphere of influence."

"Or you can choose to help us by playing along nicely with Orson now," Doctor Rouhani said, turning up his flask to drain the last few drops.

Diya smiled. "Let Orson think he's neutralized you. Go to the peace talks with the opposition leaders. Give the world Orson's illusion of peace. For now, the illusion's better than nothing, right? And while you do that, let me and Doctor Rouhani manage the rest."

Aya took a deep breath and thought about Eve. *Will I spend my whole life hiding like Eve if I don't try to help them?*

"What path do you want to take?" asked Diya.

With a groan, Aya returned to the table. "I'll help you. But, Diya, if Orson finds out you want to expose him—"

"Don't worry about me. I think we're both tough girls and can handle this." Diya looked at her watch. "Well, let's get out of here, shall we? Before our absence becomes conspicuous." She grabbed Aya's hand and looked sideways at the old man. "See you around, Doc."

He toasted her with his flask, an inebriated grin on his lined face. "To the revolution, eh?"

Diya smiled and squeezed Aya's hand.

A moment later, they reappeared in the living room of their hotel suite. Resuming her typical business demeanor at once, Diya straightened her skirt and pushed her hair behind her ears. "We can do this," she said, with a wink at Aya. Without another word, she hurried out the room and shut the door.

Exhausted, Aya dropped onto the bed, overwhelmed by a foreboding feeling. She wasn't at all sure she could succeed.

# 12

Media from all corners of the globe gathered in Reykjavik for what everyone expected to be a historic meeting between the Coalition and the two largest opposition groups in the world. Despite the attacks in Beijing, Orson and the Coalition leaders continued with the peace talks, thanks to some strong words from Aya.

"Will these talks become a repeat of the infamous failed Treaty of New York," read one headline Aya saw while scrolling through the new social media profile Diya had created for her. As she read the article, she recalled learning about the important meeting convened at the former UN Headquarters ten years ago in New York for the purpose of convincing the United States to join the Coalition. But none of her history teachers had called it "infamous" or a "failure." Rather, her teachers had referred to it as a milestone in the fight against the Coalition. During the flight from Beijing to Reykjavik, Aya asked Orson about it, and he launched into an elaborate summary of her country's troubled past with him and the Coalition.

"At the Treaty of New York, the U.S. refused again to join the Coalition. Their refusal to unite with us marked the final deathblow to an already declining empire and the beginning of your country's self-inflicted isolation from the global stage. The U.S. cut itself off from the world, all to spite me," he said, shaking his head. "In the following years, your country's power waned, but they maintained their military bases across the world. But, at the unanimous request of the Coalition member countries, Unified International Security Forces soon overtook all the military bases outside the U.S. and decommissioned them. We met little push back on that front, since the U.S. armed forces had turned their focus internally.

"Of course, it didn't take long for the U.S. to look externally again and plant the seeds of hate against me and the Coalition. I became the convenient scapegoat for all the problems in the U.S., from their shoddy elections to their power grid failures. The opposition grew there, blaming the Coalition for the demise of their country and the economic depression. They claimed I'd somehow fixed the markets in favor of fusion." Again, he shook his head and smiled. "We didn't give up on the U.S., not entirely. Through later efforts, I convinced the governments of California, Oregon, Alaska, and Washington to join us. As you know, that region became part of the Coalition, while Hawaii declared itself an independent nation and readily joined the Coalition."

Aya listened with rapt attention as he spoke, although she knew the rest of the story. The remaining states refused to join the Coalition and fell into horrid conditions. Hunger, violence, disease. The few wealthy Americans in these states lived in gated communities protected by private security. Her father had driven them near a gated community north of Chicago one time and instructed them never to venture to that area without him. The community was hostile to outsiders and known to shoot anyone they viewed as intruders. As a military officer in uniform, he was safe visiting the wealthy enclave, but he only did so when required for work.

"Once prosperous cities like where you grew up fell into decay. One after the other. It was a tragedy to witness, Aya," said Orson, gazing out the window at the clouds. "The interior states from Idaho to New Mexico became the Western Wastelands, which now are failed states where militias, criminals, religious zealots, and cult leaders control everything."

Indeed, all Aya knew of the Western Wastelands was that Jesús was born there, and her mother had died there after leaving Eve's safe house many years ago.

"Meanwhile, in the east, President Lopez's power has been hanging on by a thread. With the impending war between her Eastern Front and General Harris' Midwest Front looming, it seems like the opposition might destroy itself from within."

It intrigued Aya to hear the story of the fall of the United States told from a different angle than the one she'd heard from her father and others. She noted Orson's word choices, putting them together as if they'd reveal a clearer picture of the man. *Were they—her father, Eve, and Diya—all right about him? Why did Diya still work so closely with him if she didn't trust him?* Questions swam around her mind as she listened to him talk.

"But today the two opposition armies will put aside their differences to meet with us. This is a momentous occasion, a historical moment, Aya."

The conversation stuck with her as they arrived in Reykjavik and made their way to the meeting. She watched him smile and shake hands with journalists and local leaders once they reached Iceland's Parliament House. He hadn't even looked this exuberant in China. This was his moment to prove the opposition wrong, she surmised, his moment to show that he could save them from themselves.

After exchanging greetings and pleasantries, the day started with a closed-door meeting attended by Orson, President Sonani, Diya, President Chen, Nigerian President Onye Alabi, President Sonia Lopez of the United States, and General Gwendolyn Harris of the Midwest Front. Top military officers from the Midwest Front, state government officials, and delegation members representing the Midwest and Eastern Front armies accompanied General Harris and President Lopez. Eight people all together, the largest share of leaders from a single country.

"They travel like packs of wolves, don't they?" Blade whispered to the Nigerian president.

Orson shot him a warning glance, hoping President Lopez and General Harris hadn't heard the quip. He needed this meeting to go off without a hitch. He smiled at the Americans and offered a nod as they walked to the vacant seats next to him.

General Harris and President Lopez both wore something between a grimace and a frown. Without so much as a "good morning" or an apology for their tardiness, they joined everyone at the long table in the cramped room.

Sitting at the head of the table, Orson scrutinized the two women, noting the stress lines around President Lopez's eyes and the unyielding look on General Harris' worn face. He took in all the faces around the table. Blade's scowl revealed his disdain for the Americans. The beads of sweat rolling from President Chen's pale forehead undermined his otherwise calm expression. President Onye Alabi appeared to be in an upbeat mood, a warm smile highlighting the middle-aged woman's smooth face. The Midwest Front officers, two men who looked every bit as rigid as General Harris, sat next to their delegation members. The delegates seemed at ease and perhaps even bored.

"Aya, it's an absolute treat to meet you," said President Lopez, suddenly beaming at Aya who smiled in return. "I'm still floored by the daring rescues you carried out in the Midwest. So many lives you saved from those extremists."

General Harris groaned, and her furious eyes flitted from Aya to President Lopez.

At last, Orson looked at Diya, and she smiled. Her smile sent a bolt of hope through him, and he relaxed. "Would you all like any tea?" he asked, turning to the others. He gestured to a young man standing at the door.

The timid man hurried out the room and returned a minute later with a tray holding teacups, tea bags, and a teapot with steaming hot water.

As the delegates and the military officers helped themselves to tea, Orson exhaled and glanced at Aya. She was sitting up straight and looking a bit uneasy, casting furtive glances at General Harris. He couldn't blame her for being nervous. The tension in the room was thick. He turned to President Lopez and General Harris and smiled. "It's early so I thought we'd drink some tea instead of pints. I wouldn't want you all to think I'm a lush."

President Lopez cracked a smile that faded almost the instant it appeared.

General Harris kept a stony face. "I think of you as a lot of things, Orson, but to call you a lush would be a compliment."

Orson's green eyes flashed on her. "Now, I'm hoping we'll play nice today, general. This is a joyous day for us all."

"Mr. Remington, these talks are historic. Obviously. This is the first time in years the Coalition has granted us an audience. But I still don't trust you, your Coalition colleagues, or…" said President Lopez, pausing and turning to General Harris. "Or you, Gwendolyn."

General Harris shuffled in her seat and cut her eyes at the president before returning her attention to Orson.

Orson chuckled. "Well, on that warm note, let's get started, shall we?"

General Harris' hard stare didn't falter, even when she nodded.

"Great. Hearing no objections from others, I now call this meeting to order. I'd like to begin by saying I'm positively delighted to have you all here. What a special occasion this is."

Blade's smoker's cough came out of nowhere and startled a few people. He mouthed an apology, indicating for Orson to continue.

Orson gave Blade another warning look. He understood Blade's dislike of the Americans but not his need to be so obvious about it. *This has to go well*, he thought, with a glance at Diya. "All right. First order of business...let's agree to keep this civilized."

Taking their silence as agreement, Orson laid out the agenda.

To no one's surprise, least of all Diya's, the meeting devolved into a shouting match. President Chen remained quiet, watching General Harris and Blade yell at one another across the table, their faces inches apart as they leaned over the table and swapped verbal jabs. The timid server, standing near the door next to Thomas, retreated from the room as the arguing escalated.

With a frustrated sigh, Diya loudly cleared her throat and raised her hands to silence them. "Listen, we'd like a peaceful end to this conflict between the opposition and the Coalition. To achieve that, we're going to have to stop screaming and listen to one another."

President Lopez cursed under her breath in Spanish.

"This is why our people chose Iceland as the meeting place. You don't wield power here, Mr. Remington. We're not stupid."

"Madam President—" Diya replied, her hands still up.

But President Lopez, staring holes into Orson, went on as though Diya hadn't spoken. "How can we be assured that you won't continue your covert operations against us, Mr. Remington?"

"For the first time, I agree with Madam President," said General Harris, sitting. "How can we trust you to keep your word?"

Diya took a deep breath and sat. "Look, we can waste time tossing around conspiracy theories and hashing out years of resentment between all parties involved here today. Or we can talk about the future."

General Harris slammed her hand on the conference table. "You're out of your goddamn mind if you think I'll sign anything. The faders are the reason we're all in this predicament, so why would I negotiate with one?"

Ignoring General Harris' outburst, Orson directed his next comment to President Lopez. "Madam President, I'm quite aware that after the major attack in Chicago, the Eastern Front and Midwest Front are on the brink of war. A war that wouldn't help either of your causes and, in fact, would further drain your scarce resources. The Coalition is extending an olive branch to you and General Harris. I would advise you to take it."

General Harris shot up. "We've done fine so far without you."

"Shut the hell up, Gwendolyn, and let the man talk," said President Lopez.

Looking as though she'd been slapped, General Harris sat and whispered something to the military officer at her side. They turned an icy stare on Orson and President

Lopez.

Orson smiled. "Why thank you, Madam President. I'm simply asking you to agree to a new ceasefire deal with us and to let us deploy our wealth of resources to help you pick up the pieces and rebuild." He rose and walked to the front of the room. "We have certain things we can offer that would be beneficial to you and the people of your country."

"Like what?" President Lopez regarded him with incredulity.

"I'm glad you asked. At least someone at this table has some decorum. Many of your country's obsolete nuclear reactors are in a state of utter disrepair or offline. You barely have enough energy to meet the needs of your population. In all respects, your country is on its last leg. We're offering you the opportunity to have Coalition contractors replace your outdated energy infrastructure with fusion reactors. We'll also provide you access to the Q. In time, if you play nice enough, we may invite you to formally join the Human and Post-Human Coalition for Peace."

"What's in it for you?" asked General Harris.

"Your agreement to this offer today would signal to the opposition around the world that there is no need to resist the Coalition. I'm sure the separatists in China and opposition groups in Brazil and Pakistan would follow your lead. And the Coalition countries also would benefit from open trade with the U.S." Pausing, he held General Harris' gaze. "Ultimately, this agreement would be the right and logical step to ensure peace and prosperity for us all."

As General Harris rubbed her chin and pursed her lips, Diya knew it was a lost cause. There was no way Orson would get her to sign on to the peace agreement. The woman was unmovable.

"My answer is no," said General Harris, with a note of finality that caused others in the room to sigh and shake their heads.

Orson looked disappointed but unsurprised and turned to President Lopez. "What about you?"

"Will this agreement require us to accept your surveillance system, the Q as you call it?"

"Madam President, I should think you'd want access to our Q system to track illegal post-human activity. This would certainly reduce your populace's fear of post-humans and provide them some peace of mind."

President Lopez looked from Orson to General Harris. "I'm sure Gwendolyn likes the idea of tracking faders. But not everyone in our country harbors irrational fears of faders."

"I understand. However, the Coalition expects any nation we transact business with to register in the Q. So, yes, purchasing access to the Q would be a requirement, Madam President."

Leaning back, President Lopez regarded him for a moment. "From everything you've said, it sounds to me as though you're asking us to give up a lot, including some degree of our independence, privacy, and self-governance, while you give up nothing. In my experience, a treaty of sorts should usually involve a compromise, both sides sacrificing something."

General Harris smirked and nodded, her eyes on Orson. "Exactly. Where's your sacrifice in this little proposal?"

Diya shifted in her seat, noticing a change in Orson's demeanor. She saw the wrinkle in his forehead that only appeared when he was angry and losing patience. She noted his shoulders were slumped a bit, and he'd stopped pacing. Diya leaned forward, hoping to catch his eye, but he was focused on General Harris and President Lopez. "Orson—"

"With all due respect, you lot are in no position to

bargain. General, I could have you tried in the Global Coalition Court of Peace and Justice for the persecution and slaughter of post-humans. And President Lopez, I'm truly disappointed in you. Not only would you doom your country to permanent third world status by rejecting this offer, but you would let down this girl here," he said, with a glance at Aya. "You praised Aya as a hero, said she stood for the possibility of peace between the U.S. and the Coalition. Now you'll throw all that in her face? She took you at your word, President Lopez. Make no mistake, I'm here offering you this generous deal as a favor to Aya."

The two women said nothing but glowered at him. Neither of them looked at Aya.

"So you're both firm on this? You're refusing the offer?" said Orson, disdain dripping from his voice. "So sad. I suppose we'll move on to option B, shall we?"

"Option B?" General Harris and President Lopez asked in unison. They looked at the agenda on the piece of paper before them and then at Orson once more.

"Here we go," Blade mumbled to Diya sitting next to him.

"Orson—" said Diya. But it was too late. Items in the room levitated off the table and floor. Framed paintings hanging on the wall shook as the room itself vibrated.

Glancing sideways, she noticed Aya was frozen, staring in fear at Orson. Diya grasped Aya's hand and tried to be strong for her. *It's okay, Aya. It's okay.*

President Chen and President Alabi gaped in disbelief at the floating objects and papers hovering before them. General Harris clutched her chair, which rose a couple inches off the floor. President Lopez held onto the table so firmly her nails dug into the wood. Her aides grabbed the wheelchair to keep her from falling over as it lifted.

In the next moment, President Lopez's hands went

around her throat and she made ragged wheezing noises. Her aides along with the American delegates and military officers watched in horrified silence as President Lopez and General Harris gasped for air.

While all this was happening, Diya glimpsed Thomas looking at his watch and leaning against the doorway. Thomas' nonchalance unnerved her, but not as much as the sound of Orson's voice in her head.

*If you don't accept this generous offer, you can rest assured that I'll receive a vote of confidence from the General Assembly to affirm that the American opposition, also known as the Midwest Front and the Eastern Front, represent the greatest threat to peace and prosperity in the world. The Coalition will authorize intervention, which will include bombing all your remaining domestic bases and military strongholds back to the Paleocene Era.*

*In fairness, we may have no need to bomb your bases as we have talkers who can easily access your minds, as I'm doing right now, and compromise your soldiers without dropping a single bomb. Our talkers are the greatest in the world. We can easily access all the intimate details and military secrets you hold dear. You'll have lost this fight before it even started.*

"You're—you're threatening us? You can't do this," said General Harris, her eyes wide and her voice trembling.

*But I can. And I'll make sure you're tried and convicted by the very post-humans you hate so much, General Harris. As for you, Madam President, this time the assassin's bullet won't miss your heart. I don't want to do any of this, but I will if you leave me no other choice. As they say, the ball is in your court.*

When the room stopped vibrating and items fell to the table and floor, Diya breathed a sigh of relief. President Chen, President Alabi, and Blade took deep breaths, shaken and speechless. For some time, silence filled the room.

Diya looked at the terrified face of General Harris and watched President Lopez try to compose herself by brushing her hair behind her ears and straightening up in her seat. As Diya turned to Orson, she took a mental snapshot of the excited glimmer in his eyes. She'd seen this side of him on other occasions, albeit infrequent, and it never ceased to petrify her.

"Where do I sign?" asked President Lopez, interrupting the eerie silence.

General Harris nodded. "Me too."

Both women were still rubbing their throats and trying to regain their composure.

A joyous smile parted Orson's lips. "Oh my, what a momentous occasion this is. Today, we've made history."

Hoping her hands weren't shaking, Diya laid a paper and pen before General Harris and President Lopez and returned to her seat across the table.

They wore blank expressions as they signed the peace treaty documents. In a daze, they shoved their folders inside briefcases and, with the help of the aides, exited the room. Looking as worried as the Americans, President Chen and President Alabi congratulated Orson before hurrying from the room.

"Good job, Mr. Remington. The Americans only understand one language, brute force. Although, they're more accustomed to being on the serving end of it. You handled them well," said Blade and slapped Orson on his shoulder on his way out the room.

Diya stood next to Orson near the table.

"We'll celebrate in a more proper way tonight, my love," whispered Orson, kissing Diya's cheek and running his hand along the middle of her back.

She winced as he touched her and hoped he didn't notice.

Wearing a satisfied smile, he turned to Aya. "Thank you for being here, Aya. We have a press conference in thirty minutes, and you can be sure I'll sing your praises."

Aya nodded, her arms wrapped around her and looking more anxious than usual. She caught Diya's eyes and lowered her gaze. Something about the moment broke Diya's heart.

But not noticing Aya's distress, Orson smiled and went to Thomas across the room. "Can I have a word with you outside?"

Once both men were gone, Diya stared at the door, her mind racing. *President Lopez was right: treaties require compromise. This is no treaty. Orson made absolutely no concessions today.*

*What are you saying?*

*Huh?* Realizing Aya was in her head, Diya looked at her and held her gaze. *What Orson did today was seize total control of what he perceives as the last threat to his power. With no major opposition left to counter him, he'll be unstoppable now.*

*What do we do, Diya?*

She looked from Aya to the door and exhaled, disappointed that she hadn't seen Orson's plan from the start. *The Americans only said yes to this meeting because, without fusion, they're in the dark literally.*

Aya sighed and rolled her eyes, looking exhausted. *I didn't come all this way to take down Orson. I came for his help. How do you know this agreement won't help?*

*An agreement reached through coercion is an act of domination. It's doomed to fail. The only way you can help your country is by taking his power, Aya. Fusion is the one thing he has that the Americans need. That's his power, and we must take it from him. We have to figure out how to start the ignition, and we need to do it sooner than later.*

At the press conference, Diya stood among a crowd of reporters, leaders, and local officials as Orson announced the signing of what he was calling the Reykjavik Agreement. His face glowed with excitement. In all the time she'd known Orson, she'd never seen him show raw vulnerability in a public setting. But his voice wavered as he spoke, and he wiped his eyes once. As he took pauses during the emotional speech, she couldn't help but wonder how much of the emotion was genuine.

He concluded his speech by thanking Aya, who stepped forward and gave an awkward wave to the crowd before ducking behind him again. General Harris and President Lopez wore barely disguised looks of defeat and anger as the crowd cheered.

Did Orson not wipe their memories of what had happened other than their signing of the agreement, Diya wondered? In other rare instances where she'd observed him use his telepathic ability, he'd made sure the individuals kept no memory of what he'd done to them. "At least cover your tracks," Diya had recommended years ago. "A man who wants to be a peacemaker and diplomat can't have people terrified that he'll mind control them. No one will ever agree to a face-to-face meeting with you."

But as Diya studied General Harris and President Lopez, a realization sent chills through her. Of course he hadn't wiped their memories. He wanted them to remember his threat and never forget it. He wanted them to remember how he took their power from them, to understand he was capable of worse. This was about winning and conquering. That's all it had ever been about with Orson. Had he absorbed any of her advice all these years, or had he been merely appeasing her?

The troubling question remained with Diya as they walked by the harbor outside Harpa Reykjavik Concert Hall that evening.

"My love, why did you drag me out of the symphony?" asked Orson. "I'm sure Aya doesn't appreciate being left there with Thomas. She's not his biggest fan."

"Michio's there with her. She's perfectly happy for now."

Staring at the water, he smiled. "They're fond of one another, aren't they? I should arrange more opportunities for them to visit."

"Orson, you made a death threat to the Americans to get them to sign the peace treaty."

His smile receded as he turned to her. "Ah, that's what's bothering you."

"I've been telling you for years to make peace with the opposition. You finally had your chance to do it in a diplomatic manner and instead you went all alpha on them. They could retaliate against us in the future, Orson. It was wrong to do what you did today."

"I tried to play nice, but you and I both know politics doesn't often work that way. What does it matter? We have a peace agreement now. We can be done with this opposition nonsense and get on to more important matters. Like Ares One and—"

"Orson, what did you tell me when you hired me as vice-counsel?" She stepped forward and reached for his hand, speaking softly.

"That I didn't want people to think of me as a tyrant."

"Exactly. You've done a stellar job meeting people in the middle, peacefully coming to agreements with so many leaders who were initially hostile to you and the Coalition. Yet today you acted like what your opponents fear." She stopped and looked into his eyes, searching for something to grab onto and pull him from the darker path he'd turned down beginning with the Beijing attack.

But try as she might, she couldn't find anything to hold, to keep him restrained a little longer. The strange gleam in his eyes disturbed her. Whenever he looked at her, it was always with such softness and affection, unlike the way he looked at others. Now, she detected something else, something dangerous.

He dropped her hand and gripped her arm.

As his fist tightened, Diya's heart quickened. "Orson, what are you doing? You're hurting me," she whispered, glancing around to make sure they were alone.

He jerked her close to him, bringing his face a few inches from her face. When he spoke, the gentle tone was gone. "You're my adviser, but I make the decisions. It would behoove you to remember that from now on."

She nodded as her eyes clouded with tears. "I'm sorry. I meant no disrespect. I was simply reminding you of what you told me years ago. I don't want you to lose sight of your vision. I—"

He released her arm and cast her a withering gaze. Until this moment, she hadn't believed Orson would hurt her. Yet, as she rubbed her stinging arm, she wondered how she'd been so naive. How had she convinced herself she might be the exception?

With a last lingering look of fury, he walked away, leaving her in dumbfounded silence.

# 13

Over the next five days, Aya attended secret daily meetings with Diya and Doctor Rouhani. To avoid raising suspicions, she and Diya met during the lunch hours on Macclesfield Bridge in Regent's Park and walked to Primrose Hill. Each time, they arrived atop Primrose Hill, they teleported to Diya's apartment where Doctor Rouhani was waiting for them.

"Are you sure Orson isn't curious about your outings with Aya?" Doctor Rouhani asked during their second visit.

Diya smiled. "I told him I'm just trying to get to know Aya and help her acclimate to life here, taking her to museums and such. He's thrilled about it."

"Well, let's just keep being careful," said Doctor Rouhani, taking a seat at the kitchen table. "We can't take any chances of him finding out."

Each day they met, they strategized how to go ahead after Orson's antics at the Reykjavik meeting and whether to reach out to General Harris and President Lopez about their plan. Aya voted against contacting General Harris, whom she believed harbored too much anti-fader sentiment to be trusted to help them.

Diya suggested it might be necessary eventually for

Aya to take a public stand against Orson. But Doctor Rouhani cautioned against such extreme measures and, instead, encouraged Aya to get Orson to reveal how to start the fusion ignition.

The whole situation—the secret meetings, the lies, and planning—tired Aya so much she found herself daydreaming about teleporting to Eve's farm and never leaving again. She distracted herself from this notion, however, by crocheting in between meetings and naps. Increasingly, the hopefulness she'd felt upon arriving in London seemed like the distant past.

One early afternoon, she woke to a knock at the guest room door. She lumbered from the bed, yawned, and opened the door.

Iris greeted her with a warm smile as usual. "Dear, Thomas is waiting for you in the drive."

"Thomas?" Aya said, wiping sleep from her eyes. "What does he want?"

"How should I know? I told him you'd have to freshen up a bit, and then you'd be right down. Hurry up then."

Annoyed that her nap was being interrupted, Aya slipped her feet inside some sneakers, grabbed her backpack—never comfortable leaving it anywhere—and braced herself to interact with one of her least favorite people. What did Thomas want today? Usually, either Diya or another low-ranking Coalition security officer stopped to check on her. She walked past the kitchen, doubled back, and plucked a croissant from the pastry basket before waving goodbye to Iris and Lily.

When she arrived outside, she found Thomas leaning against the car and reading something on his phone. As usual, he didn't smile when he saw her.

"The Chief Minister would like to see you." Not

bothering to offer anything beyond this vague greeting, he opened the door for her to climb inside the car. During the short trip, Aya observed Thomas, noting his cat-like demeanor, how he looked like he was always on the prowl, searching for his prey.

*Is he a fader?* Why hadn't she asked or wondered before? She considered doing a scan but decided against it upon realizing she didn't want to know what was passing through the mind of a man as unsettling as Thomas. The thought of what she might find out spooked her. What was that her father had told her? *Curiosity killed the cat?*

In complete silence, they rode until the car stopped at the Coalition headquarters, where Thomas escorted her to Orson's office.

Aya's heart raced when she entered Orson's office, and she stared at the scene. Orson sat facing the window and looking at the city below, while a woman huddled on the floor in a corner at the far end of the room. The woman sat with her knees against her chest and hid her face. Aya looked from Orson to Thomas, who appeared to register no shock about the sight of the woman. *Oh no…*

"Thank you, Thomas. You can leave us now," said Orson, still looking out the window, facing away from Aya.

Thomas turned to leave but cast a fleeting look at the woman in the corner. A devious smirk curled his thin lips but vanished in an instant.

As he shut the door behind him, Aya drew closer to the woman and stared at her. *Diya?* Her stomach turned.

Disheveled with tears and mascara running from her eyes, Diya peered at the wall and folded her arms around herself as though to ease the shivering.

At once, she ran to Diya. "Are you okay?"

Diya moved her lips to speak but seemed to think better of it. She hung her head.

253

Aya stood, trying to piece together what she was seeing. Something was telling her to run away as fast as possible. But she tightened the backpack straps, remained still, and turned to Orson. *He knows.*

Silent, she kept her eyes on him and retreated until she bumped against the door.

When he turned around at last, his cold eyes flashed on Aya, but he went to Diya. Squatting before her, he brushed back Diya's hair and shook his head. "One of my most trusted and loyal confidantes has become my very own Judas, Aya. I admit I saw this coming, but I'd hoped I was wrong." He lifted her chin with his index finger and looked into her huge eyes. She trembled as he placed his hand on her shoulder. "She worked so hard to erase her old life, to create a new life for herself. But it was just a brand, a costume."

Diya sniffled.

"I think Diya can tell you better than I can," he said, lifting her chin. "By all means, my love, tell Aya who you really are."

Diya kept her eyes lowered and sniffled again, tears spilling onto her knees.

"Diya." Aya came forward but she stopped when Orson raised his hand and shot her a warning look.

Gripping Diya's chin, he turned her face to Aya. "Tell her who you are, Diya. She deserves the truth."

"Three years ago," she began, staring at Aya through bloodshot, watery eyes, "an opposition camp in an East Pakistan village along the border of India was destroyed. There was a young man there who claimed to be an alpha. He said he'd lead the opposition in Pakistan to victory over Orson and the Coalition. The villagers exalted him. They thought he'd be the one to take down Orson. But when mercenaries captured him, it was discovered that he wasn't an alpha, just a regular post-human. The mercenaries tortured and killed him. They burned the camp, killing everyone in the village. Old people, children, everyone."

Aya's hand covered her own mouth as she imagined the horror the villagers experienced. She thought about the attack in Chicago and how her friends and neighbors had suffered a similar fate.

"I told you that you and I were alike. That village was my birthplace. One of the opposition leaders they killed was my father. Aya, I'm sorry I didn't tell you about my father, about how he died. You deserved to know the truth but not this way."

Aya retreated more until she was pressed against the wall. She stared at Orson as Diya continued talking.

"Before my father died, I'd thought I could change things from within the system. I'd thought that by working with Orson and the Coalition, I could use my abilities for the good of us all. That I could help the opposition and Orson come to some sort of truce maybe, with minimal bloodshed." Her tone changed as she wiped tears from her cheeks. "Before the attack, I warned Orson to resolve things peacefully, that the young post-human was harmless as were the villagers. But Orson ordered the strike anyway, although he denies it. He unleashed his dogs on my people and destroyed my home. What's worse...he used it to inflame tensions between India and Pakistan. He made it look like a neighboring village just across the border had carried out the attack. Till this day, Pakistan blames India for the attack, but I know it was Orson."

Aya looked at Orson's cold face. His empty eyes. His actions in Iceland had startled her, for sure. But now she was terrified of him.

"I wanted to believe Orson didn't do the attack. I wanted to believe the anti-post-human groups in India were responsible. It would've been easier to hate them instead of

Orson. But I knew better. Orson isn't interested in peace, in bringing humans and post-humans together in harmony," Diya went on, her voice more venomous with each word. "He doesn't care about any of that. It's about him. It's always been about him and his precious image."

"Despite Diya's colorful monologue—mostly lies, of course, since I'd never attack innocent people—I'm afraid she still hasn't reached the point. So allow me to tell you who she is...a traitor. She's a member of the opposition." He paused, still looking at Diya as he spoke to Aya. "It's come to my attention that she's been aiding the opposition terrorists in Pakistan and elsewhere. It turns out she's funneled money, outdated firearms, and weapons to the opposition across the globe for years, all in a foolish effort to take me down. She deceived us. I shouldn't be surprised. She's always been a master of deception. It's how she used her telepathy before we met, manipulating people to get what she wants and driving those who'd wronged her to madness."

Aya remembered Diya's words about having gone down a "dark path" in her younger years.

"I thought she'd changed. But, you see, a leopard never loses its spots," said Orson, sneering at Diya.

Aya took some deep breaths, trying to devise a way to get Diya to safety. In her gut, she knew what would happen if she didn't act fast. She needed to stall him. "If you killed her dad, her people, she has a reason to hate you."

He ignored her. "Everything I've done has been in the name of making this world better. Look at what you and I have accomplished in such short time. Everything I've done made the Reykjavik Agreement possible."

Aya took a cautious step toward him. "So that means you can let her go."

"She's committed treason against the very organization she spent years building up."

"Orson—"

"No wonder you always wanted me to approach the opposition so diplomatically," he said, glowering at Diya. Without warning, he grabbed a fistful of her hair and pulled her up. "You really thought your little coup would work?"

"Stop. You're hurting her." Aya's hands reached forward in a begging gesture.

"Did you ever care about me?" His voice shook as he stared into Diya's fearful eyes. "Was any of it real?"

Startled, Aya watched his demeanor change from anger to defeat. Never had she seen him exhibit anything akin to sadness or heartbreak.

With her head held back and her neck contorted due to his grasp around her hair, Diya sneered at him and managed a choking laugh. "Remember that supper with your mother, and she started on about too many 'backward foreigners taking over Britain'? Remember how quickly you ended supper, sent her away, and apologized to me? You'd been so eager for me to make a good impression, but she embarrassed you. You want to know what I was thinking as you told me you loved me that night?"

He looked at her, confused and hanging onto her words.

"I was thinking your mother's a right hateful cunt, and the apple doesn't fall far from the tree." Frowning, she spat at him, and it landed on his cheek.

Tightening his fist around Diya's hair, he wiped his cheek with his free hand and looked at Aya. "I believe Diya needs to learn a valuable lesson about loyalty. What do you think, Aya?"

Aya's arms dropped to her sides. "Let her go, Orson." She searched for a hint of compassion in his eyes but found none. The kind man she'd met when she arrived in London was gone.

Ignoring Aya, he clinched his fist around Diya's hair and she winced, tears spilling over. "To be betrayed by the one person I trusted the most in this world, someone I thought would always stand by me." He brought his face closer to Diya's and kissed her lips.

They held one another's gaze for a moment, not saying a word. All the while, Aya froze in terror, looking for a way to defuse the situation she knew was a second away from becoming deadly.

A moment later, he slammed Diya to the floor. It was too late.

The loud thud seemed to echo in Aya's head, and it took her a while to focus again. Diya's left arm lay at an unnatural angle, and flecks of blood dotted on the floor. *No, no, no.* She rushed to Diya's side and helped her stand, holding her unsteadily.

"Move away, Aya," said Orson, raising his hand. As he waved, she levitated away from Diya. "I'm not done yet."

Diya floated in the air, her limbs dangling like a broken doll.

When Aya tried to move forward to intervene, she couldn't lift her feet. As she watched Orson, one of his hands still raised toward her, she feared the worst. *He's stronger than me, Diya. I can't beat him.* The realization hit her like a bag of bricks.

Diya's hair cloaked her face as she released a bone-chilling laugh, her body convulsing violently. "You want to know something else, Orson?"

His eyebrows went up in surprise.

"Every time I kissed you, I thought about how sweet it would feel to expose you for the scum you are. How amusing it would be to see your face when you finally realized you'd been brought down by the poor little brown girl whose people you slaughtered."

He turned to Aya, his face impassive. "Do you see why I told you we're different? We alphas aren't so caught up in our feelings, are we? We see the bigger picture. We see our duty to the world and recognize that sacrifices sometimes must be made."

"We? I'm not like you. And why sacrifice Diya? How does hurting her make the world better?"

Diya caught her breath and stopped laughing as she locked eyes with Aya. "You know he gave the order on your home in Chicago, Aya. You know it in your gut. If he was willing to do it to my people, he was willing to do it to yours. It was his mercenaries who burned down your home. He assumed you'd come out of hiding once everything you knew and loved had been destroyed."

"That's rubbish. She's trying to manipulate you, Aya. It's the only thing she's good at. The attack on Chicago was the work of the Eastern Front."

"Just like he gave the order for the attack on the fusion reactor in Beijing. Chaos is his strategy because it helps him play hero and stay in power," said Diya, looking at Aya.

Orson's face reddened, and he looked furious. "Nonsense."

Like someone had flipped on a switch inside her, Aya moved her right foot, then her left, not sure how she broke through his bind.

Bewildered, he gawked at her.

Not taking her eyes off Orson, Aya raised her hand and Diya fell to the floor.

Using her unbroken arm, she crawled to Aya and staggered to her feet. "I'm so sorry."

"It's okay. Let's just go n—" Before Aya could finish her sentence, Diya rose off the floor again and floated toward Orson. The helpless look on her face was more than Aya could bear.

As Aya stared at a scowling Orson, she knew this was the last chance, her last moment to save Diya. Without thinking, she met Orson's eyes and his scowl transformed into a look of surprise.

Diya sank lower to the floor.

Satisfied by the stunned look on Orson's face, Aya grabbed his arm and kept her gaze fixed on him. The longer she did this the closer Diya sank to the floor.

*Aya, it's too late for me. You can't stop him from doing this.* Diya's voice rang in Aya's head.

*Yes, I can. I'm an alpha, too.*

*It doesn't end here for you, Aya. You must go.*

Diya rose higher off the floor, and Aya tightened her grip on Orson's arm. He looked altogether flabbergasted.

*You're messing up my concentration, Diya.*

*Let go. I knew what could happen to me if he found out. It's okay.*

*But...it's not right. It's not fair.*

*I know, dear.*

Aya closed her eyes and released Orson's arm. He retreated from her and approached Diya's floating body.

For a fleeting moment, Aya heard Diya's thoughts again.

*Go to my flat. You'll find Doctor Rouhani there—he needs to leave as soon as possible before Orson's people get there. You may not realize it, but you have everything you need to defeat Orson.* Her face red and tears pouring, Diya stared at Aya. *You gave me a reason to hope again.*

Diya's telepathic communication stopped, cut short when Orson telekinetically slit her throat with the precision of a surgeon's scalpel. Blood squirted across the office floor, and Aya screamed as Diya's lifeless body fell limp to the floor.

Standing as still as a statue for what seemed to her like forever, she stared at Diya's body. She sat and cradled Diya, rocking back and forth, all her emotions breaking through the dams she'd erected.

While she stared into Diya's lifeless eyes, something like a sonic boom reverberated throughout the Coalition headquarters. Aya cried out. With each cry, the shockwave grew stronger, so much that it knocked Orson through the window and flung him clear across the street into the adjunct skyscraper. As the office crumbled around her, Aya sat there, crying and rocking her dead friend.

Anger crashed through dam after dam until she screamed, releasing a second more powerful shockwave that exploded all the windows and rocked the building's foundation. Ear piercing alarms went off as people fled the offices and poured out of the Coalition headquarters.

Coming to her senses, Aya looked at the debris around her and gently laid Diya on the floor. Through the enormous hole where the office window used to be, she saw Orson watching her from a similar-sized hole in the building across the street. *I have to get out of here.* She tightened her backpack straps and closed Diya's eyes before standing up.

Not wasting another minute, she shut her eyes, pictured Diya's apartment, and disappeared.

# THE NEXT GENERATION

# 14

When Aya opened her eyes, she was standing in the middle of Diya's living room. Everything still looked tidy and in their normal places, so she assumed Orson's people hadn't arrived yet. Noise from the kitchen caught her attention. As quiet as possible, she crept toward the rattling sound and held her breath. But she stopped and exhaled as Doctor Rouhani emerged from the kitchen and stared at her in dismay.

"My God, child. Are you covered in blood?"

Glimpsing herself in the wall mirror, Aya looked at her blood-soaked jeans and shirt. Specks of drying blood on her cheeks and hands. "We have to get out of here."

"Where's Diya?" he asked. His eyes told her he already knew the answer but needed her to say it. "That's her blood, isn't it?" At Aya's lowered gaze, the bottle of wine slipped from Doctor Rouhani's hand and shattered as it hit the floor. Red wine formed a puddle at his feet.

"Orson killed her." She looked at the blood on her hands and recalled Diya's ragged breathing at the end.

Doctor Rouhani appeared to be on the verge of either vomiting or passing out. "I just saw breaking news of an explosion at the Coalition headquarters. Was that him?"

"No," she replied, hurrying to him. "We need to leave now before they come here. You're not safe here."

He looked around and drifted to a framed photograph next to the window. In the photograph, Diya was standing next to a man who looked like her doppelganger but older. Like her, the man had thick hair that hung to his shoulders and curtained a gentle face. Diya's father draped his arm over her shoulder and rested against a pale pink concrete wall while smiling just enough to avoid looking overly enthusiastic. Meanwhile, Diya wore a radiant smile, her father the focus of her attention. "I can't recall ever seeing her look so happy."

"Orson's people will show up any minute."

"Come," said Doctor Rouhani, leading Aya to the kitchen. "You can teleport objects, right? Not just people?"

"Yeah."

He retrieved a backpack from the cabinet next to the stove and smiled at the confused look on Aya's face. "I hid an emergency bag here just in case we had unwanted visitors and needed to get away in a hurry. Anyway, we need to get to my private lab quickly."

"Why?"

"I'll explain when we get there. It's in Brent, just north of the city." He slung the backpack over his shoulders and returned to her side.

Aya clasped his hand, and they teleported to Doctor Rouhani's lab. She recognized the odd machine in the center of the room. A scaled down model of the machine Orson had showed her back in China during the tour of the fusion reactor. "You built your own Remington?"

"I built it with a colleague a few years back, and I've kept it here hidden away ever since. As you know, I retired from my post two months ago, so I've been testing this machine daily ever since. Considering what's happened with

Diya, my worry is that Orson may suspect I'm involved. We need to take this to someplace that's safe."

An image of Eve's farmhouse flashed in her mind. "I know a place where we can go. Do you think there's anything here that might—"

"Show that I've been trying to figure out how to make my own fusion reactor?"

"Yes," she said, glancing around.

He smiled. "No, I don't think so. There are only the papers, my notes. And those are in my bag. I've tried to cover all my tracks."

"So you're not sure?"

"Well, I don't think there's anything—"

"That's not good enough." Aya clutched Doctor Rouhani's hand and took a deep breath. "Hold on to the mini reactor, and don't let go of my hand."

Sparks of electricity flew in every direction like fireworks. Electric bolts flowed throughout the old laboratory, creating an elaborate light show in the room.

"What are you doing, child?"

"Setting fire to your lab and any evidence of your work on the mini reactor," said Aya with the casualness of someone talking about preparing dinner. "Now let's get out of here."

They disappeared with the mini reactor, teleporting right before flames engulfed the lab.

A cool September breeze brought much-needed relief to what had been a balmy August, and Jesús took it as a chance to start up the generator. Hunkered in the basement, Jesús held a flashlight in one hand and a jug of diesel fuel in the other. He'd gained a few gallons during his last trip out west and hoped it was enough to get the generator up and running again. Cold days were fast approaching, and he dreaded a repeat of the previous winter when the generator went out in the middle of a cold snap.

A strange crackling sound and a scream pierced the silence, and he almost dropped the diesel jug. He turned around and looked toward the window. There it was again—the sound of electricity crackling, and a man yelling something in a language he couldn't understand.

Grabbing his Louisville Slugger from under the stairs, he teleported to the backyard, where he found Eve standing with a frying pan in one hand and a knife in the other. They exchanged wary glances and turned around. Shocked, they dropped their weapons.

In the middle of the backyard stood a tiny old man, with horn-rimmed glasses and a strange looking machine, stood next to a young girl with two large Afro puffs caked with what looked like blood.

"Aya!" Eve and Jesús exclaimed in unison, running to her. They threw their arms around her, and Jesús scooped her up, forgetting about the man beside her. As he released her, he stared in horror at the blood all over her. "Aya, what the hell happened? Why didn't you message me?"

"I didn't have time." She spoke in a quiet voice and fell silent, her gaze lowered.

Doctor Rouhani cleared his throat, and they turned to face him. His eyes widened. "Pardon me, but you bear a strong resemblance to Eve Cooper, the woman who—"

"Yeah, that's me," Eve replied, sighing.

His mouth dropped open.

As Aya introduced them to the scientist, Jesús regarded him with curiosity. "One of Orson's people."

"Not anymore." Doctor Rouhani wiped his glasses clean with his wrinkled dress shirt. "Where are we? Aya, have you brought me to some sort of farm?"

"You're in Indiana," said Aya, leaning against the

miniature reactor.

"The U.S. Oh my. We're a long way from London." With the back of his hand, he wiped sweat from his forehead. "I doubt anyone will find us here."

"That's certainly the point of this place," said Eve. She turned to Aya and surveyed her bloody clothes and face. "What happened to you?"

A look of sheer fury clouded Aya's face, but it faltered when tears started gushing.

She drew Aya into a hug again. "It's okay, dear. Let's go inside and get you cleaned up. We can talk about everything afterward." Taking Aya's hand, she led her inside the house and cast Jesús a concerned glance over her shoulder.

Jesús remained in the backyard with Doctor Rouhani and looked the man over. "You're not looking too good yourself. What happened?"

"It's a long story. Where can we hide this?" Doctor Rouhani pointed at the reactor, his head still spinning from being teleported thousands of miles after losing one of his good friends.

"We can put it in the shed. I'll have to get all these tools out of here to make room for this...thing. It isn't a bomb, is it?"

"Heavens no. It's a miniaturized reactor based on magnetic confinement fusion."

"Wow, that's a mouthful when you could've just said fusion reactor. But okay."

"I'll tell you more as soon as I can sit. Suffice to say, I'm just a retired scientist here to help Aya expose Orson for the fraud and war criminal he is. And that machine there is part of the plan."

"So the rumors are true?" Jesús muttered, walking around the reactor. He brushed his hand against it. "You created this to take down Orson?"

"Generally speaking, yes."

"A fusion reactor that creates pure energy from fusing atoms, just like what the sun does. It seems the universe supplies us all we need."

Doctor Rouhani smiled wearily. "You've been educated in nuclear physics?"

Jesús shook his head. "Self-taught."

"I see. Perhaps I can teach you some more."

"I'm game. But first let's get this thing into the shed and join Aya and Eve."

Aya got cleaned up and rested on the bed she'd missed. Thankful to no longer be covered in blood, she tried to relax but found it impossible. She kept seeing Diya's terrified eyes.

Instead of trying to force herself to sleep, she got up and joined Eve and Jesús at the kitchen table, where they fed her scrambled eggs and toast for dinner. She didn't realize how much she'd missed scrambled eggs—Iris only ever made sunny side up eggs—until the first forkful. In silence she ate, hoping they'd spare her questions she didn't have the energy to answer at the moment.

Doctor Rouhani appeared after his short nap and joined them at the kitchen table. Eve poured him a glass of water and offered him the last piece of toast. For a minute, he looked around the room at the old wallpaper, the deep farmhouse sink, and the discolored refrigerator. "If I was crazy, I'd wonder about whether I've been transported back in time."

"Come again?" said Eve, closing the book she was reading.

He smiled. "Oh, nothing. It's just that a few hours ago I was sitting in a kitchen that looked the exact opposite of this one. Diya was such a minimalist. She kept her flat sleek, modern, and with very little furniture or decorations. I always felt there was something a bit cold about her home, to be honest. Kind of like her in a way. But this kitchen and this house…it's so warm and…inhabited." Doctor Rouhani laid his hand flat on the table, causing it to teeter for a moment. For some reason, this seemed to make him smile more. "A wobbly table. Diya never would've had anything so imperfect in her flat. It's difficult to believe I'll never talk to her again, never have tea with her, or talk about all her grand ideas for making the world better."

"I'm sorry about your loss," said Jesús.

The doctor's smile disappeared, and he looked at his hands. With a sigh, he told them about how he and Diya had become close friends years ago because of their heated intellectual debates about science and politics. He'd never met anyone as astute as Diya, he explained, detailing their ten-year friendship. "We experienced it all, from hopefulness about a peaceful post-human future to the disillusionment that came over us after Orson attacked her village in Pakistan."

"And she kept working for him? After all that?" asked Jesús, shaking his head.

"She was dedicated to destroying him, by whatever means."

Eve rested her palms on the book and fixed a disbelieving look on Doctor Rouhani. "So, why don't you tell us exactly what the fuck happened? I mean, pardon my language, but I need to know why Aya arrived looking like an extra from *28 Days Later*."

"What's *28 Days Later*?" Aya said, turning to Jesús.

He suppressed a laugh. "One of Eve's old DVDs."

Doctor Rouhani sipped his water and spoke to Aya. "I think you'd do a better job of telling them what happened."

Not excited about having to recall the violence she'd

seen, Aya provided an abbreviated description. As she described the explosion and more, the words tasted like sand in her mouth, and she wondered if she might choke before getting them all out.

Doctor Rouhani then explained the plan he and Diya had devised to remove Orson from power. "So, as you can see, we were quite far along in our plan until this happened."

"That means Aya's a target now?" asked Eve, with a worried look at Aya. "Orson will do anything in his power to get her back under his influence and control."

Jesús groaned. "Kendrick was right to be pissed at us. We shouldn't have let her go there."

"As I've told Aya, I think if we can start the mini reactor and create a sustained fusion reaction, we can take from him the main leverage he has over every country, even those within the Coalition. This energy can be given to people across the globe, for free and without stipulations. If we make that happen, Orson will lose his grip. He'll lose what's arguably the core source of his political power and wealth."

"Hmm-huh." Eve scrunched up her lips. "And what's in this for you, Doctor Rouhani?"

His eyes watered as he looked at his empty glass. "I could rest easier knowing Diya didn't die in vain."

"We're supposed to feel sorry for a woman who worked as Orson's closest confidante? Even if she made some effort to stop him in the end? Come on," Jesús scoffed. "She enabled him."

Eve leaned back. "He's right, you know. I'm just not feeling much sympathy for your girl."

"My girl? She was a friend, my best friend and a woman who tried to do right when it counted." He glared at them, his hand tightly gripping the empty glass.

Jesús and Eve shrugged.

"I promise you Diya felt great regret for her actions over the years and wondered if the means justified the ends. Her only reason for staying close to Orson was to restrain his most dangerous urges until she could find a way to dismantle his power. She tried to keep Orson on a tight leash, and she succeeded in that until today. Believe me when I tell you she was his conscience, the only check on his power." He stopped at the sound of a knock at the front door, and a horrified look shaded his face. "They couldn't have found us alr—"

"Of course not. This place is completely off the grid." Eve rose and looked out the kitchen window. "It's just Carmen."

"Eve's girlfriend," Aya clarified to a frantic Doctor Rouhani.

Exhaling, he grabbed the piece of toast. "This day has been enough to bring a man my age to his deathbed." He took an exasperated bite of the toast and frowned. "This has no butter. Why are we eating dry toast?"

"Commodities like butter are expensive outside the Coalition areas," said Jesús. "I'm getting us some goats."

"Didn't you tell me you can teleport like Aya? Why don't you just teleport to shops in the Coalition West and buy what you need?" asked Doctor Rouhani.

"That costs money. As you may have noticed, we're not loaded with cash," Eve replied. "And stealing, even while invisible, draws unwanted attention."

Doctor Rouhani shook his head and took another bite of the toast.

Aya laughed as they watched the old man begrudgingly eat and mumble to himself in Farsi.

In the days that followed, the Coalition moved its headquarters to the old Palace of Nations in Geneva. As the

Coalition's Minister of Information, Cornelius Remington was in full damage-control mode, feeding the international press various theories about the possible perpetrators of the attack. It didn't take long for the press to connect it to the attack in Beijing, giving Orson and the Coalition reason to take a harder line against the opposition despite the Reykjavik Agreement.

When the international press gathered three days after the attack to observe the second all-day convening of the Coalition's emergency session, Orson knew this was his chance to publicly take his boldest stance yet against the opposition. It was his chance to turn a disaster into the opportunity of a lifetime. He fielded questions about Diya's death, calling the global opposition "vicious terrorists" who had "murdered one of the most dedicated members of the Coalition."

After Coalition members spent the first half of the day paying their respects to their fallen vice-counsel, they voted to imbue the Chief Minister with the power to act unilaterally in response to the "terrorist attack" in London. Official unilateral power over the Coalition's security forces, what Orson had always wanted.

In the dusty old assembly hall that was quite a contrast to the modern style of the old Coalition headquarters, Orson approached the podium to deliver his first public statements since the attack. Before he spoke, he locked eyes with Cornelius and felt a rush of gratitude for his younger brother's swift action cleaning up this mess. Cornelius gave him a serious nod.

He grasped the sides of the podium and looked at the concerned faces. "The Human and Post-Human Coalition for Peace formed with one goal in mind. Peace. That's our only reason for being. It's what brought us together so many years ago during dark times. To this end, we recently held a historic meeting with leaders of the U.S. opposition groups and came away with the Reykjavik Agreement. A truly unprecedented moment for us all."

Whispers rippled through the crowd, but Orson raised his hand to silence them.

"The agreement was supposed to be the turning of a new leaf, so to speak. It should help us all reach a sustained and authentic peace. But the violent terrorist attack that happened on Monday can only be described as a vile and disgusting rejection of the olive branch we've so kindly extended to the opposition. My dear friend and vice-counsel died in the attack. The second alpha, Aya Wright, has been missing since that afternoon. Thankfully, there were few other injuries and none life-threatening due to the prompt action of the headquarters' security team and the brave UISF officers stationed there. I salute these heroes for their service."

Light applause interrupted Orson as a few people rose and turned to pay their respects to the UISF officers in the room. Orson raised his hand, and they resumed their seats.

"The attacks in China and now London make it abundantly clear that the opposition terrorists do not wish to accept our gracious offer of peace. As such, with the power granted me by the General Assembly's unanimous vote yesterday, I declare the Reykjavik Agreement null and void."

This time the crowd exploded with exclamations of "Oh my God," "Oh no," and "No."

"Their attack on the Coalition's headquarters is an attack on the primary symbol of peace in the world. The very stability and peace we have worked so hard to create depends upon our unambiguous rebuke of their attack. What's more, we believe they still hold captive Aya, a young girl whose only crime was wanting to make the world safer for the people in her country that has been devastated by opposition terrorists and their violent hatred of post-humans.

"Today, let us honor not only Diya Narang's lifelong dedication to the Coalition's mission but also Aya's steadfast dedication to post-human rights. Let us honor them by sending a firm message of peace by any means. Let us honor Aya by working together to find her so that she may return safely to her family. Let us set aside grievances during this important moment and stand by our vision etched on the front of the old Coalition headquarters—humanity forward together."

After a round of applause, Orson walked away from the podium and proceeded down the aisle in the center of the room. He tried to not appear distracted as he thought about Aya and the prospect of her reappearing and exposing him. He couldn't allow this to blow up in his face, not when he finally had the momentum he needed to squash the opposition. *I must find her.*

Unlike Orson's London office, this one was small and sparsely decorated on the ground level of the building. He took a seat behind the desk and sighed.

"Sir, there have been no sightings of Aya in any of the Coalition countries," said Thomas, seated across from him. "It's safe to assume she's gone into hiding. It's also come to my attention that Doctor Rouhani has not been seen since his retirement. Given our intel—"

"Yousef Rouhani? What does he have to do with this, Thomas?" asked Orson, pushing the power button on the computer.

"Our theory is that Diya used her abilities as a talker to convince people like Doctor Rouhani to provide her access to your sensitive documents and encrypted files. It appears the target was our fusion reactors and possibly the Q system." Thomas stopped and drew closer to the desk. "From our interrogations of his colleagues, we've determined he had some sort of relationship with Diya. While it's all circumstantial right now, we don't believe it's a coincidence she sought the confidence of your top nuclear scientist."

Orson turned and stared at the lush green courtyard. "I should thank you, Thomas."

"It's my job, sir," said Thomas, standing up straight.

"No, for being right about her."

A brief silence followed Orson's morose statement. Still staring out the window, he cleared his throat and spoke in a different tone. "I think it's about time we pay Aya's family a visit." He walked to the window and turned to Thomas. "But tell your cys we want her father and brother alive."

"Yes, sir. And what about the opposition? You said we needed to respond with force to send them a message. What is the plan?"

Orson's eyes grew colder than usual. "Send our operatives to take out the remaining energy plants in military-controlled areas in the U.S. We have no more need for General Harris and President Lopez. I knew the day would come when I'd have to dispose of them. They never planned to abide by the agreement, as you well know. As it turns out, Aya has spared me the tedious task of having to pretend to tolerate them any longer."

"Sir, if I'm understanding you right, you want to take out the remaining power plants in the U.S. like you did in Europe during the Great Turn?"

"It's time to free your country from these terrorists. At Diya's beckoning, I negotiated with these savages and played their games for long enough. I won't make that mistake going forward. Shutting off their meager power supply is a necessary step before we can remove this menace for good." Orson turned to the window and stuffed his hands inside his pants pockets.

"Got it, sir," said Thomas, turning to leave.

"Thomas, please emphasize to the operatives that I want Aya's brother and father brought to me alive. They're no good to us dead," Orson added. "The girl will come out of hiding when she realizes we have them."

"I told you a long time ago that everyone, even the invincible, has a weakness. Yours was Diya."

A sad smiled settled on Orson's face. "And Aya's is her family."

Thomas nodded and exited the office.

Orson remained standing at the window, his eyes closed as he thought about Diya's betrayal and Thomas' observation. *Even gods have weaknesses.* But he'd defeated his weakness, he told himself. There was nothing left but power, and it was his now. Smiling, he opened his eyes and gazed at the world beyond the office window. It was his now.

Aya stepped outside and spotted Eve and Carmen cuddled together on the porch swing. The sun kissed Carmen's dark face while Eve rested her head on the woman's shoulder. They smiled at Aya as she headed to the porch steps.

"Where are you going?" asked Eve, sitting up straight.

Aya shrugged as Baldwin purred at her feet. She bent, scooped up the cat, and petted his head. "Thought I'd go to the barn and tend to the chickens."

"The chickens don't need any tending to at the moment." Eve rose and approached Aya. "Have a seat so I can get your hair together. You've moped around here long enough looking like a crazy person."

"Carmen, can you braid my hair?" asked Aya.

She smiled and sipped red wine. "I suppose I can pop home and get my braiding kit, but we're talking eight hours of work. How about I plan to do it next time when I'm not tipsy?"

With a sigh, Aya sat on the second porch step and cradled Baldwin in her arms. Eve sat behind her and ran her fingers through Aya's knotty hair, continuing to remove the bands from her ponytails. All the while, Aya gazed at the barn trees beyond the barn. The cool breeze rustling through the dead leaves sounded smooth and constant, almost like running water. She'd forgotten this sort of quiet.

"What was it like being in the Coalition world for the first time?" asked Carmen, interrupting the silence. "Eve told me you just got back from a trip."

"It's okay, Aya. Carmen knows to keep the information she hears here to herself."

Carmen smiled. "I remember when I moved from Arkansas to Oakland. It took me a while to get used to life in a Coalition area."

After a moment, Aya launched into a description of the strange world she'd experienced in the Coalition countries. She described how people seemed to be happy with having everything provided for them, not worrying about their next meal or if someone would persecute them for being a post-human. Lighting up, she described the tall buildings in Beijing, the holographic billboards selling all types of things, the museums in London, and the self-driving cars.

"What was Orson like...I mean, besides being a psychopath?" Eve laughed.

Aya's expression hardened, and she tried not to think about Diya's body being lifted into the air as Orson choked her. "He talked a lot about alphas, always saying we had a responsibility to be stewards of humanity. He believes alphas are gods, like we have a duty to save humans from themselves." She paused as a lump settled in her throat. *He*

*doesn't know about you, Eve? I didn't even mention you.*
*Good.*
*How is it he never found you? If he found me in Chicago…?*
Eve smiled. *After years of endless interviews and having my face plastered on television as "the voice of faders," I walked away from it all. I came to the middle of nowhere and never showed my face on another television screen. Nobody knew I was an alpha, even if they suspected I was a little different than other faders. So nobody had much interest in looking for me. Orson and everybody else moved on to more important things.*

Aya considered Eve's words and realized she now understood why Eve left the spotlight. The attention had worn on her, too, after a while. When she caught Carmen staring at her with a confused look, she cleared her throat and said, "Anyway, he thinks he's a savior. But for someone who talked so much about saving people, he had no problem killing his girlfriend."

"Doctor Rouhani mentioned Diya felt guilty about helping Orson come to power," said Eve.

Aya fell silent for a moment. "She was a good person."

Using her index finger, Eve parted Aya's bushy hair along the middle of her head. "You plan to finish what she and Doctor Rouhani started, don't you?"

"If I don't, he'll keep looking for me. He'll come after Dad and Malik. He'll hurt everyone I care about, just like he did to Diya's family and the people in her village. Just like he did to South Shore."

"Wait." Carmen leaned forward. "Orson attacked Chicago? He admitted it?"

Aya shook her head. "He didn't come right out and say it, but everything Diya said…I know it was him. He hunts other people he believes may be alphas, people who might challenge him."

"How do you stop a man who has all the power in the world?" asked Eve, wrapping the band around one of Aya's Afro puffs. "Even if you and Doctor Rouhani manage to recreate Orson's fusion tech, that still leaves us with a pissed off demigod-wannabe. How do we destroy him?"

Aya petted Baldwin's stomach before he leaped from her lap. He slunk toward the barn door where Miss Sandy was lounging. "I don't know."

"Well, let me give you a suggestion that might help. Ask yourself what Orson cares about more than anything. The answer to that is how you stop him for good." Eve finished Aya's hair and looked at her. "All right, your hair is done. I'll have Jesús scrounge up some new clothes for you. You look like you've grown an inch since you left."

Carmen smiled with admiration at Aya. "Taking on Orson Remington. You got guts, that's for sure."

Eve pulled Aya into a tight hug. "And you won't be alone this time. Meanwhile, we should contact your father and let him know you're fine. He's been mad at me ever since I let you run off to London."

The thought of talking to her brother and father again invigorated Aya, and she remembered she still needed to finish Malik's scarf.

"Now," said Eve, releasing her. "Let's figure out what clothes you need and find Jesús. I haven't seen him all day. He's always off somewhere nowadays."

Carmen laughed. "You know he's probably visiting that boyfriend of his in Atlanta."

"He and Rashaad broke it off."

"They're talking again. At least, that's what Jesús told me last week," Carmen replied, lighting a joint. "These kids nowadays never know what they want."

Aya looked from Eve to Carmen, her brow furrowed in confusion. "Rashaad? That guy in Atlanta? Jesús never told me they were dating."

"Probably because that's grown folks' business," Eve said, rejoining Carmen on the porch swing.

"Why does everybody treat me like a kid?" Aya folded her arms across her chest. "I just blew up the most powerful man in the world. I don't see any of you doing that."

Eve chuckled. "Touché. I'm sure Jesús will tell you all about Rashaad as soon as he's home."

As silence elapsed between them, images of Diya's lifeless eyes returned to Aya. She thought about Diya's last moments and whether she could've saved her.

"Aya," said Eve, regarding her with concern now. "You okay?"

She smiled and nodded. Yet when she looked up and met Eve's worried face, she shook her head. *What if he's too powerful, Eve?*

"I've never met Orson, but I've known powerful men, and I've taken them down. They're all fallible," said Eve, aloud.

Aya considered this and looked at her hands, surprised not to see blood there anymore. "But those men weren't alphas."

"True," said Eve.

*And I watched him kill someone he cared about, Eve. If he can do that to her—*

"He'll do much worse to anyone else. Definitely. You're right to be scared. But can I tell you a secret? I think you're stronger than him. You have people and a community you love and care about, that you'll do anything to protect, and he has none of that. He's an empty man, as far as I can tell."

After considering this statement, Aya half-smiled. *All Orson cares about is his power and how the world sees him.*

"Then take both of those things away from him," Eve

said. "And you'll win."

Silence passed between them while Aya pondered Eve's advice. But soon her thoughts drifted to her brother and father. "Eve, I want to visit my dad and Malik. Jesús said it's too dangerous now that Orson's after me."

Eve sighed. "It's best to keep Kendrick and Malik in the dark. If Orson finds them…"

"Like all alphas, he's a talker, so he'll read their minds. Yeah, that's what Jesús said," said Aya, her shoulders dropping in defeat.

"Don't worry. I've already told Jesús to check in on Kendrick and let him know you're safe. That's all your dad needs to know for now." She patted Aya. "Let's focus on Orson, and then we'll figure the rest out. Okay?"

Aya nodded, feeling a rush of determination as her mind swam with thoughts about taking down the most powerful man in the world.

# 15

Kendrick slowed to make a right onto North 54th Street off Lansdowne Avenue. He tried not to daydream about his daughter, relieved to hear from Jesús that she was safe. He wondered if maybe it was time for him and Malik to return to Eve's farmhouse, since the situation had worsened in Philadelphia. It was a risk, but he assumed the People's Army and the Midwest Front had other things to worry about now—namely Orson's escalation against the opposition—besides looking for him.

As he cruised in his pick-up truck, he glimpsed a soldier pacing along the dark street. The city had turned off the street lights a few days ago to preserve energy as demand ratcheted up during last month's heat wave.

"Why the hell is he out here by himself?" Kendrick muttered, glancing in the rear-view mirror until he was too far away to see the soldier. It was foolish to patrol the streets alone on foot, especially since the recent attacks on power plants in New Jersey and Maryland that left a dozen soldiers dead.

The recent attacks forced nearby towns to rely on outdated generators, while towns farther north in New York remained without any electricity. Taking preemptive measures, city leaders in Philadelphia discussed community solar microgrids to reduce reliance on the one power plant serving the city. But nobody was sure how quickly they could obtain panels and installation equipment.

While city leaders wrangled over what to do about the power grid, Kendrick worried about how the city would survive another hit. He suspected Orson was behind the power plant attacks. Kendrick feared the attack on the Coalition's headquarters a week ago and Orson's press conference blaming the opposition meant there would be more assaults like the one in Chicago. The New American Army was less organized and less ruthless than the Midwest Front, less willing to take preemptive action against Orson. It pained him to admit it, but as much as he loathed her, he respected the value of a more merciless leader like General Harris.

A larger attack like the one in Chicago would obliterate this city and nearby towns. Groaning, he thought about the others—former politicians, former high-ranking officers from the old U.S. military, and international traders—all living in Gladwyne and University City, where they're heavily protected by the New American Army's soldiers and what was left of the Philadelphia police department. They'd be safe if Orson attacked, but he and everyone else would be screwed. There are barely enough guards and soldiers to spare for the other areas of the city.

After making a quick left turn, he stopped at an old rowhouse and parallel parked the truck. He sat there for a while, lost in dreadful thoughts and wondering when the last time was that he'd had a decent night's sleep. He glanced at the second-floor window of the small room he and Malik shared, certain his son was sleeping like a log. Kendrick was lucky if he managed four hours a night.

With a yawn, he turned his mind to upcoming

tasks...like making himself some tea and sitting on the porch with a good book. Reading novels had become an effective strategy for warding off the feelings of impending doom. Sometimes reading helped him sleep. On a good day, he might doze off while reading and catch a couple of hours of sleep.

Yawning again, Kendrick exited the truck and looked at the dark sky. The typically disquieting hour before dawn seemed eerier than usual. Was it the stillness of the air and the absence of birds chirping that sent a chill through him? Or was it just exhaustion and his mind wandering to far-off unpleasant corners?

It was likely the fact that the New American Army, fearing an attack, had moved many of the residents to so-called safe zones at the city's outskirts. He exhaled. Of course that was the reason for the strange quiet. This house was one of only two inhabited houses on the block.

Shaking off the bad thoughts, he removed his gear from the truck bed and fixed his mind on his morning tea.

When Kendrick entered the house, dropped his gear bag on the floor, and shut the door, another chill went through him. Something wasn't right.

For a moment, he stood still and listened. He cursed himself as the realization hit him too late.

With his hands up, Kendrick turned around and faced the man who was pointing a gun at his head. A pink-faced man with a buzz cut looked at him. He noticed the man's gun wasn't a traditional firearm but something much more high-tech. Kendrick's heart dropped.

As a man who'd always followed his instincts, Kendrick silently chided himself for not leaving Philadelphia when the thought had occurred to him after the attack in New Jersey last week. He could've packed his truck and driven to Eve's farm. Now he was staring at the barrel of a gun, not sure if he would be alive for more than a few more minutes.

His thoughts turned to Malik, and his chest constricted and grew hot. Was Malik still in the house? Was he alive? Where were Ruthie and Dylan?

Kendrick looked at the man's stony face, and rage flooded him.

The man drew closer until the gun was a mere foot or so from Kendrick's forehead. He looked at Kendrick the way a wolf stares at prey and, with his free hand, adjusted his earpiece. "I have him, sir," he said, his voice rough and monotone.

"Are you here on General Harris' orders?" Kendrick asked, fearing the answer. "You're not Eastern Front, are you?"

The man made no movement or response.

Kendrick's mind raced. He had to take his moment now. In one swift movement, he stepped aside and reached for the man's gun before punching him in the face. As the man stumbled, the gun hit the floor with a loud clang.

With a glance at one another, they lunged for the weapon. Kendrick's longer arms and bigger size worked in his favor, allowing him to knock the man back and grab the gun.

A closer look at the gun informed Kendrick that it was a handheld railgun. Before he could figure out the gun's mechanism, the man seized his leg and applied enough pressure to make Kendrick cry out. Keeping his grip tight around the gun, Kendrick landed a kick to the man's face and struggled to free himself.

When he looked at his leg, he noticed the man's hand was prosthetic. "Cys," he groaned, recalling the ambush on Aya in Chicago.

Not wasting another second, he fired the railgun, hitting the cyborg twice in the face.

As the man went limp, Kendrick scrambled away and heaved in and out. His mouth hanging open in horror, he looked at the deceased cyborg. The power of the blast had severed his head, leaving a bloodied headless corpse. Kendrick looked at the gun he was still holding and then at the dead man.

Two more cys rushed into the kitchen with their weapons drawn. One man's face was half steel and half flesh, with a vibrant, amber-colored eye on his machine side. The other man's metal prosthetic arms bulged from his fatigue jacket.

The one with the half-metal face fired at Kendrick, who rolled away from the line of fire just in time. The single shot created a gaping hole in the cabinet he'd been leaning against.

"Fool, he's to be taken alive," said the second man, grabbing his partner's hand and glaring at him. "What the hell is wrong with you?"

Thinking only of staying alive and finding his son, Kendrick returned fire at the two men and leaped to his feet. They moved faster than Kendrick had ever seen anyone move. The one with the metallic arms punched him hard in his chest, knocking him through the kitchen wall, right into the living room on the other side.

Lying among the broken drywall and debris, Kendrick coughed blood and clutched his burning chest. Retrieving the 9mm from his left leg holster and pulling himself up, he scanned the room and hobbled to the kitchen to find the men. "Where is my son, goddamn it?"

They watched him but kept their weapons lowered. "Surrender now," the one with the half-metal face yelled. "You can't win this."

Kendrick shot at the window of the front door. The flying glass shards distracted the men long enough for him to lunge at the nearest one, causing the man fall through the door and land on the sidewalk.

On his feet in a flash, Kendrick fired once at the metal-faced man still in the kitchen but missed. "Fuck."

Before Kendrick could try another shot, the man delivered one powerful kick to his chest. The impact of it sent Kendrick flying across the room, crashing into a wall.

"Boss said not to kill you, but he didn't say anything about not hurting you," the man taunted.

When Kendrick fired at him again, the man took a bullet directly to his amber-colored robotic eye and another to his forehead. He dropped to the floor and moved no more.

Catching his breath, Kendrick called his son's name as panic swept over him. As he got up, his legs shaky and his body aching, two arms wrapped around his chest.

"That was a mistake," said the man with metal arms as he pulled Kendrick through the front door.

Summoning all his strength, he reverse-head-butted the man over and over. To his surprise, it worked. The man loosened his grip. Kendrick collapsed onto the floor of the front porch as the man, holding his bloody nose, staggered backward. Seeing an opening, he tackled the man, punched him in the chest, and stomped his legs.

But the man rose weakly and backed away, trying to block his face from the blows.

Flooded with rage, he threw three quick jabs and landed an uppercut and charged him, knocking him off the porch. "Where the hell is my son?" yelled Kendrick, his hands wrapped around the man's neck.

*Over here, Kendrick.*

He looked around for the sound of the voice. Had he heard the voice in his head, or was he hallucinating? He listened for the voice again. As he pulled himself to one knee, his heart dropped.

A man dressed in all black tactical gear stood ten feet away with Malik at his side. Malik was silent and as still as a statue, his eyes unfocused as though he was in some sort of trance.

"First Sergeant Kendrick Imara Wright, former U.S. Army Ranger, enlisted in the People's Army, and now a proud member of the New American Army, or NAA," said the man in black. "You're pretty beaten up, Go."

He squinted to get a better look at the man who was calling him by his nickname. He picked up the gun lying next to the unconscious cyborg and aimed it at the man's chest. "Who are you?"

"I'm Thomas. You can lower the gun."

Kendrick didn't move but kept the gun pointed at the man. Thomas smiled. "You singlehandedly took out three cys. Very impressive. I see where your daughter gets it from."

Trembling, Kendrick pulled himself up and kept the gun pointed at Thomas' chest. "You're one of his people, aren't you?"

Thomas nodded.

"What have you done to my son?"

"Your boy's fine. He's just under my control temporarily."

Kendrick moved toward the man, but there seemed to be iron weights in his shoes suddenly. His whole body seemed to have turned into an anvil. He couldn't move an inch. Then, through no intent of his own, he lowered the gun and dropped it.

"And so are you," said Thomas, still smiling.

"Where are my friends, Ruthie and Dylan? What have you done to them?"

As if he was talking about something as benign as the weather, Thomas replied, "The people who own this house?

We had no need for them."

Tears pooled in Kendrick's eyes as he pictured his friends' last moments. At the same time, an excruciating pain went through his head, and his vision blurred. As his knees grew weak and the pain overwhelmed him, he collapsed. A bloody baton hit the ground next to him, and the cy was smirking.

Struggling to keep his eyes open, Kendrick watched Thomas and Malik vanish.

Aya appeared at the door, handed Doctor Rouhani a glass of water, and sat next to him on the porch stairs. Before anybody could stop her, she grabbed the joint from Doctor Rouhani and took a couple of deep drags.

As she coughed and gasped for air, Jesús snatched the joint from her. "¡Meirda!"

"What?" she said, still coughing. "I'm not a kid. I wanted to try it once."

"Yes, you are. You're lucky I don't tell Eve about that. But she'd just blame me for you being stupid."

She reached for Doctor Rouhani's water and took a large gulp to ease her sore throat. "I don't see why you like that stuff anyway, Jesús," she said, wheezing.

"You'll find out when you're older, but until then, you keep your hands off it. Anyway, Doctor Rouhani still can't figure out his science project over there."

Doctor Rouhani sat on the stairs and looked at the miniature reactor. "I feel like I'm no closer to figuring this out than I was a couple of years ago. The deuterium will not work to start the ignition. Helium 3 isn't a realistic choice even for someone like Orson to obtain."

Jesús took a drag of the half-smoked joint.

"We need more energy to get a sustained reaction long enough to create positive net power output. But I'm banging my head against a wall here as to how on earth we find or hold that much energy. How did Orson achieve this?" He took the joint as Jesús passed it, took a couple of puffs, and exhaled.

When Aya offered Doctor Rouhani the almost empty glass of water, he waved it away and continued staring at the reactor in the shed across the yard. She turned her attention to the reactor.

"Doc," said Jesús, standing up. "Whatever you're going to do, you're going to need to do it fast. I got those two biofuel generators to supply extra energy to the house so that you have the energy you need from the main generator to run your tests. Those generators probably only have a few more days in them."

"I understand." Doctor Rouhani wiped the sweat off his brow and cleaned his glasses on his stained t-shirt. He looked at Aya. "You immediately recognized this machine when you saw it in my lab. I have no idea why I didn't ask you this before. I suppose I had no reason to assume Orson would discuss something as complicated as nuclear fusion with a fifteen-year-old girl. But didn't you say before that Orson essentially viewed you as a pupil of sorts?"

She nodded, distracted by Jesús who'd wandered to the reactor and was squatting to examine it.

Doctor Rouhani rubbed the top of his head. "Did he ever talk about the Remington reactor?"

"He talked about a lot of things. He likes to hear himself talk."

"But did he ever say anything about how the reactor works? How he started it?"

"He just talked about it being created through magnetic confinement or something." Staring at the miniature reactor and watching Jesús, she rummaged through her memory for any clues that could help Doctor Rouhani. "It was sort of hard to keep up with him most of the time. When he showed me the Remington in Beijing, he talked mostly about how he gave the world energy, like he was some huge savior or whatever. Then he said something about the quantum computers, and he started blabbing again about how alphas are more powerful than all humans, blah, blah, blah."

As they continued their conversation, Jesús took off his sweaty shirt and tucked it in his jeans pocket. "You'd never know it was September and not July right now," he remarked, fanning himself a bit as he approached them. "Today's sun reminds me of my Sedona days."

"What did you say?" Aya looked at him.

He shook his head and gathered his long hair into a ponytail. "Nothing, just talking to myself about Arizona. Anyway, I'm about to go inside the house where it's cooler. This sun's frying me."

"Oh my God," she exclaimed, jumping to her feet. "You're a genius, Jesús!"

Looking perplexed, he smiled. "Thanks, I guess."

Forgetting her own strength, Aya grasped Doctor Rouhani's arm and almost yanked his arm out its socket.

He yelped and gawked at her.

With an apologetic look, she released his arm. "My bad."

"What's going on, child?" Doctor Rouhani caressed his tender arm and followed her to the makeshift lab inside the shed.

Aya ran her hands along the reactor. "I know how to start it. Orson's the source, and that means me and Eve are also the source."

Still rubbing his arm, a confused look came over his face. "Are you still feeling the effects of that marijuana?"

"Huh? No, I'm serious. That day Orson did tell me something. He told me a story about when he was a boy."

Doctor Rouhani's confusion transformed into curiosity. "Go on, then. Explain."

"He said he had the power of the sun in his hands, that he could channel the power of the sun just by thinking about it. When he was young, he did it accidentally while playing soccer with some other kids."

"Are you saying that one of Orson's abilities is that he can create fusion?" Doctor Rouhani's eyes widened.

"It put him in a coma for three days and gave him third-degree burns the first time. But he healed."

Doctor Rouhani stepped away, looking from the reactor to Aya and stroking his chin. "He's never shared this story publicly. It's the first I'm hearing of it. Are you quite sure, Aya?"

"I don't think he wanted other people to know. His parents covered up the accident to protect him."

"So, you're saying—"

"The secret to the fusion reactors has been locked away in Orson's mind. That's why nobody else has figured it out," Jesús said, staring at Aya. "If you ask me, it was pretty stupid for him to tell you."

Without warning, Doctor Rouhani hugged Aya. "He underestimated you, child. Like all fools, he underestimated his enemy."

She nodded. *If I'd known I was his enemy at the time, I would've paid more attention.*

As the afternoon arrived, the temperature rose to a balmy ninety degrees. Jesús guzzled water while Doctor Rouhani appeared unaffected by the stifling heat. Indeed, he'd been light on his feet and buzzing since Aya's revelation.

Standing in the shed and wearing welding helmets now, Jesús and Doctor Rouhani stared at the reactor.

Aya brushed her hand against the reactor, gazing at it

and thinking about the bigger one she'd seen in Beijing.

"You think you can create plasma just by thinking it, huh?" asked Eve, standing next to Aya.

"If this works, we can finally take down Orson or at least level the playing field. This might be the most exciting day I've had in years," said Doctor Rouhani.

Eve looked over her shoulder at him and glanced at the electronic tablet he was holding. "Well, you've been wearing that weird grin for a couple of hours, so I'll take your word for it."

"He killed my friend. The sooner and the harder he falls, the better." He looked at the tablet and then at Aya. "We're ready when you are, Aya."

After a deep breath, she faced them and repeated the instructions they'd agreed upon during lunch. "As Doctor Rouhani said, I'll focus the energy beam there." She pointed at the base of the reactor. "Eve will hold a protective energy field around me and the machine. That'll give him time to check the stability of the readings on his tablet. Did I get all that right, Doctor Rouhani?"

He nodded at Aya but fixed an ominous look on Eve. "If you don't hold the protective field, every piece of metal within a fifty-mile radius will be coming our way, flying at the speed of sound. Destroying everything in its path, including us."

Jesús took another step back. "Sounds like the description of a tornado."

"I promise you it's much worse, son."

Jesús' expression went from alarmed to downright terrified. He swallowed and retreated farther.

"We won't let that happen," said Eve, nodding at Doctor Rouhani.

After an uncomfortable silence, Aya exhaled and made herself erect. "Okay then. Let's do it. Doctor Rouhani and Jesús, get to the porch and pull down your helmets. Take Baldwin with you and keep Miss Sandy over there." She pointed at the cat grooming himself near Jesús' feet. "Eve, when they're far enough away, you can set up the energy field. Make sure it's focused on me. Doctor Rouhani, you hit the power when I say ready."

He nodded and followed Jesús to the porch.

"Oh, Jesús," said Aya, before they exited the shed. "Where did you get welding helmets from anyway? You weld?"

Jesús smiled. "I stole them years ago. At the time, something in the universe told me they might come in handy one day. When the universe speaks, I listen."

Eve shook her head. "You're the definition of a stoner."

With a shrug and a wink at Eve, he departed with Doctor Rouhani and hurried to the porch.

"You ready?" asked Eve, touching Aya's shoulder.

Aya smiled, not sure how to answer Eve's question. If Orson could do it, couldn't she do it? "I'm ready."

Stepping back, Eve put five feet between herself and Aya. She extended her hands as though she was reaching for something and, with the most subtle flick of her wrists, a large purplish energy field manifested around Aya and the machine.

The warm sensation of Eve's energy field comforted Aya as she rubbed the cold steel of the reactor. Doubt nagged her. *What if it doesn't work? How can we stop him?*

*It'll work.*

Aya closed her eyes and recalled Orson's story about the day in the park. "The power of the sun in my hands," she mumbled, repeating his words and picturing her own words. She opened her eyes and looked over her shoulder at Doctor Rouhani and Jesús who were standing far away on the porch.

"Hit the power!"

Jesús flipped the switch that connected all the heavy-duty power cords to the generators powering the miniature reactor. Within seconds, the reactor began to roar like a lion awaking from a long slumber.

Clinging to Orson's childhood memory, Aya held out her hands in a cup-like formation as a strong magnetic field emanated from the reactor. Tiny flashes of light formed above her open palms. The flashes of dazzling light grew larger with every passing second until they congealed into glowing embers.

Clumped together, the embers created a ball of pure plasma. It looked clear with shades of blue, sort of like the energy ball she'd used to disperse the guards when she first arrived at the Coalition headquarters. But this ball of energy felt warm rather than cool.

Stunned and trying to ignore the increasing intensity of the heat, she directed the beam into the reactor's doughnut-shaped chamber. Almost overcome by the searing pain in her burned hands, she closed and locked the chamber telekinetically to trap the energy inside the reactor. The pain made her dizzy, and she stumbled away and leaned against the wall. On the verge of collapsing, she peered across the yard at Doctor Rouhani. Had it worked?

He removed his helmet and looked at the tablet. As he noted the reading and looked at Aya and Eve in the distance, his mouth hung open. "I have a stable reading," he yelled, giving her a thumbs up signal.

Jesús looked from Doctor Rouhani to Aya to the reactor. "It's stable. You can stop now, Eve."

Concentrating on keeping the energy field, Eve looked sideways at Jesús and Doctor Rouhani. "You sure?"

They gave another thumbs up signal.

The energy field vanished. She dropped her arms to

her sides, exhausted and breathing heavily.

Doctor Rouhani hurried to the shed and stopped at the door. "The super conducting magnets are now focused on the plasma. So the magnetic field has inverted into the chamber."

"I feel like I've run a mile," said Eve, exhaling. She put her hands on her hips to steady herself. "Did it work?"

Jesús removed his helmet as Aya staggered to her feet. He gasped, causing Doctor Rouhani and Eve to turn to Aya. Eve's hands flew to her mouth, and Doctor Rouhani stared in horror at the severe burns covering Aya's arms and hands.

She stopped a few feet from them, fearing that if she moved another inch she might pass out from the pain. Yet...was she imagining it, or was the pain already subsiding? She looked at her arms and hands. Were the burns healing, or were her eyes tricking her?

In the minute or so they stood in silence gaping at her, Aya felt the pain pass away and watched her arms and hands return to their previous smoothness. Why was she still conscious?

Eve came closer. "My God, Aya. You...how...? Are you okay?"

Distracted by her thoughts, Aya muttered to herself. "This landed Orson in the hospital when he was a kid. I don't understand."

"I guess that means you're stronger than him," said Jesús, staring at her in amazement.

Still dizzy, she swayed and held out her arms to balance herself. *It worked.* The room spun faster, and she dropped to her knees. As Jesús picked her up, she smiled until everything went black.

Kendrick woke in a fit of panic and drenched in sweat. He jerked his head left and right, looking for the man named

Thomas. The blinding white walls and strip light on the ceiling caused him to squint and look down. That's when he saw Malik beside him, sound asleep.

Overwhelmed with relief, he clutched his chest and tried to catch his breath. "Malik, wake up. Are you okay?"

Stirring, Malik opened his eyes and wiped away sleep. He smiled at his father, but the smile faded when he looked around the room. "Where the hell are we?"

Kendrick drew his son into a bear hug, squeezing him tight and kissing the side of his head. He sniffled.

"I'm okay, Dad. Are you?"

He released Malik and got to his feet. He checked himself for any wounds and injuries. "So far," he said, walking to the only exit in the room, a large steel door. The door didn't budge when he pulled the latch. "It's probably dead-bolted from the outside."

"Maybe you can knock it down, like in the movies."

Kendrick rolled his eyes. "What do I look like? A cy?" He went to Malik and sat, the pain from his encounter with the cys returning to him. "I don't know where we are, son. Hell, I don't even know how long we've both been knocked out. But I know we're not going anywhere until whoever's on the other side of the door says we can."

Malik scooted closer, and Kendrick draped his large arm around his son.

"Malik, did the man in black, the one named Thomas, say anything to you? Did he say what he wanted?"

"What man in black?"

"The one...when we were outside in the middle of the street." Kendrick remembered Malik's unfocused eyes and sighed. "You don't remember, do you?"

He shook his head and bit his nails. "Dad, these aren't People's Army soldiers, are they? They'd know you. They wouldn't have us here, right? Even when they were after

Aya, they treated us better than this."

"You're thinking like I've taught you, son. Your gut is telling you these people aren't our friends, and you're right. This is Orson. I'm sure of it," he said, lowering his voice as he considered the place might be bugged.

Malik looked at him with frightened eyes. "Does that mean Aya's here? I thought you said she was safe. Do you think they've hurt her?"

Kendrick whispered, "No. My gut tells me she's still safe. Orson's people have been looking for her since the attack last week. Last I read, they're still searching." His heart sank as a realization hit him. "It's why they came for us. They're going to..." He stopped and looked at Malik. The boy didn't need to hear the rest. He didn't need to know what Kendrick now suspected. What he suspected because it was a strategy he'd used while serving in the People's Army. Forcing an enemy out of hiding required threatening what the enemy held most dear. Family.

For the first time, he understood the reality of their predicament. Fear replaced the temporary relief he'd felt upon seeing his son alive and unharmed.

"Dad, I'm scared."

He squeezed his son's hand. "Me too, son, but don't worry. I got you."

They sat in silence, staring at the walls and talking in hushed tones until they drifted to sleep.

The sound of keys unlocking the door snapped Kendrick awake. He leaped up, faced the door, and instructed Malik to stand behind him. With no weapon, he knew he wouldn't be able to overcome another cy, but he decided they'd have to kill him before getting to Malik. He assumed a left-handed boxer's stance.

The moment the door creaked open, Kendrick went

into attack mode and swung at the first guard who entered the room. He delivered a left hook to the man's jaw and watched him stumble. Not missing a beat, he landed a left jab to the man's face and grabbed his shoulders to knee him in the midsection. The dazed guard fell on the concrete floor in the middle of the doorway.

Three more guards rushed Kendrick and knocked him over. When he saw their batons, he shielded his face with his arms. They rained down on him with their steel batons as he lay curled up on the floor.

"Stop it!" Malik hollered, still on the bed.

The sound of his son's plea lit something inside Kendrick. He kicked one guard in the leg, and the man collapsed. As he continued covering his face to avoid the baton blows, he mustered his last bit of strength to grab one of the guard's batons. With his fist tight around the baton, he met the guard's surprised eyes and kicked him in the shins. The guard dropped to one knee.

Holding the baton, Kendrick felt fresh adrenaline pump through him.

The guard left standing tried to punch him in the face, but he blocked it and head-butted the man. The resulting pain that shot through Kendrick's head was like no other, but it got the job done. Blood spurted from the guard's nose and dripped from his lips and chin as he leaned against the wall and sunk to the floor.

"Malik, let's go," said Kendrick, reaching the door.

Something caught his ankle. He gripped the doorframe with one hand to keep from falling. The guard he'd head-butted was holding his ankle. Frowning, Kendrick looked at the man's blue eyes and bloody face, and rage filled him. He kicked the man's face twice until his grip loosened.

Looking over his shoulder, he wondered why Malik hadn't moved an inch. "Come on! We need to move, Malik."

"Dad, the man behind y—"

As Kendrick spun around, something hit his chest with enough force to knock the wind out of him. Thomas hit him a second time, and the force of it sent Kendrick smashing into the concrete behind the bed. When he landed on the bed, it buckled instantly from the impact.

As if observing an exotic animal, Thomas looked at an immobilized Kendrick who lay tangled within the folded mattress, bent steel, and debris from the busted wall.

"Dad?" Malik cried out, kneeling at his father's side.

All the while, a second man in a well-tailored gray suit approached and stood in front of Thomas. He looked around and took in the damage Kendrick had inflicted upon the guards.

Malik looked at the towering man who was every bit as tall as his father. "You're Orson."

Kendrick gently squeezed Malik's hand, fear consuming him. "Quiet, son."

"Thank you for sorting that, Thomas," said Orson. "Either we're overpaying these guards, or this Kendrick here is one tough bloke."

Wrenching his hand from Kendrick's grasp, Malik stood and stared daggers at Orson. "Fuck you, asshole. Leave my dad alone."

"While it's adorable you want to stand up for your father, how about you do us all a favor? Be quiet and stand in that corner over there."

"You can't tell me what to do."

Orson smiled and looked past Malik, shifting his attention to Kendrick. "How lucky of you to have such a brave son. I see bravery runs in the family. Allow me to introduce myself—"

"Orson Remington. I know who you are," said

Kendrick, groaning as he disentangled himself.

"I don't appreciate the mess you've made of my guards. They were merely bringing you lot a bite to eat." He paused and looked Kendrick over. "You're quite impressive. It's a shame you fight for the wrong side. I could use a man like you in the UISF."

One of the half-conscious guards on the floor rolled over and bumped Orson's foot. He twitched and scowled at the guard. "Thomas, get someone to remove these men lying around. Bloody normies are useless."

"Yes, sir," said Thomas and left.

Orson turned his attention to Kendrick again. "Your nickname is Go, right? So I can call you that?"

Kendrick frowned.

"I've invited you here as my guest because I'm very worried about your daughter. She's missing, you see."

"If you touch Aya, I'll kill you myself."

Orson smiled. "Take a number, mate. I'm accustomed to idle threats by you opposition people."

As Kendrick floated off the bed, Malik screamed and reached for him.

"The truth is Aya's a little upset about the death of my vice-counsel. Diya's death was a tragic loss to us all." Orson lowered his eyes in plain sadness. "Your daughter ran off after that incident, unfortunately."

Kendrick grimaced from the pain shooting through his shoulder. "You killed your own vice-counsel, didn't you? And tried to pin it on the opposition."

"Go, I feel we're getting off on the wrong foot here. Your daughter is a uniquely talented girl. You Americans failed to realize her true potential, and that's why I want her to return to where she belongs. To the one person she's most like. Me."

"You're out of your mind. You're actually crazy," said

Kendrick, shaking his head.

Orson ignored this interruption and continued. "You can't fathom what it's like to have this type of power. We both share the pleasure and burden of being at the pinnacle of Mother Nature's crowning achievement in human evolution."

Malik burst out laughing. "Dad, this dude talks like a comic book villain. The pinnacle of Mother Nature's crowning achievement?" He held his stomach as he convulsed with laughter.

Still suspended in the air, Kendrick smiled at his son. "The boy's right, Orson. You sound ridiculous."

"Thanos ass nigga," Malik cackled. "Darkseid ass fool in a James Bond suit. And what in the multiverse is up with his hair? Looking like a fake ass Bruce Wayne."

"Let me translate what my son is trying to say. My daughter may be an alpha, but she's nothing like you, Orson. I could never raise anyone so corny." The anger on Orson's face pleased him. "You're not so special. Aya's just the beginning, and I think you know that, don't you? One day there'll be more alphas. Then you won't be the sole person at the top of the food chain. How tough will you be then? I'm thinking my daughter's existence brought you down to reality, and you're scared of what's next."

After a pause, Orson's sly smile returned, and Kendrick crashed to the floor. Before he could catch his breath, Orson's foot was on his throat.

Kendrick's arms flailed about, and Malik screamed.

"You're just a soldier and a normie," said Orson, applying enough pressure to choke but not kill him. "Your primitive brain couldn't comprehend what I'm capable of, you fucking ant." Smirking, he lifted his foot and stepped back.

Malik ran to Kendrick and wrapped his arms around

him as though to shield him from further attacks.

Orson adjusted the cuffs of his sleeves. "But I respect the fact that you're Aya's father. If you weren't, I'd blow past you so fast you'd be dead before you knew what hit you."

With a smug smile, Orson turned away and exited, leaving Kendrick moaning in pain on the floor, in the arms of his son.

Sitting on the floor in the living room, Aya rubbed Baldwin's furry stomach while Eve and Doctor Rouhani discussed next steps. She hadn't felt this hopeful since the day she'd arrived in London. But this hope felt more tangible. She was going to change things now. She was going to change things not by sitting in a bunch of meetings or press conferences but by exposing the source of the instability, the person who had caused so much of the turmoil into which she'd been born. *Orson.* Each time his name rang in her mind, a fresh wave of rage and determination swept over her.

"How about we record a video of the fusion reactor and upload it to Aya's social media accounts?" Eve suggested.

"We could go out there tomorrow, capture Aya creating the energy ball again, and then upload—"

"We need a few more days to run tests," said Doctor Rouhani. "I have to be sure that the energy output can be sustained."

"Look, I know you're a very cautious and meticulous man."

"Yes, I am. And I'm a little worried the Coalition's satellites may be able to track the energy signature. So we need to limit how often we run it for now."

Eve sipped her wine as Doctor Rouhani poured himself another glass. "You and Jesús built a giant lead box over my shed. It's a total eyesore. The sooner I get my shed back the better. And from what you've explained, it shouldn't be detected."

"Are you worried about your neighbors?" Doctor Rouhani shot her an amused smile.

"The last neighbor left this town years ago."

"Exactly. So there's no need to rush this."

"Look, it's just so ugly to look at, and I used to feel proud of that shed. A lot of hours and days went into putting that shed together."

He laughed. "You put it together yourself? Your carpentry skills are better than mine, that's for sure."

"Hey," said Aya, interrupting them as Baldwin jumped off her lap. "Where is Jesús?"

Eve rose and opened the window to let some cool night air inside the muggy house. "He's on a mission. He should be home before too late this evening." She looked out the window and turned around with a smile, the glass of wine dangling in her right hand. With a wave of her other hand, the old CD player on the bookcase came on and salsa music flooded the room. Her hips swayed with the music as her arms rose. "Jesús taught me a bit of salsa over the years. Come on, Doctor Rouhani." She extended her hand for him to join her.

"I know nothing about salsa."

"Neither did I." Eve grinned before taking another sip of wine.

Relenting, he got up and danced toward her.

Aya moved to the now vacated sofa, where she watched and cheered them on as they danced drunkenly in the middle of the living room. Baldwin curled up next to her and purred, while Miss Sandy wandered into the living room and sprawled at her feet. Yawning, Aya leaned against the sofa and thought about Jesús' mission.

She didn't realize she'd fallen asleep until Jesús said her name.

"Aya, something's happened."

Opening her eyes, Aya looked at Jesús and her eyes swept around the room. The music was low, and Eve and Doctor Rouhani were gone. "How long was I asleep? Where's everybody?"

Doctor Rouhani and Eve came stumbling through the door, holding one another up.

"Oh, you're home, Jesús," said Eve, her speech slurred. "Doctor Rouhani and I decided to take a walk through the field after I taught him salsa. The man has two left feet, you wouldn't believe it. It's such a nice breeze outside. You want to walk with us?"

"The size of the rats in that field...the stuff of nightmares," Doctor Rouhani added, stuttering.

Aya looked at the joy in their faces and the happiness emanating from their inebriation. She'd never seen Eve let loose like this. It was nice.

As Eve held Jesús' gaze, she waved her hand to turn off the CD player. Eerie silence filled the room.

Jesús inhaled, casting Aya a sad look. Something about his look sent shivers through Aya.

"I'm sorry, everyone. I hate to shit on your party, but I have some news." He started pacing and running his hands through his hair.

"What's going on, Jesús?" Eve asked, her voice low and her speech less slurred this time.

Jesús stopped and his foot tapped against the floor. "Kendrick and Malik have been taken by Orson's people."

The empty wine glass Eve had been holding slipped from her hand and shattered on the hardwood floor.

Doctor Rouhani sank into the nearest chair.

"Are you sure?" asked Eve, clenching her hands together. "Are you sure they've been taken and that it was Orson?"

Jesús looked at Aya, who hadn't broken eye contact with him since he started talking. "When I got to the house in Philly this evening, it was all dark. I knew something wasn't right. The front door looked like someone had taken a battering ram to it. So I ran inside. The place was so wrecked, and the smell." *Like rotting flesh and burned electrical wires.*

Aya heard his unspoken thought, and terror ripped through her.

"I saw the bodies of two dead cys in the living room," he said, growing paler as he spoke. "Thinking the worst, I rushed to check out the rest of the damage on the first floor. I found the owners, your dad's friends, dead upstairs. But Kendrick and Malik weren't there."

Eve clasped her hands together. "My God."

Jesús turned to her. "I didn't realize Orson's people were still there watching the house, probably expecting Aya to show up. I had to put down a guard before I could get out of there. The whole scene...it was so...." He trailed off, lowering his eyes as he sat on the coffee table.

Eve folded her arms across her chest. "That bastard took them to lure Aya back to him. He knew this would bring her somehow."

"His cruelty has no limit," said Doctor Rouhani. "If he can kill his closest confidante, he'll kill Aya's family as well."

Her fist balled up and her chest heaving in and out, Aya rose and took a deep breath. "No, he won't."

"How do you know that?" Eve regarded her with curiosity.

"Because we're getting them back," said Aya, trembling. She didn't want to imagine the alternative outcome.

Jesús nodded. "We'll need some backup for this mission? This is a rescue mission in Coalition territory. You and I can't do it alone like we did the prison breaks."

"You all won't be alone," said Eve, confidently. "I'm coming with you, to make sure you don't mess things up."

Aya and Jesús ogled her.

"You're wondering why the change of heart? Well, I visited Carmen yesterday, and we talked about—"

"You visited Carmen? In Oakland? You actually left this house?" Jesús stared at her in disbelief.

"We talked about a lot of things, about how I kind of retreated here to this place and let all the people I loved leave because I was too afraid to go out anymore. I gave up." She looked at Aya with a sad smile. "You were right to be disappointed in me before. But I'm not letting you all go into the lion's den alone. Not anymore."

"Well, I will offer you all my moral support from the comfort of this house," said Doctor Rouhani. "Someone has to watch the reactor out there."

Aya approached Eve. "Are you sure about this?"

She retrieved the wine bottle from the fireplace and poured the rest in a new glass she summoned from the kitchen. After taking a sip, she looked at Aya. "I've been cooped up in this house for far too long, child. Visiting Oakland helped me realize that. I'd actually forgotten what other places smell like, what it's like to be around so many strangers. Besides, I had a few adventures back in my day. I think there's still a little gas left in the tank."

Aya hugged her. *Thank you, Eve.*

"No, thank you," said Eve, teary-eyed.

After a moment of silence, Jesús cleared his throat. "Glad to have you along, Eve, but…uh…I think we're still going to need some additional backup." He tapped his fingers against the table.

"I'll ask Lee to join. He's always down for some action."

As Aya returned to her seat and they began discussing the mission, she looked at the team around her. Diya's face drifted to the center of her mind, and she replayed her lasts moments, what she could've done differently. It all had happened so fast, she remembered. She couldn't save Diya. Alone, she couldn't save Malik and her father.

But with her friends…? Perhaps it was possible. With her friends, she could beat Orson. Or, at least, she wanted to believe it was possible…

# 16

Eve woke from a brief nap in the lounge chair on the back porch. Aya was sitting next to Jesús in the grass and engaged in a deep conversation, and she assumed it was about the upcoming mission.

"When did you get here?" asked Eve, rising as she spotted a dark-haired man in the middle of the yard.

Lee Kwon turned to her, and a big grin spread across his face. "About five minutes ago."

When she reached him, she thrust her arms around him. "It's been too long."

"Still letting the locs grow out, huh? And look at those guns," he said, squeezing her well-defined biceps and triceps when she released him. He surveyed her outfit—jeans, sneakers, and a black tank top—and smiled. "You're cosplaying Sarah Connor? I dig."

"That's what almost twenty years of farming does to a girl. You're looking good yourself, Lee. I see you've embraced longer hair and a bit of beard stubble."

He stroked his beard. "You like?"

"Indeed. You're still breaking hearts in Atlanta, I assume?"

"Well, there's no Mr. or Mrs. Kwon yet," he replied,

winking. "You know, if you and Carmen ever want a third, I'm your guy. I'll just leave it at that."

"Carmen's got me trying this whole monogamy thing for now. She's not into the poly life. I tried to tell her she's missing out." As Eve laughed, she caught a glimpse of Doctor Rouhani in the shed running tests on the reactor. His hair and clothes looked more tousled than ever.

"So what's all this about?" Lee asked, following her gaze. "The old man explained a bit, but I'm still lost. He called it a mini-Remington."

"It's a small fusion reactor. Doctor Rouhani's trying to make sure it's stable."

Stepping back, Lee looked at the device and Doctor Rouhani who was approaching. "Are you serious?"

Eve nodded, smiling as Aya came to her side.

"But Orson's company has the patent. How did you even—"

"I developed the technology for Orson's fusion reactors," said Doctor Rouhani, stopping next to Aya. "It's a long story. All you need to know is that machine is a game changer."

Smiling, Jesús looked at Lee and slapped his bat against his palm. "But more importantly, we hope you're down for some trouble today."

"Damn right I am," said Lee, looking confused but excited. "Any way to stick it to Orson is fine with me, especially after his attacks along the east. But this is going to be a dangerous rescue mission. Orson's attacks have been devastating to militia strongholds. We're mostly living on backup generators now, severe food rations for the past week, and limited supplies." Lee paused and said to Eve. "Are y'all sure Kendrick and Malik are still alive?"

Silent for a moment, Eve glanced at Aya and turned her gaze to Lee. "Aya believes they're alive, and she knows

Orson better than any of us. So, yes, I think they're alive."

Aya nodded. "I think he's holding them at the Human and Post-Human Coalition for Peace headquarters in London. There's an area in the basement. I don't think I was supposed to know about it, but I got lost one day when I was bored and ended up in the basement. There were a lot of guards there, more than usual. It seemed weird. I was invisible, so they didn't see me."

Lee regarded her with uncertainty but sighed. "Well, I'll take your word for it. You know more about that place than we do. If we're doing this today, we'll need guns. I can hop to Atlanta and get a few more guns and ammo."

"Eve and Aya are alphas, so they have all the guns they need. As for me, I'm fine with my trusty baseball bat." Jesús spun the Louisville Slugger in the air and caught it.

Aya looked at Eve. "I'm assuming you don't care who knows you're an alpha now?"

"Lee and I go back a lot of years, so he already suspected as much," said Eve, with a wink at Lee before turning to Aya. "Look, I don't care who knows at this point. I just want to stop this maniac and help Kendrick and Malik."

"May I?" Doctor Rouhani, looking worried, raised his index finger to get their attention. "You all know there's no going back if you do this? Orson is nothing if not relentless against his enemies. Unless you take him down, he'll never stop hunting you."

Aya pushed out her chest and held her head high. "Then we'll take him down."

Lee looked at Aya with admiration and muttered to Eve. "Prison breaks and pissing off the People's Army. Infiltrating Orson's team. And now this? The girl's got guts, huh?" He muttered to Eve, while staring in admiration at Aya.

Eve felt transported back to the days with Mauricio,

AJ, Samuel, and Niles. Once, she believed anything was possible, that she could make the world better. Perhaps this was her chance to finish what she'd started. She smiled at Lee. "You heard the girl. Let's get it done."

Half the crowd jeered, and the other half applauded while Orson stood at the podium in the middle of the Palace of Nations' assembly hall. After the final vote for Coalition General Assembly president, Blade had won a second term. Just as Orson expected, half the Coalition was not happy about the election result.

The British Prime Minister stood and glared at Orson. "I'm concerned about the lack of transparency during this election."

This prompted President Chen to stand and second the British Prime Minister's statement. Chatter erupted around the room as President Chen turned a fiery look on Orson and resumed his seat.

President Alabi of Nigeria, standing to address the contentious crowd, raised her hand in a futile attempt to quiet them. "I voted for President Sonani because he is a fine choice. He served the role so nobly over the past four years. During this troubling time, we need the sort of stability he has demonstrated in his leadership of the General Assembly. He has my vote of confidence." As she sat, she gave Blade a reassuring nod.

The shouting match continued as everyone tried to speak over everyone else.

"I knew this wouldn't be an easy outcome. President Sonani and President Chen are both exceptionally worthy candidates." Orson's voice boomed as he spoke over the crowd. His eyes flashed on Blade sitting in the front row a few seats away from President Chen. "I know you're worried and looking out for what's best for your own countries."

The crowd grew more restless and irritated, and Orson's patience waned. *So what if Blade receives another term? Chen can try again in a few years and, if he's proven his loyalty, I'll make sure he wins. Have some bloody patience.* He often asked himself why he bothered with the veneer of elections and democracy anymore, since people never seemed to appreciate it and always found something else to complain about. He'd only chosen this path because of Diya's suggestion that he employ a peaceful strategy. Now that she was gone, should he trust her advice anymore?

President Chen shouted, "This is punishment for the Beijing attack. We're being punished for the acts of opposition groups. How is this fair?" He turned to Blade Sonani. "You wouldn't have received the majority were it not for the bombing at our fusion plant. I find it highly suspicious, the timing. How do I know you didn't have something to do with it, President Sonani?"

Blade glowered at him. "You're out of your mind, man. To launch accusations of this nature without a shred of evidence. You think you're fit to lead this Coalition with that temperament?"

At this point, President Alabi was on her feet again and wagging her finger at President Chen. The noise in the hall increased as others joined Blade in dismissing the egregious accusation from President Chen.

"Oh, for fuck's sake," Orson groaned under his breath. He raised his hand and silence fell over the crowd.

President Chen and others clasped their necks, as their lips moved but no sound came out. Looks of horror clouded their faces as they stared at Orson, who lowered his hand.

"Calm yourselves. I don't appreciate having to use my abilities on Coalition members, but these are desperate and unstable times, and we don't have the luxury of disunity right now. Need I remind you all of what happened in London not even two weeks ago? Opposition terrorists are attacking us, whether it's in London or in Beijing, because they believe we're weak. Shall we avoid proving them correct?"

Some people sat and cast him looks that ranged from approval to disdain.

"President Sonani received over fifty-two percent of the votes. He's the democratically-elected leader. As with all our elections, there has been full transparency in the process. Democracy doesn't always deliver the desired results, but it is the best system we have for fairness and peace. It is foundational to the Coalition. If you have issues with this process, you're free to withdraw from the Coalition. But if you choose to withdraw, just know that when the opposition threatens the tranquil peace your country has known for so long as a Coalition member, you'll need the support of this body."

The room was silent.

Pleased, Orson adjusted his tie and combed his fingers through his hair. "Now, our next order of business is the continued opposition campaign against the Coalition. Some of you in this room believe we shouldn't send further support and supplies to the Unified International Security Forces. However, I'll remind you that we're in this fight together. The recent attacks were not only against the Coalition, but against the free world and all that we stand for."

Reluctant applause spread around the room.

"As members of the Coalition, you all signed a pact to build this world for the better. The tactics our UISF officers are employing against these terrorists are necessary to ensure the vision of the Coalition. If you don't want to be a part of that vision anymore, you're free to withdraw. But, as the agreement you all signed outlined, that will require you to take your fusion reactors offline as well as relinquish access to the Q and the NeoNet." Orson stopped, lifted the telekinetic hold on the crowd, and peered at them. "I implore you to remember that we're stronger together. We're on the verge of finally overcoming those who threatened our freedom and democracy. The efforts of the UISF officers right now, while not the ideal approach, are necessary to creating the world we can be proud to leave our children."

Hushed chatter rose, while many people looked around in silent concern.

Orson observed them, aware of their concerns about the UISF's attacks on the east coast of the United States, attacks that had left dozens of civilians dead. He cleared his throat. "I want to be clear to all our guests from the press who are here today. UISF drones do not rain fire from the sky, despite what the tabloids have erroneously asserted. The brave members of our UISF are being strategic in their approach, and their top priority is ensuring no innocent civilians are harmed. Unlike the opposition, our goal is not terror but a better tomorrow." Pausing for effect, he cleared his throat once more. "Our goal is peace and progress. Onward together, forward."

Cheers and chants rippled through the crowd as everyone, including President Chen, rose and applauded.

Satisfied that he'd unified the members, Orson smiled and descended from the stage.

"Sir," said Thomas, just above a whisper so that only Orson could hear him. "There's been a breach at the headquarters in London."

"You're my head of security, Thomas. Do your job." Orson loosened his tie as he made his way through the aisle toward the exit, Thomas trailing behind him.

"Sir, we believe it's Aya."

He stopped, not turning to Thomas. "Are you sure?"

"Yes, sir."

Orson smiled, feeling hopeful for the first time in days. *Perfect.*

When Aya arrived in the Coalition's lobby, she remained invisible and looked around. Construction crews, working day and night to repair the damaged building, had cleared the place of debris, installed new windows, and repaired or replaced busted floors and walls.

*Keep quiet and hold on to me or Eve,* Aya communicated telepathically to Lee and Jesús. *Let's go through that side door right ahead. Stay invisible.*

She grasped Jesús' hand, while Lee held Eve's and they walked through the solid steel door leading to the main lobby. Once on the other side, Aya and Eve surveyed the area to ensure they were alone.

"I don't know if we can teleport in here," Aya whispered to them. "I tried to teleport the day I got lost walking around and I couldn't."

"I've heard of tech that can block our abilities. But this place is busted, so whatever security tech they had probably isn't up right now," Lee suggested.

"No way Orson would leave this place vulnerable," said Eve, incredulously. "If they had tech up preventing teleportation, you can bet it's still up and running."

Jesús tapped Aya's hand. "There's a stairwell here. Look to your left."

"Good. Let's get out of this open area," replied Eve. "I'm getting a bad feeling right here."

Not wasting another moment, they advanced toward the stairwell past an unoccupied desk. But Aya stopped when she saw Eve, Jesús, and Lee. "We're not invisible anymore." She looked at her own dark brown hands.

Jesús' head swiveled around, and he grabbed the bat

from his backpack.

"Anti-teleportation tech wasn't the only feature of their security." Lee readied his shotgun by pumping a shell into the chamber. "We're going to have company."

Aya pointed at the ceiling. "What's that? It wasn't flashing before we were visible."

Eve looked at the small camera-like device wedged in the corner of the ceiling. There was one in each corner of the room. "Maybe that's the anti-fader tech." She extended her hand, motioning for Lee to hand her his shotgun. He did and, one by one, she shot each device. As she handed Lee the gun, she stared at the devices that were smoking now. "See if that worked. Try to fade ag—" She stopped as a swarm of UISF officers stormed the foyer and lined up in attack formation.

The officers aimed their handheld railguns at them, not moving or making a sound.

A light flashed amid the officers, and they parted. When Aya looked into Orson's eyes, her stomach dropped.

"He's a showy one, isn't he?" Eve whispered to Aya. "I don't think I've ever seen someone create a flash of light when teleporting. Who's the guy behind him?"

*Thomas. His security guy.*

"What a relief to have you back here, Aya. You've had the world on pins and needles worried about your safety." Orson's smile extended only to his lips; his piercing emerald eyes as cold as ever. He stopped ten feet away from Aya and looked at the three people behind her. "Who are your friends?"

She narrowed her eyes on him.

"You may have realized we have regular and infrared sensing quantum cameras installed throughout this building just in case some disgruntled post-humans plan an assassination attempt or whatever sort of thing these terrorist blokes like to get up to nowadays. Despite the damage you did to the building, I made sure those cameras remained operational. You didn't think being unregistered would allow you and your friends to circumvent our surveillance did you?"

Although Aya remained quiet, Eve stepped forward. "Unregistered?"

"Post-humans don't have to be registered in the Q for our surveillance system to detect their presence here," he explained.

"You know why I'm here," said Aya, tugging Eve and signaling her to stand down.

He pushed his hair behind his ears, smiling smugly. "You're here because this is where you belong, Aya. Not with these terrorists." As he looked at Eve, his head tilted to the right and the smile seemed to spread to his eyes. Closing all but a foot of the space between himself and Eve, he reached for her hand and brought it to his lips. "You are stunning. Have we met before?"

Eve looked at him with disinterest and pulled her hand back.

The officers inched forward, and Orson signaled them to continue holding their fire. All the while, Thomas watched like a cat waiting for any hostile movement.

"You have my brother and dad. I want them. I can't sense their presence anywhere. I can't hear their thoughts."

"Aya, I know the last time we crossed paths it was a less than pleasant experience. The circumstances were not ideal. I was wrong for forcing you to witness it, but I assure you Diya's death brought me no pleasure."

As a gloomy look shaded his face, Aya was surprised that it seemed more genuine than his smile. "Give me my family, and we'll leave."

"Only in exchange for your promise to remain here with us where you belong. I'm asking you nicely to stay. But if you're unwilling to accept this invitation…well, it's been a while since we've had long-term guests in holding here."

*I was right. They're in the basement*, she communicated to Eve, Lee, and Jesús.

Orson sighed. "So you found out about the basement? Another leak from Diya, I suppose."

"How did you—are you in my head?"

"Like Diya, you've done a decent job of closing your mind to me all this time, Aya. But not to Thomas here. You see, having a head of security whom no one knows is a telepath is truly a gift that never stops giving. Though Thomas tells me you blocked him most of the time. You're a smart one."

*That's how you found out about Diya? It was me.*

Orson smiled again. "I've tried to reason with you and offer you an easy path, but it looks like that's not what you want. You know I've secured the votes for you to become the Coalition's first ever Youth Ambassador. Imagine the good you could do, the life your brother and father could have if you accepted it. The world's two alphas working together and steering the Human and Post-Human Coalition for Peace."

Aya frowned.

He looked at her with great disappointment. "Well, you leave me no other choice, Aya. Since you destroyed something I love—this place, what it represents for the stability of the world—it's only right that I return the favor. I will say, though, your father's one tough man."

"What have you done to him?" When he responded with a smirk, fury bubbled to the surface. With a quick wave of her hand, she telekinetically threw Orson backward. He crashed into the officers.

Eve looked from Aya to Orson, who was being helped to his feet by the officers. "If I'd known I'd witness the most powerful man in the world get tossed like a rag doll by a one-hundred-pound teenage girl, I'd have brought a camera."

"That was impressive," said Orson, ignoring Eve's snide remark. He glanced at Thomas. "Get rid of her friends. Maybe then she'll come to her senses. I'm going to check out my new office." He disappeared, leaving Thomas alone with the remaining UISF officers.

Thomas went to a bench, unbuttoned his jacket and sat. When he cued the sergeant, the officers readied their weapons and, within seconds, fired upon Eve, Lee, and Jesús.

Terrified, Aya shut her eyes as the loud sound of their guns firing drowned out all other noise. After a moment, she opened her eyes, wondering why everything had become quiet and she wasn't in excruciating pain. She examined her body and noticed shattered projectile debris on the floor around her. As she looked at Eve, she sighed with relief.

With her arms extended out, Eve had created a protective energy field around the four of them, causing all the projectiles to shatter upon contact with it.

Adrenaline pumped within Aya, and her rage and determination returned. She glared at the faces of the officers and waved her hands. Their guns melted. The officers screamed and gaped at their blistering, red hands. Eve removed the energy field and stepped back, standing at Aya's side.

"Now!" Lee shouted and fired at the officers.

Jesús teleported amid the officers and swung his bat, knocking out one man and disorienting another. An officer grabbed him, but he teleported from the man's grasp only to reappear behind him. He struck the officer with a clubbing blow of the bat.

As the officers charged toward Aya, she catapulted them in every direction. Three officers crashed through the new lobby windows, while one lay unconscious on the floor.

Eve looked at Aya. "Orson basically gave away their location, right? That mention of the basement?"

"Yeah, the basement's a secret jail or something."

Eve shook her head. "I have to say I'm impressed by his gall. Agent Grobeck had a Guantanamo on the West Side of Chicago, which was kind of predictable if you knew Chicago in those days. But this guy has nerve…to keep a secret jail in the headquarters of the Human and Post-Human Coalition for Peace. The irony is just incredible."

Aya shot her a blank look, and they spun around at the loud sound of something metal hitting the floor. Lee had dropped his shotgun and switched to his two 9mms. As projectiles flew at him, he ducked and took cover behind the large desk.

"Lee, you think you two can wrap this up?" Eve yelled.

"Yeah. Now find Aya's family while we finish these assholes and the good ole boy over there," he answered, nodding toward Thomas who was still watching from the bench.

Aya winced as she watched Jesús fighting off two officers.

He dodged one officer's right hook and came back with a swing of his baseball bat.

"Are we sure we should leave them, Eve?"

She took Aya's hand. "Lee's an old pro at this. Let's find your family."

Without another word, Aya breathed in and turned away from Jesús and Lee. She squeezed Eve's hand, and they teleported.

Standing side by side Jesús and Lee faced the officers. A thick silence enveloped the dark room lit only by the lights of the officers' railguns.

"You think Eve and Aya are fine?" Lee kept his eyes on the officers.

"I'm more worried about us, man."

An officer gripped Jesús' long ponytail and pulled him to the floor. Two other men joined in and raised their feet to stomp Jesús, but he teleported in an instant. With his bat, he landed a gut blow to the man who had pulled his ponytail, sending the man collapsing to the ground in agony.

The other officers lunged at him, but he teleported behind them.

"Come on, do we really have to fight? This is fun and all, but I can think of other ways to—" He dodged a punch from the larger man, who powered forward to attack him but met a baseball bat to the temple instead. The last officer standing punched Jesús squarely in the jaw. The power of the punch knocked Jesús off balance, giving the man an opportunity to tackle and slam him against the wall.

Lee glimpsed the officer delivering another punch to a wobbly Jesús. "Hey," he hollered, rushing to help Jesús. But before he could reach Jesús, an officer blindsided Lee and sent him tumbling to the floor. Two more soldiers approached as he scrambled for his gun that had flown out of his hand during the fall.

The gun was at least five feet away, too far for him to grab it before the officers reached him. He took a deep breath and stood. "None of y'all are faders. Orson sent a bunch of regular men to capture some faders."

The officers watched him, their guns drawn and aimed at him.

"Have you ever heard of 'enhanced learning'? Some people refer to it as 'extreme adaptability'. You see, some faders can learn new things quickly, faster than any non-fader. Faster than most faders even."

Quiet, they kept their guns aimed at him.

322

"Y'all are probably wondering what any of this information has to do with this situation?" He noticed the officer in the middle looked more interested and curious than the others, so he turned his gaze to him. "Are you trained in any of the martial arts?"

The officer shook his head.

"Good. Neither am I. I was just stalling," said Lee, assuming a fighting stance.

One by one, their guns flew out of their hands and landed across the room. Lee smiled at Jesús, who had faded, sneaked up, and disarmed the officers. The men exchanged petrified looks before lunging at them. Lee dodged and stomped one officer until he stopped moving. When another officer threw a wild right hook, Lee stepped back and kneed the man in the stomach before punching him in the chest. The officer bent over and wailed in pain. A stiff elbow to his head brought the officer to his knees, and he fell face forward against the floor.

The remaining officer struck Lee in the side with a strong left hook and came back with an uppercut. Staggering, Lee steadied himself and dizzily grabbed the man. He slung the officer to the floor and kicked him twice in the ribs. "Fuck," said Lee, rubbing his sore side. "You know I don't like this hand-to-hand fighting shit. I'm a guns guy."

Teleporting behind an officer, Jesús clubbed the man a few times with the bat until he collapsed. "How was I supposed to know these guys would be so tough? It's been a long time since I broke a sweat while fighting." He pulled a cloth from his pocket and wiped the bat.

Lee was still rubbing his side and frowning. "Tell me about it. That one had some bite."

Jesús' gaze swept over the bodies of unconscious or squirming officers scattered about the room. "You know, we should get drinks after this. I'd say we've earned it."

An eerie, slow clap came from behind them, and they spun around prepared to fight.

Lee's hand went to clutch his gun on its holster but grabbed nothing but air. "Fuck," he groaned, glancing at his gun on the floor across the room.

Jesús' fist tightened around the bat.

Thomas stood and took off his jacket. He methodically folded the jacket and placed it on the bench. "I want to congratulate you for an entertaining show. It's even more entertaining that you think you've won."

"That accent," said Lee, "Where are you from? Georgia? Alabama?"

"Texas. And after I'm finished, you're going to wish you'd never left whatever backwater you crawled out of." He rotated his neck left and right and ended with a big stretch.

"So, you're like the big scary super villain who's the muscle for the evil mastermind. I get it," Jesús quipped.

Thomas rolled his eyes. "Am I the only one who didn't grow up caring about stupid comic books?"

Lee and Jesús looked at one another, turned to Thomas, and nodded.

As Thomas placed his hands behind his back and approached, Lee dove left for his 9mm. Before he could reach the gun, Thomas was there with his foot on it. "I haven't seen a person move that fast in years," said Lee, standing up.

Thomas delivered a hard jab to Lee's chest, and the force of it sent Lee sailing twenty feet across the room where he smashed into the desk.

Jolted into action, Jesús teleported behind Thomas and swung the bat. Yet Thomas spun around and grasped the bat with his right hand before it contacted his head. Jesús' eyes widened in alarm.

"The old Louisville Slugger P72 model," noted

Thomas, gripping the bat and studying it. "You know Derek Jeter used this bat throughout his entire career right up until the day he retired from the Yankees." With the slightest application of pressure, the bat crushed in his hand.

Jesús' eyebrows retreated into his hairline. "What the fuck…?"

A kick to the chest slammed Jesús against the wall next to the elevator. Moaning, Jesús lay on the floor, clutching his burning chest.

As Lee reached his gun lying near the desk, Thomas' hands wrapped around his neck. He lost his grip on the gun and gasped for air as he stared at Thomas through frightened, bloodshot eyes.

Like a ragdoll, Thomas flung Lee across the room.

This time, Lee landed on his back but staggered to his feet within seconds and caught his breath. He retreated a few steps as Thomas stepped over the bodies of unconscious officers to reach him. Inhaling, Lee assumed a fighting stance. He went for a punch to the face, but Thomas dodged it with ease.

As Jesús watched, he noticed Thomas looked comfortable dodging all of Lee's blows, like he was playing with a child. Growing weary but refusing to give up, Lee went for a kick to the shins and regretted it in the next moment. Thomas grabbed his leg and threw him toward the elevators where Jesús still was recovering. When Lee went for another punch to the face, Thomas grabbed his arm and bent. The sound of the bones breaking and Lee's scream pierced Jesús. Before Lee could crumble to the floor, Thomas picked him up and threw him next to the elevator near Jesús.

Lee's body contorted at an unnatural angle as he hit the floor.

Too shocked to move, Jesús watched the next sequence as if in slow motion.

Thomas rushed toward a semi-conscious Lee, picked him up, and gave him lightning-fast body punches to his torso. Jesús counted at least ten punches in less than two seconds and met Lee's eyes, which were wide with both surprise and fear.

"Lee!" Jesús shouted, as his friend stumbled, leaned against the elevator door, and coughed up blood.

Approaching Lee like a tiger stalking its unsuspecting prey, Thomas tilted his head and looked at the man. He blocked the sloppy punch that Lee aimed at his face and closed the space between them. With one hand, he grabbed Lee's neck and snapped it.

"No," Jesús murmured, too stunned to yell or scream. He stared at Lee's lifeless body slumped against the elevator door. "Lee?"

He wasn't sure the moment could get worse until Thomas turned to him and smiled. Hot rage coursing through him was all the adrenaline Jesús needed. In one swift movement, he pulled himself up and backed away from the man.

Thomas lunged, but Jesús teleported across the room. While Thomas recovered, Jesús retrieved a gun from one of the soldiers.

"I guess I'm not the only fast person in here. You know you're only making this harder on yourself, boy." Thomas dashed forward at the exact moment Jesús fired the gun.

Dropping the gun, Jesús teleported quick enough to leave Thomas looking left and right for him. He stood behind a weakened Thomas and noticed a spot growing in the middle of the man's back.

Feeling his luck might not run out, Jesús did the only thing that made sense. He put Thomas in a rear chokehold and teleported them out the building. They reappeared in the air amid a sound-splitting freefall, heading straight to the Tower Bridge. The one nearby landmark Jesús could remember on the fly.

"*¡Vete a la verga!*" said Jesús and teleported, leaving the wounded man in a solo free fall twenty feet to the ground.

He reappeared on the sidewalk as Thomas smashed into an empty self-driving bus, and other cars braked to avoid collision. From sheer exhaustion, Jesús collapsed and lay in the middle of the sidewalk.

Aya and Eve teleported to several different basement rooms of the Coalition headquarters, searching for Kendrick and Malik. In an enormous room filled with quantum servers as far as the eye could see, Aya looked around in bewilderment.

"Aya, I thought you knew the building. You said there were holding cells down here."

"I don't remember that well, but I know we're close to the right place. We should've confronted Orson in his office."

Eve shook her head. "The plan was to get your family out and then we come back to deal with him."

"What about Jesús and Lee? That was a lot of soldiers and Thomas—"

"They're grown men. Besides, they're just taking out his henchmen. We need to stay focused on finding Kendrick and Malik."

Marveling at the strangeness of the room, dimly illuminated by blue ceiling lights, Aya tried to remember how she'd spoken telepathically to all the people in the first prison she and Jesús had liberated. Eve had knocked out the anti-fader security upstairs, but it still seemed to be operational—at least partly—down here. *Maybe I can break through it.* Squeezing her eyes shut, Aya focused her thoughts in a desperate attempt to find her father and Malik before it was too late.

Meanwhile, Eve approached one of the quantum servers and looked up. It dwarfed her by a foot or more. "I'm no techie, but I'm wondering if this is the heart of the Q database system. All that data on every registered person walking the face of the earth. This type of knowledge would make anyone think they're a god." She paused and examined the computer. "Why would he put the servers here in the Coalition building? It's the first place anyone who hates him or the Coalition would target. The man's a fool. Or he wants it close because he doesn't trust anybody else with it. He really doesn't have a single friend, does he?"

Silence elapsed between them as Aya entered a trance-like state and twitched, her eyes shut while she searched for her father and Malik. Yet the sound of steps charging towards the double doors halted this quiet moment.

"Aya, you better find them fast."

Aya's eyes rolled so far back that only the whites were visible. Then, she opened her eyes and cast Eve a panicked look. "I need more time."

"Meaning I need something to stall the officers," said Eve, looking around. She touched the server and jumped when sparks flew, knocking out the power. In the pitch black, the voices of the officers yelling at each other and banging on the doors filled the room. "Aya, with the power out, the security system should be disabled."

Seizing the moment, Aya returned to a trance-like state, twitched, and focused on her brother. *Malik...? Shrimp? Aya?*

The lights flickered on again, and she opened her eyes. A large black spot appeared over one wall of the servers and a smile curled her lips. Aya ran to the other wall and touched the servers. Again, the power blinked out but only for a few seconds this time and a huge burn spot appeared over the servers.

As the officers banged on the door, Eve went from wall to wall destroying the servers.

Knocking the door down at last, the UISF officers rushed into the room and surrounded them. But Aya grabbed Eve's arm, and they teleported.

They reappeared in a long hallway where six officers blocked a reinforced double steel door. When they fired their weapons, their projectiles exploded upon contact with the energy field Eve had erected. Aya telekinetically slammed them against the wall hard enough to knock them out. The officers dropped to the floor, and Aya leaped over them, to get inside the room.

The room looked like a bomb had gone off in it, and a pungent odor filled the air. Yet none of that mattered to Aya when she saw Malik, dirt and grime caked on his face. He sat up and looked at his sister, his mouth hanging open in shock. A look of pure joy spread across his face.

Kendrick tried to rise to a sitting position, and Eve hurried to help him up. He rested his large frame against her, while Aya hugged him. Malik thrust his arms around her and cried.

"How did you two find us?" asked Kendrick, in a hoarse voice.

"We'll fill you in later. Let's focus on getting the hell out of here first." Eve lifted him to a standing position, and he moaned in pain. "Are you all right, Kendrick?"

"I'll be fine." He grinned, but it looked more like a frown.

Malik pulled one of Aya's Afro-puffs. "Missed you, sis!"

"I missed you, too, Shrimp. More than you know. I have a lot of stuff to tell you," she said, watching her father stumble as he got up.

"All right. Ready to get us out of here, Aya?" asked Eve, taking Aya's hand.

Aya held her other arm out to Malik, and he grasped it with both hands. "Hold on to me and don't let go, Malik. It's going to feel a little funny."

Holding them and feeling a rush of happiness, Aya closed her eyes and waited for the familiar tug in her stomach.

# 17

Eve patched up Kendrick and sent him upstairs to her bedroom to get some rest. In the living room, Malik lay asleep on the sofa while Eve relaxed in the recliner chair and Aya dozed off with a book in her lap. Rubbing her temples, Eve stared at the ceiling. Her head throbbed, and she wondered how she'd had such boundless energy for these missions in her younger years. All the sleepless nights she'd spent with Mauricio, AJ, and Niles on the run. The rescue missions she'd led when she created this safe house years later, after Chicago and most cities became unsafe for faders. It was exciting then because she felt she was changing things, that a better future was possible.

When Jesús appeared in the center of the room, blood spatter on his shirt, Eve jumped up. The book slipped from Aya's lap as she got up and stared wide-eyed at Jesús. Although the thud of the book hitting the floor caused Malik to stir, he merely turned over and continued snoring.

"Are you all right?" asked Aya, reaching for his arm to support him.

Eve helped Aya guide him to the chair, and he plopped down. Sliding her hands under his tattered tee, Eve checked for broken ribs. "Looks like you've seen better days."

He brushed back his disorganized and sweaty hair. "You should see the other guy."

"I bet." Eve grinned and sat on the coffee table facing him. "We didn't think we'd be home before you."

"Where's Go?" he asked, glancing at Malik.

"He's upstairs. But what happened to you?"

"I think I passed out on the Tower Bridge or something. When I woke up I was in an ambulance."

Eve looked at him incredulously. "And they didn't fix you up better than this?"

"I didn't give them time to. I knew the authorities wouldn't be too far behind, so I got out of there."

"Well, you could've gotten taken care of by some professional medics first. Now you're stuck with me and Aya," she said, patting his leg.

Aya, standing next to Eve, looked around. "Where's Lee? Did he go to Atlanta?"

Jesús lowered his gaze. "I didn't think I had time to go back for his body."

They fell silent for a while as Aya's eyes filled with tears and Eve stared at Jesús.

"The guy who kicked my ass got to Lee first. I got lucky. Only thing he broke was my bat." He wiped his face and mumbled to himself, "That bat was the only thing I had left from my dad."

Biting her bottom lip and trying to fight tears, Eve stood and breathed in deeply. "I never should've let him come with us." She caught Aya's eyes, realizing the girl probably was wracked with guilt. "I'll let his militia comrades know," she said, sighing and wiping her damp cheeks.

Jesús nodded. "Maybe I should go find his body."

"Not in the shape you're in. Leave that to me. In the meantime, I'll find some more rags and athletic tape to wrap you," Eve replied and hurried out the room. But she stopped when Aya spoke in a hushed tone. Standing outside the room, Eve listened to their conversation.

"You think she'll be all right, Jesús?"

"She's lost so many people, so many friends. It's why she stopped leaving this house, and now the first time she does a mission after all these years, she loses another friend. I don't know."

A brief pause followed until Aya said, "Orson keeps hurting good people. I hate him."

She noticed the weariness in Aya's voice. It wasn't right that any child should have to feel the weight of the world. Suppressing tears, Eve headed up the stairs, their words echoing in her mind.

Aya stared at the reactor while Doctor Rouhani paced, mumbling to himself.

He stopped and scratched his head. "We still have to figure out a way to show people this working fusion reactor that doesn't belong to Orson or the Coalition."

"Why can't we just broadcast a video of it on the NeoNet? It'll go viral in a heartbeat," asked Eve, leaning against the door of the shed.

"That's what Malik did with the video of me jumping from the cultural center."

Doctor Rouhani stopped pacing and shot Aya an exasperated look. "And that's also how Orson found you, isn't it? If we upload a video, he'll intercept it and use it to pinpoint our location. Not only will he scrub the video from the NeoNet before more than a handful of people have the chance to see it, but he'll send every UISF officer in his employ our way, especially after last night."

Aya looked at the reactor, combing her brain for an idea. "What if we put it on a lot of different sites, not just

Aya's social media accounts?"

"We'd have to do a simultaneous international broadcast. But that's quite impossible. With this rural infrastructure here there's no way to connect to the NeoNet, and it's too risky to try to transport the reactor to Chicago." He resumed pacing, brushing his hand over his balding head. "Our technological limitations are hurting us here. Even if we uploaded the video to the old web, Orson would take it down at once. The processing powers of those quantum computers are astounding, and they have IT spies still tracking the old web. I personally trained some of them." When Doctor Rouhani stopped pacing again, tense silence enshrouded them.

Malik ducked under Eve's arm to enter the shed, and his jaws dropped when he saw the reactor. "No way. That's not a miniature magnetic confinement fusion reactor, is it?"

Doctor Rouhani regarded him with raised eyebrows. "How old are you?"

"I'll be eleven soon."

"How do you know about fusion reactors?"

"Technology is kind of my thing," he said, strolling toward the reactor.

"He spent a lot of time in the library," Aya whispered to Doctor Rouhani but loud enough for Malik to hear her. "I think he's really smart or something." She smirked at Malik and stuck her tongue out, teasing him.

Rolling his eyes at his sister, Malik touched the reactor and leaned closer to look at it. "I used to read books on all types of technology, but I mostly liked the stuff on communication and energy." Like an excited kid on Christmas day, he prodded the reactor and examined it.

"Do you know how to upload a simultaneous international broadcast?" asked Aya, stumbling upon an idea.

"You mean a simulcast? Yeah. Why?"

Eve and Doctor Rouhani exchanged an excited look, and Aya explained to her brother the importance of revealing the reactor to the world. Malik pointed to the tablet Doctor Rouhani was holding. "That's a quantum tablet, isn't it? Are you getting a wireless signal?"

Doctor Rouhani glanced at the screen. "Not at the moment."

Malik sat on a stool next to the reactor and stroked his chin as though he had a full beard rather than the hairless face of a scrawny sixty-pound boy. "So you need to stream a live video on the NeoNet, but we can't connect to a wireless signal strong enough to process the quantum power of that tablet?" When Doctor Rouhani answered in the affirmative, Malik sprang up and snatched the tablet. He skimmed through the settings and grinned. "I can get you guys a signal."

"How?" Eve asked, with a look of disbelief.

He sat on the stool and swung his short legs. "Same way I got Aya's video up on the NeoNet. I'm a superhero, too."

"Malik, I know you're jealous of me, but you don't have to make up stories."

"Wait. Aya, let the boy talk. What do you mean, son?" asked Doctor Rouhani, coming forward.

Malik threw Aya a mean glare before turning a smiling face to Doctor Rouhani and Eve. "I can connect to traditional wireless signals and then transfer the signals to connect to the NeoNet. I can even connect directly to the complex quantum computers and holographic televisions in the Coalition countries. It happens when I touch things like this tablet or a cell phone."

"You were in the library reading about communication technology so you could understand how to use your ability?" asked Aya.

He stared at her and, after a moment, said, "I wanted to get good at it before I told you."

Eve looked from Doctor Rouhani to Malik. "Fascinating. Even I don't know how to do that. I mean I can get a few channels on the TV sometimes if I focus hard enough, but that's it. I don't know any other faders who can—"

"Tap into electromagnetic and quantum fields and waves to interact with our quantum communications devices?" finished Doctor Rouhani. "Neither do I."

In the next moment, they gasped when Malik's eyes rolled to the back of his head, and an electrical hissing sound emanated from the tablet on his lap. All the while, his small hands kept a tight grip around the tablet.

"Malik?" said Aya, taking a cautious step toward him.

As his eyes focused again, he smiled with satisfaction and handed the tablet to Doctor Rouhani. "I can hold that connection for a little while."

"Wh—" Doctor Rouhani stammered, looking at the tablet and noticing the wireless icon showed strong connectivity. He removed his eyeglasses, wiped them clean with his dingy shirt, and put them back to make sure he was seeing things clearly. "We can broadcast the livestream across the globe to the old web and NeoNet. This signal is strong enough to allow us to transmit the powerful processing speeds of this tablet. Amazing."

"Best to film it inside the shed, right?" Aya asked, looking at Eve.

"Of course. We don't want to give away our location. Now, let's not waste any more time." Eve motioned for Malik and Doctor Rouhani to retreat several feet from the reactor. "Get the tablet ready to record. Be sure you have Aya and the reactor in the frame, and the volume's up."

Standing near the doorway with the tablet, Doctor

Rouhani gave a thumbs up.

Eve fixed the collar on Aya's shirt and fluffed her ponytail. "Remember the speech you practiced?"

"I think I need more time to prac—"

"We don't have time, Aya. You heard Malik. He can only hold the signal for so long." She lifted Aya's chin and offered her a reassuring smile. "Remember what that monster has done to your friends, to Diya and Lee. To your family. Do this for them."

*Eve, I'm sorry about Lee.*

*You don't have any reason to be sorry. He was brave. Now I need you to be brave.*

With a nod, Aya took a deep breath. "I'm ready."

In his Geneva office, Orson dug the tip of a pencil into the desk as he looked at a holographic image of Aya standing next to a small reactor in what appeared to be an old shed or storage room. "He's a liar, a terrorist, and a murderer," she said, staring at him. As she went into detail about the Q database system, Orson dropped the pencil and laid his hand flat on the desk. He seethed as he watched her take a sledgehammer to the world he'd spent decades creating.

"The Q doesn't just search for illegal post-human and terrorist activity. It tracks and monitors every post-human and human in the Coalition countries. But that's not the worst of it. He's not just tracking you. He's attacking communities that go against him. He's destroyed villages and cities, like my home. Like the home of Diya Narang."

At these words, Orson's anger mixed with horror. He closed his eyes for a moment, knowing what was next.

"Orson made me watch as he tortured Diya and slit her throat. He killed her because she wanted peace, and she knew there would never be peace with a tyrant like him in power. He didn't stop there. He kidnapped my brother and beat my dad to punish me for standing up to him. Orson's a monster." Aya stopped and approached the fusion reactor. "I'm talking to you today because, like you, I thought Orson cared about peace, about protecting post-humans, about bringing us together. But I was wrong. You have the right to know that your world isn't so free, not with Orson in charge. The Coalition isn't about peace, not with Orson in charge.

"But that can change today because we all know the source of Orson's power, where it all began. Fusion. The only reason you need his fusion is because he destroyed power plants across the world during the Great Turn. Diya knew this, and it's part of the reason he killed her. You know who blew up the Beijing fusion construction site? Orson. But as of today, Orson is no longer the only one who knows how to create fusion energy, and this mini reactor is proof. With this, the power is in our hands now. We don't need him."

Orson's mouth hung open as he watched her do what he'd done in the park so many decades ago. Her skin darkened and blistered as she held the glowing ball of energy in her hands, but she channeled it into the reactor at once. Once the reactor was ignited, she wobbled a bit and turned to him again. Within seconds, the blisters disappeared, and her skin returned to its normal dark complexion.

"She can heal instantly," Orson said, stunned.

The broadcast ended a minute later—with her calling on the world and the Coalition to reject him—and her holograph vanished. Yet he kept staring at the spot where she'd been standing. Rage soon returned, displacing shock and horror. As his phone buzzed against the desk, he groaned, realizing he'd missed no less than sixty calls in the past five minutes.

Cornelius burst into the room, out of breath and red in the face. "Orson, you've seen? Why are you not answering your phone?" he exclaimed, rushing to his brother who was seated behind the large desk. "She somehow broadcast it across the world. Everyone with a wireless connection or a television has seen that message. The number of reporters ringing me—"

"I've seen the message, Cornelius," said Orson, his voice low and calm. He looked out the window at the courtyard. "She's a clever girl, isn't she?"

"Orson," said Cornelius, confused by his brother's calmness. "Billions of people watched the video in real time. It's already trending on every major social media site. The public will be quick to react to this, especially to the bit about the Q system—"

"The Q is down. The break-in at the headquarters yesterday resulted in substantial damage to the Q and the backups. It's not functional at this time. I've spent half the day responding to Coalition members about the disruption."

"Well, when will it be back online?"

"The system has been disrupted indefinitely, Cornelius. I have no efficient means of tracking opposition troublemakers now, no way to quell dissent."

Cornelius sat in the chair across from Orson's desk and sighed, rubbing his temples. "Brother, why didn't you alert me about the Q system failing? What if a reporter had contacted me about it? You're not making my job easy by withholding information."

Orson faced him, looking at the half-empty bottle of whiskey on his bookcase. A thought occurred to him, and he laughed. "Of course," he muttered.

Alarmed, Cornelius leaned forward. "Are you quite all right?"

"Diya was truly a gift to the opposition. It was she who convinced me to place the Q database and the backup servers in the Coalition's headquarters. She knew I distrusted leaving it in the hands of anyone else, so she suggested I establish it in my home base where I could control it and ensure it didn't fall into the wrong hands." *But it was all part of her schemes.*

Cornelius shook his head. "I'll confess I never thought it was a bright idea, brother."

"Our mother was right about Diya. She's been right about all these people, hasn't she? They're ungrateful, treacherous—"

"Orson." Cornelius shifted in his seat, looking uncomfortable. "It's not true, is it? What the girl said about you killing Diya. That's not true, is it?"

He met his brother's blue eyes and studied him. Was it surprise or fear? Perhaps both, and pity. He cleared his throat and waved his hand in a dismissive gesture. "Leave me, Cornelius. I must make some calls."

"But—but we need to discuss a unified response to this controversy before you speak to anyone about it."

"I trust you'll develop talking points and share them with me within the hour. Now, leave me."

Cornelius stared at him in dismay but stood and buttoned his blazer jacket. "I assume you realize this is not the time to retreat and try to go it alone. I know that's your default during crisis, but I strongly recommend that you do not lapse into that old habit. Can we please discuss this before you make any calls?"

Orson turned to the window, thinking about the chaos that would ensue no matter what steps he took next.

"Very well," said Cornelius, taking Orson's silence as a negative. He gave an exhausted sigh and left the office.

Orson's mind wandered through jumbled thoughts. Thomas was gone. Diya was gone. His reputation in shambles. *Is this grief? Mourning?* This feeling was new to him, and he didn't care for it. He preferred anger. Anger led to action.

He wiped away tears and looked at his wet fingertips. *Grief is for the weak.* He got up and went to the bookcase where he poured a shot of whiskey and gulped it. He repeated this two more times, enjoying the warmth of the liquor.

After capping the bottle of whiskey and placing it on the bookcase, he went to his desk and grabbed his phone. Instead of returning any calls, he dialed his mother and left a message warning her not to believe anything she'd seen on the news. As he pocketed the phone, he took a last shot of whiskey.

With vengeance on his mind, he spared one more look at the office and teleported to Chicago.

At Chicago's old city hall, one of the few buildings to survive the recent attack, General Harris organized a meeting of People's Army and Midwest Front leaders to discuss how to respond to the rise of violence within the city. With her hands resting on the conference room table, she looked more tired than usual. Her face bore more wrinkles than ever before, in stark contrast to the jet black locs that flowed down her back in a neat ponytail.

While Terry Jackson spoke, General Harris nodded absently. Worn out and distracted, all she could think about was the little girl with the big hair, the little girl who had slipped through her fingers months ago.

All this trouble had started with Kendrick Wright's daughter. From the cy attack that killed her top scientist, the prison breaks, the attack that wiped out the entire South Shore area, the growing tensions with the Eastern Front, it all began with that child. If she'd followed her instincts and locked Aya Wright away the moment she was discovered to be a fader, perhaps she could've spared her people the turmoil of recent months. The humiliation of being outsmarted by a child enraged her.

Yet everything happened for a reason, she supposed, grateful that the girl had pierced the heart of the Coalition, Orson himself. Maybe it had all been worth it to watch Orson and his empire fall.

"General Harris?" said Terry Jackson, snapping her back to the present.

Clearing her throat, she replied, "You're right, Commander Jackson. We have limited supplies and a very desperate civilian population that's getting restless. What with the trauma of the past months and the dire food scarcity we're seeing, we can be sure the violence will get worse. I'm in talks with the leaders of the Coalition West now about an agreement around food imports. They're more willing than usual to consider business with us, as they're still honoring the Reykjavik Agreement, despite the London attack. But I'm not sure we have enough time to wait for the outcome of those talks."

He rubbed his bald head. "If I might suggest, why not impose an earlier curfew across the city?"

"You can only restrict a person's freedom of movement so much before they react, Commander. We need another solution."

Before anyone could respond, a thunderous boom resounded from above, shaking the room. The terror-stricken people around the conference table leaped from their seats, drew their weapons, and looked for the source of the disturbance. They received their answer when, following a flash of light, something crashed from the ceiling and landed in the middle of the table. Debris flew in every direction, sharp shards puncturing anyone not fast enough to duck for cover.

As ash and dust rained down, an unsettling silence swept over the room.

Having retreated to a far corner, General Harris got

up now and aimed her gun at the center of the room. She pointed it at the pile of rubble that, moments earlier, had been the conference table.

The smoke cleared and revealed bodies strewn about the floor, all of them as still as boards.

Coughing and still struggling to see through the haze of smoke, she stiffened as an imposing figure appeared in the center of the room. From what she could discern, the man was dressed in an all-black suit and at least six feet tall.

"Don't move!" She shouted, aiming at the man's chest and trying to see him through the smoke. As the smoke cleared, she found a man with thick chestnut-colored hair and piercing green eyes staring at her. Her grip tightened around the gun, and her trigger finger twitched. "You son of a bitch."

"It's good to see you too, General," said Orson, his voice low and menacing.

Realizing time was of the essence, she looked at her peers. "Fire at will!"

But Orson raised his hands, and they froze, unable to move or blink. "Lower your weapons."

Confused, they lowered their guns and looked frantically from General Harris to Orson.

"Turn them on yourselves," he said, his eyes fixed on General Harris. "Except for you, General. We have a lot to talk about."

They placed the barrels against their temples and stared at one another in abject horror. As she looked at their terrified faces, she recalled she'd only felt this helpless once before. During the Reykjavik meeting. With a look of pure desperation, she said, "Orson, what are you doing?"

"I don't have all bloody day," he scoffed. "On with it."

As gunfire rung throughout the room, General Harris closed her eyes and her heart dropped. The thud of her fellow soldiers falling to the floor in unison reverberated in her mind. She wondered if she'd ever not hear that sound again.

Cupping his hands behind him, Orson stepped over dead soldiers and advanced toward General Harris.

She stared at the blood and bodies around the room, her voice cracking when she spoke. "Don't come any closer."

To her surprise, he stopped and smiled at her.

"You know there'll be reinforcements and air support soon," she said, retreating.

He glanced at the dead soldiers at his feet and looked at her. "Does it look like I'm at all worried, my dear?"

Meeting Orson's cold eyes, she straightened her posture and tried to lift her gun to point it at him once more. But her arm might as well have been broken because she couldn't move it an inch. "Why are you here?"

"Gwendolyn, may I call you that? 'General' feels too formal, and I think we're quite past formalities at this point."

She looked daggers at him.

"I've always admired your steadfast dedication to your utterly futile mission."

The smirk on his pale face sent waves of wrath crashing over her. "If you're going to kill me, just shut your goddamn mouth for once and do it."

"Defiant to the bitter end, Gwendolyn. It truly is admirable. I could have used someone as ruthless as you on my side."

When he touched her shoulder, she pulled back, pressed herself against the wall, and spit at him.

Chuckling, he removed a cloth from his pocket and wiped the spit from his face. "It's too bad you're such a hateful cunt. The power we could've amassed together, you and me. I realized that in Reykjavik, you know. This world needs strong men. And it needs strong women like you. The people don't want to admit it, but they prefer to be ruled by the strong."

"You tried to rule the world with a child by your side, and she exposed your sorry fader ass. Even she can see what I saw from the first time we met. Weakness. You're no strong man. You're just an asshole with too much power."

As she spoke, she lifted her arm at last. But when she tried to smack him with the butt of the gun, he caught her hand mid-swing. He squeezed the gun, causing it to contort and fall apart.

"Let's go for a walk, shall we, Gwendolyn?" Not waiting for her answer, he took her hand and led her through the rubble and bodies until they arrived outside the building.

Standing on Washington Street, they watched at least six helicopters fly overhead. People's Army soldiers and armed civilians advanced with guns drawn, and General Harris noted the snipers positioned atop the city hall. Thirty-year-old tanks lined the streets in each direction.

"Are you sure you want to do this, Orson? There are far more of us than you."

Before he could respond, a sniper's bullet pierced Orson's chest. A spot of blood appeared at once, and he rolled his eyes. With a wave of his hand, guns flew from the hands of the snipers, soldiers, and armed civilians trying to kill him. The guns hovered inches above their heads.

General Harris experienced a sinking feeling when she saw the same look of fright on their faces that she'd seen on the faces of Terry Jackson and the other people in the conference room.

"I would've aimed for the head," he said, waving his hand again. The guns disappeared this time. "But don't worry. You'll soon be reunited with your outdated weapons."

Some young soldiers charged toward Orson, while others scrambled to find other weapons. General Harris knew it was all hopeless. She knew she'd be staring at a street full of dead soldiers and civilians within minutes. These young people with so much promise would be dead in seconds, and there was nothing she could do to prevent it. Before any of them reached Orson, he waved his hand again, tossing some of the people in different directions. Helplessly, she watched him wave his arms this way and that way, as though he was a conductor leading a symphony.

Two soldiers smashed into the helicopters soaring above. The impact damaged the helicopters, sending the gunners leaping out. The helicopters crashed less than a block away, killing all the soldiers and civilians too slow to run for cover. Shards of glass and debris shot like missiles in their direction and General Harris wondered why she wasn't hit, until she realized Orson had placed some sort of protective field around them.

"Secure the general!" yelled a middle-aged sergeant.

A group of soldiers, armed with knives or whatever piece of gear they could turn into a weapon, rushed to attack a man they'd only known as some far-off enigma until this moment. The mysterious head of the Coalition they'd heard about for so long. Now, this man was there in the flesh, wreaking havoc on what little remained of downtown Chicago.

Orson put his arm around her shoulder and waved his hand one more time. All the soldiers, armed civilians, remaining helicopter pilots above, and snipers within a mile, vanished. The pilot-less helicopters fell from the sky and burst into flames as they hit the ground. General Harris shielded her head and face, forgetting she was within Orson's protective shield.

"What—what did you do?" she said in a weak voice. "Where did everyone go?"

"It's called telekinetic teleportation, if we want to be scientific." He looked into her petrified eyes. "In other words, they've been reunited with their weapons."

"Where…?" She stammered. "Where are they?"

"Rapidly approaching the bottom of Lake Michigan."

Her heart quickened. "No. No, bring them here. My God, what have you done?"

"'My God'…what an interesting choice of words," he said, smiling a cruel smile. "Today, you're the one to bear witness to my destruction, to tell the world what I can do. That is, if the world believes you."

"Why didn't you kill me?" She sniffled.

He patted her arm as though she was a dog. "My dear Gwendolyn. You will live with this. You will live with this day for the rest of what's left of your sorry life. Just like I need to live with knowing that some little brat from your city took so much away from me," he said, pausing and straightening his blazer jacket. "But I don't hate her. She's young, and I underestimated her. That's my own fault."

Still unable to move, General Harris sniffled as she studied the towering man next to her, realizing she'd made the same mistake. She'd underestimated him.

"I don't hate Aya, but today I'll finish what I started here." He looked at the wreckage around him and smiled.

General Harris, still unable to move, called him every foul name under the sun.

When he released the protective shield and she realized she could move once more, her face lit up with fury. Before she could connect a right hook with his chin, he stepped back.

"Sleep," he said, smiling a sickly smile.

She felt her legs give out, and there was darkness.

On command, General Harris collapsed onto the sidewalk

and lost consciousness. He crouched and looked at the sleeping woman, wondering where he should send her. As he landed upon an answer, he smiled, and the woman vanished.

Standing up, he headed down Washington Street, consumed with thoughts about his years-long quest to find another alpha. How desperate he'd been to find someone else like him, to not have to feel so alone anymore. Yet finding another alpha had reduced his life to rubble and left him more alone than he'd ever known possible.

Aya had taken away Diya, Thomas, and perhaps his Chief Minister position in the Coalition. They would certainly set up an investigation around her claims, and how would he counter it without force and violence? Was he a weak man, as General Harris said?

He stopped at an intersection and recalled what he'd told Aya during the tour of the Beijing reactor. The power of the sun in my hands.

As he cupped his hands, a small ball of pure plasma energy formed between his palms. The heat seared the skin off his hands and face within a matter of seconds. But he ignored the pain. Instead, he closed his eyes, gathered all his rage, and released it.

When he opened his eyes, he was standing in the middle of his bedroom and burned beyond recognition, his whole body in pain. He hadn't felt this kind of pain since that day in the park. He fell onto the bed and cried in agony until he lost consciousness.

While Orson slept, his burned body regenerated.

All the while, journalists around the world scrambled to understand what had caused an unconscious General Harris to suddenly appear on the White House lawn before the mysterious blast that wiped out ten square miles in Chicago, obliterating the thousands of remaining inhabitants in the city.

# 18

Aya gazed at the clouds, a couple of puffs of white in the blue sky, and sipped iced tea. She stretched her legs on the porch swing as a cool September breeze picked up.

Malik and Doctor Rouhani sat slumped over a small table and staring at a chess board. Gleefully, Malik captured one of Doctor Rouhani's pawns, to which the old man groaned and smacked his lips.

"I've never beat Malik at chess," said Aya, grinning. "Looks like you won't either."

Doctor Rouhani's tablet buzzed, and he cast an annoyed look at it before picking it up. Thanks to Malik, the tablet was still connected to the NeoNet, allowing Doctor Rouhani to stay plugged in to his world. Prior to Malik's fix, Doctor Rouhani had spent no small amount of time complaining about feeling isolated from the events and goings-on in his world. But he'd tired of the tablet's incessant buzzing with news alerts.

As he scrolled his finger along the tablet now and brought up a holographic headline, he muttered several curse words in Farsi.

"What's going on?" asked Malik, regarding the man with alarm.

Doctor Rouhani rose as quickly as his old body would allow and darted inside the house. Aya and Malik gestured to each other and followed the man. He stopped in the living room where Jesús, Kendrick, and Eve were discussing how to bring the reactor to Chicago.

Clutching the tablet and resting his other hand on his knee, Doctor Rouhani hunched over and struggled to catch his breath. "There's been an attack."

"Another one?" Aya asked, fearing the worst.

Eve and Jesús looked at Doctor Rouhani, while Kendrick—still wearing an arm sling and recovering from his injuries—struggled to stand up.

"What are you talking about?" Eve approached Doctor Rouhani and extended her hand to help him stand up.

"There was an explosion in Chicago, a bomb they think. I felt a little rumble a few hours ago but thought nothing of it." Doctor Rouhani's chest heaved in and out, but he stood straight. "They're saying the Americans are warring with each other. But I don't think they'd start nuking each other now, not after the Reykjavik Agreement, no matter how much the Coalition wants to nullify it."

"What do you mean by 'nuking'?" asked Kendrick, eyes wide.

Doctor Rouhani wore a grave look and responded by looking away.

"How many people died?" said a quiet voice that made everyone turn around to Malik. His usual smile and lightheartedness were absent.

Doctor Rouhani looked at Eve and Kendrick. "I don't know."

"Can we rewind? Are you saying someone's essentially nuked Chicago?" Jesús joined Eve by her side.

"Look," exclaimed Doctor Rouhani, shaking his head. "If it were a nuclear attack we'd be baking in high radiation right now. I pulled up the app I use to watch our reactor. The app can trace particles over a hundred kilometers, uh, miles. I've been using it to ensure that Eve's energy field is shielding the particles when we test the reactor, so that the Coalition can't find us."

"Are you approaching a point, Doctor Rouhani?" Eve said, sighing.

"What I'm saying is the particles in Chicago match the particles that were used by Aya to start the reactor."

Growing impatient, Jesús folded his arms across his chest. "Still not following, man."

Doctor Rouhani sat in the comfy chair vacated by Eve. "It wasn't a nuclear attack that just wiped out ten square miles of Chicago. It was a sudden release of a highly charged plasma burst." He turned to Aya with a look grimmer than any she'd seen on his face before. "It was an alpha who just leveled your hometown."

"Hold on. Orson's capable of something like that? Of destroying a whole city?"

Heavy silence followed Kendrick's question as they all exchanged horrified looks.

"I think I need to sit down." He released Malik and Aya and made his way to the sofa.

Jesús, on the other hand, jumped into action and retrieved a baseball bat—a new one Eve had gifted him—from the hall closet. "It's time to stop this maniac."

"No, you all aren't going anywhere. You're still injured," Eve said, taking the bat from Jesús. She returned it to the closet and went to Aya. For a moment, they met one another's eyes. A shared understanding passed between them.

"Eve and I are the only ones who can stop him. We're the two alphas here." Images of South Shore flashed across Aya's mind. Her home was not just damaged now. It was gone. As she looked at her father, her heart shattered.

She went to him and reached for his hand, squeezing it to reassure him. Or was she trying to reassure herself? "I have to do this, Dad."

Fighting back tears, Kendrick looked at his daughter and brought his palm to her warm cheek. "It's been six years since I lost Valerie, but I feel like I'm seeing your mom again. She had the same will and determination."

"I know you don't want me to go—" Aya began, but he shushed her.

"Your mom would be so proud of you." He kissed her forehead and brushed his thumb against her cheek. "Go do what you need to do, baby girl."

Malik sat next to him and gave Aya an encouraging nod.

After wiping her eyes, she smiled. "I'm coming home, Shrimp."

"You better." Malik stuck out his tongue before winking.

Kendrick squeezed Aya's hand one more time. "And give him an extra kick in the you-know-what for me."

With that, Aya turned to Eve. "You're sure about this?"

Eve, looking full of energy, half-smiled. "You bet." She gave Jesús a fist bump and held his gaze for a moment. "Make sure our guests eat this evening."

He shot her a worried look but nodded.

Aya took Eve's hand and waited for the familiar tug in her stomach.

Pushing aside the fear that she'd never see her family again, she concentrated on one thing only. Bringing down Orson Remington III, even if she had to die trying.

They teleported to London and, invisible, tiptoed through Orson's quiet apartment. To her relief, Iris appeared to be out for the moment. As they proceeded along the hallway, Aya recalled how odd it had felt when she first arrived there. How surreal it had felt to live in so much luxury, like she'd been transported to a wonderland. As exciting as it all was at the time, she'd never gotten comfortable in this place.

*I'm sure he's here. If he used plasmakinesis to blow up Chicago, he'll be here recovering.*

*I hope you're right, Aya. I'd rather not have to deal with any UISF officers this time.*

*There's a room at the end of the hall on the right. His home office. If he's not here, we can go back to Geneva.*

They scurried down the hall, walking as lightly as possible, and stopped at the door. Aya leaned close to the door to listen for any noise indicating he was in there. She couldn't be sure, but she thought she could hear a faint gulping sound followed by a groan. She took Eve's hand, and they passed through the door.

An unkempt Orson sat behind a desk, drinking from a bottle of whiskey. He wore a dress shirt and jeans, not his usual well-tailored suit. What's more, his eyes looked bloodshot and his skin blotchy.

He sat the bottle on the desk and stared at the ceiling. As he pushed his hair behind his ears, he closed his eyes.

Aya had to cover her mouth to keep him from hearing her audible gasp. She could hear his thoughts.

*Eve, I can hear him. He's...sad. He's thinking about Diya and Thomas. He feels alone now that they're gone.* The very thought that this man could feel genuine sadness about anything, much less a person, surprised Aya. *He's worried about potential uprisings from Coalition members and opposition groups, everyone turning on him. The destruction in Chicago made him happy for a while, but his happiness is gone again. He feels powerless because he can't undo the deaths of Diya and Thomas...because he can't just destroy everything.*

*If he did that, destroyed everything, then he'd be truly alone. He knows that, Aya. He feels trapped now. He knows you've won.* Orson walked to the window, looked at the dismal gray sky, and turned up the bottle once more. As he prepared to take another swallow of whiskey, he paused as though distracted by something. The pause lasted mere seconds before he turned up the bottle, took a swallow, and released a long sigh.

"I hope you enjoyed the lovely bonfire in your city," said Orson, staring out the window. "It seems Chicago can't escape the fate of always burning."

Aya made herself visible and glared at him. "You killed thousands of people just to get at me."

When he turned around and saw Eve, he ran his fingers through his hair and smiled. He took another swig from the near-empty bottle and sat it on the windowsill. "I don't believe I caught your name the first time we met."

"Eve Cooper."

"Apologies for my appearance, Ms. Cooper. I'm in mourning." He sat on the desk, letting one foot remain flat on the floor. "Wait a minute. Eve Cooper? You're the one who leaked out to the press about the existence of post-humans. You leaked that torture video in the U.S. over twenty years ago. I searched for you for years. I didn't recognize you with your hair like that."

Silent, Eve smiled and nodded.

He ran his fingers across the desk, looking at Eve with increased curiosity. "Aya, I didn't know you kept company with someone so infamous and...even more beautiful in person. She's the sole reason the world knows about post-humans. Bravo to you, Eve. You changed everything."

Aya stared at him.

"You exposed the global conspiracy of governments

using faders as guinea pigs and lab rats, as human weapons—
"

"I thought the world needed to know the truth," said Eve, interrupting Orson. "But in the end, I lost almost everyone I ever cared about. It was pointless because people are eternally stupid and power-hungry."

Aya looked sideways at Eve. "You told me you lost everyone. But you never gave me the details. Why didn't they teach us about you in school?"

"Right now isn't about me or my past. It's about that asshole sitting over there. He was in the British Parliament when I first leaked that information. He knew his fellow faders were being used as weapons and experimented on. He knew everything but stood by, tricking my old friends like Mauricio into working for him. You remember Mauricio, the man you convinced to join the project you were funding? The project you used to create chaos so you could gain power?" She looked at Orson with intense loathing. "You see, Aya, all Orson ever did was play us like puppets and bide his time until he could rise to power."

Orson listened in amusement as Eve spoke, tapping his fingertips against the desk and fixing his gaze on her. "I read the file SPI had on you. Typical fader with a couple of abilities. But Agent Grobeck and Charles Ford noted your paranoia tendencies. I see how right they were."

Eve glared at him.

Turning to Aya, Orson smiled. "I assure you I had nothing to do with the government torture program Eve is speaking of. I ended it once I took office as PM. As for the Harmony Project, our intentions were good if not poorly executed. When I stepped down from my post, I became the world's biggest advocate for post-human rights."

"Yes, the world would've ended if you hadn't swooped in on your white horse to save the day, right? Our very own real-life Tony Stark." Eve rolled her eyes.

Orson ignored Eve and continued speaking to Aya. "That whole spectacle in Chicago could've been avoided if you'd returned here to where you belong. After all I've done for you, inviting you into my home. Treating you like a guest of honor, teaching you how to use some of your abilities. I let you in on secrets I shared with nobody outside my own family. All that and you choose to run around with opposition terrorists, destroying everything I've built, taking away everyone who mattered to me."

Aya stared at him, noting that her silence seemed to increase his anger.

Red in the face, he went on. "You seem to forget I made you the celebrity you are, the teenaged alpha who charmed the world. I took you under my wing and even considered a truce with your opposition mates. I did all of that for you. And this is the way you repay me?"

"Everything is all about you, isn't it? Anyone who opposes you is a 'terrorist'. It doesn't even matter that Eve and I are both faders like you, that we want a world that's safe for all of us. You only care about people who do your bidding, like Thomas." Aya paused, trying to keep her anger in check. "You think I'm like you just because I'm an alpha. But I'm nothing like you. That's what you never understood."

An unhinged smile sailed across his face. "One day you'll realize how much we have in common. Only an alpha can understand an alpha, can know what it's like to have skills far beyond anyone else in the world. You think she understands you?" Standing up, he gestured toward Eve. "She may be a post-human, but she doesn't know what it means to be an alpha. She's not special like us."

"Oh boy. You've really had no one tell you to shut the fuck up, have you?" Eve affected a yawn and pretended to cover her mouth.

Orson returned to his desk and sat, disregarding Eve and looking at Aya. "Your friend's gotten awful bloody annoying."

Suddenly unable to move, Aya watched wide-eyed as Eve rose off the floor, higher and higher just as Diya had during her last moments. "No," Aya yelled, struggling to free herself from Orson's bind.

Eve looked both confused and infuriated. She flopped about like a fish out of water. "Put me down, asshole. Put me down, now!"

Aya turned to Orson and tried to block out the image of Diya's lifeless eyes. "Don't do it. Please don't do it," she begged, her voice trembling.

As he had with Diya, Orson made a throat slashing movement and a horizontal line appeared along her throat. Red drops trickled out and dripped to the floor.

Within moments, Eve stopped struggling and looked as though she'd fallen asleep, still hovering in the air.

Aya shut her eyes, and a cold numb feeling came over her. *No, no. It can't be happening again. Eve, can you hear me?* The silence was a symphony in her head. *Eve?* Aya's chest constricted like someone was squeezing her heart.

Orson's laughter interrupted her thoughts, and she opened her eyes.

"I'm afraid she can't hear you, my dear." With one more wave of his hand, Eve's body fell.

The loud sound of her body hitting the floor thrust Aya into a void she'd never known existed. He'd won. She'd failed.

Transported to the moment Diya died, Aya recalled the look of fear in Diya's eyes, the gurgling sound she'd made before hitting the floor. Unlike Diya, Eve looked peaceful as if she were sleeping.

"This is about balance, Aya. You took something

from me, then I took your home. You took something from me, and now I've taken something else from you." He sat on the desk and watched her with a look of satisfaction.

Able to move again, Aya ran to Eve and held her, the same way she'd held Diya. But as she looked at Eve's chest, she paused and leaned closer. Was she hearing a heartbeat?

Eve coughed, and her eyes fluttered open.

Startled, she watched Eve exhale and open her eyes wide.

Eve rubbed her throat, looking surprised as she pulled herself up. She dusted off her jeans and shirt before sliding her fingers over her throat again to check that it was healed.

Orson's jaws may as well have dropped to the ground. The whiskey bottle slipped from his hand and shattered as it hit the hardwood floor.

"You know, the throat cutting thing is really fucking tiresome," Eve said, turning to a dumbfounded Orson. "Why are people so unoriginal?"

He stood and gaped at her; his face as white as paper. "Impossible…"

A shadow of a smile parted Aya's lips as she looked at his scared and befuddled face.

"My turn now." Eve waved her hand, and all the items in the office shook. Anything not bolted down rose and levitated.

Speechless, Orson stared at her, his eyebrows disappearing into his hairline.

Standing side by side, Aya and Eve lifted their hands to their chests and glowing sparks flashed over their palms. The sparks slowly coalesced into baseball-sized balls of energy, warm and hovering inches above their palms. With a quick glance at each other, they nodded, glowered at Orson, and fired two large glowing balls of plasma at him. The beams hit him so hard his body smashed through the window and landed on the driveway below. His desk went along for the ride, crashing next to him on the ground.

They walked to the gaping hole in the office and peered at him in the driveway. He was covered in burns and struggling to move.

Orson took a minute to recover, wobbling and coughing as he got up and regained his balance. Ash and dust covered his face. Half his shirt had burned off, leaving his torso exposed. But his burned skin healed in the seconds or minutes he stood there, eyes closed and concentrating on regenerating.

All the while, Orson's head spun, thoughts running at a million miles per hour. *It can't be…it's not possible…?*

Anger surged up as he surveyed the destruction of his home. When he noticed Aya and Eve watching him from the second floor, he rolled up his tattered sleeves. From the corner of his eyes, he saw his neighbors in the adjoining flats peeking from their curtains. At once, he adjusted the shredded collar of his shirt and took a deep breath.

"My bad, Orson," Aya said with a mocking smile when he teleported into the office. "I forgot to mention Eve's an alpha, too. I guess we're not so special."

Eve smiled. "Stings, doesn't it?"

He slicked back his hair, and his eyes flitted between them. "I spent my whole life alone, not realizing there were others like me. The alienation, the loneliness. It was at times unbearable." He walked to the small bar on the right side of the room, thankful it was still intact, and opened a new bottle of whiskey. After dropping two ice cubes in a shot glass, he filled it halfway. In one gulp, he drained the glass. "You may not believe me, Aya, but I wanted us to get along. I wanted to teach you the things I had nobody to teach me at your age."

"You blew up my home and expected me to like you?

If I had known when I got to London that you were the one who—"

Eve tugged her arm and shook her head. "Don't blame yourself for not knowing he was a monster. Even I wasn't sure the rumors were true about him. He did a good job of making the opposition seem like paranoid conspiracy theorists. It didn't help that horrible people like General Harris were part of the opposition, too."

Clearing his throat, he ignored Eve and looked at Aya. "I may have acted with too much haste. But—"

"Look, man, it's over. Aya exposed who you really are to the world. I hear some leaders are already calling for you to resign from the Coalition. Soon everyone will have access to fusion. The Coalition's monopoly on it is over. You're done." Satisfaction dripped like molasses from Eve's words. "Outsmarted by a child, Orson. Doesn't it just break your heart?"

"I'm not a child. I'm a teenager." Aya shot Eve a testy look and folded her arms across her chest.

She patted Aya's shoulder but kept her attention on Orson. "And to top it all off, you're not particularly special anymore. There's three of us. For now. Who knows how many more are out there?"

"Let me tell you something," he said, approaching them, holding his rage at bay.

Eve took to a defensive pose, but Aya looked him dead in his eyes.

"What do you think is going to happen if I'm no longer the Coalition leader? Who will keep the peace and stability? Do you think the opposition can do a better job of running things? What about the normies who fear what they don't understand? They'll start killing post-humans again like they did during the Great Turn. The relative peace and stability the world enjoys right now? I did that. I united us all under the common good. They need me. You need me."

The look of pity and disdain on Aya's face pierced him like a knife through his chest.

"People will figure it out on their own without you," she said, closing the space between them and looking at him with pure loathing. "Now, let me tell *you* something. If you bother us again, we'll figure out a way to stop you. I doubt even you can take out two alphas."

Although he was almost twice her height, she towered over him in this moment and his heart sunk. He stepped back, stunned by her defiance, by the depth of her hatred for him. How had he so underestimated her just as he'd underestimated Diya?

"By 'stop you', Aya means 'stop you from breathing'. She's just too nice to say it that way, but I'm not. I could end you right now, and I probably should. But unlike you, I'm not a killer. I'd rather you suffer a miserable isolated life as a pariah. Don't make me change my mind." Eve took Aya's hand, and they exited through the door, leaving Orson alone in his partially destroyed office.

Amid the scattered debris, he saw the framed photograph of Diya he'd kept in his desk drawer. A photograph of their last vacation in Southern Spain. He picked up the cracked frame and removed the photograph, staring at it through watery eyes.

Pressing the photograph against his chest, he sunk to the floor and sobbed, his cries filling the empty apartment.

## 19

Orson sat next to Cornelius in the lavish hallway of the Aso Rock Presidential Villa in Abuja and rehearsed his comments to the African Union wing of the Coalition. Gwendolyn Harris, reportedly in a state of shock, hadn't spoken a word about the attack in Chicago. But General Harris' silence didn't matter.

Aya's video had been enough to convince most people Orson was the culprit behind the devastation in Chicago. The attack at Orson's home did little to improve his image—a week later, it was still headline news. Sentiment against him within the Coalition had reached boiling point.

He cursed himself every day for his impulsive decision to attack Chicago and, even more foolishly, to leave General Harris alive. If only he hadn't given in to anger and grief...

At his brother's advice, Orson requested a meeting with his friends in the African Union, his wall against an increasingly probable insurrection within the Coalition. Without the African Union's support, Orson knew he was finished as Chief Minister.

"Thank goodness President Alabi was gracious enough to organize this meeting at such short notice, brother.

The rumblings I've been hearing are not good. Whatever you do, keep the AU on your side," Cornelius said, barely above a whisper.

Orson nodded, looking up when he heard Blade Sonani's voice. Rather than his usual bright smile, Blade wore a severe expression and appeared less than enthusiastic as he strode toward them.

"Cornelius, do you mind?" Orson asked, gesturing for his brother to give him some privacy with Blade.

"Of course." Cornelius stood and buttoned his jacket, offering Blade a curt smile before making his way down the hall to speak with some UISF officers.

After directing his cabinet members to go on without him to President Alabi's conference room, Blade sat in the empty chair next to Orson. "I didn't expect to see you here today. I guess I know the reason for the emergency meeting now. I wondered."

"It's good to see you too, mate. You reek of cigars as always. I'm sensing Cuban, such quality those stogies have to them." Orson smiled while his eyes remained as serious as ever. "I do apologize for avoiding your calls of late, Blade. As you know, it's been a very difficult time, and I'm not just talking about the opposition riots in China right now. I've still got bloody contractors repairing my home office."

Blade leaned in closer to Orson, not wanting anyone to overhear their conversation. He made sure the hallway was clear before he spoke. "Was the girl telling the truth? Were you behind the attack on the Beijing fusion site?"

Orson tensed up. "The girl is a liar. Pathological. Nothing in that video should be believed by anyone with common sense. Why would I blow up the fusion reactor that I gifted to China?"

Blade regarded him with uncertainty and shook his head. "That video has me by the damn balls, Orson. I spent the past week in China convincing them to remain part of the Coalition." He leaned back, and an enigmatic look came over his face. "Thankfully, I was able to convince President Chen to not withdraw."

"I know things have been difficult for you, but what about me, Blade? How do you think I feel? Everything I worked so hard for has been torn apart. The European Union wing of the Coalition wants me to step down at once, and the Aussies and Japanese have renounced their Coalition membership. Russia and India are threatening to follow suit, not to mention the North American wing is coming for my head because of that child's malicious accusation that I attacked Chicago."

Blade nodded. "President Chen has even suggested that you be prosecuted in the Global Coalition Court of Peace and Justice for crimes against humanity."

"It's a bloody nightmare," said Orson, pulling away from Blade and searching the hallway. "Listen, Blade, I made you the man you are today. This is your chance to make good on that debt. I need the support of the African Union. I need you to make that happen."

"Orson, buddy, I've done what I can do, but I doubt today's meeting will change anything. This may very well be your final day as the Chief Minister. If you refuse to step down, then more and more countries will renounce their membership in protest. Your actions have made us all look bad and severely damaged the Coalition's once pristine image." Blade poked his index finger at Orson's chest. "People don't need the Coalition and your Remington Center for Science to start or run the reactors. They're looking at local government scientists and engineers to oversee the fusion plants now, and I'm sure many of them are eager to talk to that girl about consulting with them. The Q database is still offline indefinitely. I'm sorry, Orson, but you're fucked, and we'll be lucky if the people don't rise up against all our asses. We could have a damn revolution on our hands because of your alleged actions in Chicago and China."

With a long sigh, Blade rose and adjusted his shirt cuffs. Casting Orson a disappointed look, he turned away and headed to the conference room.

Orson's eyes followed Blade as he closed the door. Sinking in his seat, he replayed the conversation and considered his options. These people were all weak. He could overcome them with ease, but at what cost? He thought about the Reykjavik meeting, how he'd forced President Lopez and General Harris to agree to his terms. Why not do that again? They'd be powerless to stop him. *I could force every leader of the African Union to support me. They'd have no choice but to let me remain in my post.*

"Chief Minister," said a young assistant, appearing from the conference room. "You may join us now."

Cornelius returned and gave him an encouraging nod. "Good luck, brother. You can do this."

With a fleeting smile, Orson followed the assistant to the conference room to make his pitch to the Nigerian president and the African Union.

Orson sat in the middle of the conference room and looked at the audience of African leaders, some of whom had holographically dialed in to the meeting. Above his head, a sparkling glass chandelier hung from the ceiling and provided bright lighting. Aides who'd joined sat near the back of the room.

As he surveyed the people around the room, he mused about how they'd all worshiped him at one point. They'd been the first to receive his fusion energy and—as he spent no small amount of time reminding them—had changed the course of their continent's history. Not to mention the Q had given authoritarian leaning as well as democratic countries unprecedented access to their citizens. These people needed him, he reminded himself.

While he knew he could use his abilities to compel them to do his bidding, he hoped the relationships he'd built with them would make the African Union his natural allies in the Coalition now and enable him to keep his seat as Chief Minister.

Yet the hard looks on their faces dimmed his hopes a bit.

"Mr. Remington, we always turned a blind eye and let you and your privately-run science center handle all the reactors in our respective countries," said President Alabi, sitting at the head of the table and resting her hands on her lap. "But now we see that in Atlanta, the militia has a functional miniature reactor in their possession, and it's powering their city. Without any help or direction from you or the Remington Center. How fascinating."

Orson locked eyes with the president and tried not to frown.

"All these years, your personnel were just monitoring readings and making sure nothing exploded. It's strange that your personnel never let our state scientists observe how the reactors truly operated, never sought to train them about how your fusion technology works. In hindsight, this proprietary behavior should've given us all pause," she said, stopping as other members muttered in agreement. "At any rate, we've all learned a valuable lesson about openness and transparency. Thanks to that brilliant girl."

Silent, Orson adjusted his tie and held her gaze.

"While we appreciated your Q database," said another man with a bald head and full white beard, "the girl's exposure of it has led to broad conspiracy theories, undermining the sense of freedom in our so-called free world.

And your alleged violent tactics are more than a little unsettling."

"I'll get straight to the facts, Mr. Remington," President Alabi interjected, her tone colder now. "People are questioning whether the Coalition is the great unifier it claims to be, all thanks to your alleged behavior. We're all viewed with suspicion now."

His nerves getting the best of him, Orson chuckled and adjusted his tie some more. "Madam President, if I may...?"

The woman nodded. "You may."

"The rumors of Atlanta having a functional fusion reactor are rubbish. Why are we to believe any of that? We have waged a clandestine war against them and their sympathizers for years. They would say anything to weaken us. As for the Q rumors, they're just hearsay. Surely the opposition terrorists brainwashed the girl to say all those things."

Next to President Alabi, Blade cleared his throat. He stood and glared at Orson. "Pardon my language, but that's bullshit."

Gasps sounded around the room, and Orson's eyes widened as he looked at his old friend and ally.

"We all know that alphas like you and Aya can't be influenced or mind-controlled, so to speak. This means only one thing then: her admissions aren't influenced by any other post-humans. She hasn't been brainwashed as you suggest. She's telling the truth."

Chatter grew around the room, and leaders nodded in agreement.

Blade raised his hand to silence them. "She stated that you caused grid instability around the world by engaging in covert sabotage activities to force the world to accept your fusion, information she learned from Diya Narang. We believe her. She told us that you and your alpha abilities were the key to starting the sustained fusion reactors. We believe her. She claimed that you were behind the attacks in Chicago and Beijing. We believe her."

This caused another eruption of gasps and chatter, but Blade silenced them.

"What's more and perhaps most disturbing? She claimed you killed a fellow Coalition member, your own vice-counsel."

President Alabi cut in now, looking from Blade to Orson. "And we believe her."

The thick silence in the room pounded against Orson, who felt like walls were closing around him. Growing hot as sweat beads lined his forehead, he loosened his tie.

"The destruction you caused in Chicago is unparalleled, Orson. It's altogether horrifying and despicable. People are afraid and living in fear now, not because of the opposition. Because of you," said Blade, frowning.

Orson's face reddened as he stared at Blade. "There's no evidence to support any of these allegations. This is a final desperate ploy by the resistance terrorists to weaken and break up the Coalition just as we're on the verge of winning. Don't let them succeed."

Several people around the room smacked their lips and scoffed, regarding him with increasing suspicion.

"Today, we can show them we stand united. If the African Union can get behind me, I can weather these heinous and false allegations, and bring the Coalition out of this whole messy affair stronger and better."

To his surprise, President Alabi raised her hand to silence him. "Chief Minister, we will not be standing behind you. For you to presume we would after all you've done—"

"It's offensive to President Alabi, me, and every leader in this room," Blade said, resuming his seat next to

President Alabi.

President Alabi nodded at Blade and fixed a glare on Orson. "You lied to us from the very beginning. Your actions have brought shame upon the Coalition. Furthermore, how can we trust you not to harm one of us if we don't comply with your wishes, or—dare I say—your demands?"

Orson's face flushed beet red, and he clenched his fists. Murdered world leaders wouldn't reflect well on him, he reminded himself. Indeed, it would prove him guilty of the crimes of which he'd been so publicly accused.

He closed his eyes and listened to his breathing.

When he opened them, he looked at all the unhappy faces in the room, faces of people who had not long ago considered him a great friend. Or so he'd thought. Had one video ruined all of that?

Blade spoke next, and the words caught Orson off guard as everything else had so far during the meeting. "President Chen and I agreed that you should be tried by the Global Court, Orson."

"What power do you or President Chen have to make that happen?" Orson replied, before he could catch himself.

Blade smiled with satisfaction. "During an emergency meeting last night, the Coalition members all agreed that President Chen should assume the position of General Assembly president. And that I should assume the position of Chief Minister. The motions passed unanimously. As of twelve hours ago, you're no longer part of this Coalition."

As Orson looked at Blade, he thought about Diya's betrayal, and his fury threatened to overcome him.

President Alabi rested her hands on the table and leaned toward Orson. "What President Sonani is saying is we gave you this meeting merely as a courtesy. Nothing more."

On his feet now and looking from her to the other leaders around the room, Orson could no longer hold in his anger. "Every single official sitting in this room is guilty of crimes. Bribery, embezzlement, human and post-human rights violations. The list goes on and on. You had no problem using my Q to spy on your own people, approving my call for war with the opposition." He pointed his index finger towards his chest in a violent gesture. "I'm the reason the Coalition even exists, the reason you're sitting around this table, the reason we have light and air conditioning in this room right now. Me. You think you can do this to me? You think you can do this to an alpha? I'm the closest thing to a god on this green earth."

Everyone sat in silence and fidgeted, disturbed by Orson's uncharacteristic outburst. But Blade and President Alabi appeared unmoved by his harsh comments.

"Mr. Remington, if you're done, I will ask you to resume your seat," said President Alabi. When Orson remained standing, she smiled. "The Human and Post-Human Coalition for Peace exists to ensure that no person or member nation suffers indignation again. As our covenant says, no one person—post-human or human—shall be bigger than the Coalition. Even if that person is an alpha. You, Mr. Remington, are not bigger than the Coalition, no matter what you've told yourself."

Orson felt the wind sucked from him, and his complexion went from beet red to pale white. The room spun a little, and he steadied himself by taking a deep breath. Once more, he adjusted his tie and rubbed his fingers through his sweaty hair. "If that's the way it's going to be after all I've done for you people, then I suppose I have no choice but to accept it." He turned to Blade. "You were one of my most trusted allies. I made you."

"You hear this white man saying he made me? Can you believe it?" Blade laughed and nudged President Alabi who smiled and shook her head. He sneered at Orson and smacked his lips. "Your mistake is the mistake of so many men like you, Orson. You underestimate those who look like me."

Quiet with rage, Orson glanced at Blade. He remembered that same mocking smile Diya had given him at the end. "I could crush you all right now if I wanted to. But you wouldn't be worth the heap of rubble, bones, and ash I'd be standing on."

Three stocky guards entered through the double doors and surrounded him. "As you know, you're not the only post-human in this room, Mr. Remington. Some of us have been preparing for this day since we first met you. Tread with caution," said President Alabi, looking at him with a mix of pity and disgust. She gestured to the guards. "Please escort Mr. Remington off the premises."

As the guards grabbed his arms, he yanked away. "I can see myself out."

Outside the room, he found his brother flanked by three UISF officers. "I'm assuming it didn't go well?"

He walked past his brother, not looking at him. "It's over, Cornelius."

"Well, what about the science center?" asked Cornelius. "We can still figure out how to rebrand—"

"You can do with it what you want, brother. I'm done." Orson exited the building, stepping into the thick, humid air. No matter which way he looked at it, he'd lost.

After one more glance at the building, Orson shot into the air with no destination in mind.

From the kitchen window, Aya watched the orange sun set on the overgrown field that seemed to go on forever. The leaves of the boxelder maple tree beyond the window had lost their vivid green, changing to a deep reddish orange. The end of September had arrived and with it Malik's eleventh birthday.

Eve, Kendrick, Carmen, and Jesús sat around the kitchen table, sipping juice and watching Malik finish opening his birthday presents. Aya pushed a braid behind her ear—she'd allowed Carmen to style her hair in long braid extensions that went down her back—and smiled at her brother.

Malik held up a red and black scarf and wrapped it around him before retrieving a large stone from the gift basket. As he turned over the grayish-brown rock almost the size of his hands, he lowered his head to get a closer look. "What's this?" He shot Eve and Kendrick a puzzled look.

They shrugged and looked at Aya.

"You know how you always wanted to go to the sea? That rock is from a cliff over the sea in Scotland," said Aya. "And guess how I got there?"

"Orson took you?"

"Well, yeah. But I flew. I flew there with Orson."

"Like on an airplane? Cool!" Malik exclaimed.

Aya grinned. "No, actual flying. I forgot to mention I can fly. Oh, and I can make it rain. But only if there's a rain cloud nearby."

Malik stared at her in awe.

"I can fly, but I've never tried the rain thing," Eve said, smiling. "You'll have to teach me that one."

Kendrick, wearing his own red and black scarf, beamed at Aya. His arm was still in a sling, but the bruises on his face were healing up. He looked like his old self more each day.

Doctor Rouhani's tablet buzzed on the table, and a smile stretched his lips as he read the notification. "Malik, it looks like you, Aya, and I need to spend some time working on that new mini reactor out there. After the headlines about the original one we gifted to Atlanta in honor of Lee Kwon, the people in D.C. and Philadelphia are now asking for one. Demand is increasing."

Eve nodded. "Which means you need to get that document written supplying development details. As soon as that information is in the public domain, cities can start working on their own reactors. And I can get my shed back. I was thinking since there's so many of you all here now, I need to get started on turning it into a small guesthouse."

Kendrick looked around. "We could definitely use the extra space."

"Any word about Orson?" Jesús asked.

Doctor Rouhani shook his head.

"So they announced they were pursuing charges in the Global Court, and the man just vanishes?" said Kendrick.

Eve exchanged a knowing glance with Aya and sipped her juice. "I think he doesn't want to face the public. He's been ousted from the Coalition and his own company. Not to mention that brother of his is claiming ignorance now and has cut him off, from what I read."

"You don't think he'll try anything terrible again?" Jesús looked at Eve with concern. "Should we be worried?"

"He's done," said Aya. "The only thing he ever cared about was people adoring him and treating him like a savior. Now everybody knows he's a monster."

Finished opening his birthday presents, Malik hopped up and gave his sister a big hug around the neck. Meanwhile, the adults continued discussing recent news.

Of particular interest was the mysterious appearance of General Harris on the White House doorstep at the same time of the Chicago attack. Once the most vocal opponent of faders, General Harris now faced accusations of being a closeted fader.

"Why do they think she's a fader?" asked Aya, baffled.

Eve scanned the article. "Because Orson spared her. Authorities have confirmed Orson did the attack, but they can't figure out why she's the only person he left alive. So people are coming up with all kinds of crazy theories, one of them being that she's a fader."

Amused, Kendrick grinned. "Serves her right."

"Look at this," said Eve, laughing and holding the tablet where they could see it as she pressed play on a video.

The viral video depicted a reporter questioning General Harris about whether she was a fader. General Harris responded with a string of expletives and a swift punch to the reporter's face.

Kendrick laughed and slapped his leg with his free hand. "That woman is something else."

Suppressing laughter, Eve read more of the article, "President Lopez has cautioned the public from stoking the flames of anti-fader hate by launching unfounded accusations against General Harris."

"I apologize about changing the subject," said Doctor Rouhani, removing his eyeglasses and wiping them clean on his wrinkled shirt. "But I believe Malik and I should be finished with the new reactor in a couple of days, plus the development document is almost finished. So, in a day or two, Eve and Aya can work their mojo again and power it up."

"Okay. What's the catch, Doctor Rouhani? You have a gloomy look," said Eve.

The old man smiled. "I want to return to London. With staff and management stepping down at the Remington Center for Science and Orson's disappearance from the public eye, my safety is no longer a concern. My lab and hopefully the remaining staff members would be better suited there to aid you all with spreading this fusion energy across the globe. Plus, the Coalition still trusts me. They have no idea I participated in any of this with you all. I'm sure Orson out of sheer embarrassment of anyone finding out his top scientist turned on him kept the information to himself. With the Coalition's trust and the inside access I have, I can also make sure the Q remains offline forever or at least until I'm dead."

"Well, you're a part of our family now and my favorite drinking buddy." Eve gave him a tight hug. "You can't leave until after Jesús' big day."

Everyone except for Eve stared at Jesús, waiting for him to elaborate. "Rashaad's coming this weekend. We're getting married."

There was a moment of silence, followed by loud cheering and clapping.

Aya threw her arms around him. "Why didn't you say anything?"

He wiped his eyes. "After Lee...I started thinking about things and how Lee always told me not to pass up love like he'd done. Anyway, I popped in to see Rashaad the night you two left to confront Orson, and I asked him. He said yes."

"Oh my God!" Carmen shouted. "A backyard wedding."

Smiling, Aya sat. "I still haven't even met this guy. What's he like?"

"He's tall, dark. He has a shaved head, big eyes," Jesús said, a dreamy look in his eyes.

"You're describing my dad," Aya teased. "I like him already."

Jesús' face turned redder. "I guess he looks a little like Go. Sure. But he's not a military guy."

The conversation went on, transitioning from Jesús' impending wedding to Eve's announcement that she would split her time between the farm and Carmen's home in

Oakland. Before long, they headed to the porch, where Eve joined Aya and Carmen on the swing, while Kendrick relaxed in the rocking chair.

Kendrick took a deep breath and looked out at the vast prairie and the fall tree colors. He stroked his salt-and-pepper beard and watched Eve run her fingers through Aya's new braids. "I think we should also hit the road and go back to Chicago, see what's left to salvage."

"Dad, I thought you said we were staying this time," said Malik.

Eve leaned forward. "Kendrick, listen. You all are family to me. It would be rude of me to let you go to Chicago. You're welcome to stay as long as you want."

"But I wouldn't want to infringe upon your space any longer than we've done already." He rubbed his sling.

"You're still dealing with your injuries, and Jesús will be happy to have an ally to join him on his nightly missions—assuming Aya's still up for the missions."

"Missions?"

Eve scoffed. "This isn't over, Kendrick. We know the People's Army and Midwest Front have fader detention facilities they haven't shut down, despite the Reykjavik Agreement. There's still a segment of humans who hate faders. Jesús' missions and this safe house will remain necessary for the near future."

Sensing a pleading tone in Eve's voice, he sighed. "I can't repay you."

"You already have." She glanced from him to Aya. "And don't worry. When you heal up, I'm going to put your ass to work around here. You and Jesús are going to help me turn that shed into a guesthouse."

Kendrick chuckled. "Speaking of healing, I thought alphas could heal people. You must want me broken for now, woman."

"I figured you'd prefer the rest from healing the old-fashioned way." She winked. "That reminds me, though, I still need to teach Aya how to heal others. There are so many things she still has to learn about her abilities."

A peaceful silence passed among them as wind brushed through fall leaves and the sun peeked through gray clouds.

Once Eve finished pulling Aya's braids into a ponytail, Aya got up and hugged her father. "I love you, Dad."

When she released him, he wiped tears from his eyes. His gaze swept over her and his son, who was playing with Miss Sandy and Baldwin in the grass. Aya sat on the floor beside his rocking chair and reached for his free hand.

"Eve," she said, "Do you think Orson will come hunting for us?"

Eve pulled her own locs into a ponytail. "Even with our alpha abilities, we can't predict the future. But if I were a betting woman, I'd say probably not." She turned her body sideways and lay across Carmen's lap like a cat. "We're going to be fine."

Baldwin approached Aya and rubbed against her leg. She scooped up the cat, petted him, and smiled as Carmen leaned forward to kiss Eve. She realized it was the first time she'd seen Eve look relaxed and happy.

"These two lovebirds," Kendrick said, smiling. "I remember the times your mom and I sat on the porch in Chicago, and she'd lay across my lap like that."

Aya draped her arm around her brother and looked at her father with rapt attention, as he launched into a long story about her mother. His face lit up as he talked, and Malik joined them.

For the first time, Aya was safe. She was home.

*SIX MONTHS LATER…*

Eve sat with Doctor Rouhani at the bar inside the Ye Old Mitre Tavern, one of London's oldest establishments. March had arrived, bringing with it Eve's birthday, so she'd celebrated by giving herself a trip to London. She hadn't visited before and, now that she was getting out more, it had made her bucket list.

"You know Malik is already talking about coming to work with you someday," she said, brushing the locs that curtained her face and gave her a somewhat airy presence.

Doctor Rouhani smiled and finished the remaining red wine in his glass. "Well, now that I'm running the center, I'd be able to hire him. I'm rebuilding my work now and developing more advanced reactors, large and small. My goal is to improve upon Orson's original design from twenty years ago."

"Sounds like you have your work cut out for you. I just think it's a shame I lost my wine-drinking friend. You know I used to hate this stuff when I was in my twenties. I was a beer person in those days."

Doctor Rouhani gestured to the bartender for another glass of wine. "Well, as much as I appreciate wine, there's nothing like a good pint in a dingy old pub."

"Any of it's a good deal better than that moonshine shit Kendrick likes to drink," she said, laughing. "Anyway, don't you have an appointment to be getting to? Don't let me take all your time."

He looked at his watch, got up, and put on his jacket. "Yes, Chief Minister Sonani is relentless. He likes to know every detail of our work at the center and stay briefed. I've paid for the glass."

The bartender placed another glass of red wine before them.

"It's all yours," said Doctor Rouhani and kissed her cheek. "Enjoy some much deserved free time seeing the city. Ring me if you'd like to meet for lunch tomorrow."

She toasted him. "Sure thing, good sir," she replied in a mock English accent. As she watched him make his way to the exit, she spotted an older blond-haired man wearing a black shirt, tie, and snug-fitting jeans.

The man met her gaze, approached, and sat in the seat Doctor Rouhani had vacated. "Oi! Another glass of wine for the lady, please."

His voice was boisterous and louder than she'd expected. "Oh thanks, but that's not necessary," said Eve, smiling.

"I insist." He flashed her a smile and turned to the bartender.

"Thank you, but I'm not interested."

"Just a friendly chat with an old fart is all I ask of you. Keep an old man company, won't you?"

She sipped her wine, trying not to appear aggravated. As she looked at him, something about his striking green eyes caught her attention. Why did he seem familiar? "I'm still finishing this one, but you can give me a glass of 2006 Bourgogne chardonnay."

"I'll have what she's having," he said to the bartender, not taking his eyes off Eve.

Not a minute later, the bartender set two glasses of wine in front of them. The man lifted his glass. "Cheers to a lovely lady from across the pond."

Eve giggled, thinking about the hotel bar in Philadelphia twenty-five years ago where a good-looking British man had hit on her and left her his number. She'd never bother calling him. "You Brits always add so much flair when you hit on American women. Don't you?"

"Well, yeah, but I'm a bit out of practice. Ever since

the Great Turn, American tourism has gone down a bit. On holiday in my younger days, sure I'd have a bit of fun here and there. Tonight, however, is just friendly banter." He sipped his wine and frowned at it. "I must say I've always preferred whiskey."

She shook her head. "I don't mess with that stuff. Too much for me."

Silence elapsed between them as they sipped their drinks and looked around the bar.

Eve looked at the television over the bar and saw a reporter talking to Faye Lennox about the fallout with Orson. Although he'd been spotted a couple of times in the past six months, he still hadn't been apprehended. "That woman's on perpetual damage control," said Eve, laughing. "Serves her right for being a useful idiot for a tyrant."

A frown settled on the man's face but vanished almost as soon as it appeared. "I couldn't help but overhear some of your conversation with your scientist friend. Even after all these years, Yousef is still an arrogant bastard. Improve upon Orson's design, my pink ass."

"You know Doctor Rouhani? They say every big city is really a small town, but wow."

He smiled and took another sip of wine. "Oh, Yousef and I have quite a history, my love." As he spoke, his grayish-blond hair darkened to a deep chestnut brown with gray temples. The wrinkles in his face smoothed out, and his jaw became squarer and more prominent.

Eve leaped up and threw her drink in his face.

The bartender rushed to them. "Is everything okay, Miss?" His eyes widened when he saw the man sitting next to Eve.

Orson held up his hands and flashed the charming smile that had fooled the world for so many years. "Everything is fine, mate."

With a frightened look at Orson, the bartender backed away and hurried to the other end of the bar to whisper to his colleague.

"I deserved that," he said, using a napkin to wipe the red wine off his face and shirt. "I'm used to people launching things at me nowadays."

"Tell me why I shouldn't turn your ass in to the authorities right now."

"I can't tell you that. But let me be clear, I mean no harm to you or Aya. I just want a couple of minutes of your time, and you'll never see me again."

She scowled at him.

"Look, I didn't expect to see you here. It's just the luck of the draw that Yousef, like me, still favors this pub. This is the first time I've been here since Diya…" He trailed off and lowered his gaze.

She tapped her fingers on the bar counter, waiting for him to respond.

"Diya liked this pub. We came here for lunch often and used to sit in that booth." He pointed to a vacant booth near the window. "I was sitting there alone when you walked in."

Eve stared daggers at him.

"Shapeshifting has come in handy these days, but mostly I just stay away from London. It's easier that way. But sometimes I miss the crowd, you see."

Eve folded her arms across her chest and cast him a contemptuous smile. "I'm simply overcome with grief for you."

He turned to her again, flashing a smile that didn't reach his eyes. "Cheeky. I must say you look stunning nowadays, although I do miss the short little hairdo you had before the Great Turn. What do they call it…an Afro? It's funny we should meet again like this, eh? Given how we met two decades ago in that romantic Philadelphia bar. I believe you were posing as a redhead with far less melanin back then."

She stared at him, the realization hitting her. "That was you?"

He nodded. "I didn't realize it until I met your friend, Mauricio, sometime later."

Resisting the urge to pour another drink on him, she groaned. "Look, say what you need to say. I don't have all day."

The smile vanished, and he cleared his throat. "You know the Coalition's reputation has been damaged, so they've played it quiet for a while. But they won't play it quiet for very long. There are powerful forces who run it. I should know, since I built the damn thing. There's no telling if the truces with the various opposition forces will last. There are rumblings."

"All conjecture and you trying to stir up shit, as usual. You already know what I'll do to you if you try to maneuver your way back to power." She slid her finger along her throat and glared at him. "So why are you here?"

"Now that the world is at a relative state of peace, it's important that the Ares One project goes on."

"The what?"

He sighed. "The Mars station project. It appears that Yousef has a close relationship with Blade now. I ask that you impress upon Yousef the importance of keeping Blade focused on the space station."

"Okay, is that all? And you're taking a long time to finish that drink." She looked at his half-empty wine glass.

He reached into his pocket and pulled out a USB biometric fingerprint reader. When he pressed it, a small holographic projection appeared above them.

Eve stared at it. "What is it?"

"It's my magnum opus, you could say, my final gift to humanity. It's the design for a fusion Bussard ramjet engine. It works by basically scooping hydrogen from interstellar dust clouds in space and fusing it. It will in turn release an unlimited amount of energy in the process. Sustainable fusion that doesn't need alphas to ignite it, but it uses the most abundant element in the cosmos."

She stared at the projection.

"I might have been misguided in my methods, but I had our future in mind every step of the way. It's a cruel sort of irony that, due in large part to my downfall, the Mars station might finally materialize with this truce if it holds. Eve, it's the key to sustainable fusion."

"So why didn't you leave this information with the Coalition or the people at your science center?"

"You could say I have trust issues nowadays."

"This is leverage. You're going to try to use this information to get your power back."

"Eve, everyone's afraid of me. On the rare occasion I do come out undisguised, most people won't look me in the eyes. My brother will turn me in to the authorities if I contact him. And my own mother hasn't spoken one word to me in almost six months. I've ruined the family name, she told me. There's no coming back for me."

The tone of his voice stunned Eve. Where his voice usually dripped with arrogance, there was only deep despair now. *Good.*

Orson clicked the USB again to turn off the holograph. "So I'm giving this to you. As you and Aya continue your goodwill tour of making fusion available to everyone, please ensure that the Coalition goes forward with the Mars base. That base, along with the information on this little device, will be the key to our survival. With it, we'll no longer be bound to one small blue marble in the vastness of space."

Eve's mouth hung open as she looked at the USB he placed in her palm.

He looked at her for a moment. "For what it's worth, I'm sorry. I know those words sound hollow coming from me."

"Damn right they do." She looked at the small device and slipped it inside her jeans pocket before looking at Orson. "If I ever see you again, Orson, I'll give you a taste of what you tried to do to me. And then I'll turn you over to the authorities. I hear the Coalition's been developing some interesting ways to contain an alpha."

He chugged the rest of his wine, got up from the bar stool, and rubbed his fingers through his hair. As he did, his hair turned white again and his face changed to how it looked when he approached her. After a curt nod, he turned to leave.

Patrons watched in confusion as he headed to the door to exit the pub.

With his hand on the door handle, he turned to Eve. "One more thing. You and I are the same age. We're the only two confirmed alphas from our generation of the few thousand of us post-humans. Right?"

"Yes, that's correct. Only you and me. Now there's Aya for the next generation."

"And her abilities far exceeded mine by a long shot. Do you think there'll be even more powerful alphas that evolve with future generations of post-humans?"

Eve considered his question, a question that had crossed her mind months ago as she realized the range of Aya's abilities. "I don't know. But, if so, Aya's only the beginning."

"I'm sure you're right," he said, nodding. "Speaking of Aya, I hope she's kept in touch with Michio. He seemed like a good kid."

"She visits him now and again," said Eve. "Orson, if I ever see you again, you'll wish the Coalition had found you first."

His sad smile returned. "I know." With a final nod to her, he exited the pub.

Standing at the window, Eve watched him shoot up like a rocket across the sky. She thought back to when all this mess began decades ago, about all she'd lost and all she'd gained. Smiling, she returned to the bar and sat to order another glass of wine.

The bartender approached with caution. "Was that actually Orson Remington?" he whispered. "I can't believe he'd show his face here. Some of the patrons were getting nervous."

Eve sipped her wine and shook her head. "He was just some guy with an ego the size of Everest."

The bartender laughed. "There are a lot of those types, aren't there?"

"The stories I could tell you," said Eve, laughing along with him. The laugh came from deep within, from a place she didn't know could exist within her, from a place of freedom. At last, she could breathe. She was free.

# ACKNOWLEDGMENTS

We appreciate all our friends and fellow book lovers who served as great readers and guides for the development of this story. Thanks to our editor, Mary-Theresa Hussey, for her wonderful insights and enthusiasm for the characters. We wrote this story because we sought to create a space for unconventional heroes, particularly queer women and people of color, in the fantasy and speculative fiction space. Completing the *Faders and Alphas* universe was a long but amazing journey, and we learned so much about storytelling and the joy of co-writing. We are grateful for every invisible hero who inspired us to craft this story.

# ABOUT THE AUTHORS

**Berneta L. Haynes** was born and raised in Little Rock, Arkansas but has lived everywhere from Missouri, England, Iowa, Chicago, and Philadelphia. She has authored two novels, *Landrien Moriset* and *Eve and the Faders*, as well as short stories. An attorney and founding editor of Waking Writer, Berneta lives in Atlanta with her partner and co-author, **Lornett B. Vestal**. A Chicago native, Lornett served in the U.S. Navy and traveled the world before attending the University of Chicago. An environmentalist, social worker, and politics junkie, he runs the Evolving Man Project, a website that promotes social change through insightful discussion, activism, and idea sharing. His first novel, *Eve and the Faders*, debuted in 2021.

Official Site: www.bernetahaynes.com | Twitter: @BernetaWrites | Twitter: @EvolvingManLBV

*If you enjoyed this novel, please leave a review on Goodreads and at your favorite retailer!*